Blue Is the Warmest Color

BLUE IS THE
WARMEST
COLOR

JULIE MAROH

ARSENAL PULP PRESS

BLUE IS THE WARMEST COLOR
ENGLISH LANGUAGE EDITION © 2013 BY ARSENAL PULP PRESS

THIRD PRINTING: 2013

FIRST PUBLISHED IN FRENCH AS *Le bleu est une couleur chaude* BY JULIE MAROH
© 2010 — GLÉNAT EDITIONS

ARSENAL PULP PRESS
SUITE 202 — 211 EAST GEORGIA ST.
VANCOUVER, BC V6A 1Z6
CANADA
arsenalpulp.com

THIS IS A WORK OF FICTION. ANY RESEMBLANCE OF CHARACTERS TO PERSONS EITHER LIVING OR
DECEASED IS PURELY COINCIDENTAL.

TRANSLATION BY IVANKA HAHNENBERGER
BOOK DESIGN BY GERILEE MCBRIDE

PRINTED AND BOUND IN CANADA

LIBRARY AND ARCHIVES CANADA CATALOGUING IN PUBLICATION:

MAROH, JULIE, 1985-
  BLEU EST UNE COULEUR CHAUDE. ENGLISH
       BLUE IS THE WARMEST COLOR / JULIE MAROH.

TRANSLATION OF: LE BLEU EST UNE COULEUR CHAUDE.
ISSUED IN PRINT AND ELECTRONIC FORMATS.
ISBN 978-1-55152-514-3 (PBK.).--ISBN 978-1-55152-513-6 (EPUB)

       1. GRAPHIC NOVELS. 2. LESBIANS--COMIC BOOKS, STRIPS, ETC.
I. TITLE. II. TITLE: BLEU EST UNE COULEUR CHAUDE. ENGLISH.

PN6747.M36B5413 2013   741.5'944   C2013-904195-8

                                                      C2013-904196-6

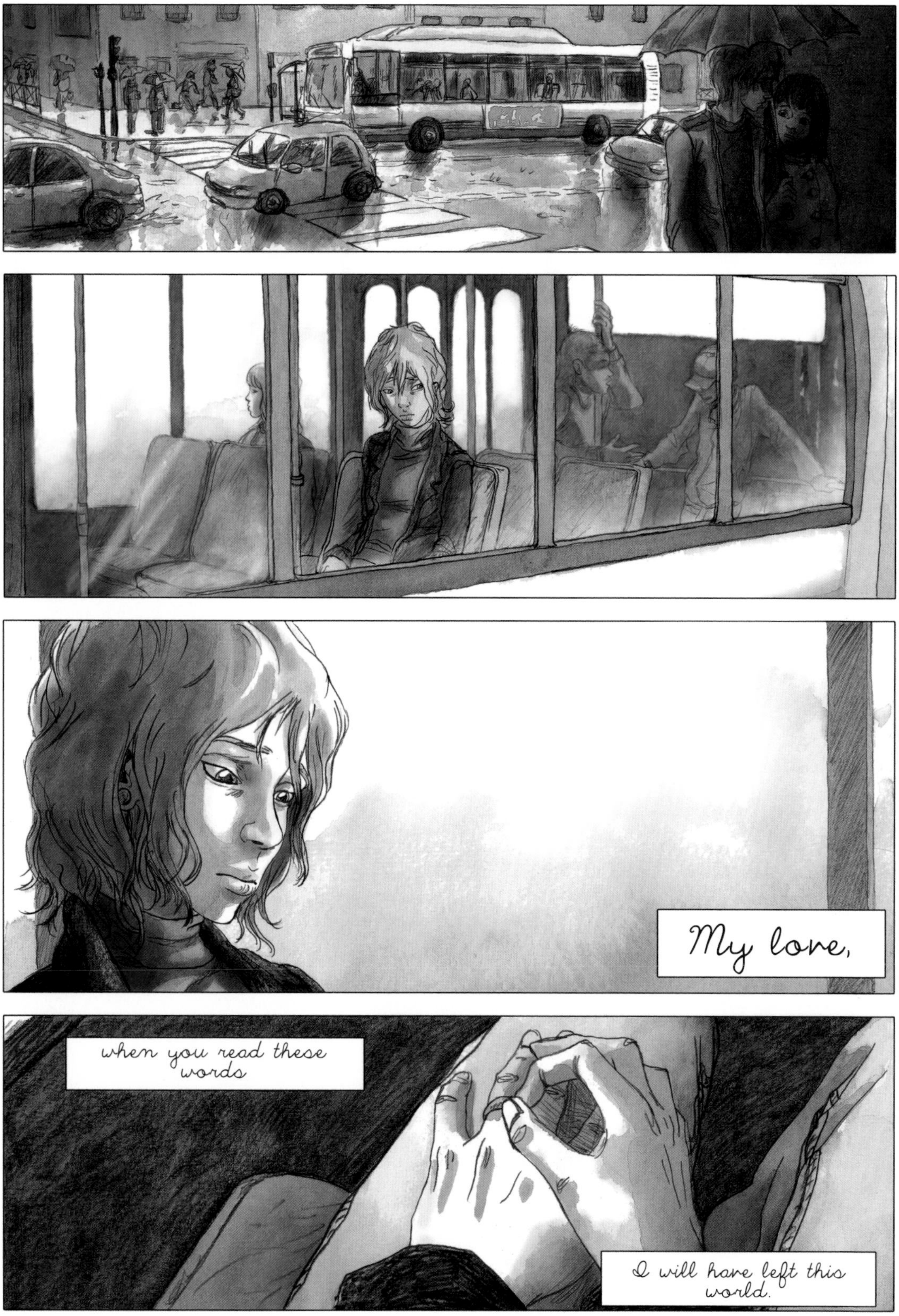
My love,
when you read these words
I will have left this world.

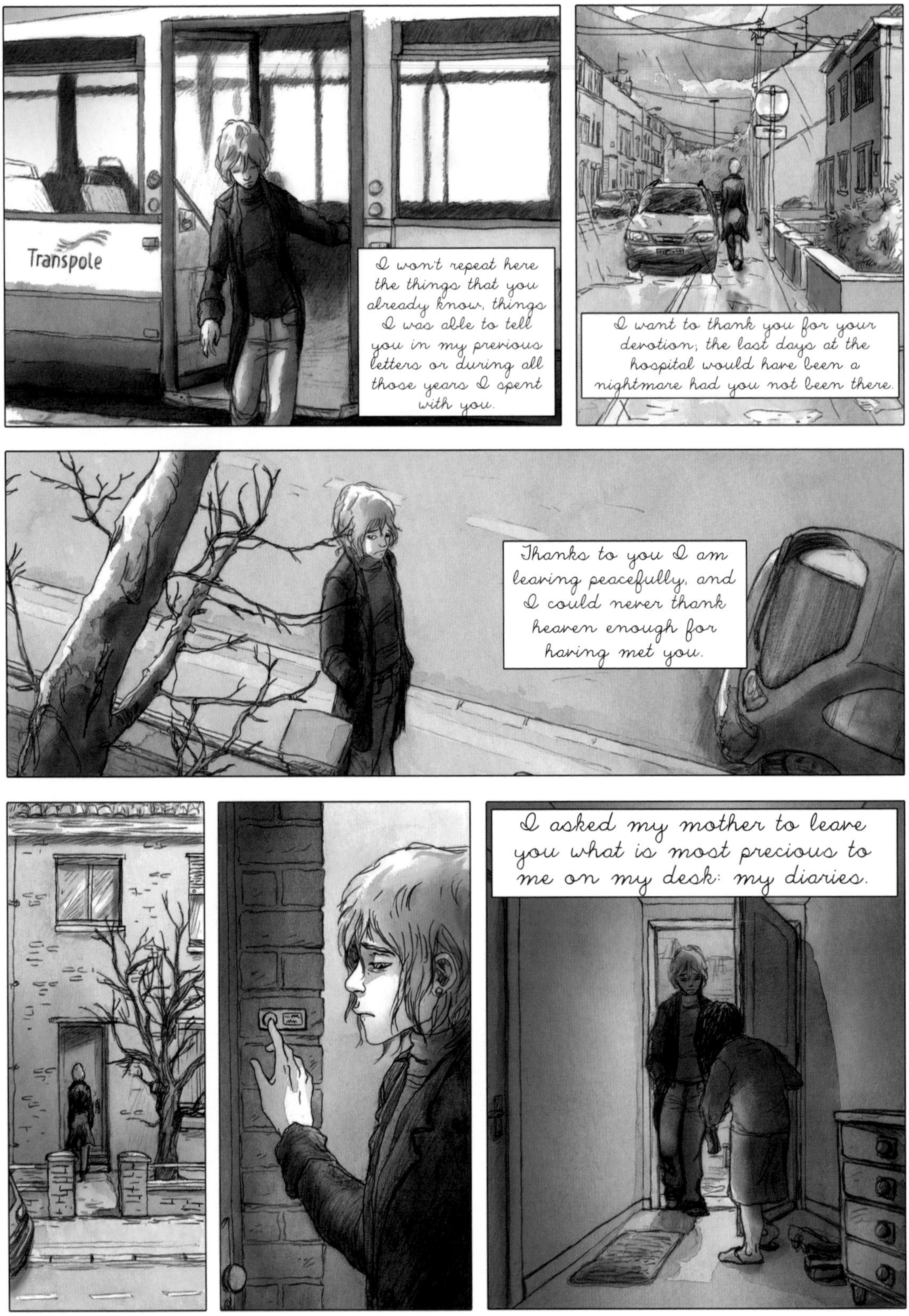
Transpole
I won't repeat here the things that you already know, things I was able to tell you in my previous letters or during all those years I spent with you.
I want to thank you for your devotion; the last days at the hospital would have been a nightmare had you not been there.
Thanks to you I am leaving peacefully, and I could never thank heaven enough for having met you.
I asked my mother to leave you what is most precious to me on my desk: my diaries.

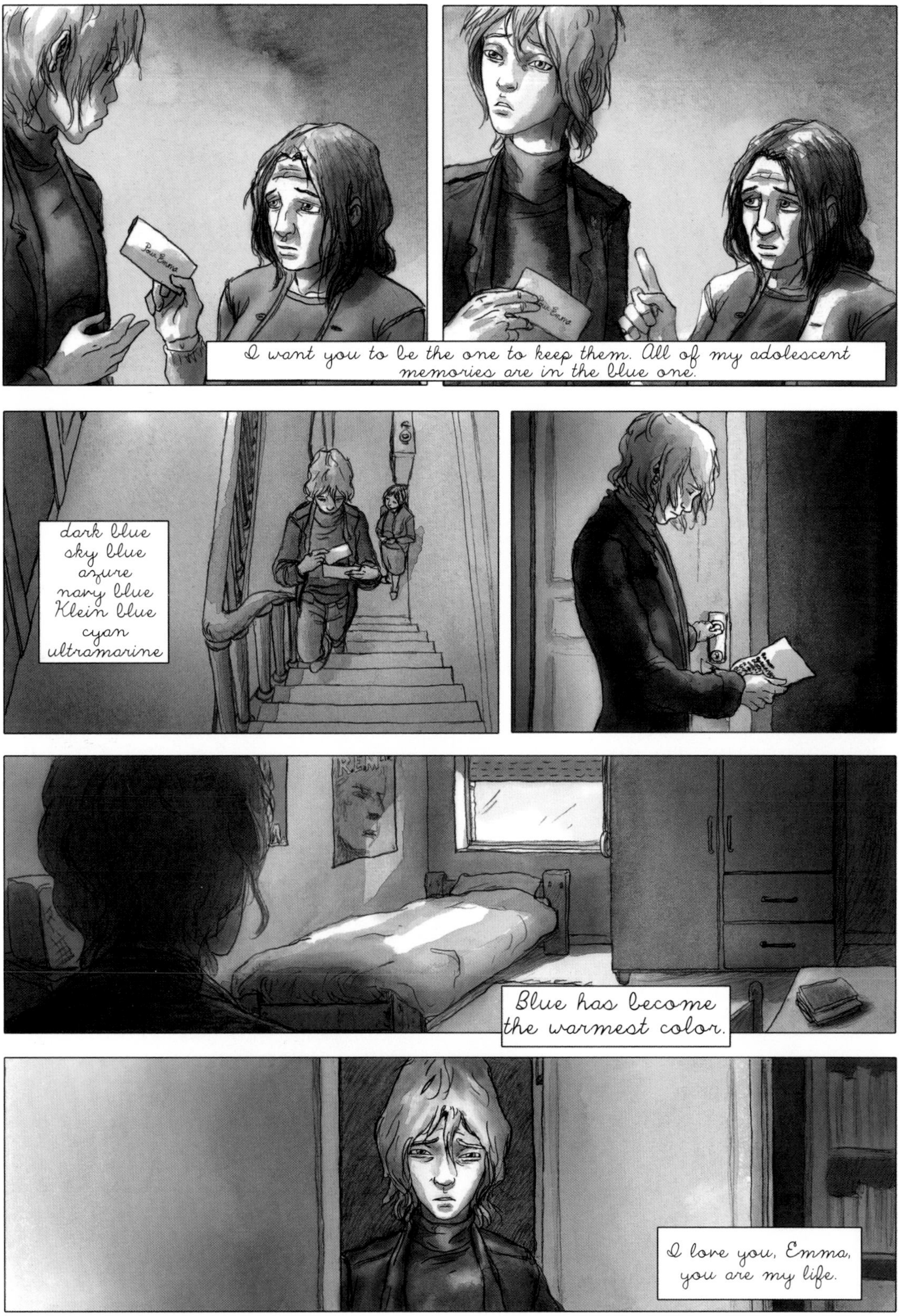
I want you to be the one to keep them. All of my adolescent memories are in the blue one.
dark blue
sky blue
azure
navy blue
Klein blue
cyan
ultramarine
Blue has become the warmest color.
I love you, Emma, you are my life.

Signed...

Clementine

DIARY

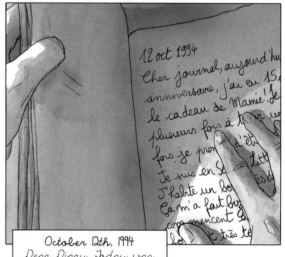

12 oct 1994
Cher journal, aujourd'hu
anniversaire, j'ai eu 15,
le cadeau de Mamie! Je
plusieurs fois à t'.. .. u..
fois, je proi... ...d'êt..
Je suis en .... Lit...
J'habite un bo......
Ca m'a fait boz
coi......mencent ...
.... très te...

October 12th, 1994
Dear Diary, Today was
my birthday. I turned
15, and you were my gift
from Grandma!

I have already tried
many times to keep a
diary but this time I
promise to stick to it!!

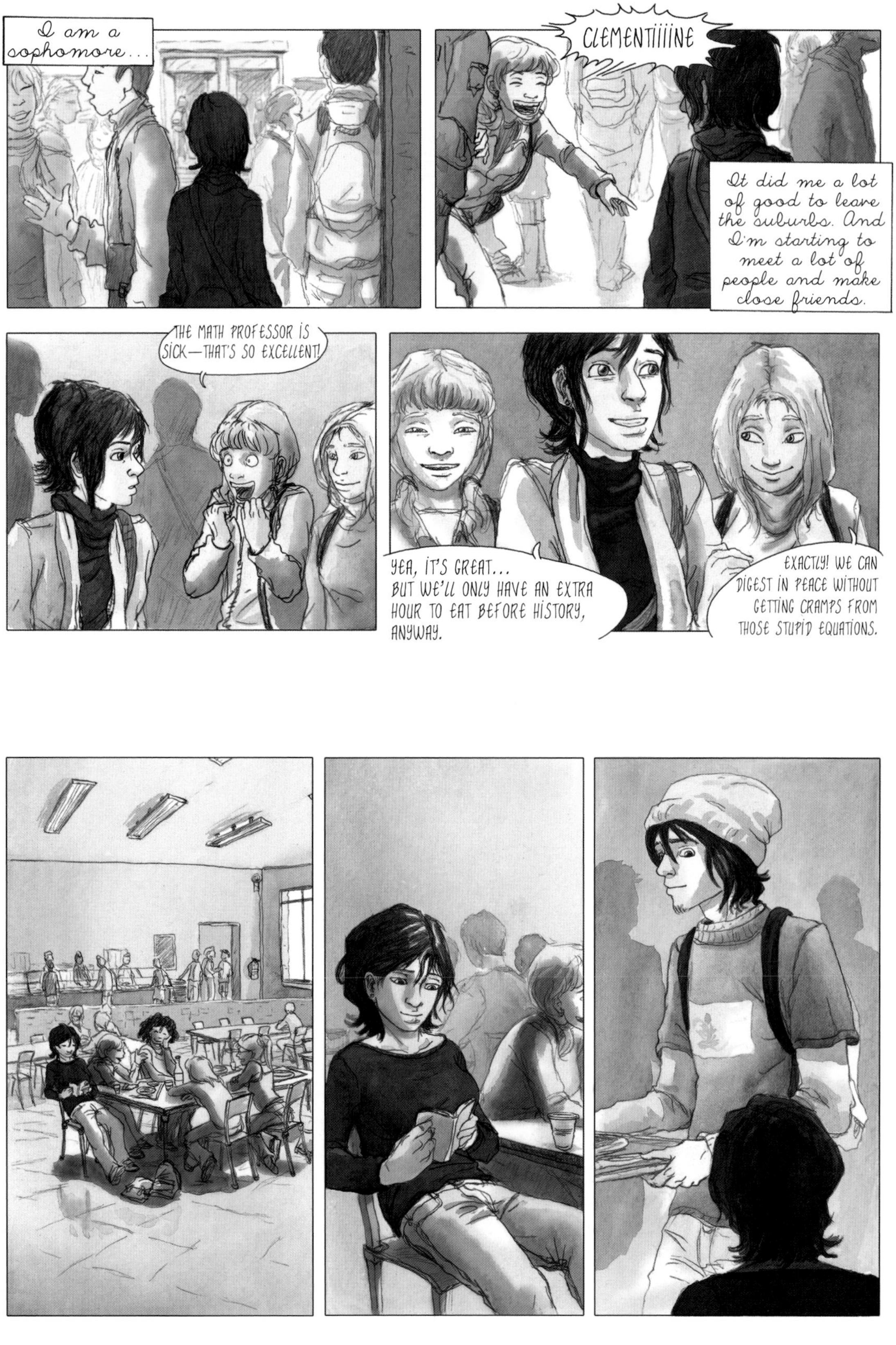
I am a sophomore...
CLEMENTIIIIINE
It did me a lot of good to leave the suburbs. And I'm starting to meet a lot of people and make close friends.
THE MATH PROFESSOR IS SICK—THAT'S SO EXCELLENT!
YEA, IT'S GREAT... BUT WE'LL ONLY HAVE AN EXTRA HOUR TO EAT BEFORE HISTORY, ANYWAY.
EXACTLY! WE CAN DIGEST IN PEACE WITHOUT GETTING CRAMPS FROM THOSE STUPID EQUATIONS.

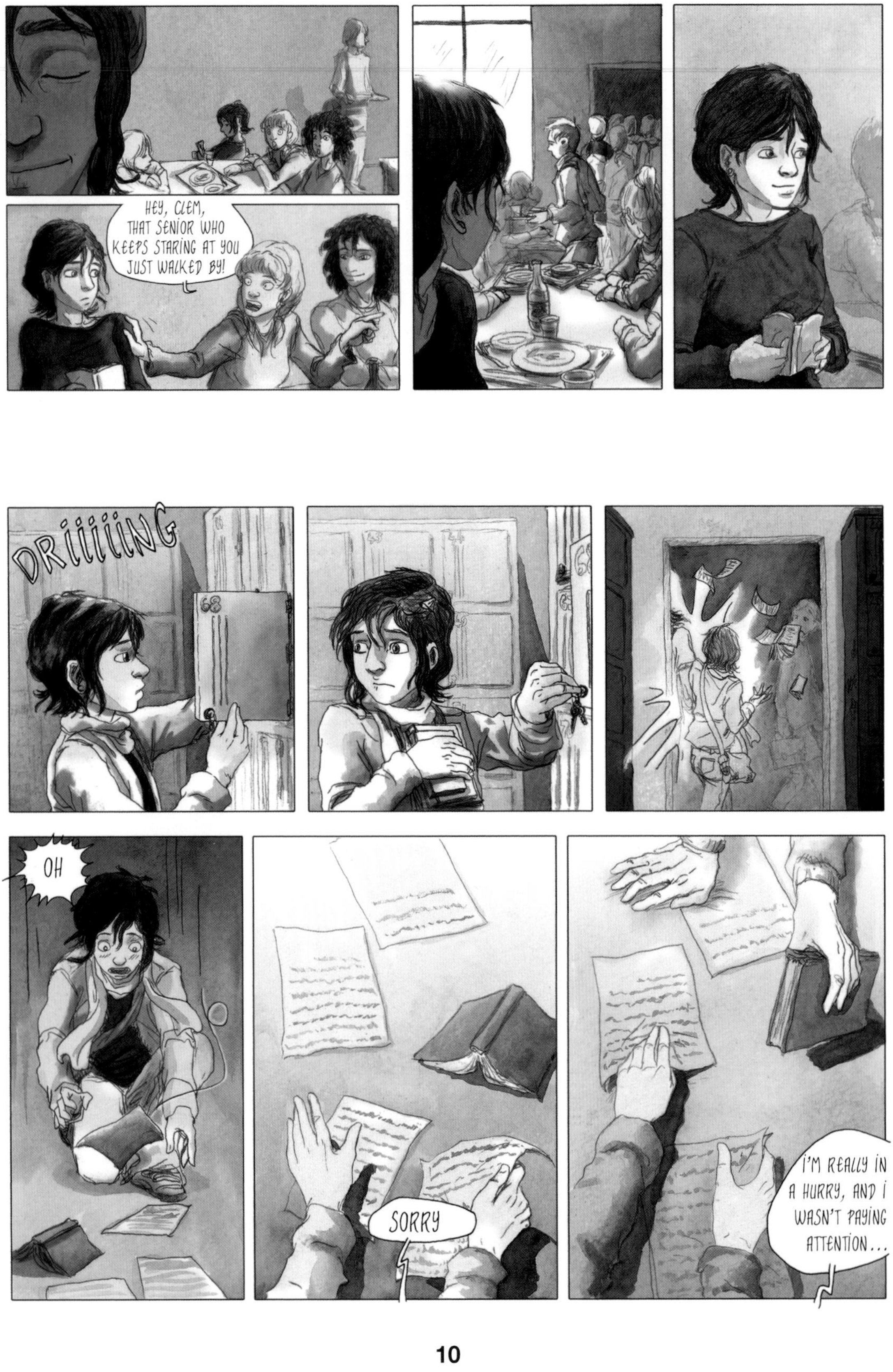
HEY, CLEM, THAT SENIOR WHO KEEPS STARING AT YOU JUST WALKED BY!
DRIIIIING
OH
SORRY
I'M REALLY IN A HURRY, AND I WASN'T PAYING ATTENTION...

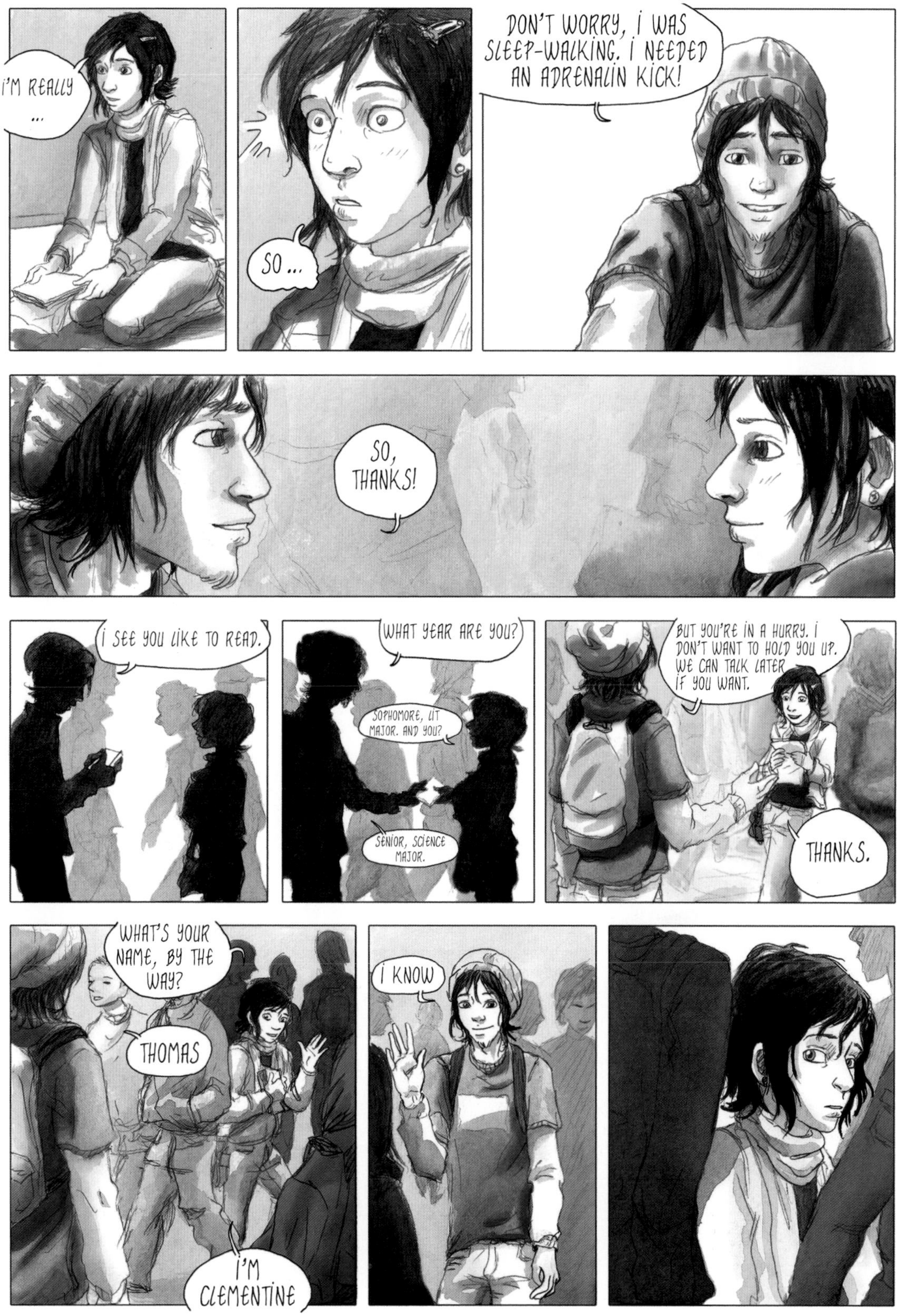
I'M REALLY ...
SO ...
DON'T WORRY, I WAS SLEEP-WALKING. I NEEDED AN ADRENALIN KICK!
SO, THANKS!
I SEE YOU LIKE TO READ.
WHAT YEAR ARE YOU?
SOPHOMORE, LIT MAJOR. AND YOU?
SENIOR, SCIENCE MAJOR.
BUT YOU'RE IN A HURRY. I DON'T WANT TO HOLD YOU UP. WE CAN TALK LATER IF YOU WANT.
THANKS.
WHAT'S YOUR NAME, BY THE WAY?
THOMAS
I'M CLEMENTINE
I KNOW

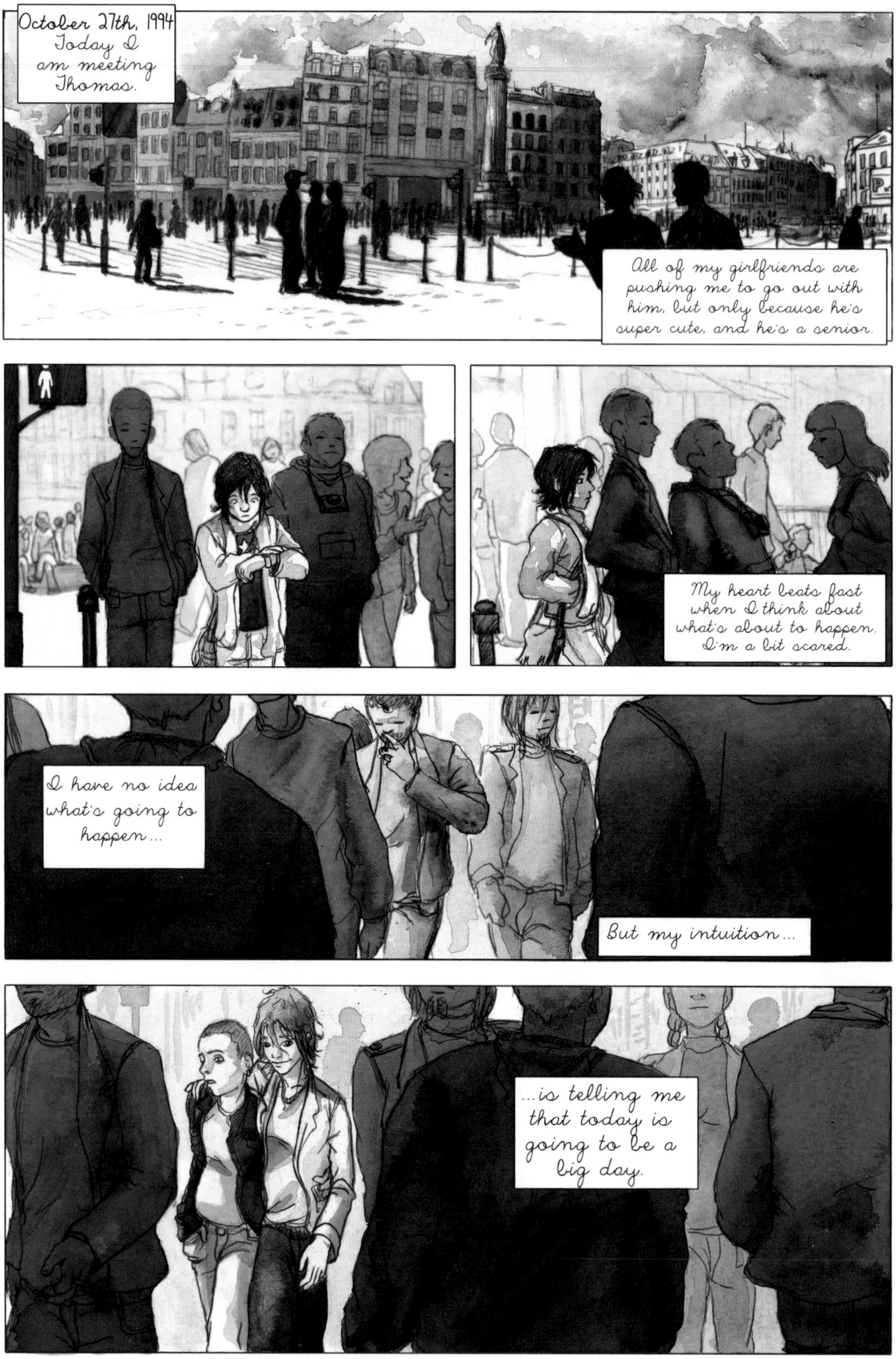
October 27th, 1994
Today I am meeting Thomas.
All of my girlfriends are pushing me to go out with him, but only because he's super cute, and he's a senior.
My heart beats fast when I think about what's about to happen. I'm a bit scared.
I have no idea what's going to happen...
But my intuition...
...is telling me that today is going to be a big day.

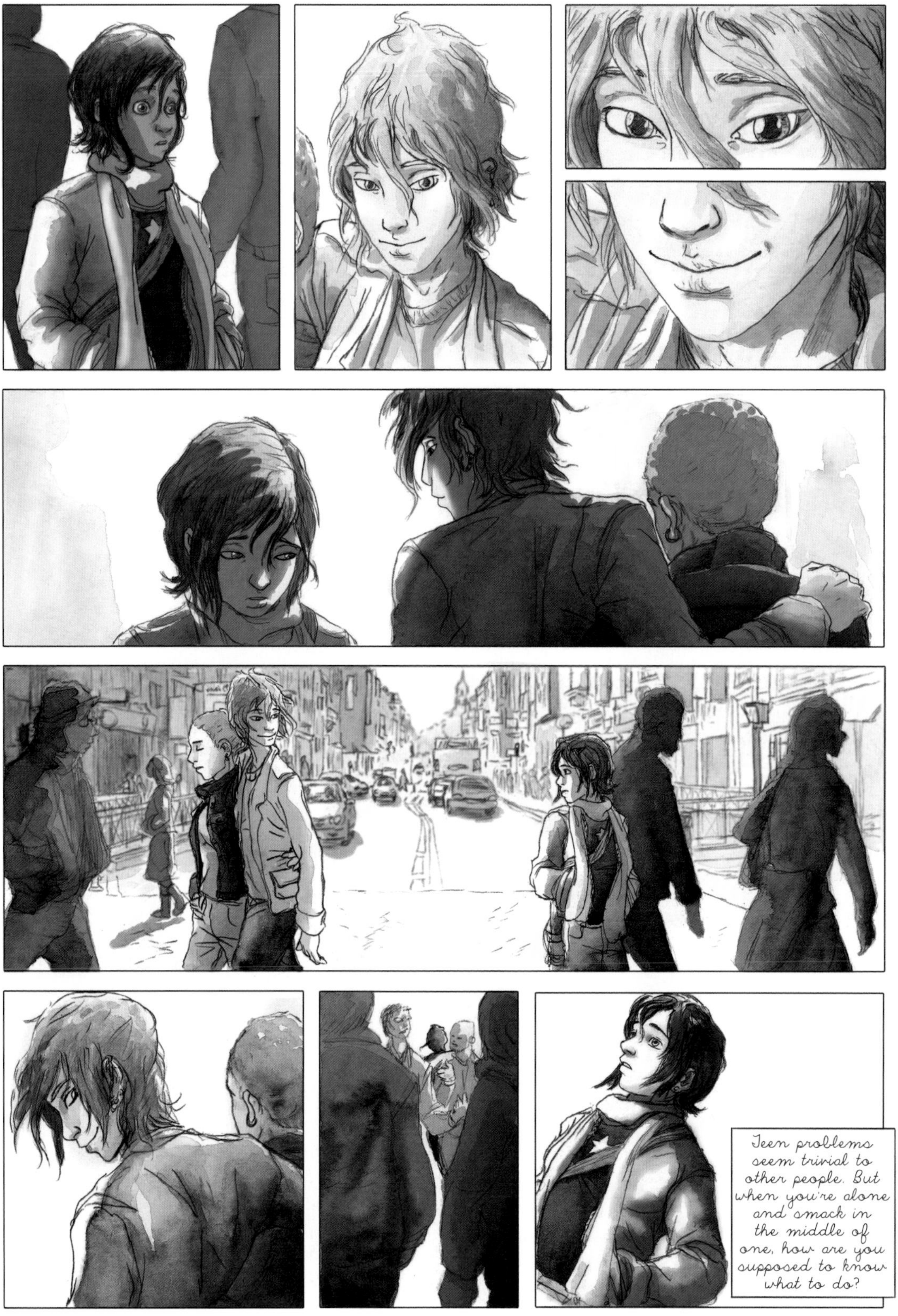
Teen problems seem trivial to other people. But when you're alone and smack in the middle of one, how are you supposed to know what to do?

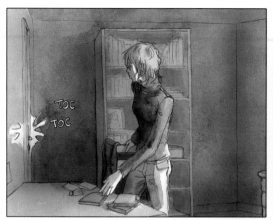

TOC
TOC

I'VE MADE YOU SOME COFFEE, EMMA.

THANK YOU, FABIENNE.

PLEASE FORGIVE MY HUSBAND. YOU CAN UNDERSTAND THAT HE'S HAVING TROUBLE ACCEPTING THE ROLE YOU PLAYED IN OUR DAUGHTER'S LIFE. I DON'T THINK YOU'LL SEE HIM BEFORE DINNER.

JUST TELL HIM THAT IF I HAD BEEN A GUY, CLEM WOULD HAVE FALLEN IN LOVE WITH ME ANYWAY.

UH ...

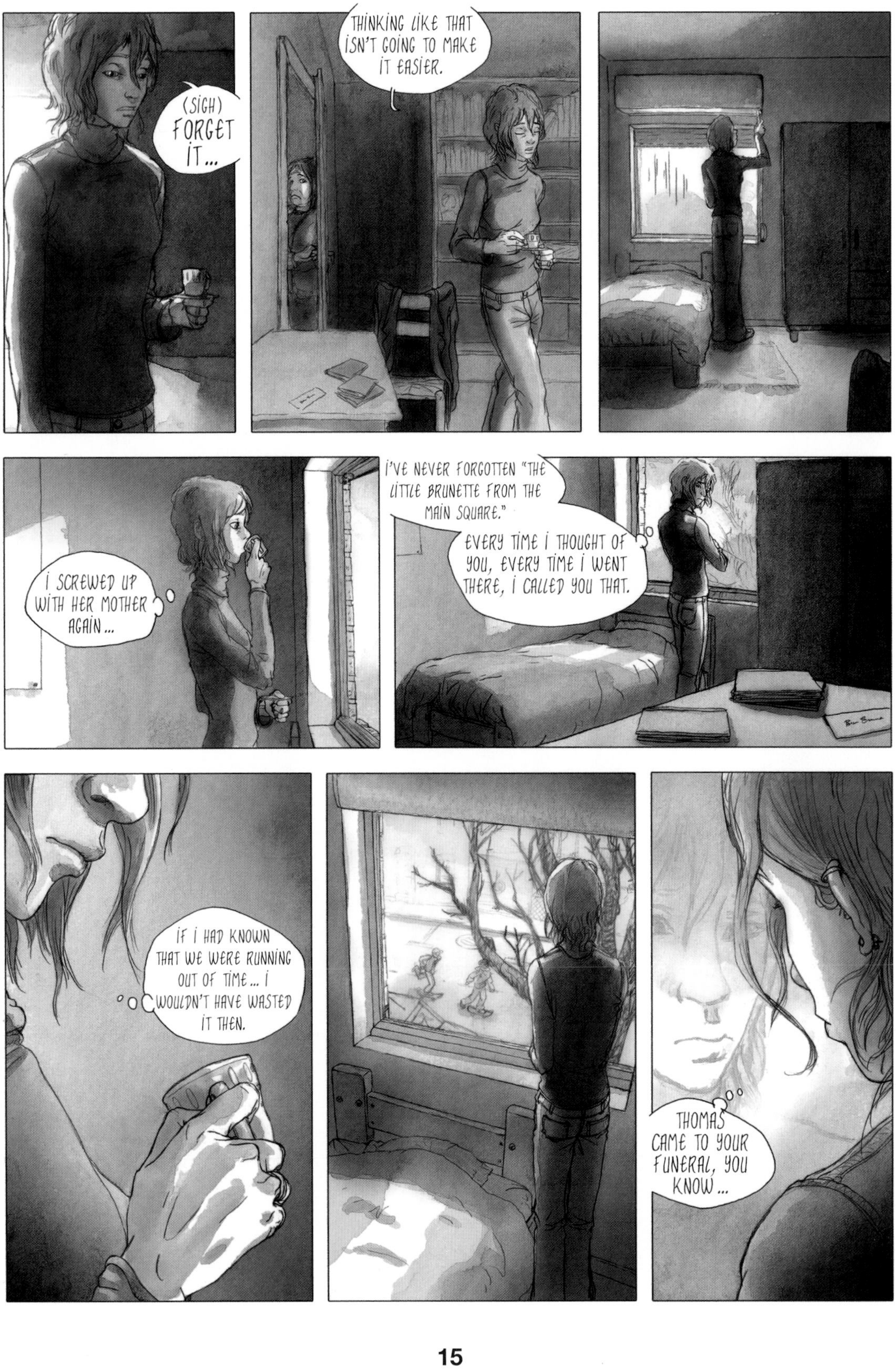
(SIGH) FORGET IT...
THINKING LIKE THAT ISN'T GOING TO MAKE IT EASIER.
I SCREWED UP WITH HER MOTHER AGAIN...
I'VE NEVER FORGOTTEN "THE LITTLE BRUNETTE FROM THE MAIN SQUARE."
EVERY TIME I THOUGHT OF YOU, EVERY TIME I WENT THERE, I CALLED YOU THAT.
IF I HAD KNOWN THAT WE WERE RUNNING OUT OF TIME... I WOULDN'T HAVE WASTED IT THEN.
THOMAS CAME TO YOUR FUNERAL, YOU KNOW...

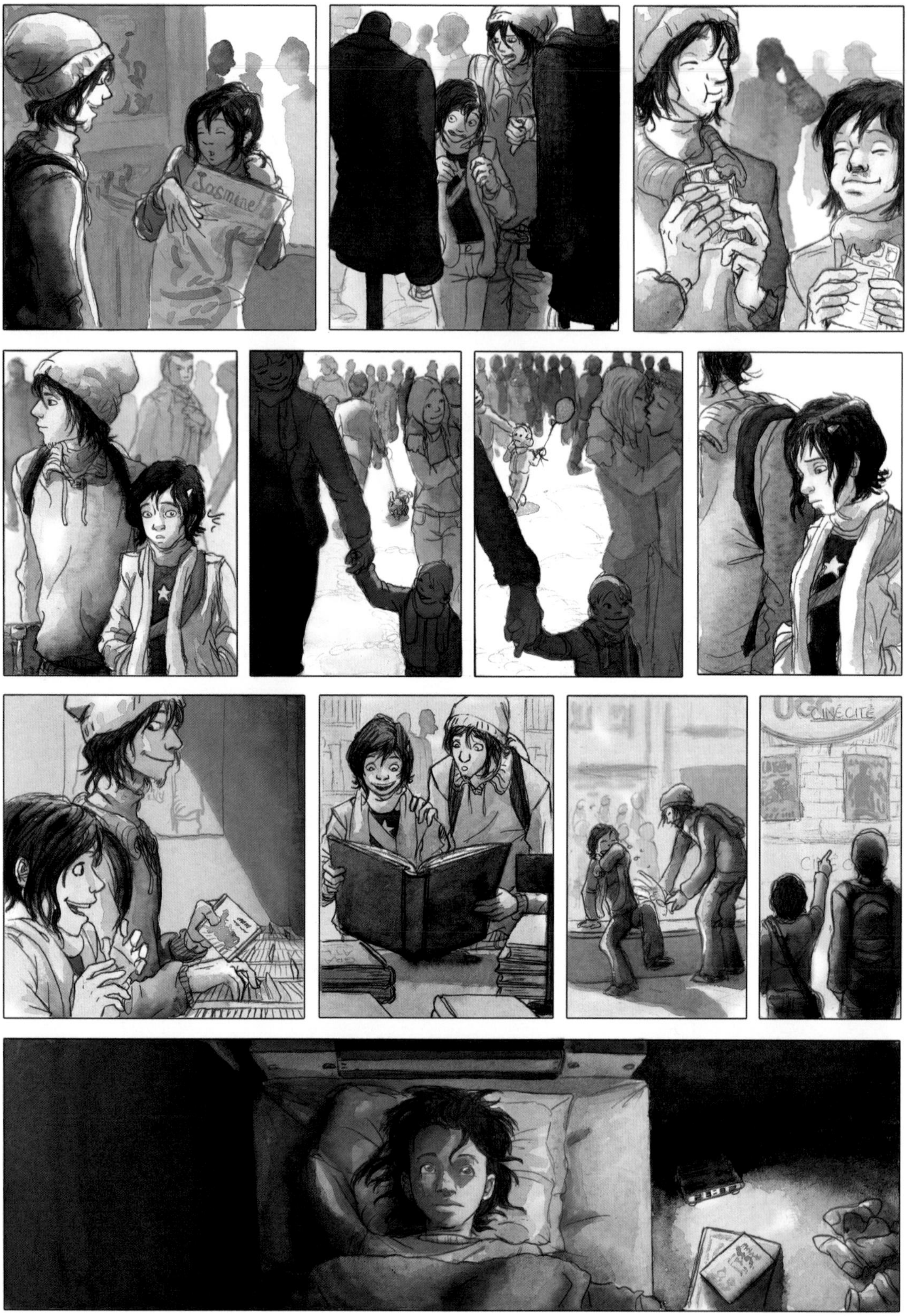
Jasmine
UGC
CINÉ CITÉ

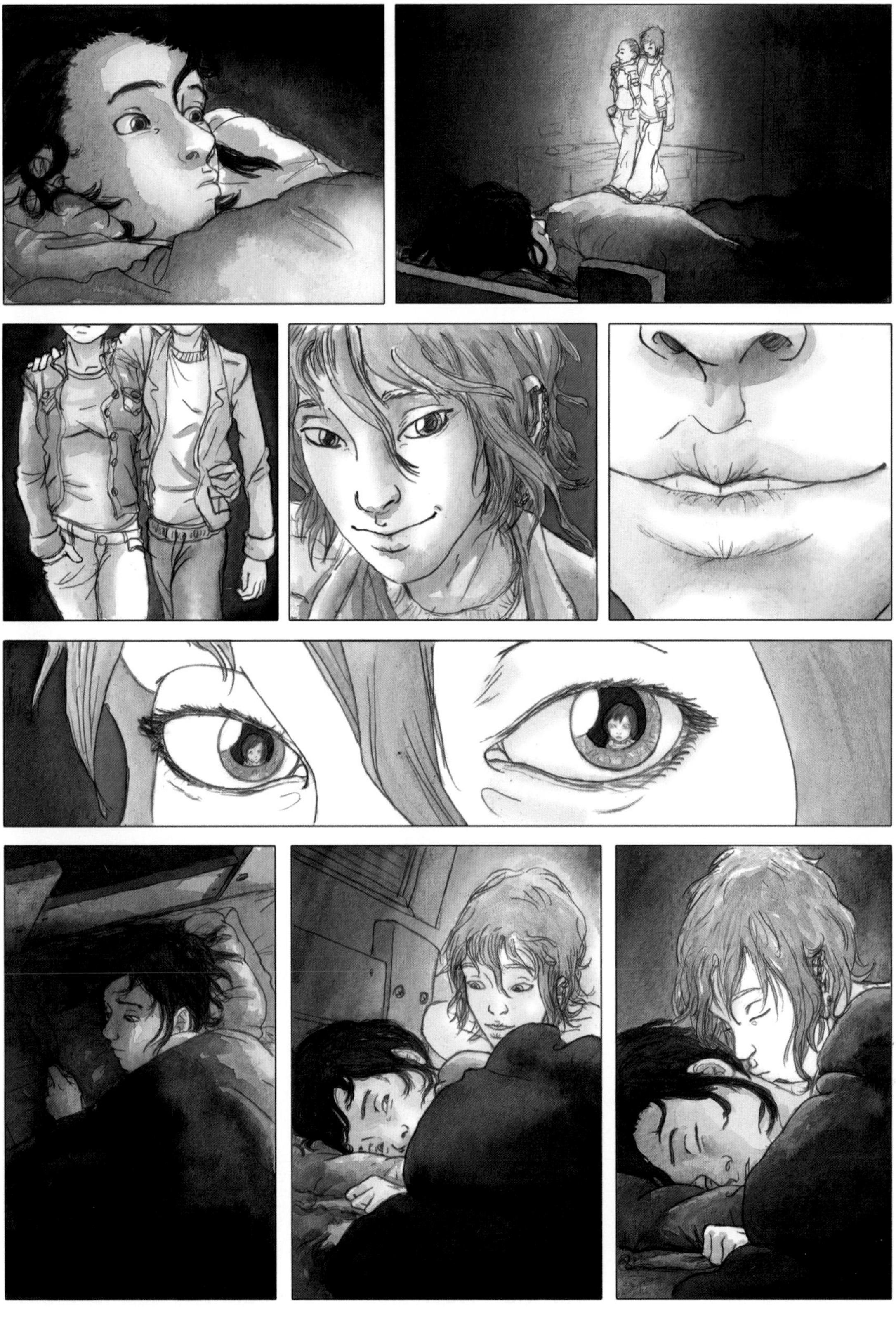

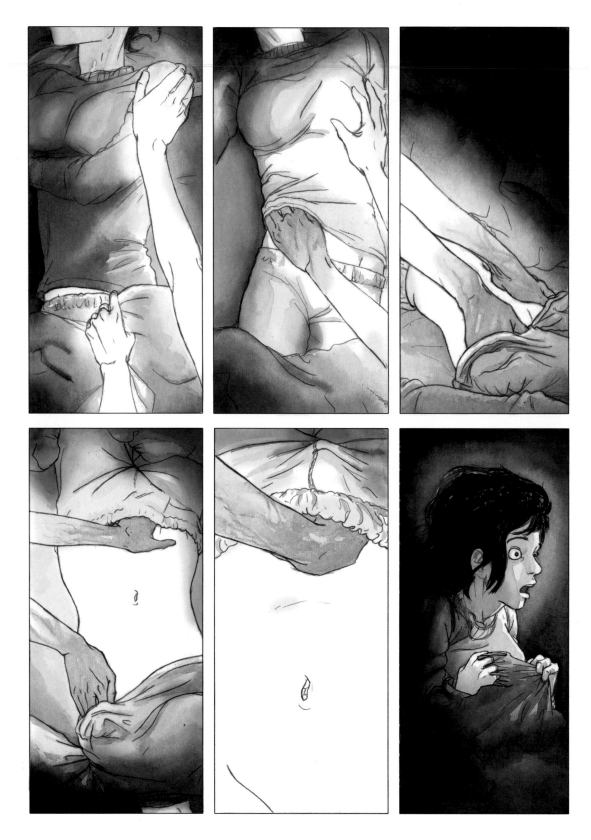

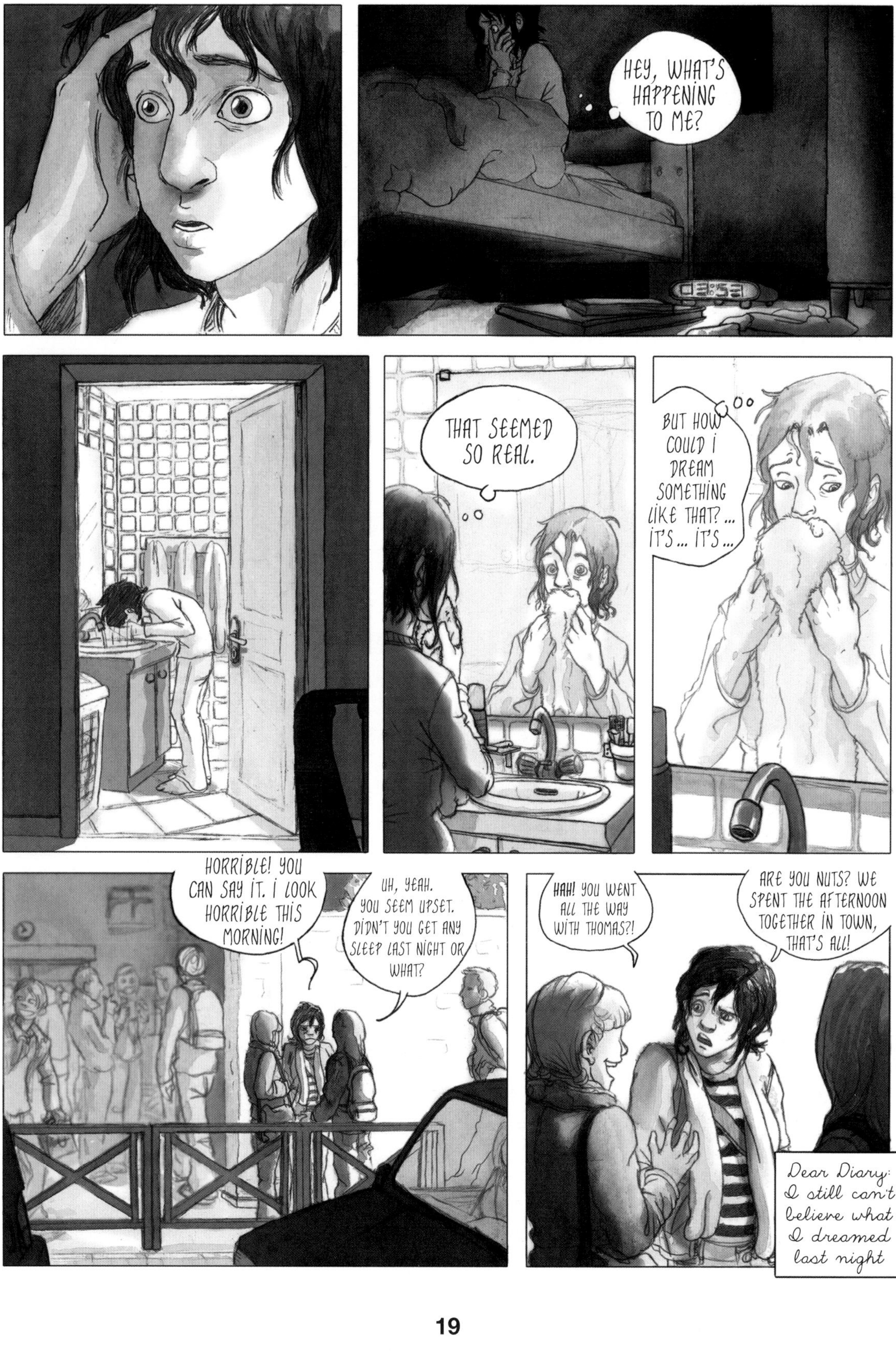
HEY, WHAT'S HAPPENING TO ME?
THAT SEEMED SO REAL.
BUT HOW COULD I DREAM SOMETHING LIKE THAT? ... IT'S ... IT'S ...
HORRIBLE! YOU CAN SAY IT. I LOOK HORRIBLE THIS MORNING!
UH, YEAH. YOU SEEM UPSET. DIDN'T YOU GET ANY SLEEP LAST NIGHT OR WHAT?
HAH! YOU WENT ALL THE WAY WITH THOMAS?!
ARE YOU NUTS? WE SPENT THE AFTERNOON TOGETHER IN TOWN, THAT'S ALL!
Dear Diary: I still can't believe what I dreamed last night

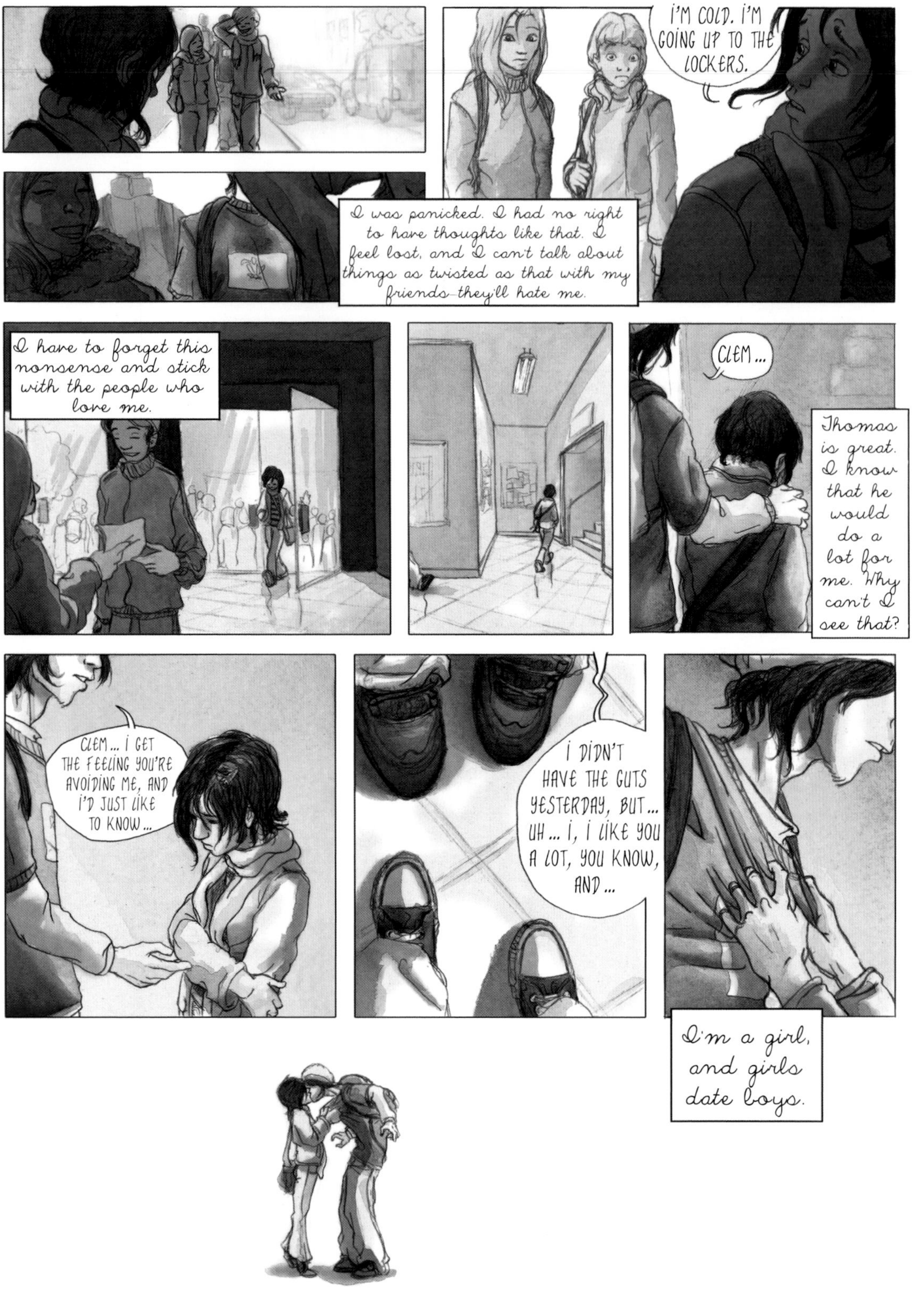
I'M COLD. I'M GOING UP TO THE LOCKERS.
I was panicked. I had no right to have thoughts like that. I feel lost, and I can't talk about things as twisted as that with my friends—they'll hate me.
I have to forget this nonsense and stick with the people who love me.
CLEM...
Thomas is great. I know that he would do a lot for me. Why can't I see that?
CLEM... I GET THE FEELING YOU'RE AVOIDING ME, AND I'D JUST LIKE TO KNOW...
I DIDN'T HAVE THE GUTS YESTERDAY, BUT... UH... I, I LIKE YOU A LOT, YOU KNOW, AND...
I'm a girl, and girls date boys.

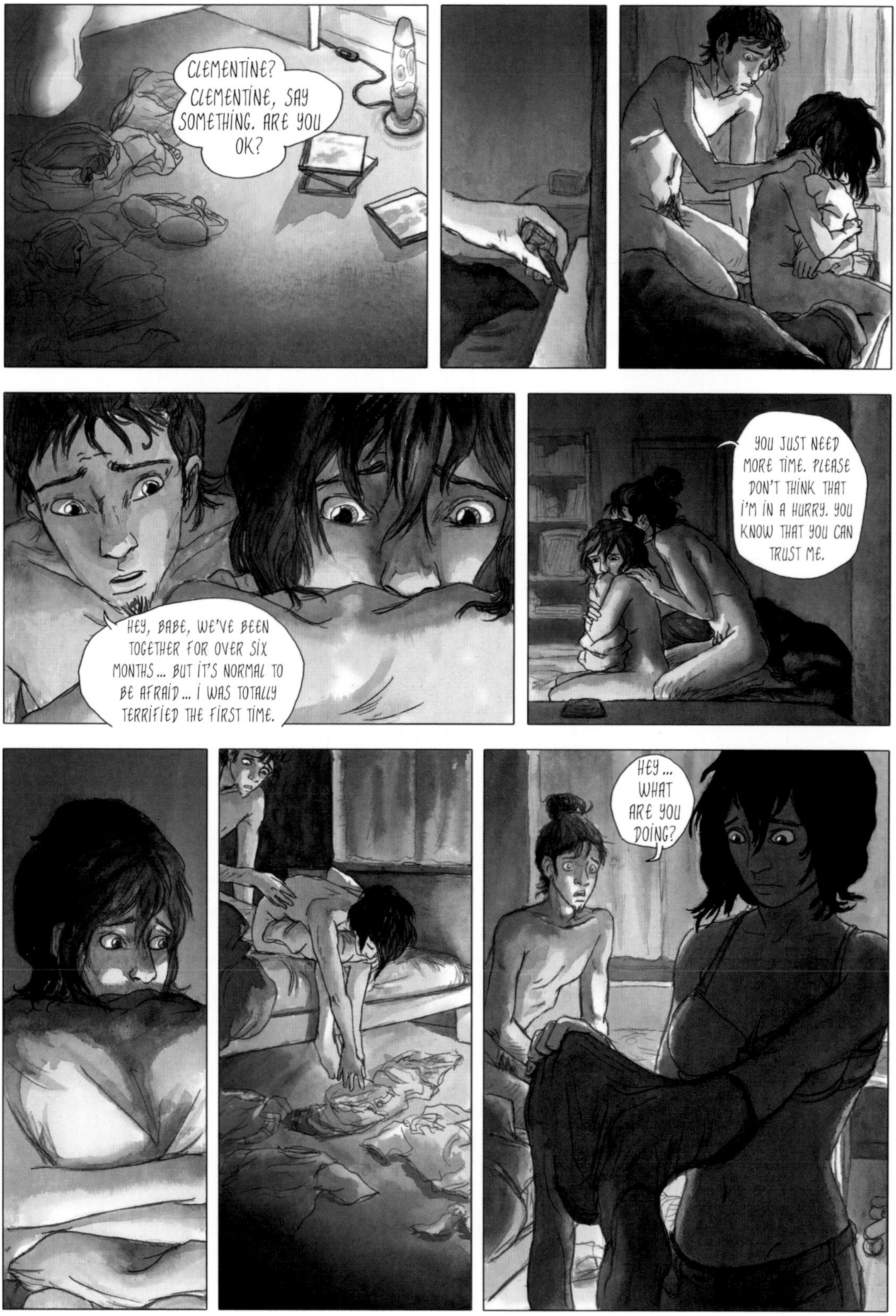
CLEMENTINE? CLEMENTINE, SAY SOMETHING. ARE YOU OK?
HEY, BABE, WE'VE BEEN TOGETHER FOR OVER SIX MONTHS... BUT IT'S NORMAL TO BE AFRAID... I WAS TOTALLY TERRIFIED THE FIRST TIME.
YOU JUST NEED MORE TIME. PLEASE DON'T THINK THAT I'M IN A HURRY. YOU KNOW THAT YOU CAN TRUST ME.
HEY... WHAT ARE YOU DOING?

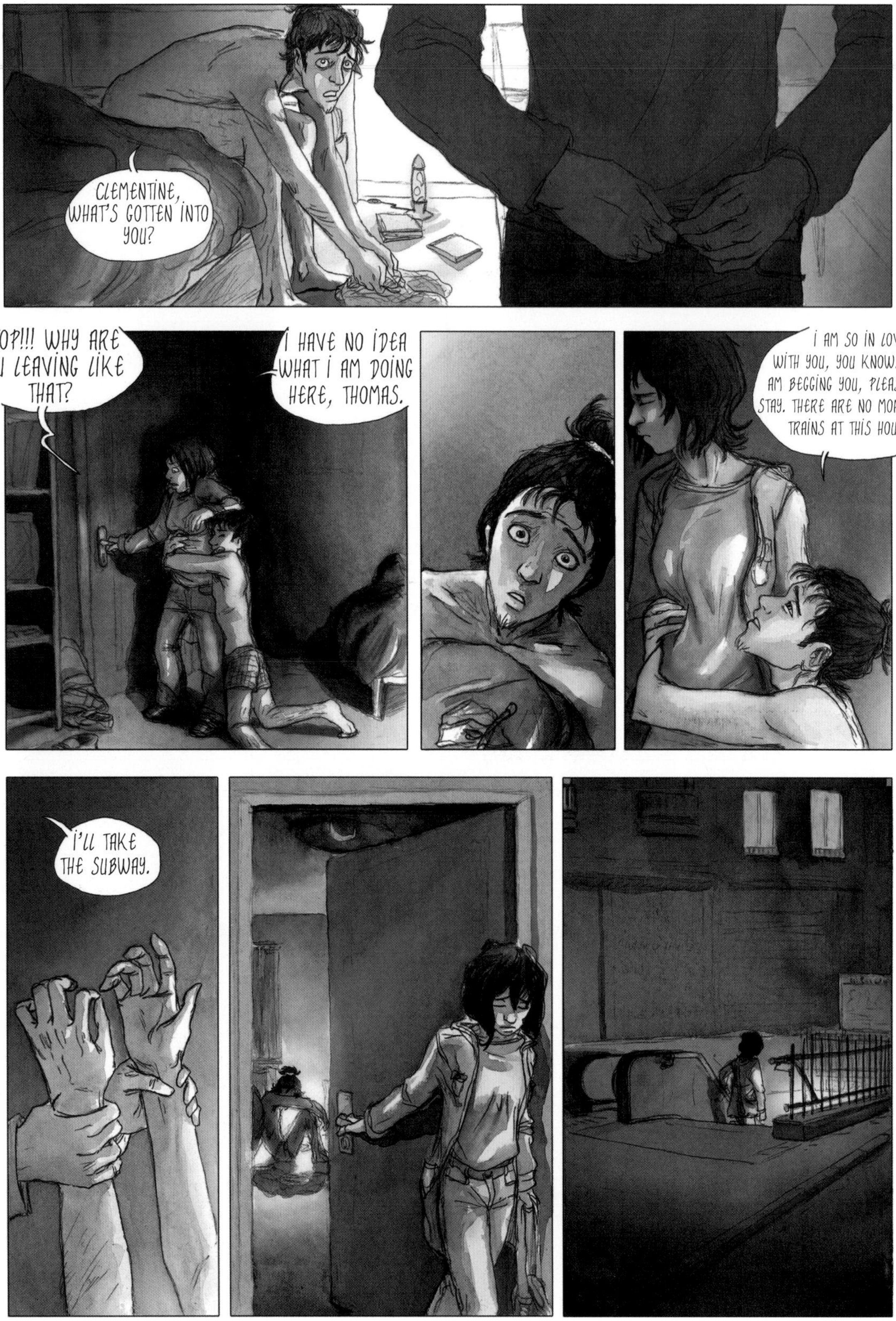
CLEMENTINE, WHAT'S GOTTEN INTO YOU?
STOP!!! WHY ARE YOU LEAVING LIKE THAT?
I HAVE NO IDEA WHAT I AM DOING HERE, THOMAS.
I AM SO IN LOVE WITH YOU, YOU KNOW. I AM BEGGING YOU, PLEASE STAY. THERE ARE NO MORE TRAINS AT THIS HOUR.
I'LL TAKE THE SUBWAY.

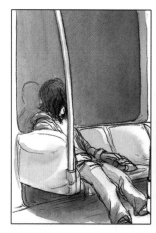

CLEMENTINE?!

MY MOTHER AND HER CHRONIC INSOMNIA...

BUT... YOUR PAJAMA PARTY AT YOUR FRIEND'S HOUSE...

WE GOT INTO A FIGHT. I WANTED TO COME HOME.

AT 3:00 IN THE MORNING?!

DO YOU REALIZE WHAT COULD HAVE HAPPENED TO YOU? REALLY, YOU ARE SO IRRESPONSIBLE!

AND WITH EVERYTHING THAT'S HAPPENING!

GOOD NIGHT, MOM.

May 1st, 1995

Dear Diary,

I've already told you about my disastrous evening with Thomas, but I still need to talk about it.

I can't stop thinking about what happened (and could have happened), and I like myself less and less.

I didn't even really want to go to his place and even less to sleep with him.

But I'm going out with him—that's what's supposed to happen, isn't it?

I feel lost, alone, at the bottom of a pit. I don't know what to do. I get the feeling that everything I do is unnatural.

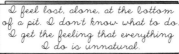

Against my nature.

Why does life work for other people and not for me?

LIFE DOES NOT WORK FOR EVERYONE ELSE, EITHER, MY DEAR HEART.

25

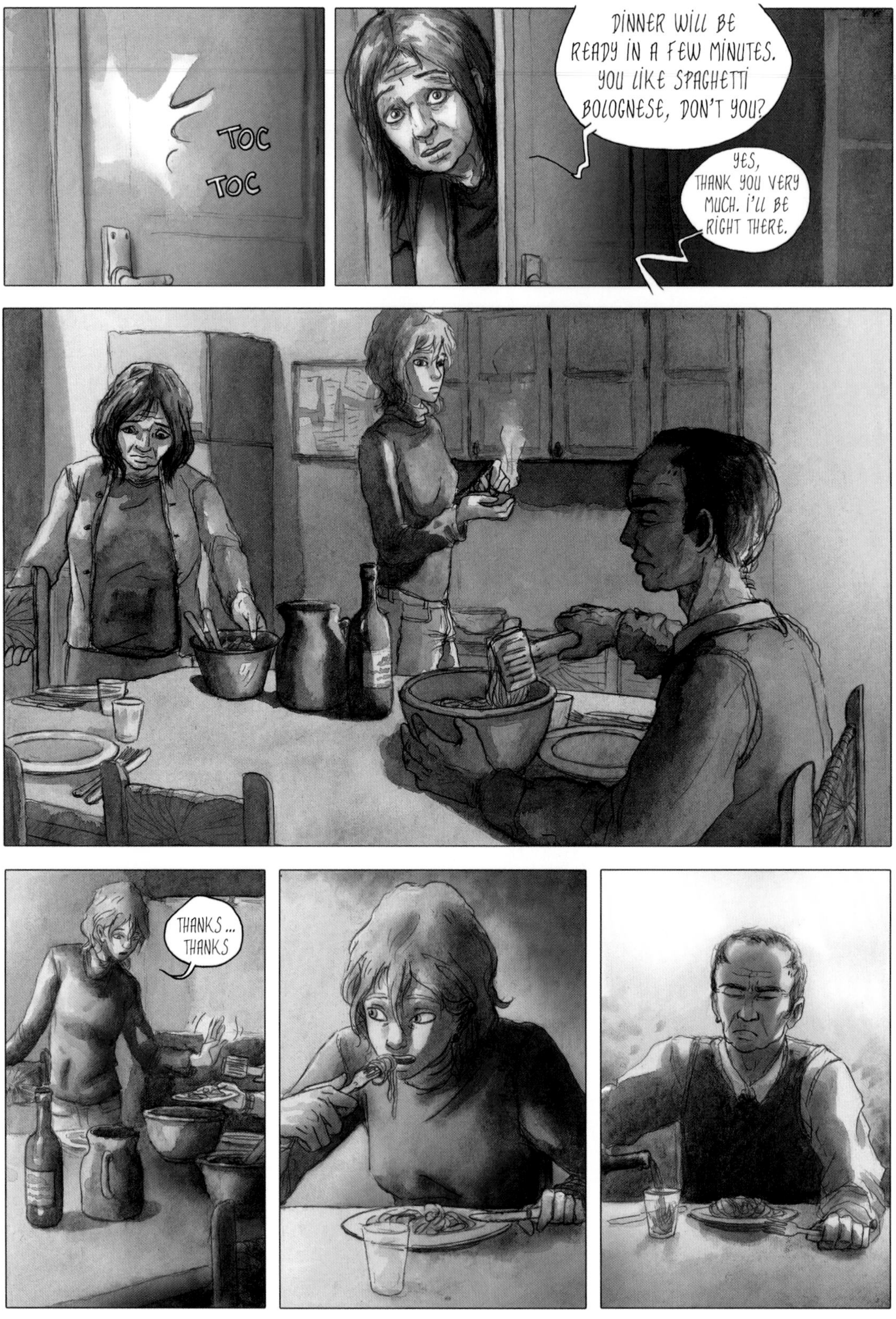
TOC
TOC
DINNER WILL BE READY IN A FEW MINUTES. YOU LIKE SPAGHETTI BOLOGNESE, DON'T YOU?
YES, THANK YOU VERY MUCH. I'LL BE RIGHT THERE.
THANKS... THANKS

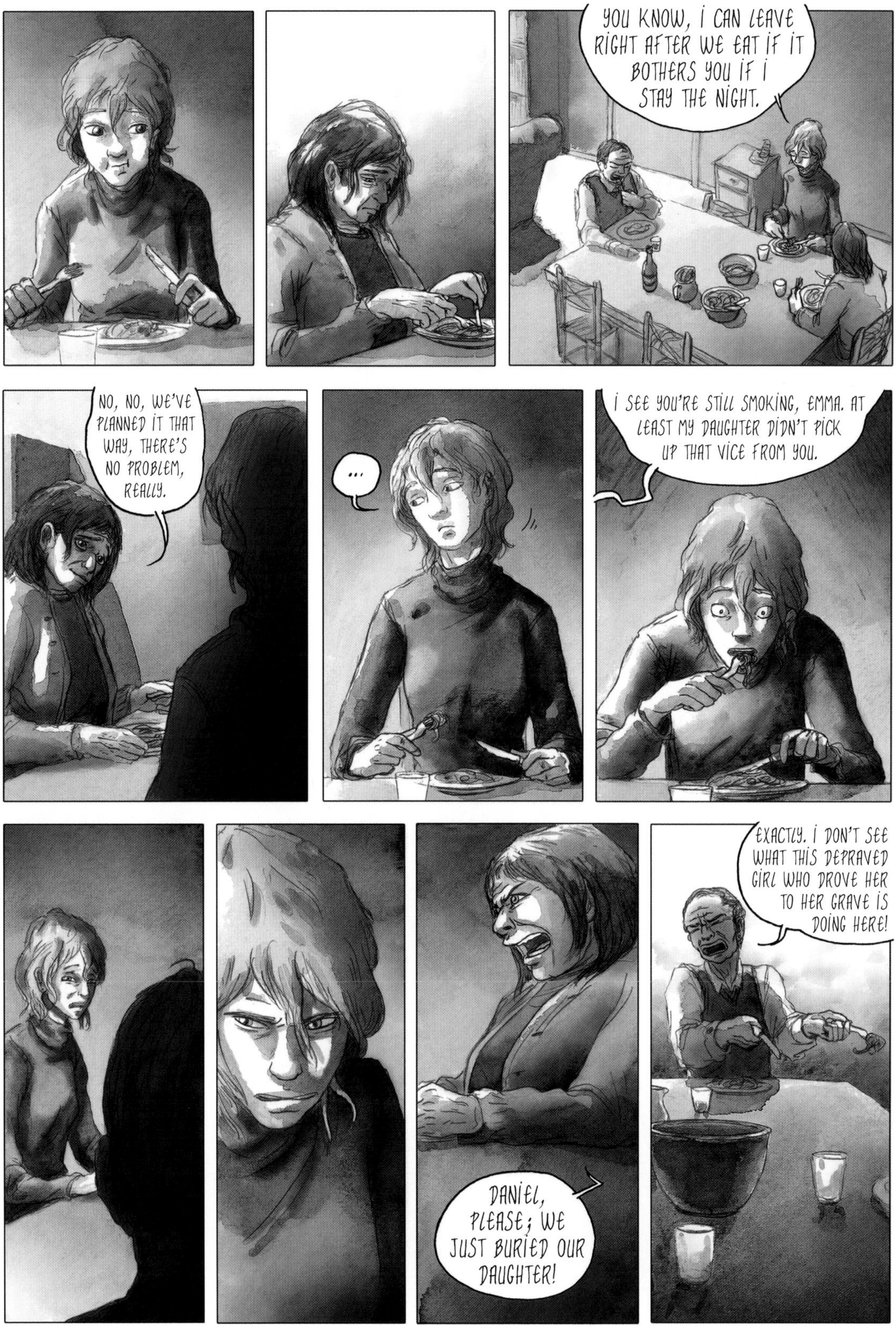
YOU KNOW, I CAN LEAVE RIGHT AFTER WE EAT IF IT BOTHERS YOU IF I STAY THE NIGHT.
NO, NO, WE'VE PLANNED IT THAT WAY, THERE'S NO PROBLEM, REALLY.
...
I SEE YOU'RE STILL SMOKING, EMMA. AT LEAST MY DAUGHTER DIDN'T PICK UP THAT VICE FROM YOU.
DANIEL, PLEASE; WE JUST BURIED OUR DAUGHTER!
EXACTLY. I DON'T SEE WHAT THIS DEPRAVED GIRL WHO DROVE HER TO HER GRAVE IS DOING HERE!

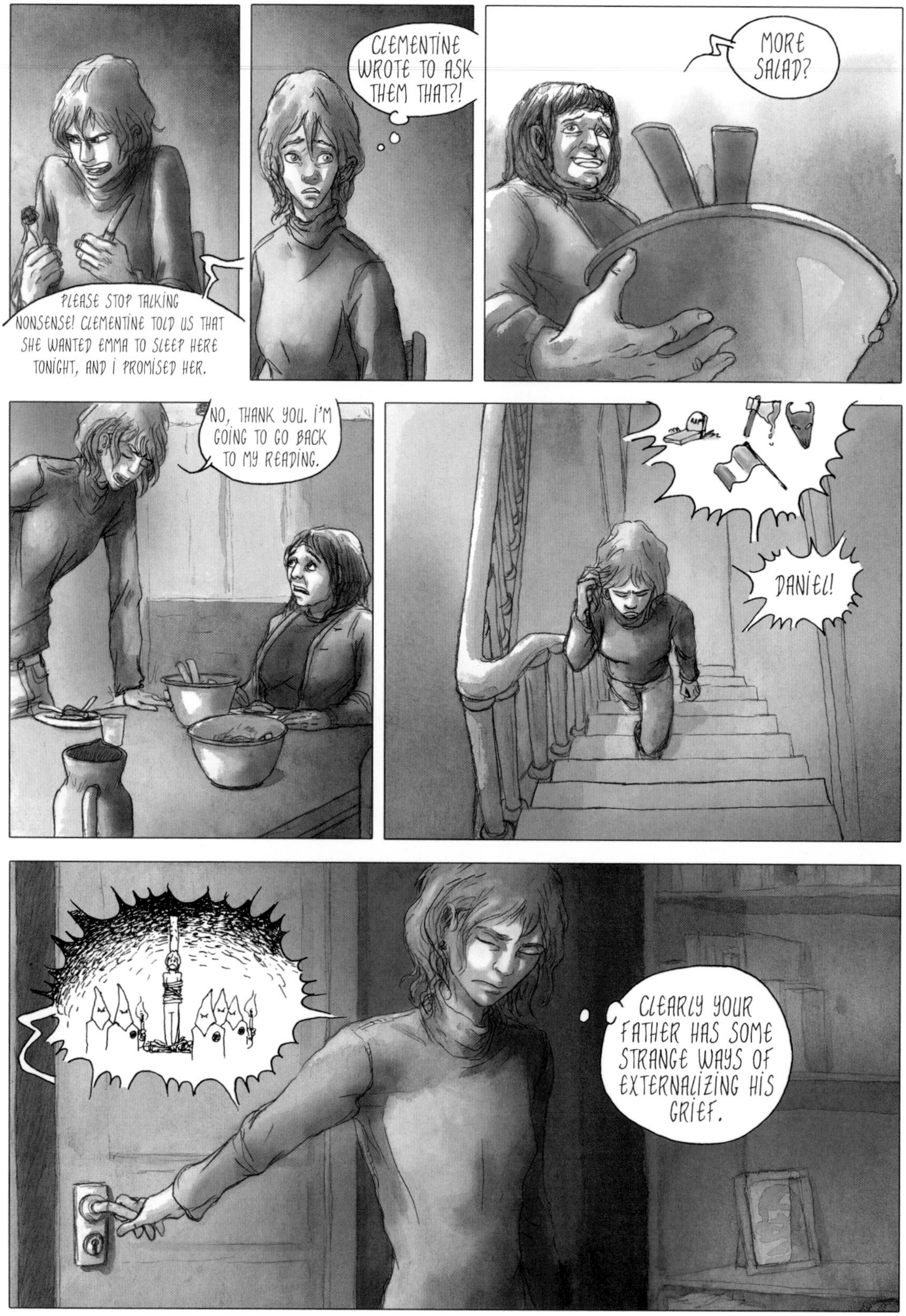
PLEASE STOP TALKING NONSENSE! CLEMENTINE TOLD US THAT SHE WANTED EMMA TO SLEEP HERE TONIGHT, AND I PROMISED HER.
CLEMENTINE WROTE TO ASK THEM THAT?!
MORE SALAD?
NO, THANK YOU. I'M GOING TO GO BACK TO MY READING.
DANIEL!
CLEARLY YOUR FATHER HAS SOME STRANGE WAYS OF EXTERNALIZING HIS GRIEF.

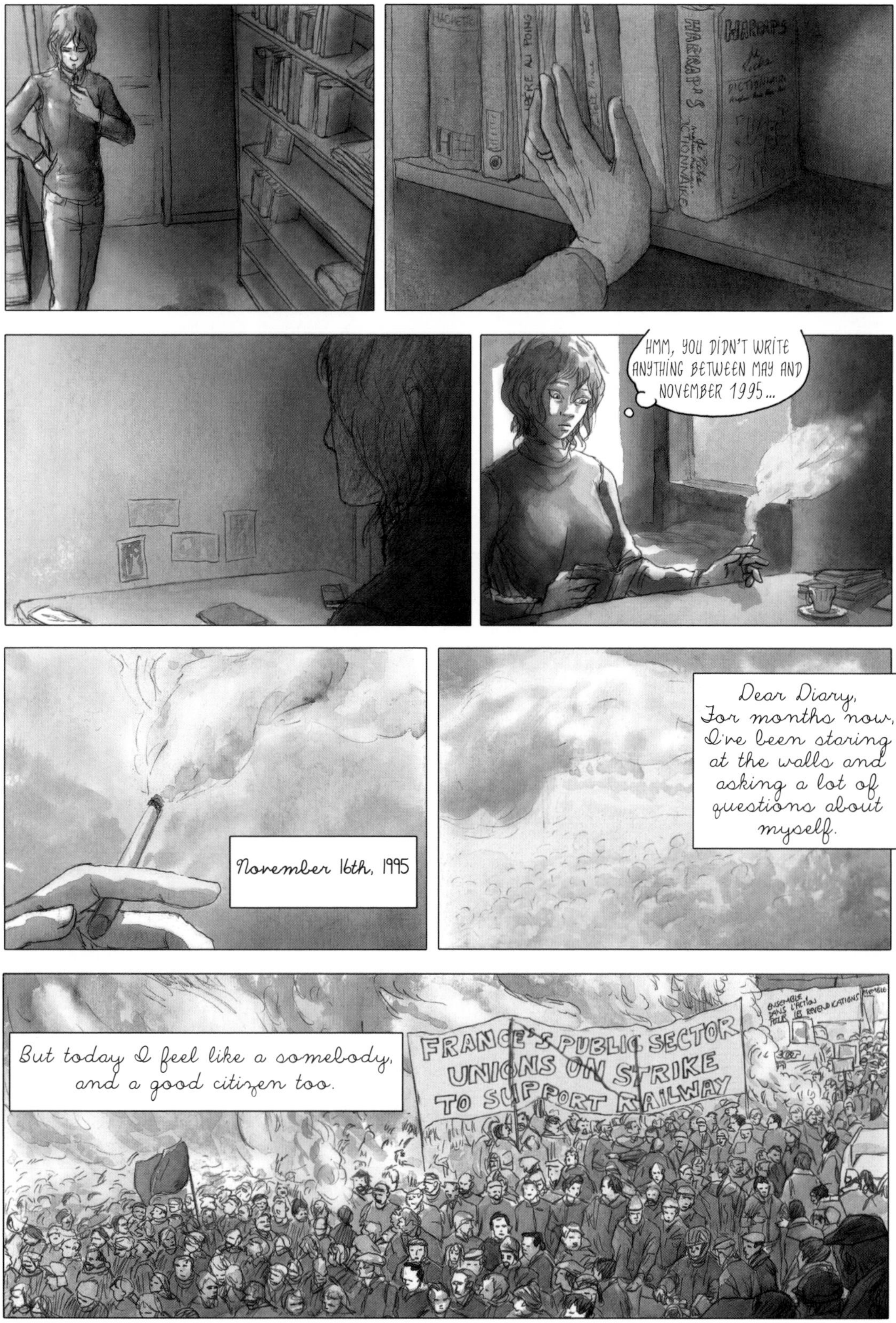
HMM, YOU DIDN'T WRITE ANYTHING BETWEEN MAY AND NOVEMBER 1995...
November 16th, 1995
Dear Diary, For months now, I've been staring at the walls and asking a lot of questions about myself.
But today I feel like a somebody, and a good citizen too.
FRANCE'S PUBLIC SECTOR UNIONS ON STRIKE TO SUPPORT RAILWAY

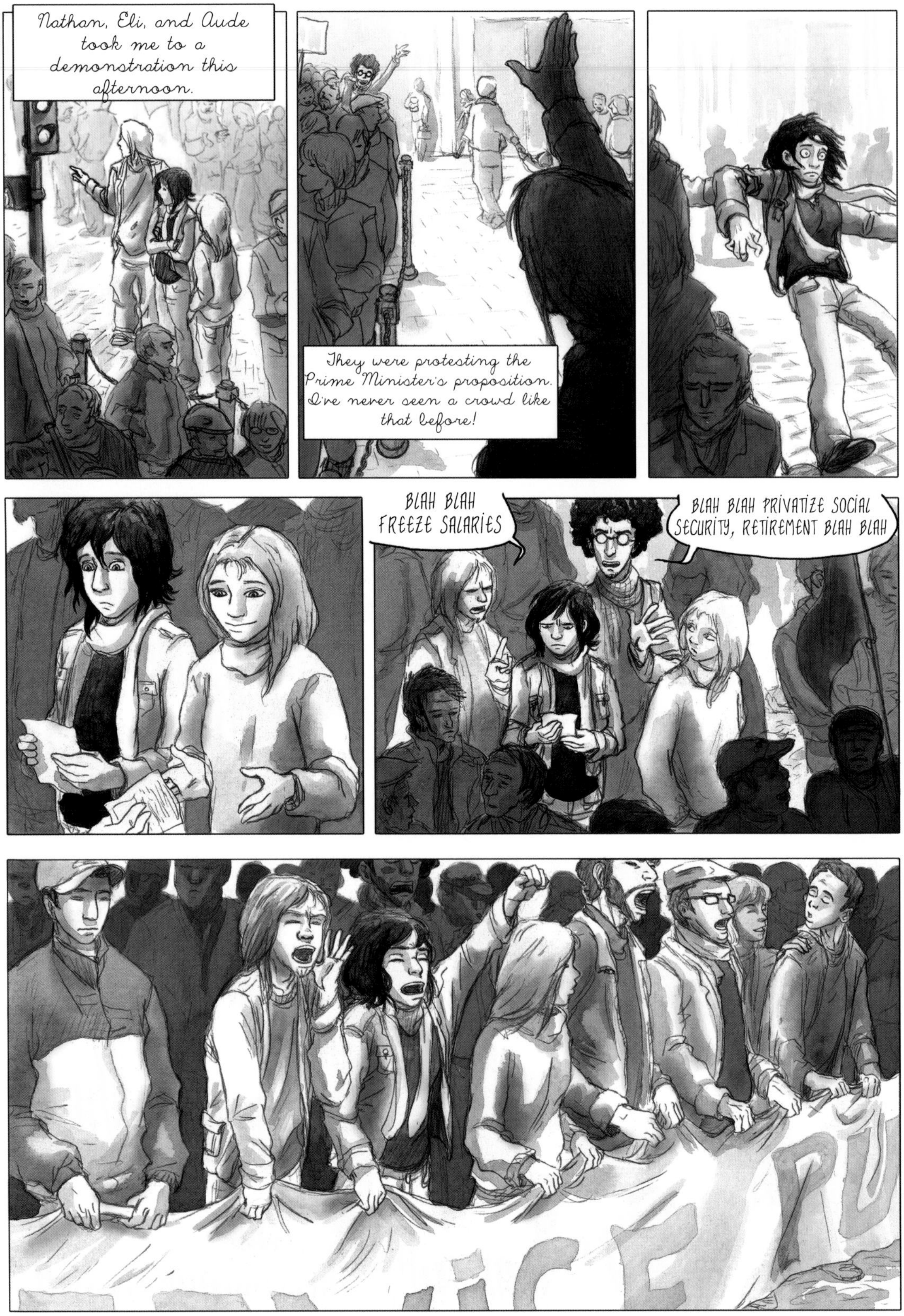
Nathan, Eli, and Aude took me to a demonstration this afternoon.
They were protesting the Prime Minister's proposition. I've never seen a crowd like that before!
BLAH BLAH FREEZE SALARIES
BLAH BLAH PRIVATIZE SOCIAL SECURITY, RETIREMENT BLAH BLAH

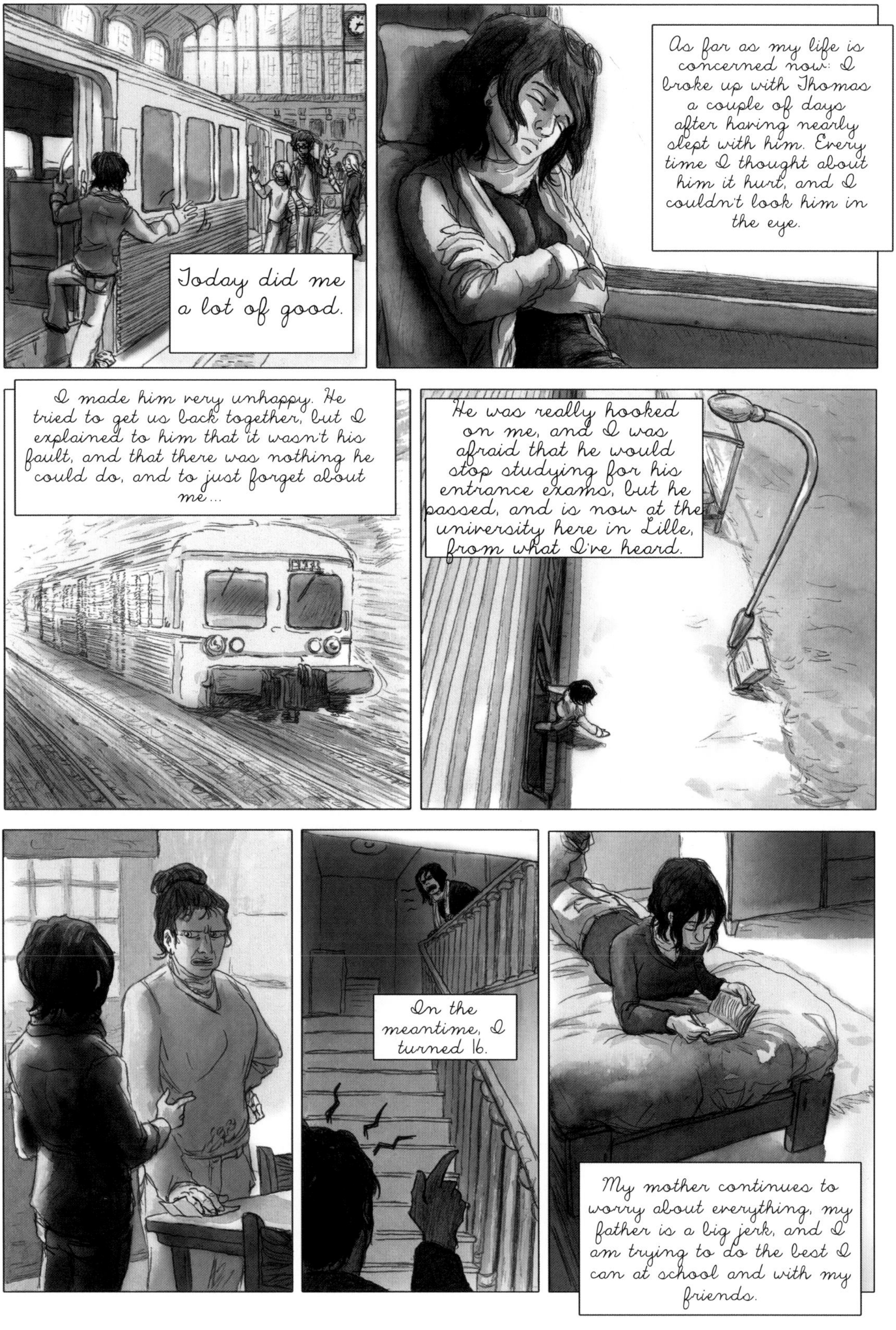
Today did me a lot of good.
As far as my life is concerned now: I broke up with Thomas a couple of days after having nearly slept with him. Every time I thought about him it hurt, and I couldn't look him in the eye.
I made him very unhappy. He tried to get us back together, but I explained to him that it wasn't his fault, and that there was nothing he could do, and to just forget about me...
He was really hooked on me, and I was afraid that he would stop studying for his entrance exams, but he passed, and is now at the university here in Lille, from what I've heard.
In the meantime, I turned 16.
My mother continues to worry about everything, my father is a big jerk, and I am trying to do the best I can at school and with my friends.

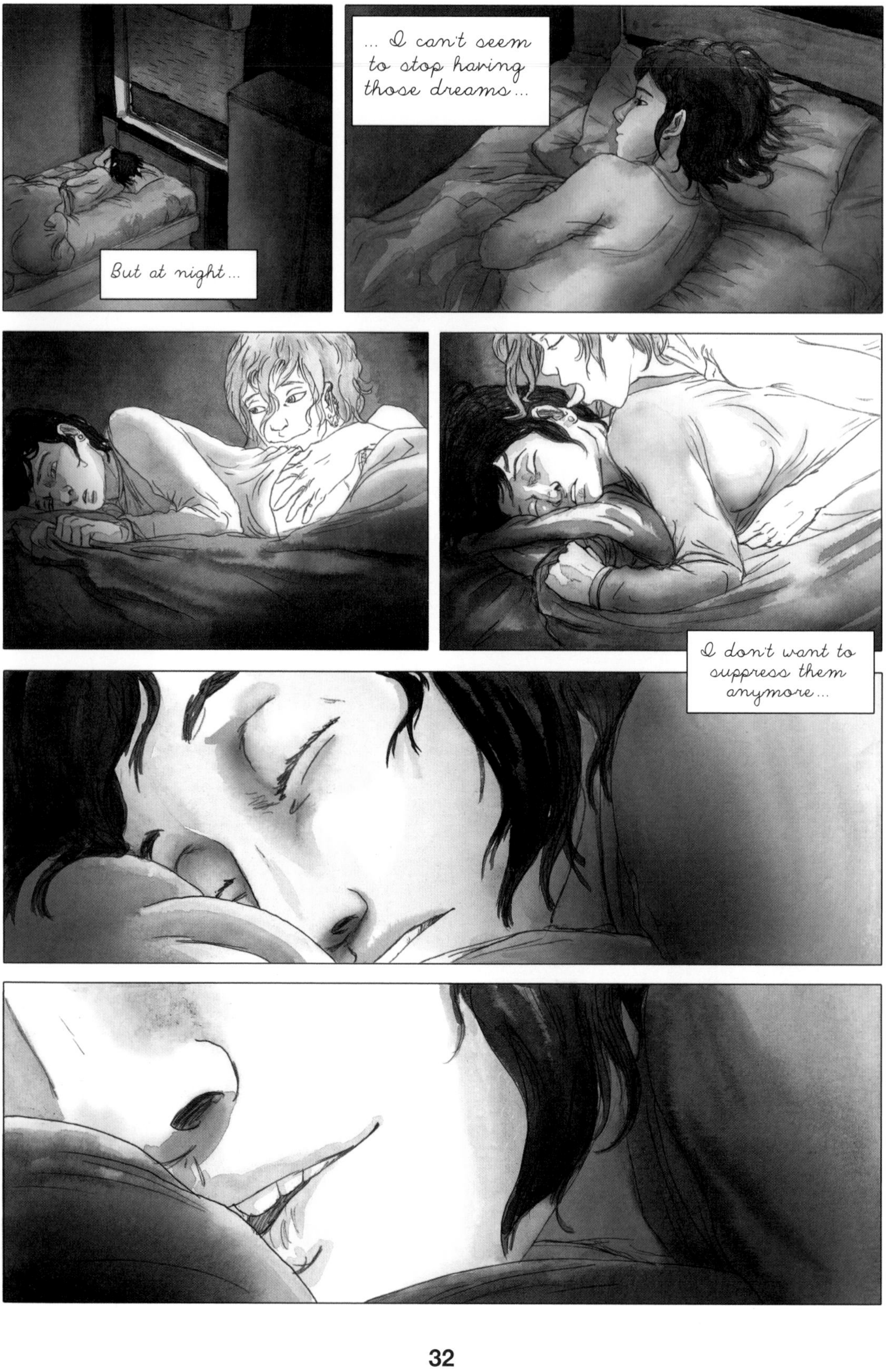
But at night...
... I can't seem to stop having those dreams...
I don't want to suppress them anymore...

December 6th, 1995

I would like to stay in my bed all day, out of the cold, floating in my dreams. I would like to have someone to share my feelings with, but just thinking about talking about it stresses me out till I can't breathe.

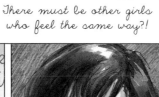

There must be other girls who feel the same way?!

DON'T YOU THINK CHARLOTTE IS SUPER CUTE?!

33

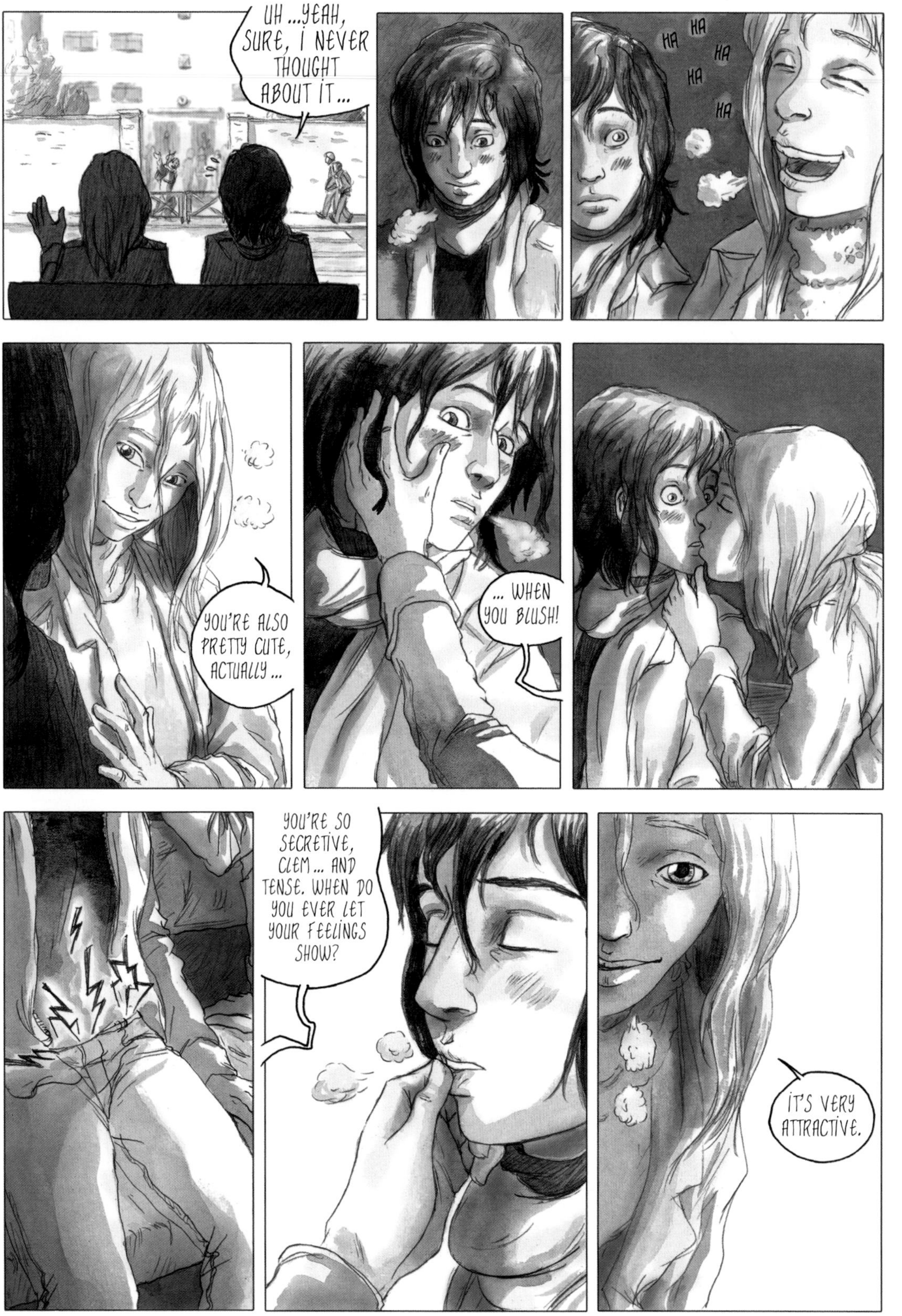
UH ...YEAH, SURE, I NEVER THOUGHT ABOUT IT...
HA HA HA HA HA
YOU'RE ALSO PRETTY CUTE, ACTUALLY...
... WHEN YOU BLUSH!
YOU'RE SO SECRETIVE, CLEM... AND TENSE. WHEN DO YOU EVER LET YOUR FEELINGS SHOW?
IT'S VERY ATTRACTIVE.

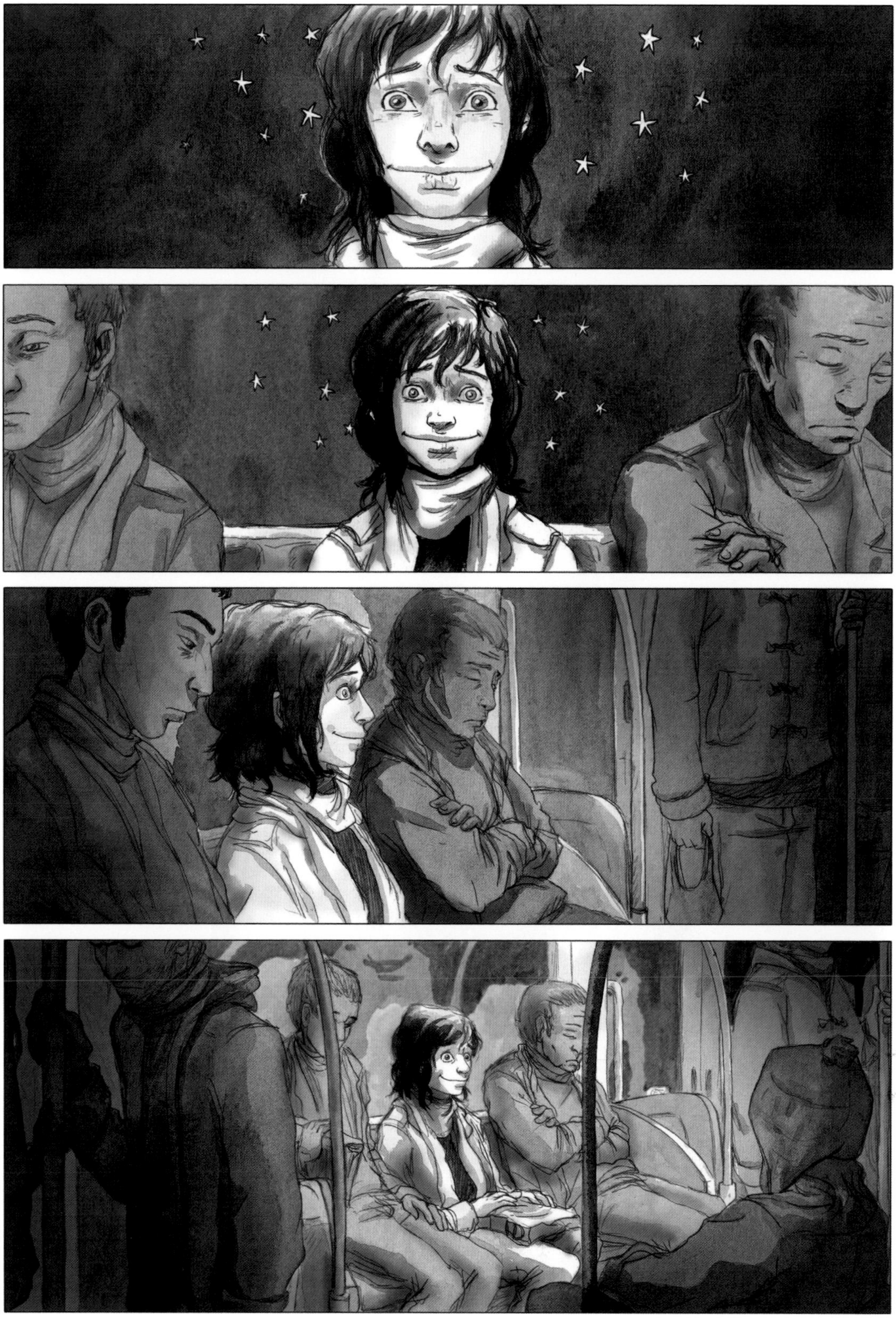

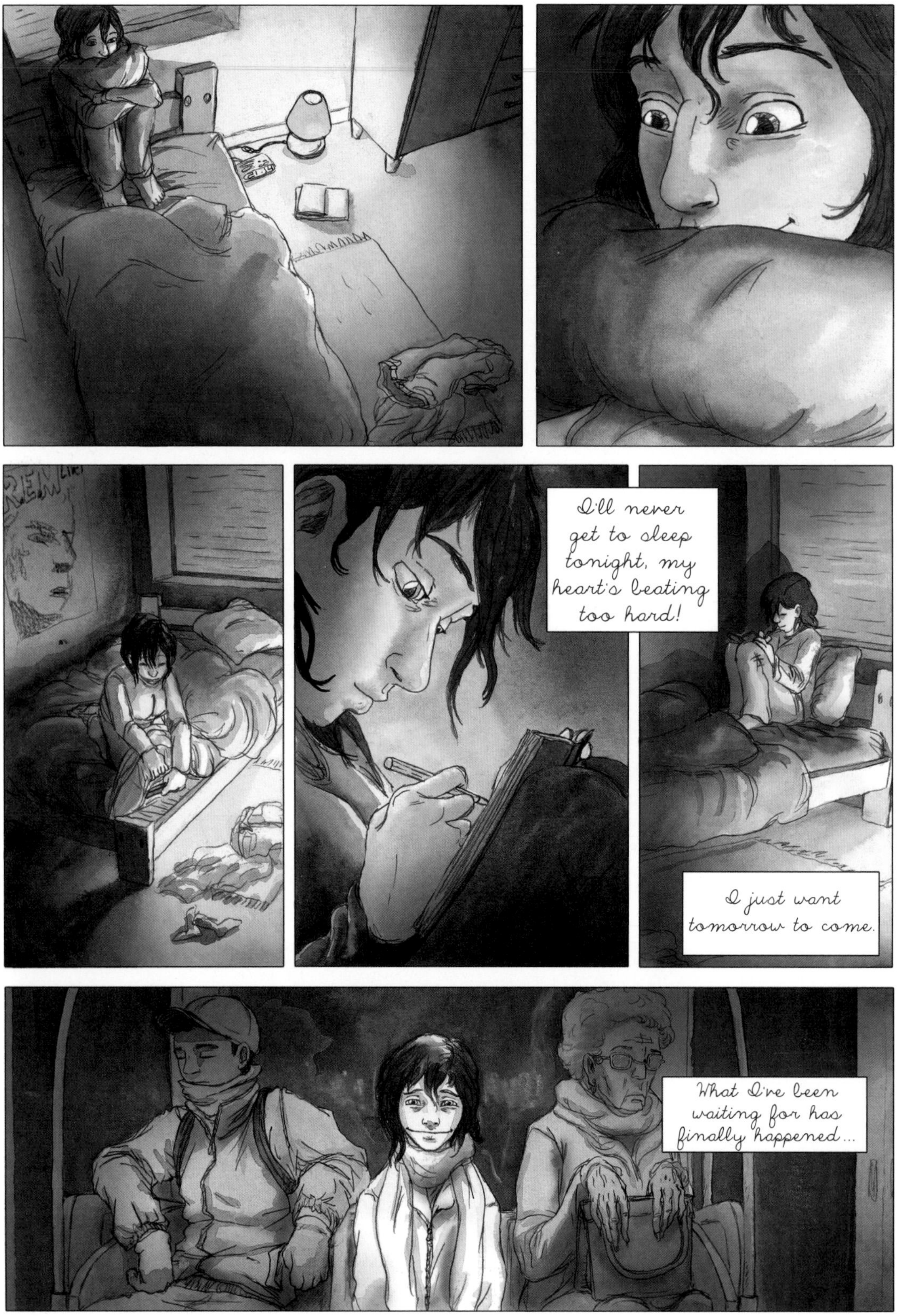
I'll never get to sleep tonight, my heart's beating too hard!
I just want tomorrow to come.
What I've been waiting for has finally happened...

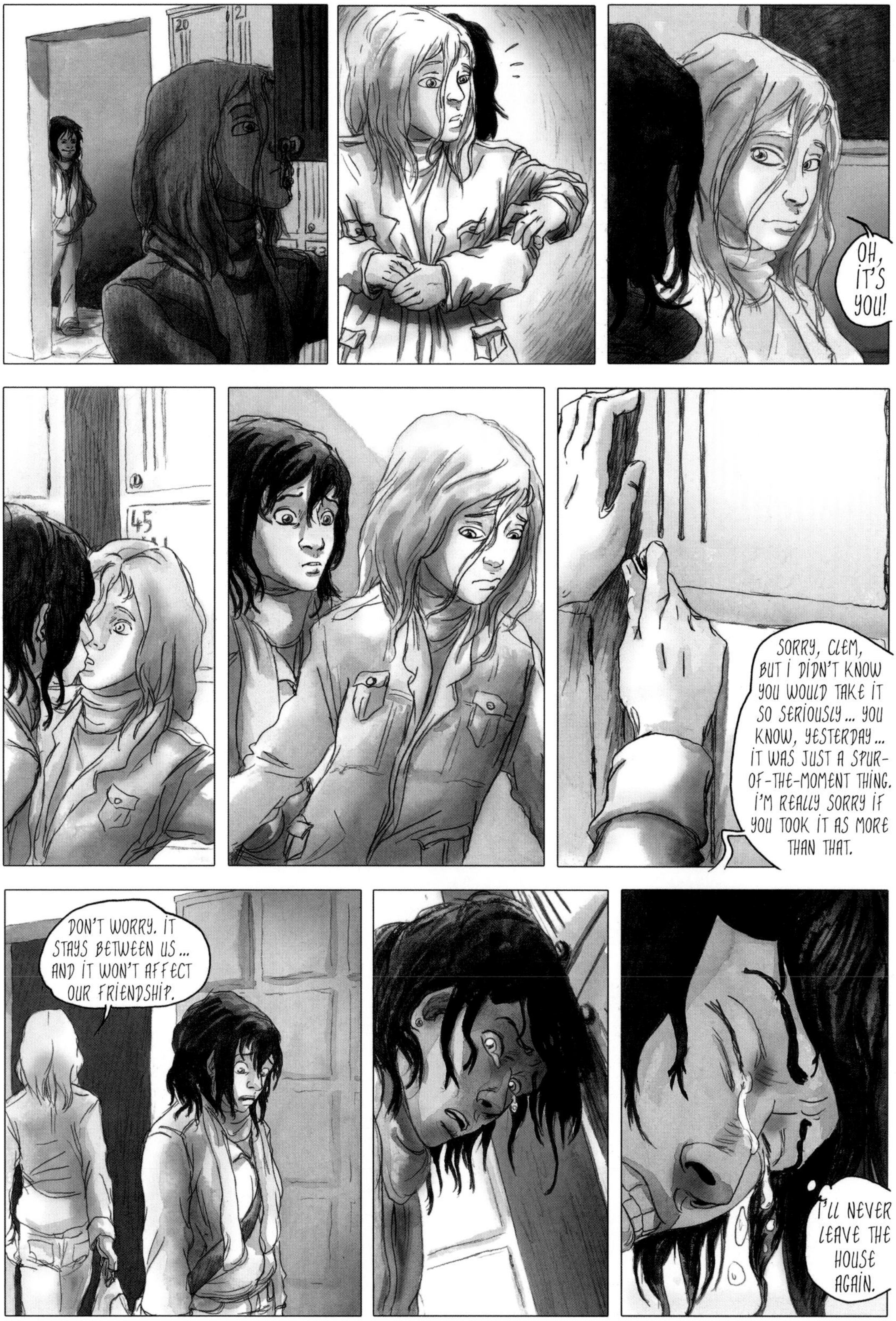
OH, IT'S YOU!
SORRY, CLEM, BUT I DIDN'T KNOW YOU WOULD TAKE IT SO SERIOUSLY... YOU KNOW, YESTERDAY... IT WAS JUST A SPUR-OF-THE-MOMENT THING. I'M REALLY SORRY IF YOU TOOK IT AS MORE THAN THAT.
DON'T WORRY. IT STAYS BETWEEN US... AND IT WON'T AFFECT OUR FRIENDSHIP.
I'LL NEVER LEAVE THE HOUSE AGAIN.

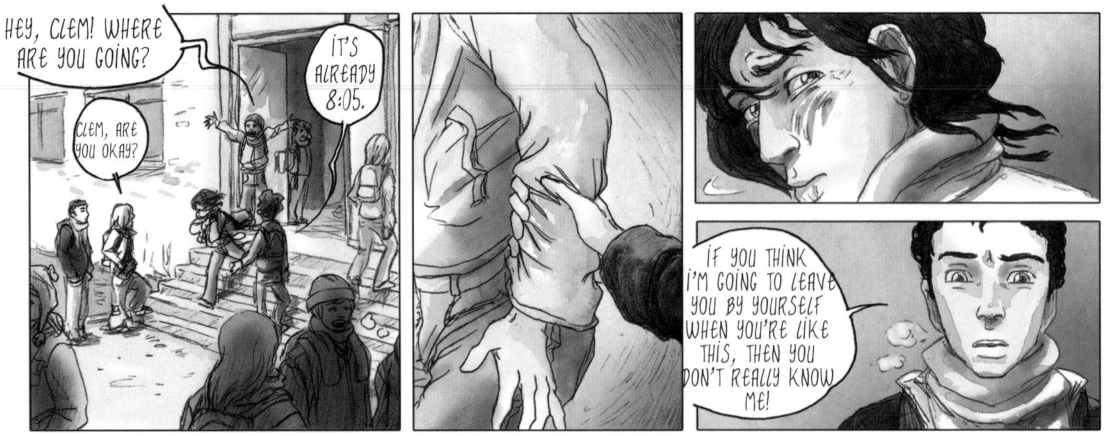
HEY, CLEM! WHERE ARE YOU GOING?
IT'S ALREADY 8:05.
CLEM, ARE YOU OKAY?
IF YOU THINK I'M GOING TO LEAVE YOU BY YOURSELF WHEN YOU'RE LIKE THIS, THEN YOU DON'T REALLY KNOW ME!

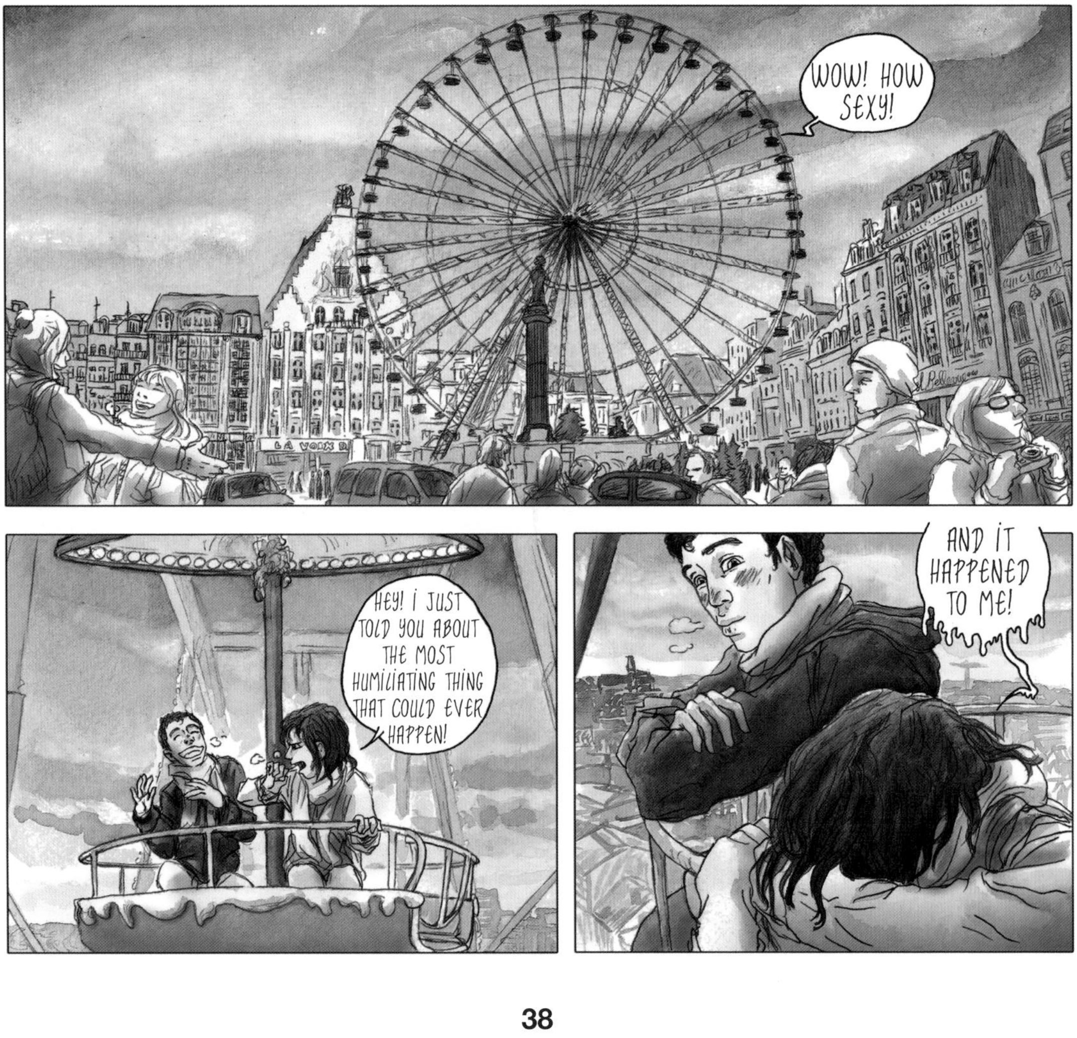
WOW! HOW SEXY!
HEY! I JUST TOLD YOU ABOUT THE MOST HUMILIATING THING THAT COULD EVER HAPPEN!
AND IT HAPPENED TO ME!

YOU KNOW, I HIT ON A GUY ONCE.

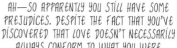

AH—SO APPARENTLY YOU STILL HAVE SOME PREJUDICES. DESPITE THE FACT THAT YOU'VE DISCOVERED THAT LOVE DOESN'T NECESSARILY ALWAYS CONFORM TO WHAT YOU WERE TAUGHT.

I'M NOT IN LOVE WITH AUDE!

YOUR VIEW OF LOVE SEEMS PRETTY LIMITED AND CLOSE-MINDED. THAT'S WHY YOU DIDN'T UNDERSTAND WHAT AUDE MEANT BY HER KISS.

THERE'S NO STRICT BOUNDARY BETWEEN FRIENDSHIP AND LOVE.

CLEM, YOU CAN'T CONTROL EVERYTHING.

WHO WAS THE GUY?

IF I TELL YOU, I'LL HAVE TO KILL YOU!

THANKS, VALENTIN.

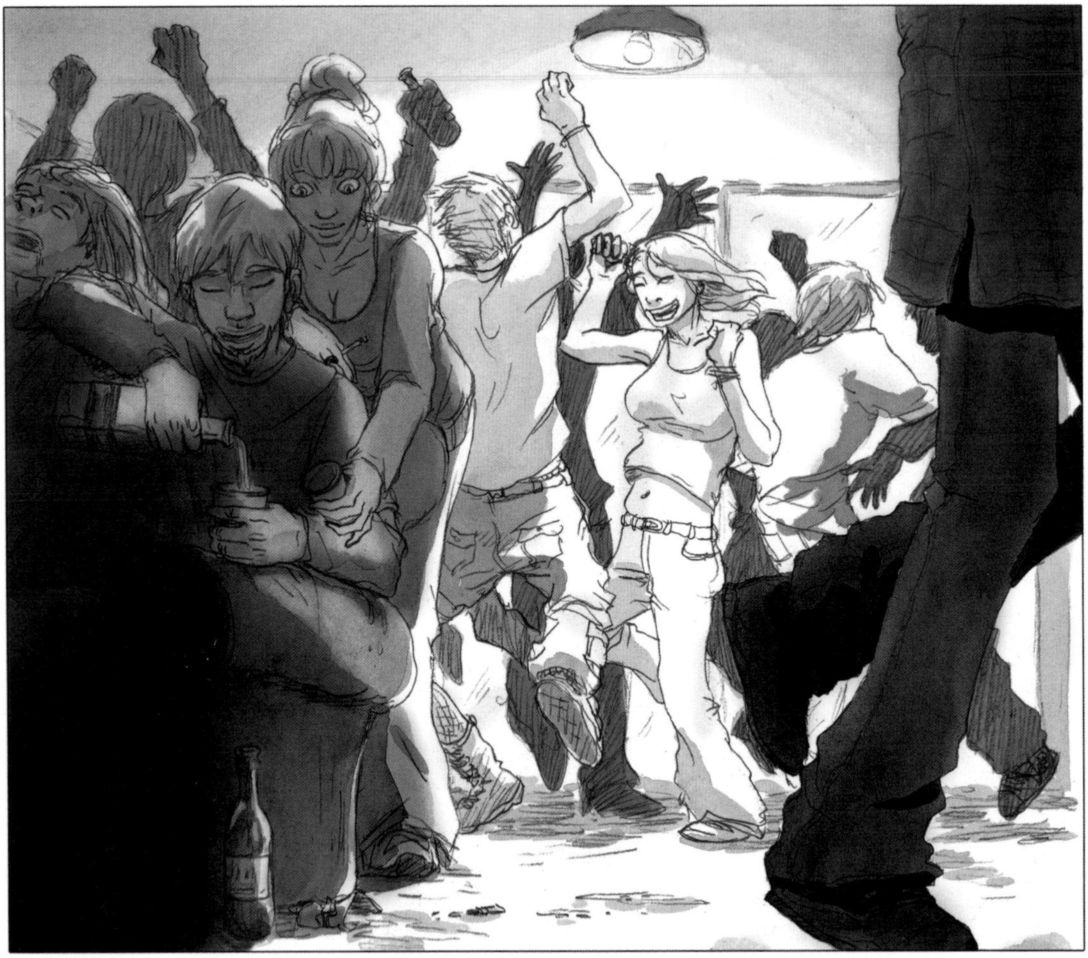

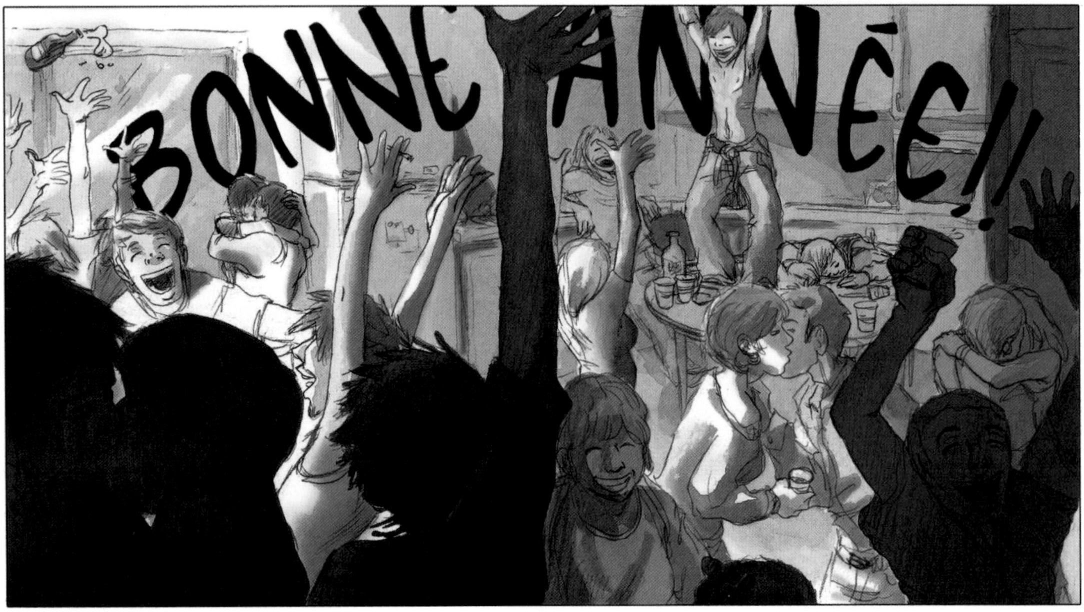
BONNE ANNÉE!!

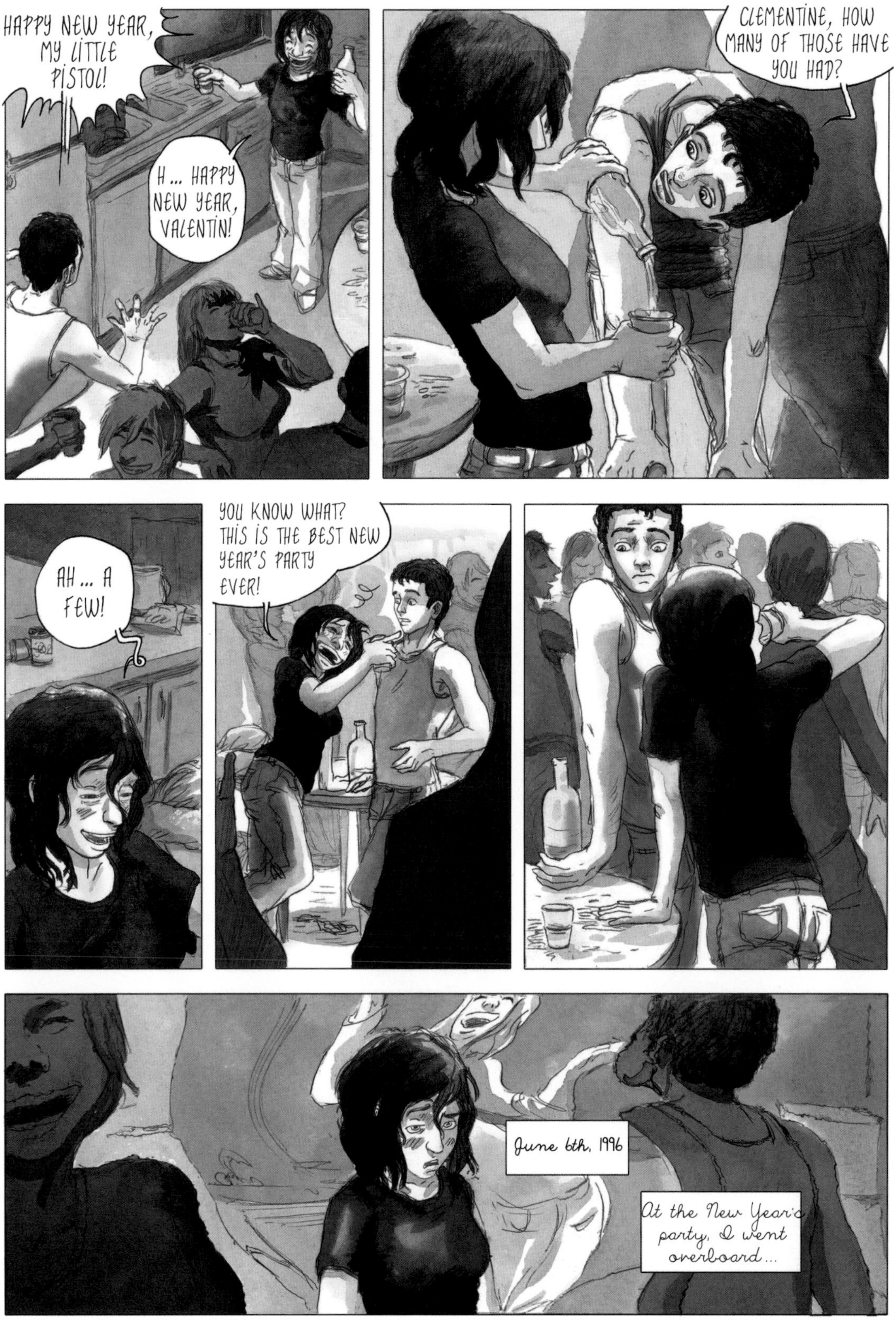
HAPPY NEW YEAR, MY LITTLE PISTOL!
H... HAPPY NEW YEAR, VALENTIN!
CLEMENTINE, HOW MANY OF THOSE HAVE YOU HAD?
AH... A FEW!
YOU KNOW WHAT? THIS IS THE BEST NEW YEAR'S PARTY EVER!
June 6th, 1996
At the New Year's party, I went overboard...

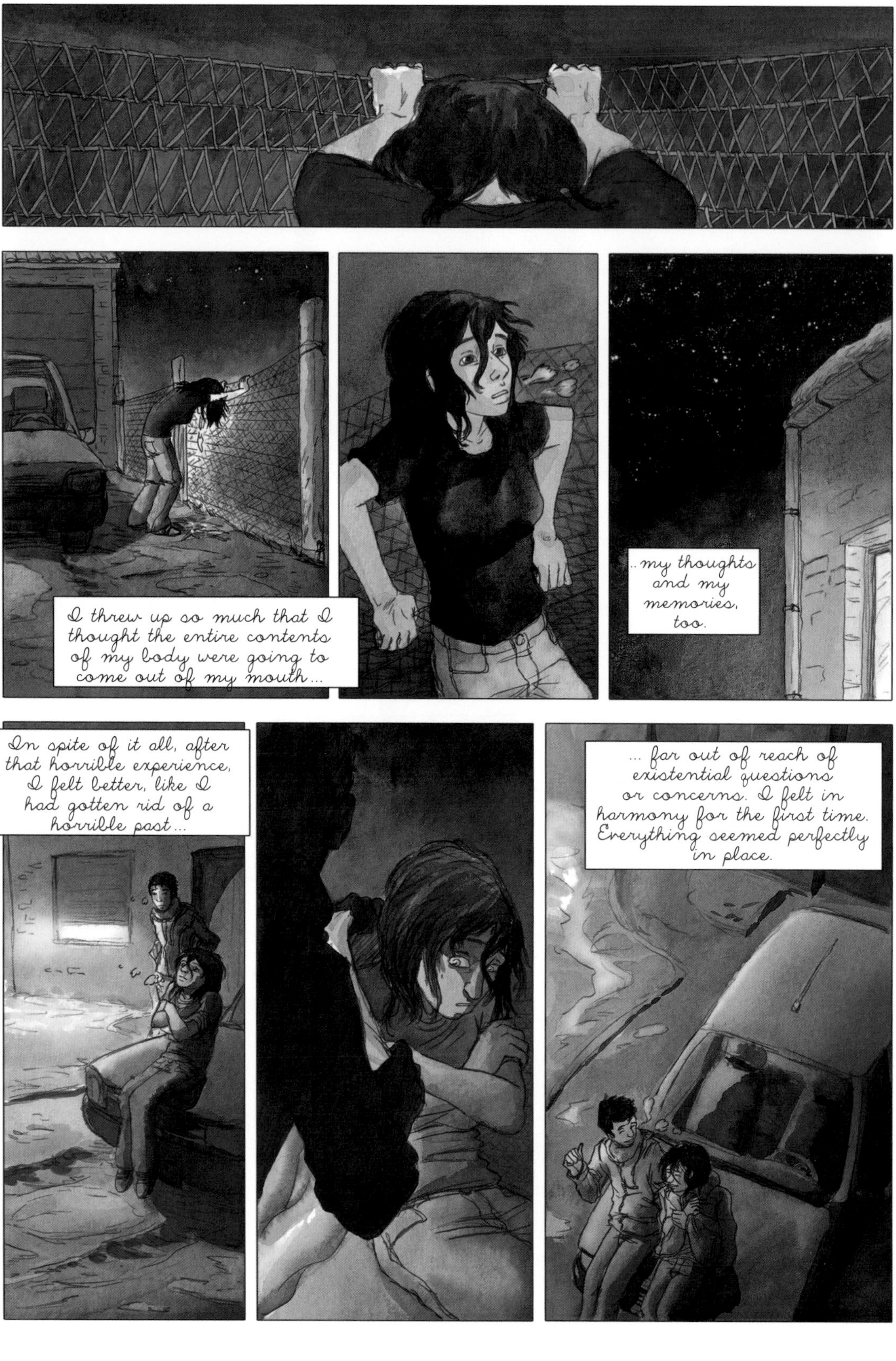
I threw up so much that I thought the entire contents of my body were going to come out of my mouth...
...my thoughts and my memories, too.
In spite of it all, after that horrible experience, I felt better, like I had gotten rid of a horrible past...
... far out of reach of existential questions or concerns. I felt in harmony for the first time. Everything seemed perfectly in place.

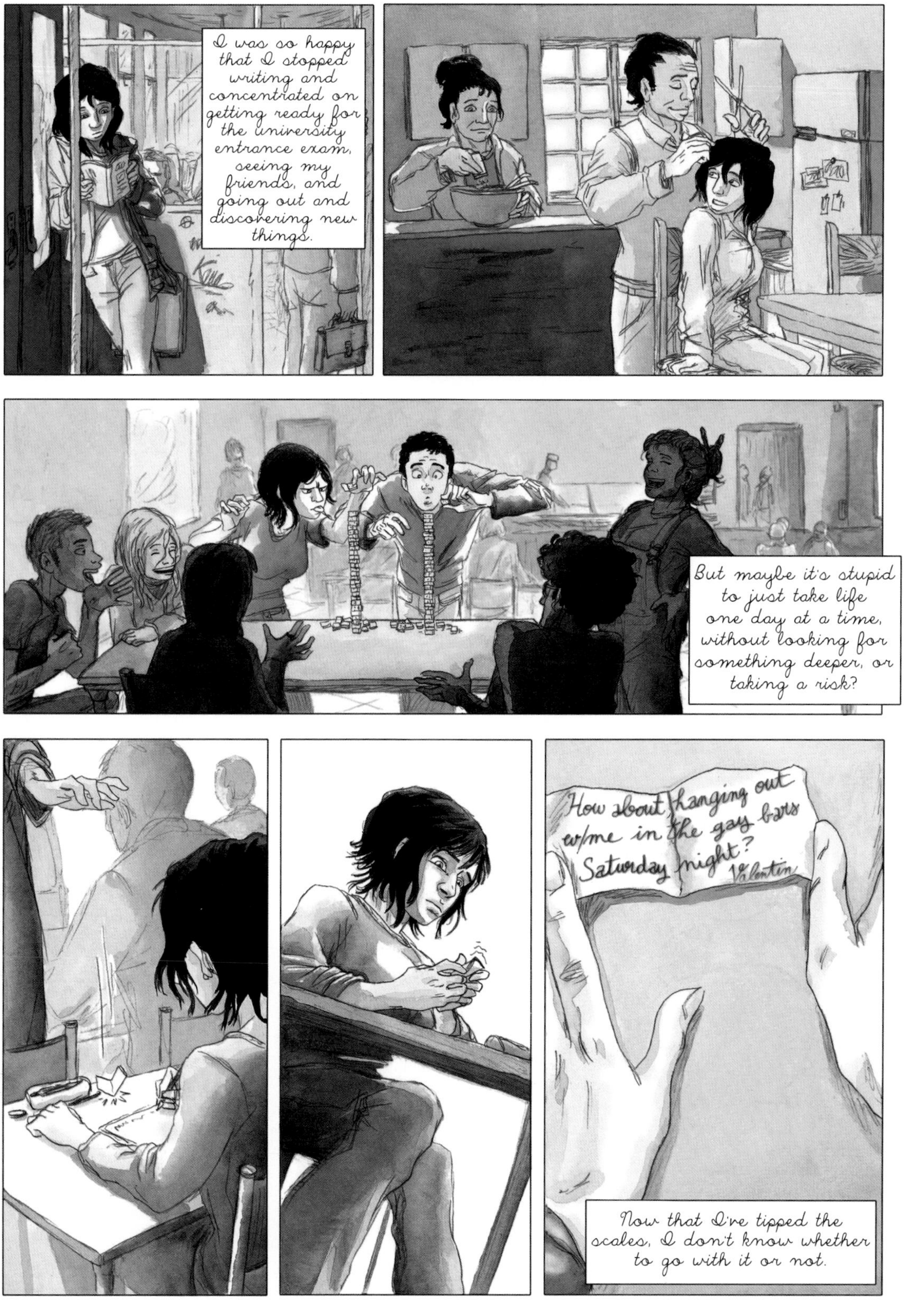
I was so happy that I stopped writing and concentrated on getting ready for the university entrance exam, seeing my friends, and going out and discovering new things.
But maybe it's stupid to just take life one day at a time, without looking for something deeper, or taking a risk?
How about hanging out w/me in the gay bars Saturday night? Valentin
Now that I've tipped the scales, I don't know whether to go with it or not.

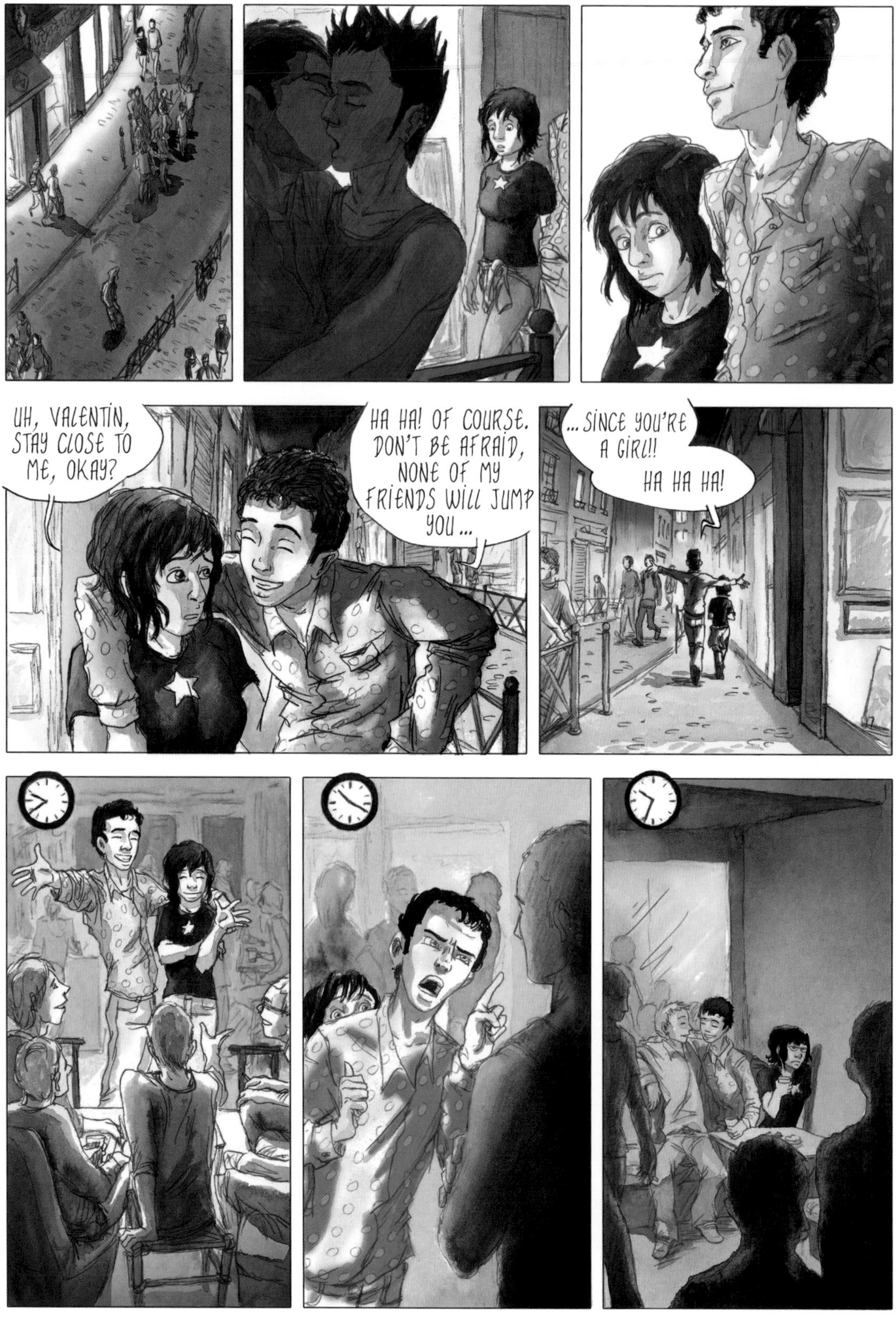
UH, VALENTIN, STAY CLOSE TO ME, OKAY?
HA HA! OF COURSE. DON'T BE AFRAID, NONE OF MY FRIENDS WILL JUMP YOU...
...SINCE YOU'RE A GIRL!!
HA HA HA!

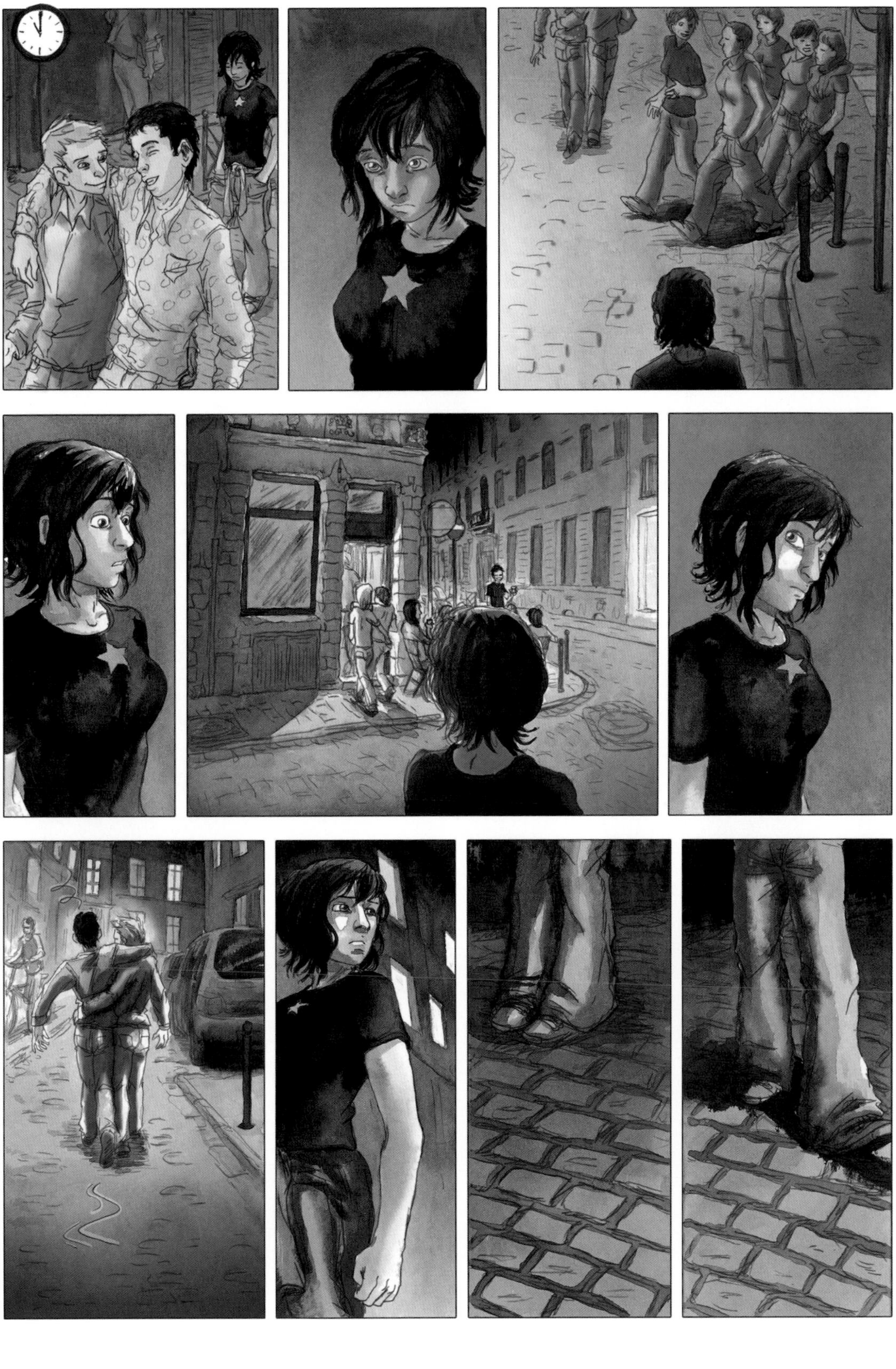

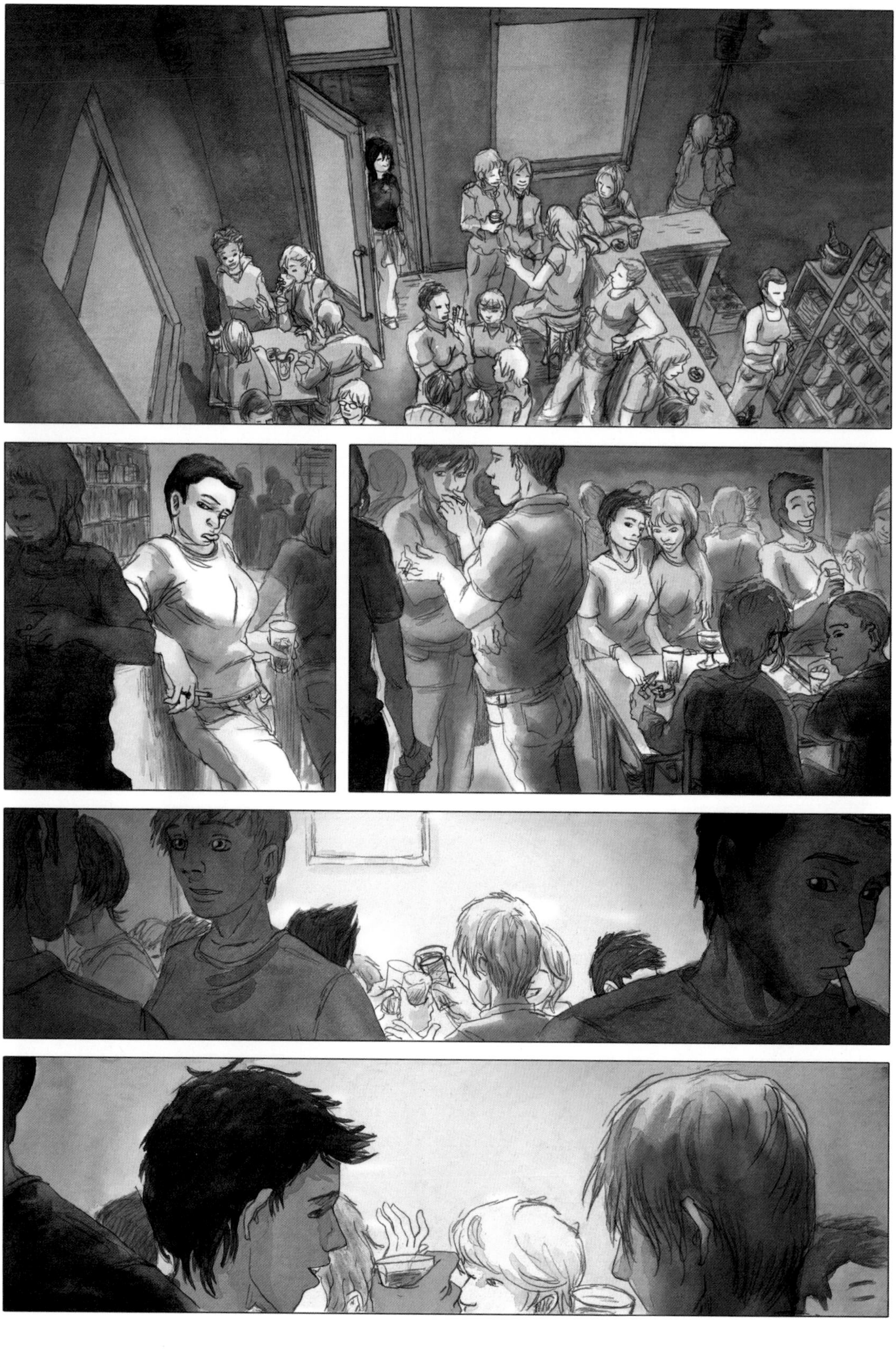

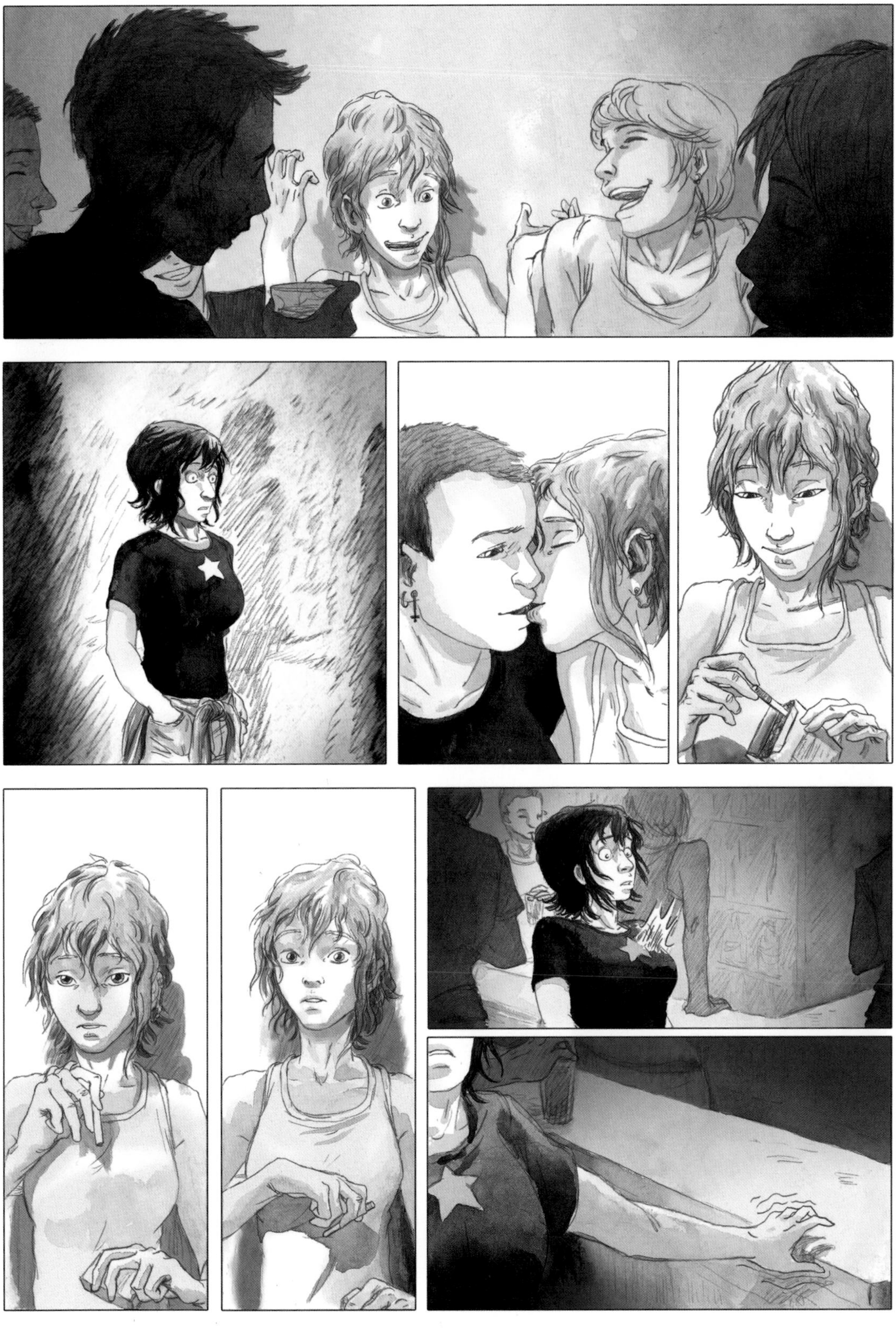

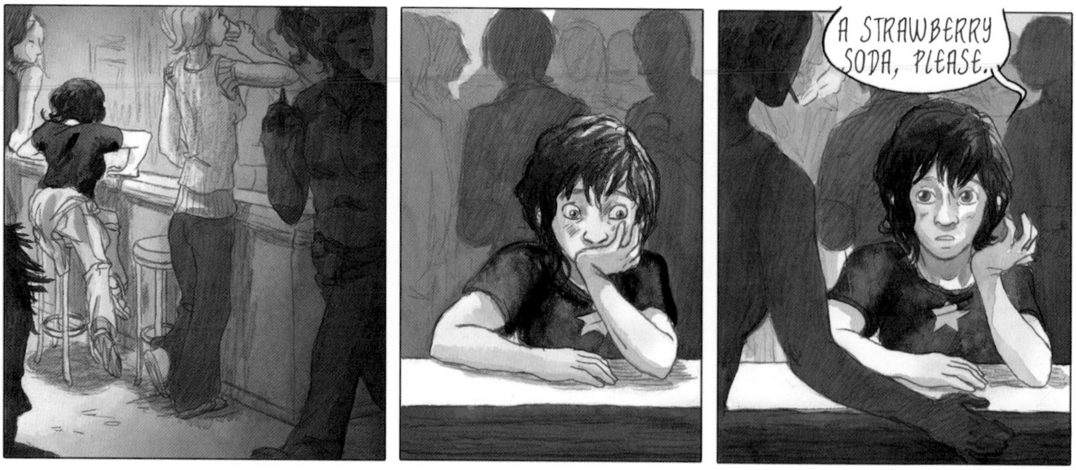
A STRAWBERRY SODA, PLEASE.

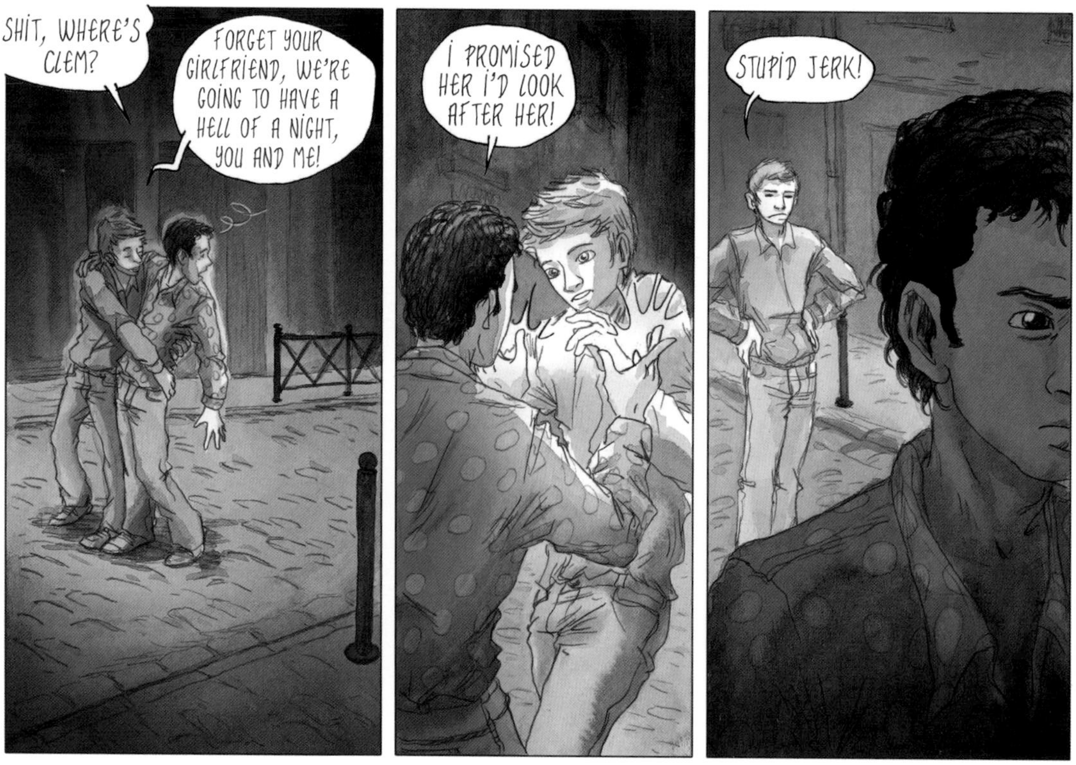
SHIT, WHERE'S CLEM?
FORGET YOUR GIRLFRIEND, WE'RE GOING TO HAVE A HELL OF A NIGHT, YOU AND ME!
I PROMISED HER I'D LOOK AFTER HER!
STUPID JERK!

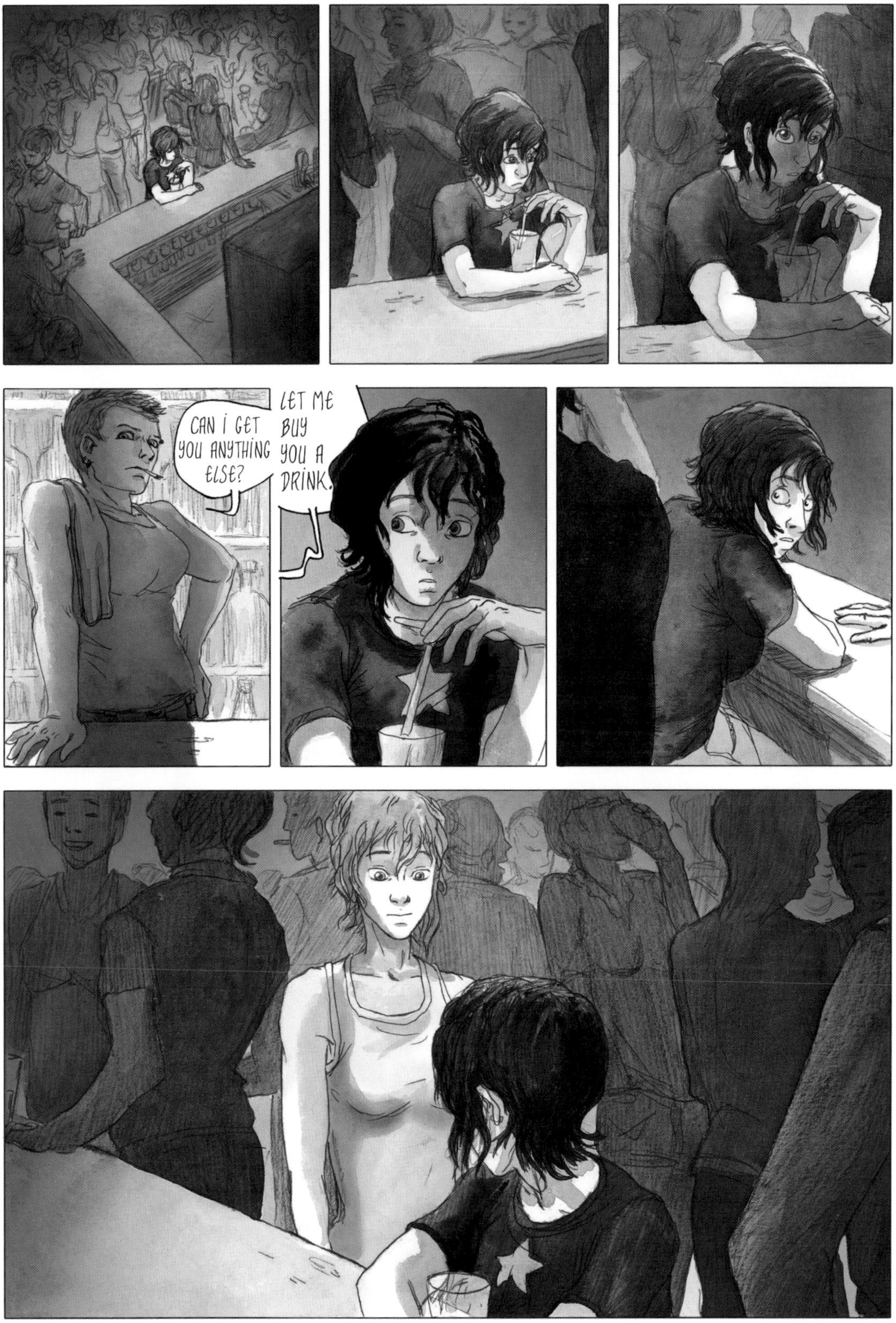
CAN I GET YOU ANYTHING ELSE?
LET ME BUY YOU A DRINK.

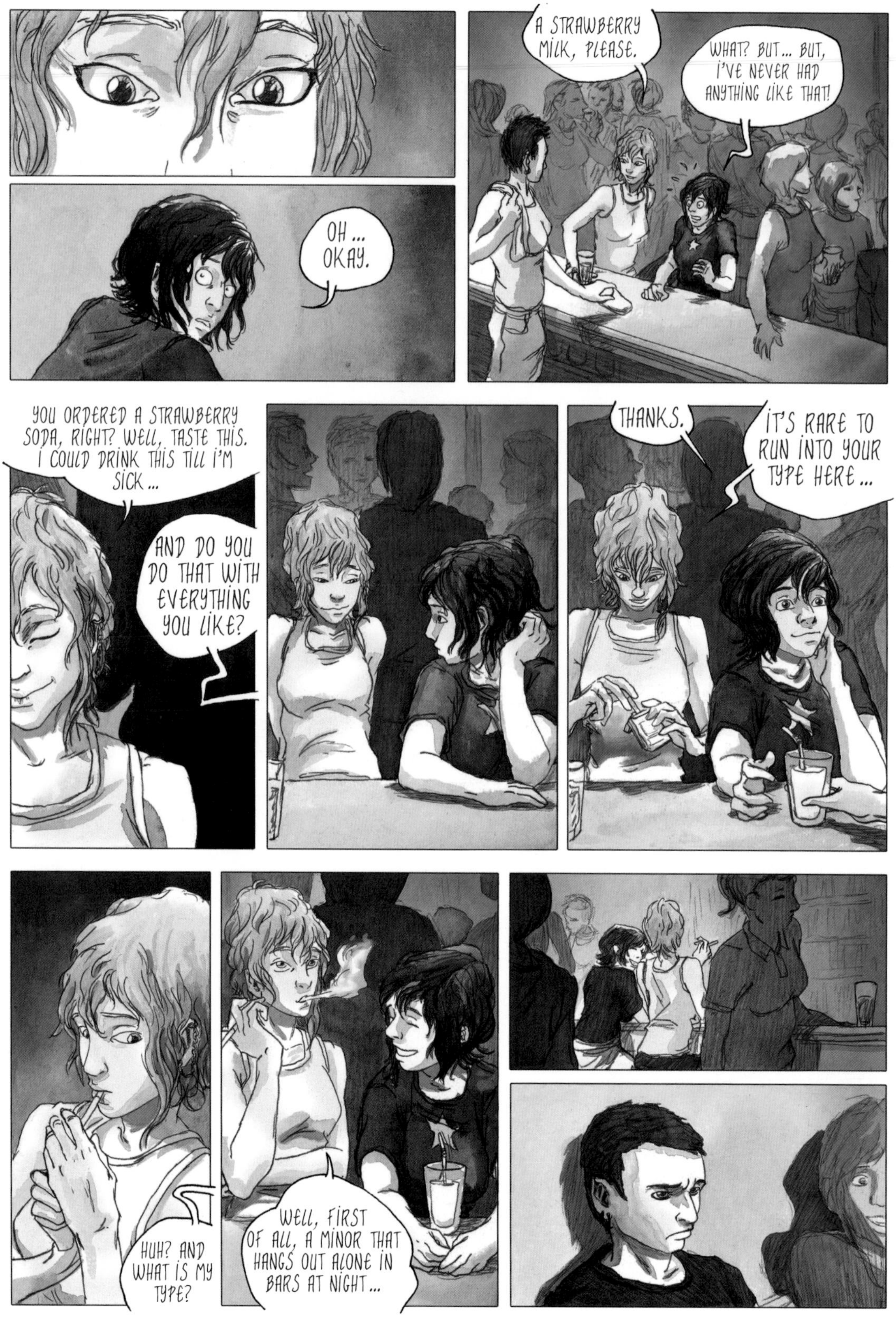
A STRAWBERRY MILK, PLEASE.
WHAT? BUT... BUT, I'VE NEVER HAD ANYTHING LIKE THAT!
OH... OKAY.
YOU ORDERED A STRAWBERRY SODA, RIGHT? WELL, TASTE THIS. I COULD DRINK THIS TILL I'M SICK...
AND DO YOU DO THAT WITH EVERYTHING YOU LIKE?
THANKS.
IT'S RARE TO RUN INTO YOUR TYPE HERE...
HUH? AND WHAT IS MY TYPE?
WELL, FIRST OF ALL, A MINOR THAT HANGS OUT ALONE IN BARS AT NIGHT...

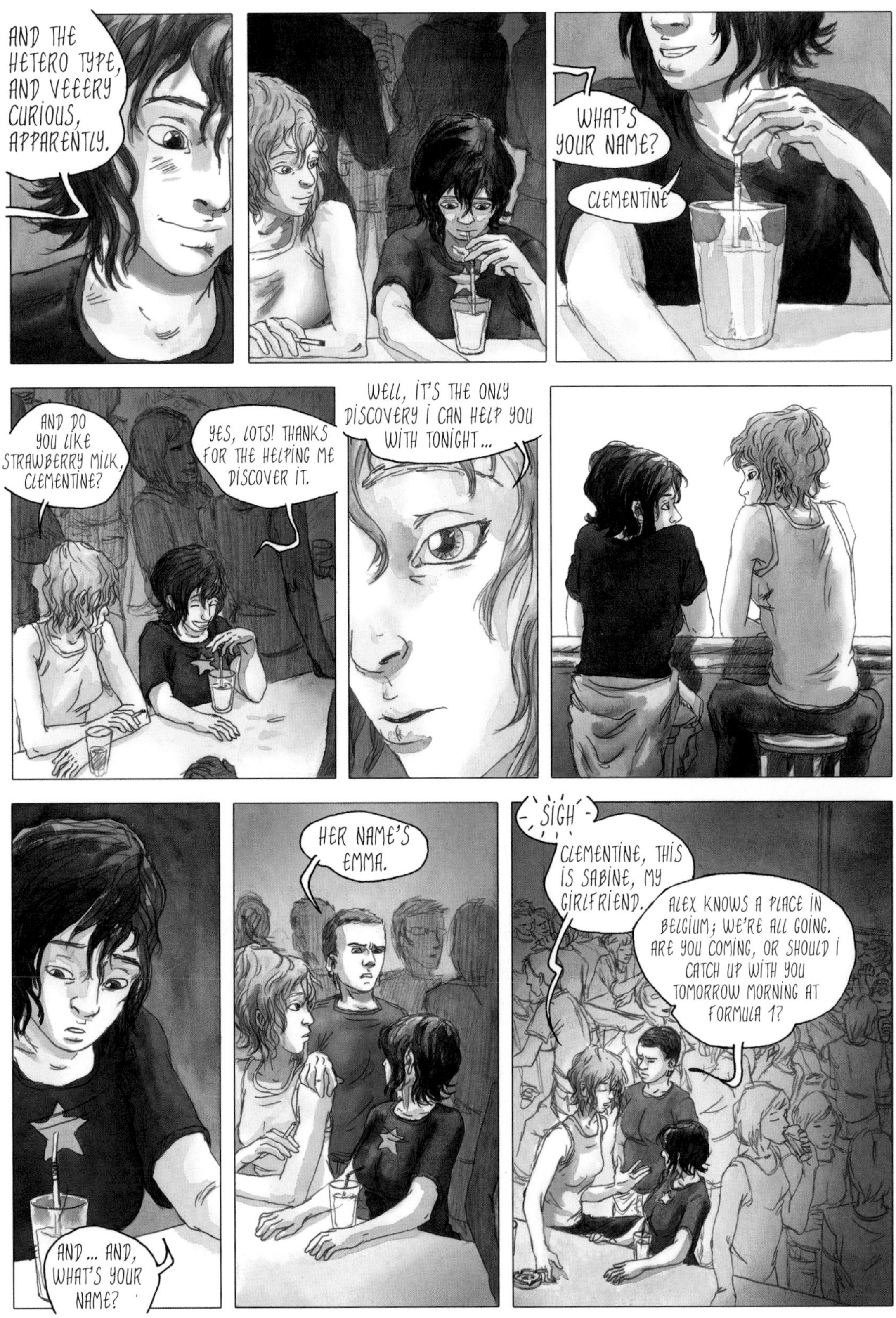
AND THE HETERO TYPE, AND VEEERY CURIOUS, APPARENTLY.
WHAT'S YOUR NAME?
CLEMENTINE
AND DO YOU LIKE STRAWBERRY MILK, CLEMENTINE?
YES, LOTS! THANKS FOR THE HELPING ME DISCOVER IT.
WELL, IT'S THE ONLY DISCOVERY I CAN HELP YOU WITH TONIGHT...
AND... AND, WHAT'S YOUR NAME?
HER NAME'S EMMA.
SIGH
CLEMENTINE, THIS IS SABINE, MY GIRLFRIEND.
ALEX KNOWS A PLACE IN BELGIUM; WE'RE ALL GOING. ARE YOU COMING, OR SHOULD I CATCH UP WITH YOU TOMORROW MORNING AT FORMULA 1?

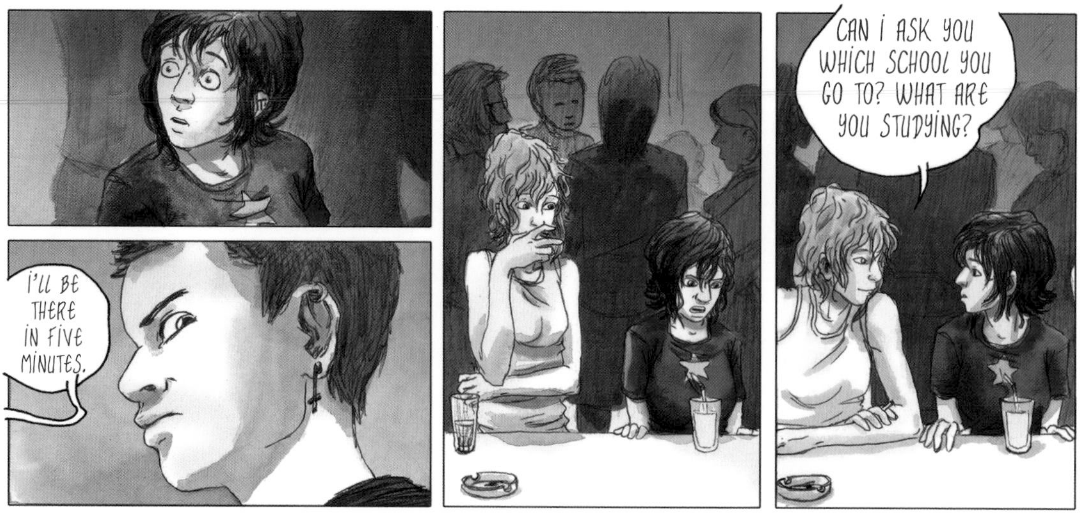
I'LL BE THERE IN FIVE MINUTES.
CAN I ASK YOU WHICH SCHOOL YOU GO TO? WHAT ARE YOU STUDYING?

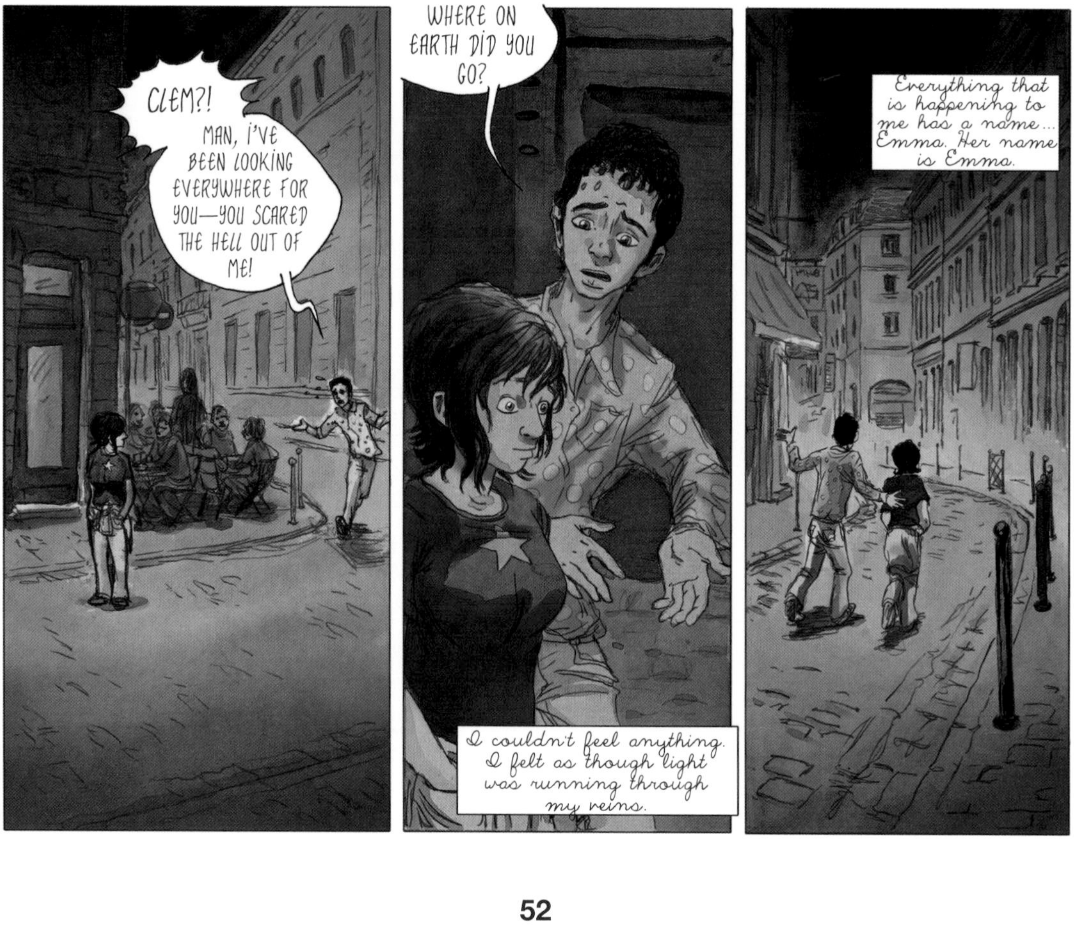
CLEM?!
MAN, I'VE BEEN LOOKING EVERYWHERE FOR YOU—YOU SCARED THE HELL OUT OF ME!
WHERE ON EARTH DID YOU GO?
I couldn't feel anything. I felt as though light was running through my veins.
Everything that is happening to me has a name... Emma. Her name is Emma.

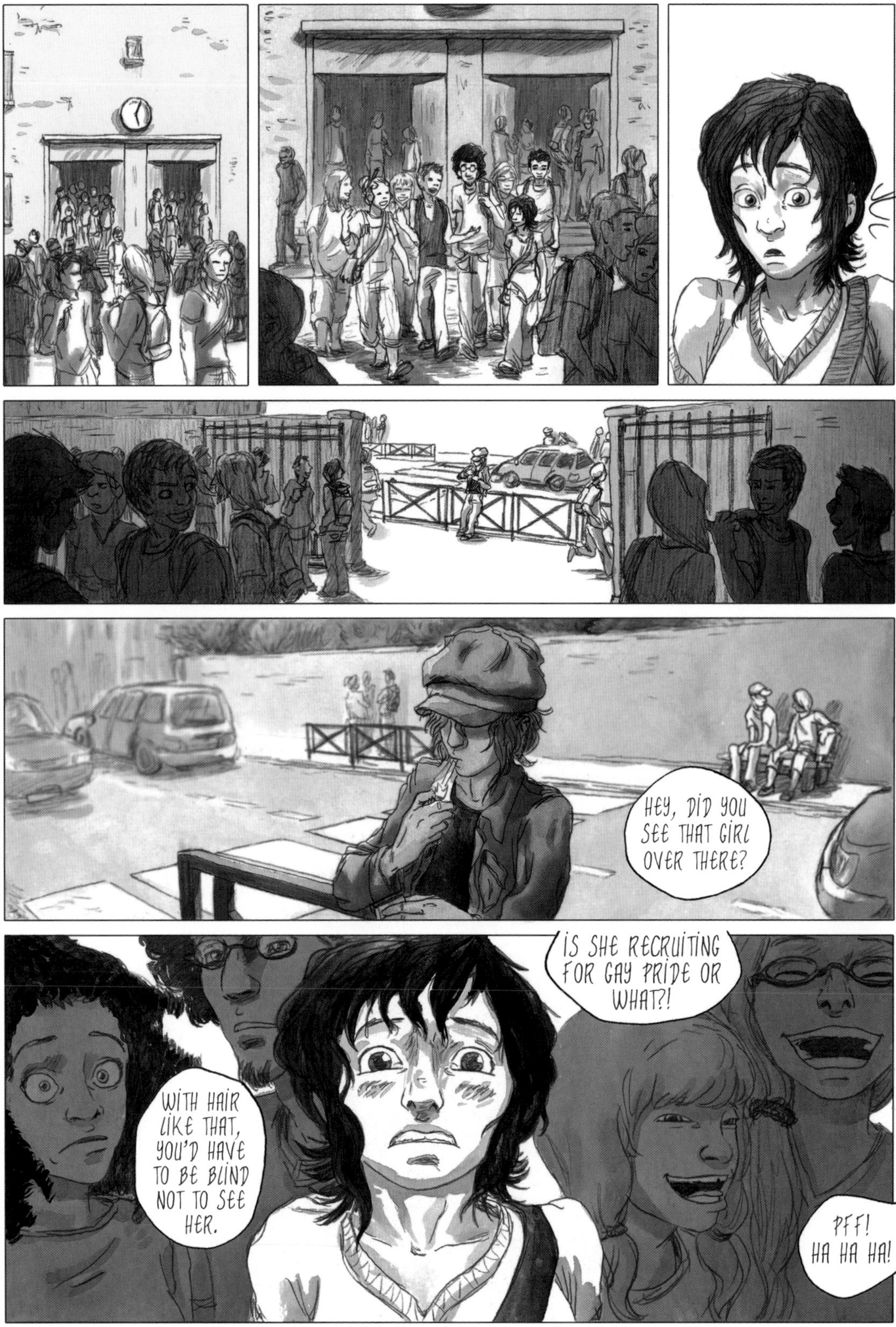
HEY, DID YOU SEE THAT GIRL OVER THERE?
IS SHE RECRUITING FOR GAY PRIDE OR WHAT?!
WITH HAIR LIKE THAT, YOU'D HAVE TO BE BLIND NOT TO SEE HER.
PFF! HA HA HA!

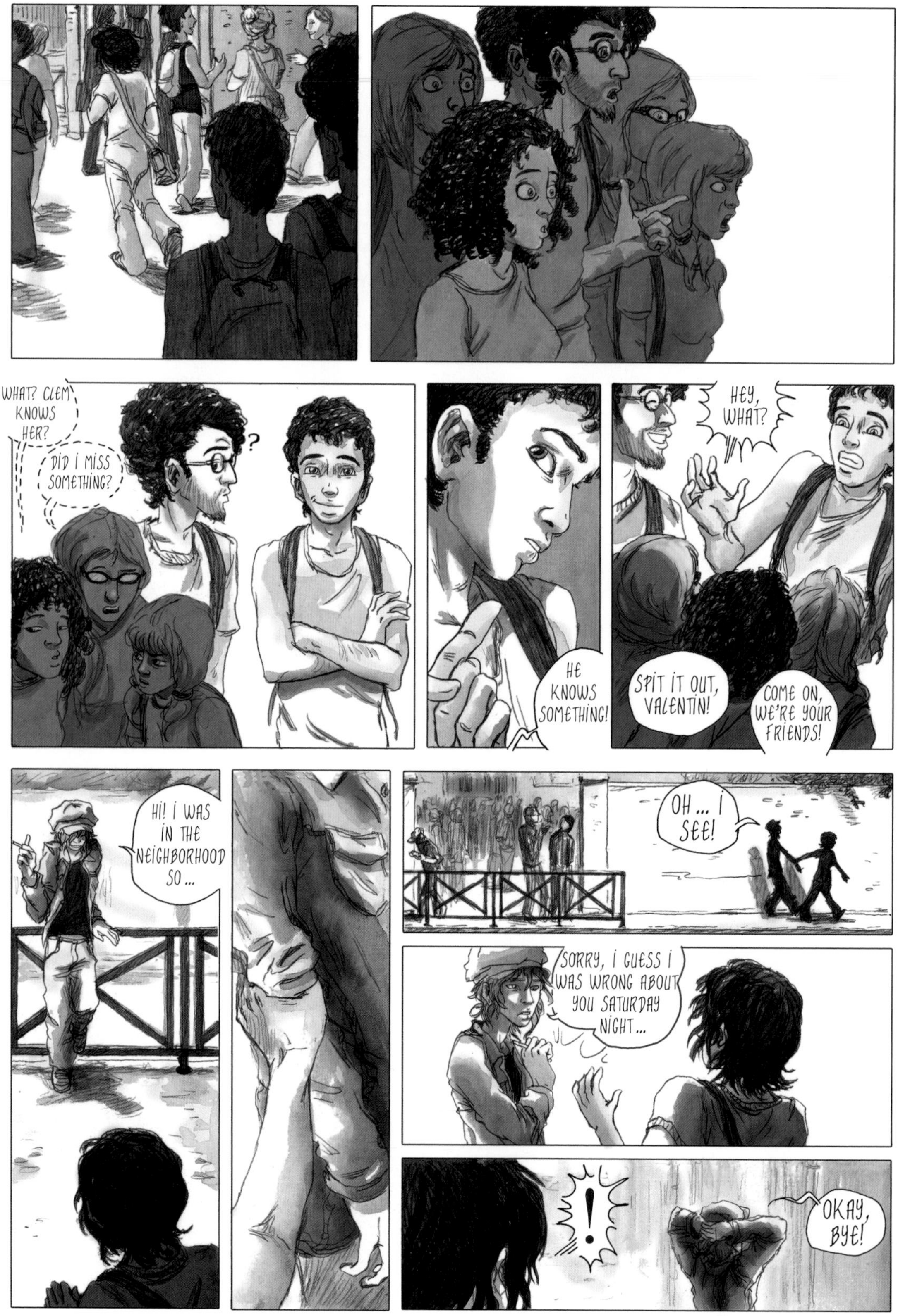
WHAT? CLEM KNOWS HER?
DID I MISS SOMETHING?
?
HE KNOWS SOMETHING!
HEY, WHAT?
SPIT IT OUT, VALENTIN!
COME ON, WE'RE YOUR FRIENDS!
HI! I WAS IN THE NEIGHBORHOOD SO...
OH... I SEE!
SORRY, I GUESS I WAS WRONG ABOUT YOU SATURDAY NIGHT...
!
OKAY, BYE!

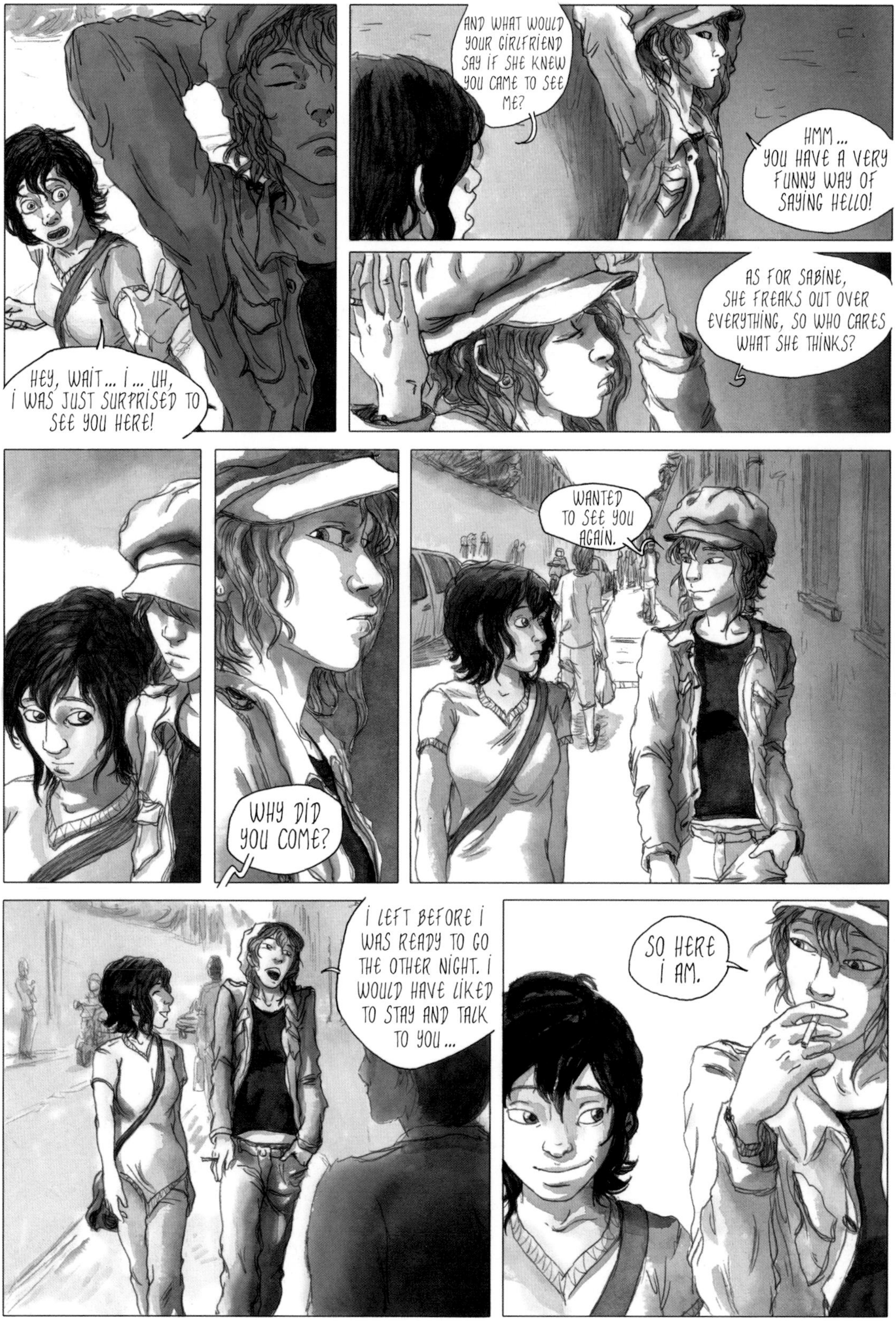
HEY, WAIT... I... UH, I WAS JUST SURPRISED TO SEE YOU HERE!
AND WHAT WOULD YOUR GIRLFRIEND SAY IF SHE KNEW YOU CAME TO SEE ME?
HMM... YOU HAVE A VERY FUNNY WAY OF SAYING HELLO!
AS FOR SABINE, SHE FREAKS OUT OVER EVERYTHING, SO WHO CARES WHAT SHE THINKS?
WHY DID YOU COME?
WANTED TO SEE YOU AGAIN.
I LEFT BEFORE I WAS READY TO GO THE OTHER NIGHT. I WOULD HAVE LIKED TO STAY AND TALK TO YOU...
SO HERE I AM.

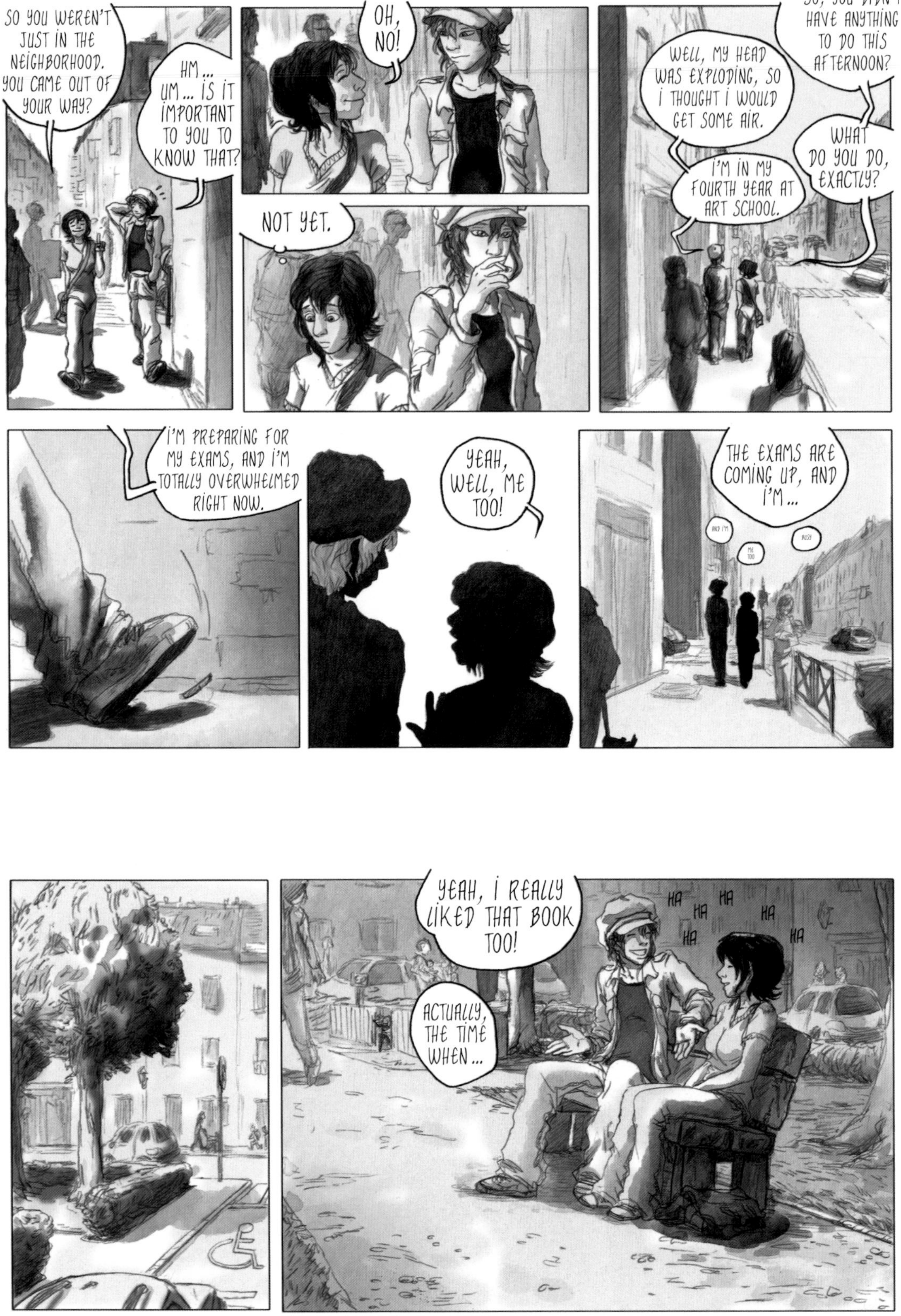
SO YOU WEREN'T JUST IN THE NEIGHBORHOOD. YOU CAME OUT OF YOUR WAY?
HM... UM... IS IT IMPORTANT TO YOU TO KNOW THAT?
OH, NO!
NOT YET.
WELL, MY HEAD WAS EXPLODING, SO I THOUGHT I WOULD GET SOME AIR.
I'M IN MY FOURTH YEAR AT ART SCHOOL.
SO, YOU DIDN'T HAVE ANYTHING TO DO THIS AFTERNOON?
WHAT DO YOU DO, EXACTLY?
I'M PREPARING FOR MY EXAMS, AND I'M TOTALLY OVERWHELMED RIGHT NOW.
YEAH, WELL, ME TOO!
THE EXAMS ARE COMING UP, AND I'M...
AND I'M
ME TOO
BUSY
YEAH, I REALLY LIKED THAT BOOK TOO!
ACTUALLY, THE TIME WHEN...
HA HA HA HA HA HA

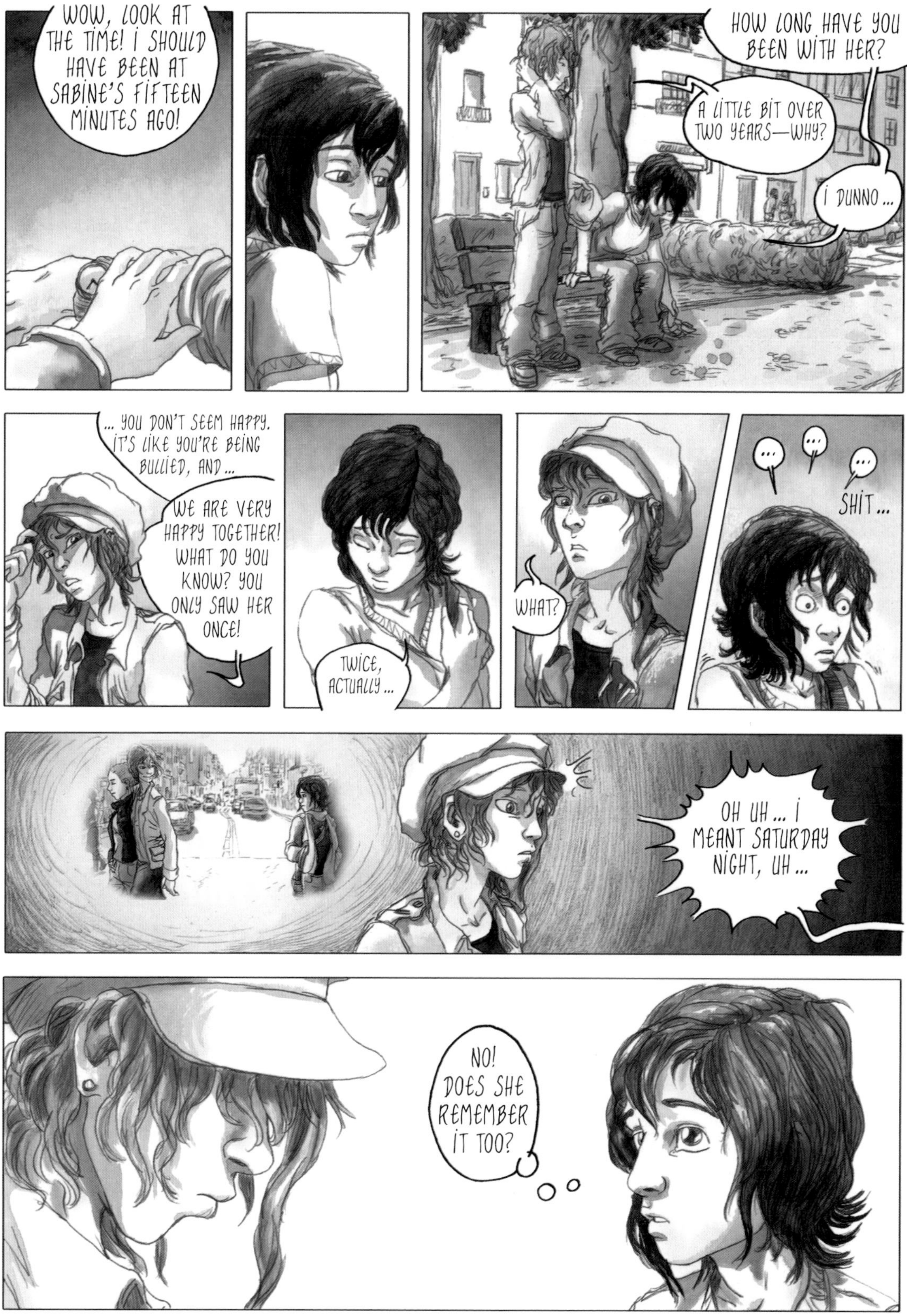
WOW, LOOK AT THE TIME! I SHOULD HAVE BEEN AT SABINE'S FIFTEEN MINUTES AGO!
HOW LONG HAVE YOU BEEN WITH HER?
A LITTLE BIT OVER TWO YEARS—WHY?
I DUNNO ...
... YOU DON'T SEEM HAPPY. IT'S LIKE YOU'RE BEING BULLIED, AND ...
WE ARE VERY HAPPY TOGETHER! WHAT DO YOU KNOW? YOU ONLY SAW HER ONCE!
TWICE, ACTUALLY ...
WHAT?
...
...
...
SHIT ...
OH UH ... I MEANT SATURDAY NIGHT, UH ...
NO! DOES SHE REMEMBER IT TOO?

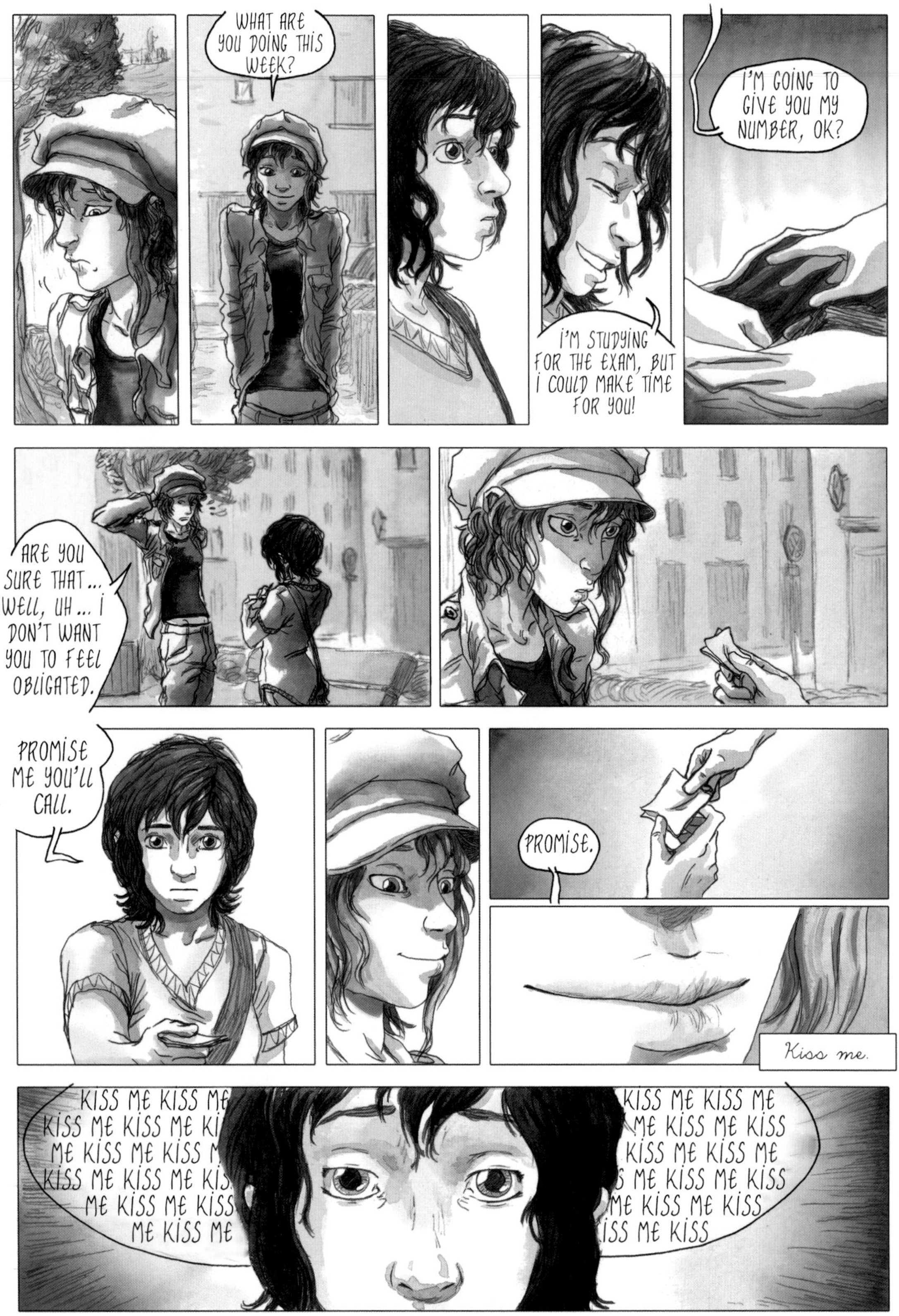
WHAT ARE YOU DOING THIS WEEK?
I'M STUDYING FOR THE EXAM, BUT I COULD MAKE TIME FOR YOU!
I'M GOING TO GIVE YOU MY NUMBER, OK?
ARE YOU SURE THAT... WELL, UH... I DON'T WANT YOU TO FEEL OBLIGATED.
PROMISE ME YOU'LL CALL.
PROMISE.
Kiss me.
KISS ME KISS ME KISS ME KISS ME KISS ME KISS ME KISS ME KISS ME KISS ME KISS ME KISS ME KISS ME
KISS ME KISS ME KISS ME KISS ME KISS ME KISS ME KISS ME KISS ME KISS ME KISS ME KISS ME KISS

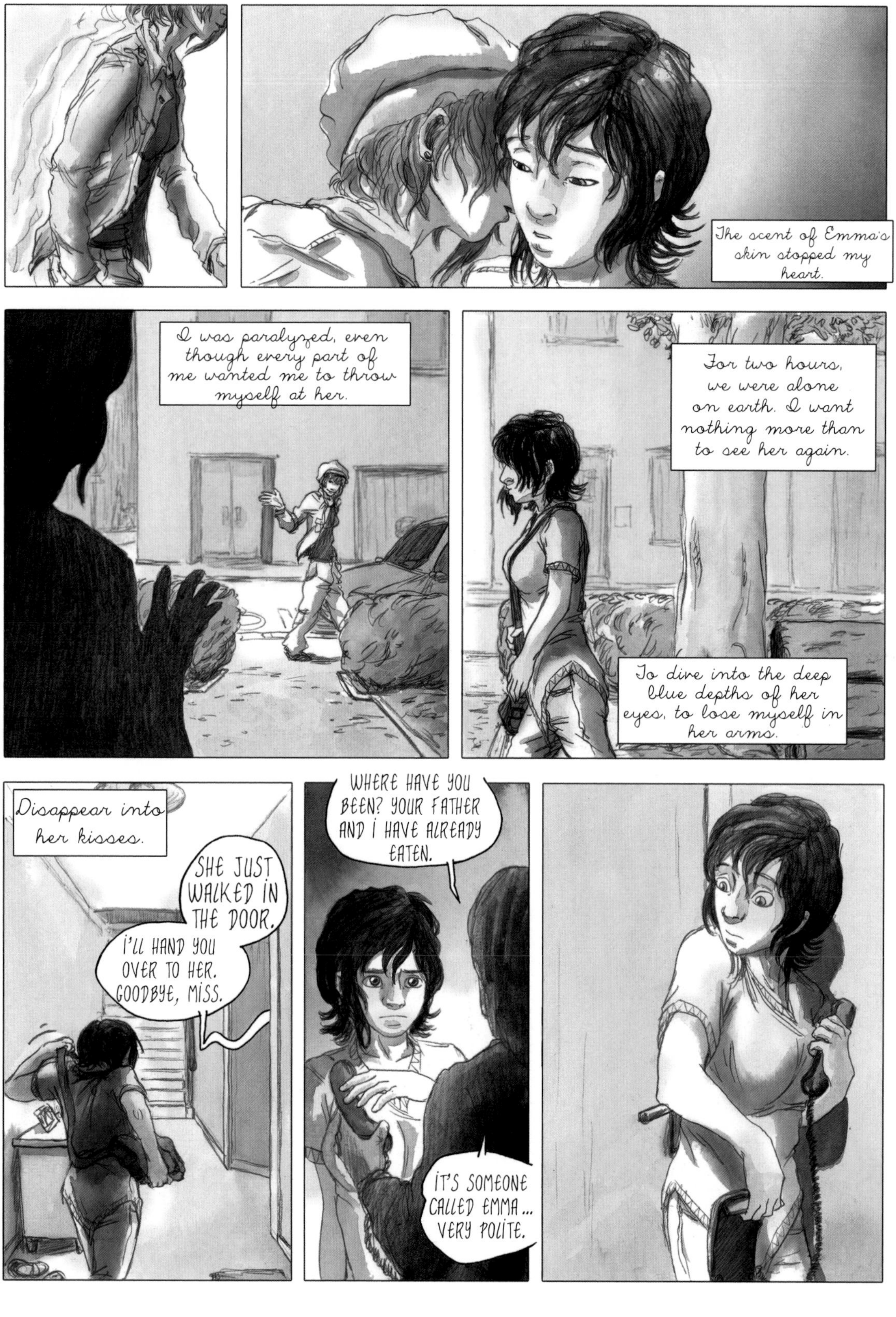
The scent of Emma's skin stopped my heart.
I was paralyzed, even though every part of me wanted me to throw myself at her.
For two hours, we were alone on earth. I want nothing more than to see her again.
To dive into the deep blue depths of her eyes, to lose myself in her arms.
Disappear into her kisses.
SHE JUST WALKED IN THE DOOR.
I'LL HAND YOU OVER TO HER. GOODBYE, MISS.
WHERE HAVE YOU BEEN? YOUR FATHER AND I HAVE ALREADY EATEN.
IT'S SOMEONE CALLED EMMA... VERY POLITE.

YOU DIDN'T WASTE ANY TIME!

I WANTED TO MAKE SURE IT WAS REALLY YOUR NUMBER.

HEH, YOU THINK THAT I'M RUNNING AWAY FROM YOU?

AH, SO YOU ARE ALSO A "TYPE"?

YEAH, THE MATURE TYPE THAT SPENDS HER WEEKENDS IN GAY BARS!

YEAH, I CAN BE PRETTY WEIRD AND DAUNTING—FOR MY TYPE. SO, YES!

HA HA HA

SO, YOU'RE COMPLETELY DIFFERENT FROM THE TYPE OF PERSON YOU SAID I AM?

YES, I THINK THAT WE ARE VERY DIFFERENT...

DON'T BE SO SURE, IT'S HARD TO TELL AFTER HAVING MET ONLY ONCE.

THREE TIMES, IN FACT...

I HAVE TO GO, I'M STANDING IN FRONT OF SABINE'S PLACE. SHE'S WAITING FOR ME. I'LL CALL YOU AGAIN SOON, OK?

WHEN?

TOMORROW?

OK! TILL TOMORROW, THEN.

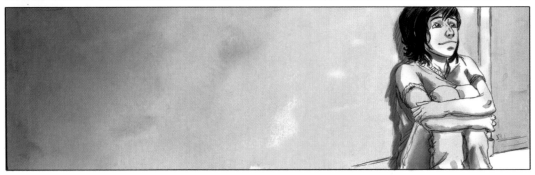

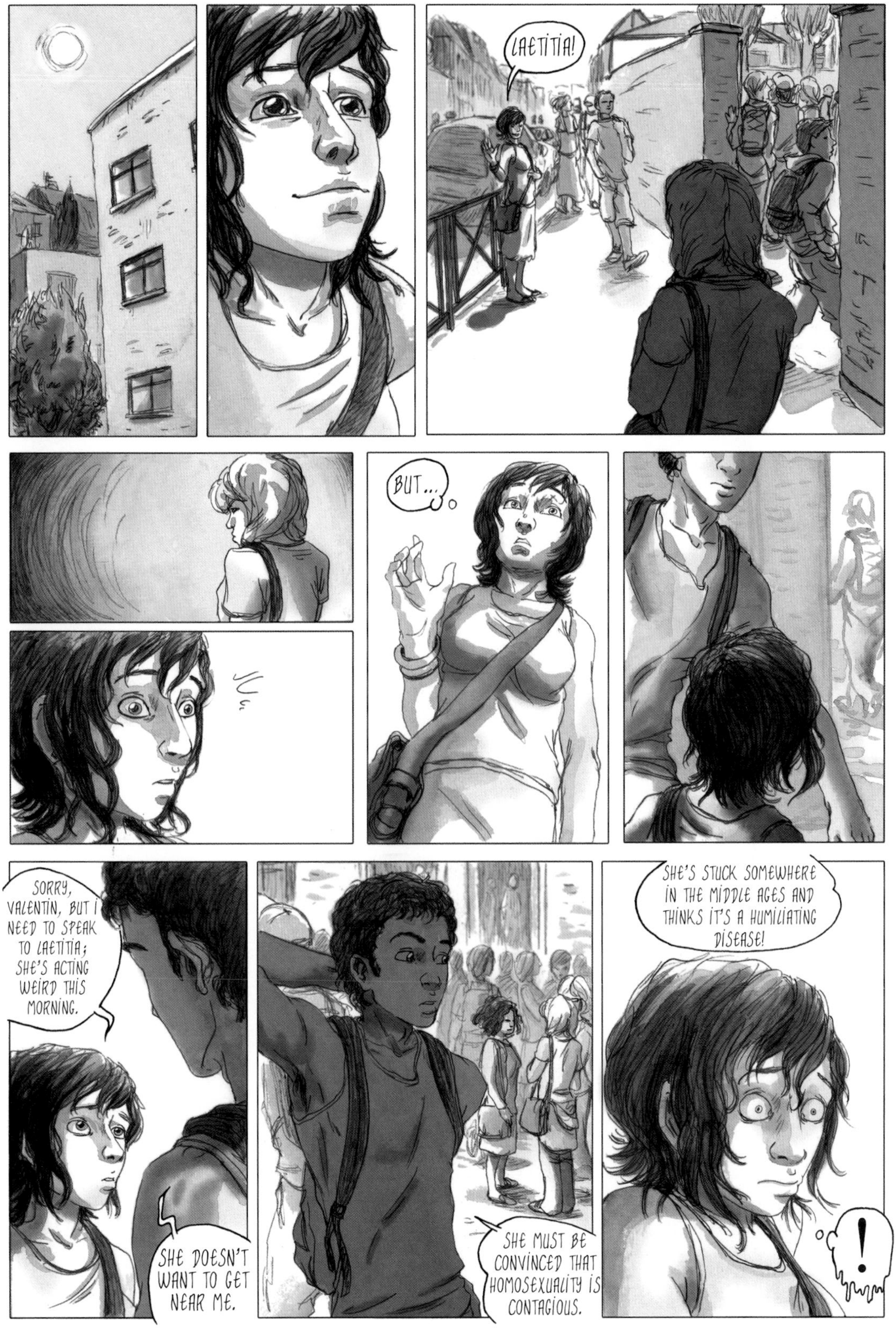
LAETITIA!
BUT...
SORRY, VALENTIN, BUT I NEED TO SPEAK TO LAETITIA; SHE'S ACTING WEIRD THIS MORNING.
SHE DOESN'T WANT TO GET NEAR ME.
SHE MUST BE CONVINCED THAT HOMOSEXUALITY IS CONTAGIOUS.
SHE'S STUCK SOMEWHERE IN THE MIDDLE AGES AND THINKS IT'S A HUMILIATING DISEASE!
!

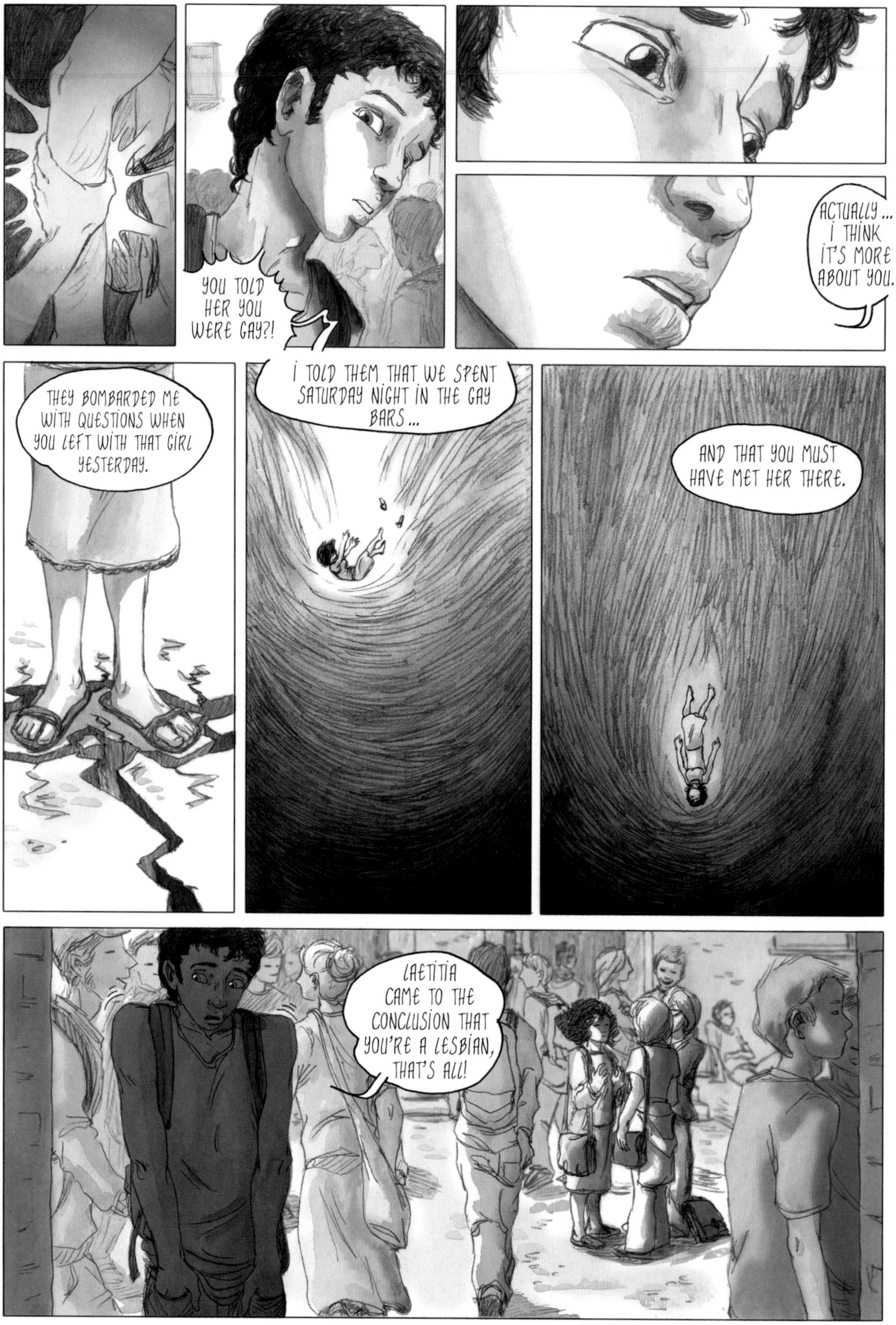
YOU TOLD HER YOU WERE GAY?!
ACTUALLY... I THINK IT'S MORE ABOUT YOU.
THEY BOMBARDED ME WITH QUESTIONS WHEN YOU LEFT WITH THAT GIRL YESTERDAY.
I TOLD THEM THAT WE SPENT SATURDAY NIGHT IN THE GAY BARS...
AND THAT YOU MUST HAVE MET HER THERE.
LAETITIA CAME TO THE CONCLUSION THAT YOU'RE A LESBIAN, THAT'S ALL!

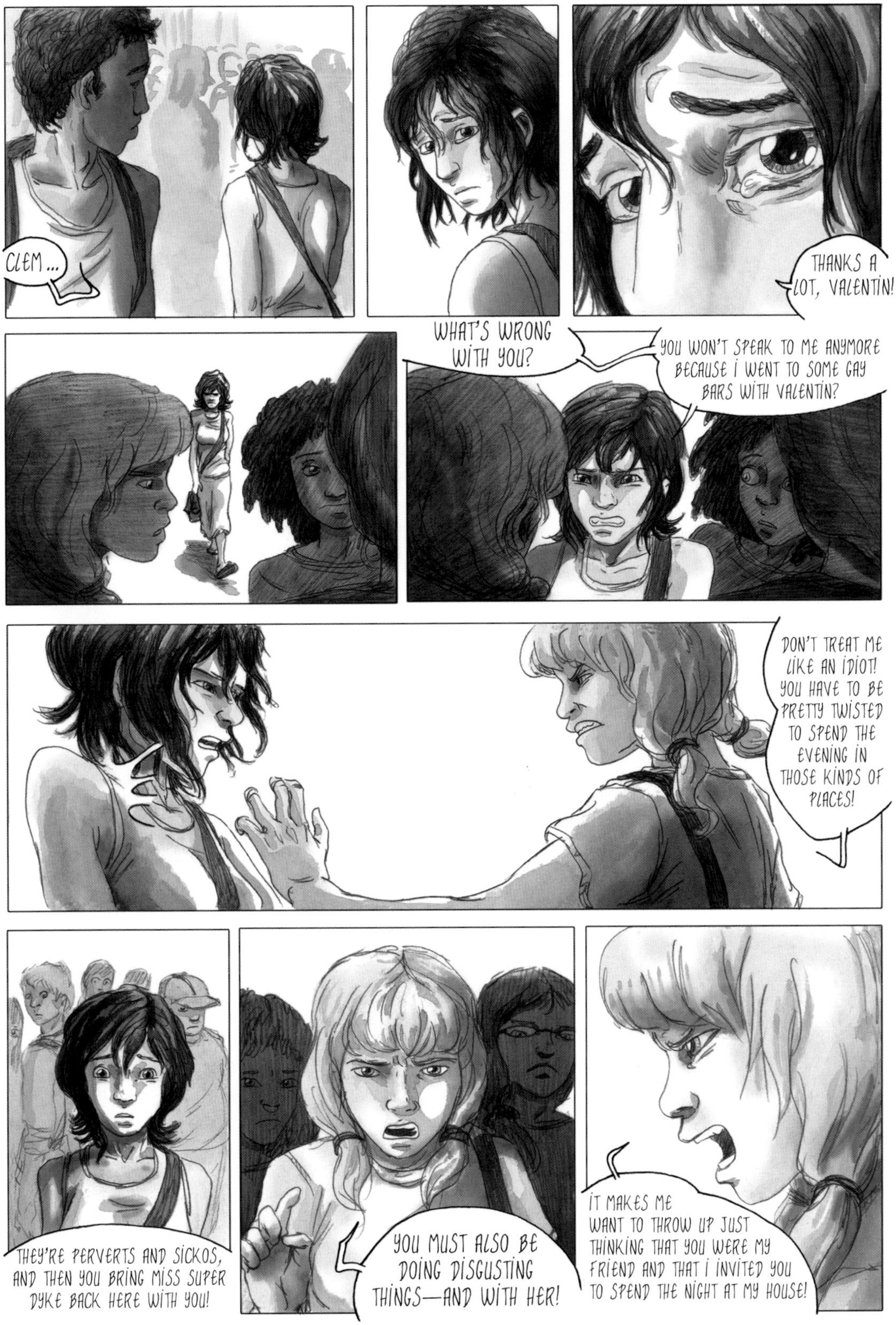
CLEM...
THANKS A LOT, VALENTIN!
WHAT'S WRONG WITH YOU?
YOU WON'T SPEAK TO ME ANYMORE BECAUSE I WENT TO SOME GAY BARS WITH VALENTIN?
DON'T TREAT ME LIKE AN IDIOT! YOU HAVE TO BE PRETTY TWISTED TO SPEND THE EVENING IN THOSE KINDS OF PLACES!
THEY'RE PERVERTS AND SICKOS, AND THEN YOU BRING MISS SUPER DYKE BACK HERE WITH YOU!
YOU MUST ALSO BE DOING DISGUSTING THINGS—AND WITH HER!
IT MAKES ME WANT TO THROW UP JUST THINKING THAT YOU WERE MY FRIEND AND THAT I INVITED YOU TO SPEND THE NIGHT AT MY HOUSE!

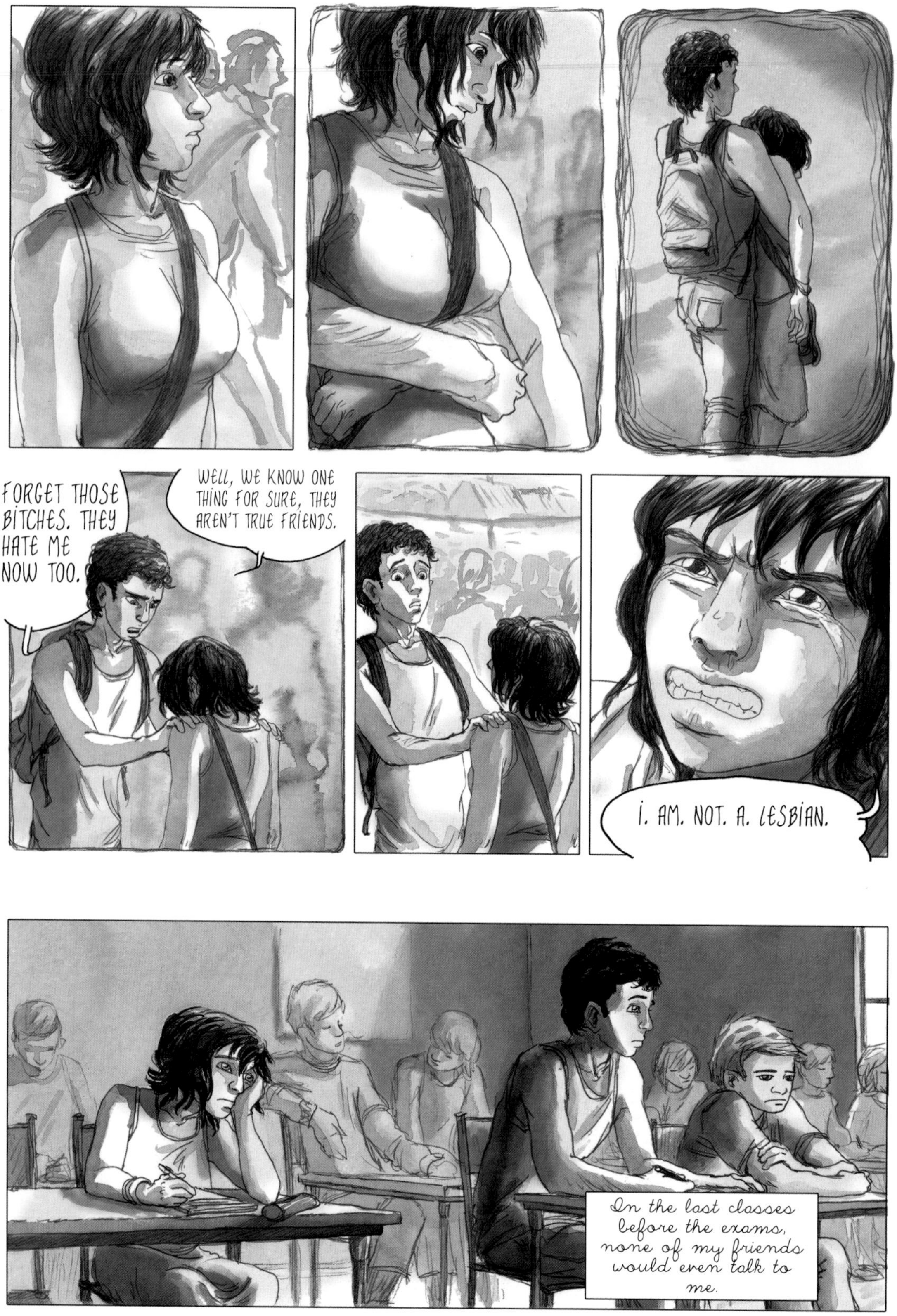
FORGET THOSE BITCHES. THEY HATE ME NOW TOO.
WELL, WE KNOW ONE THING FOR SURE, THEY AREN'T TRUE FRIENDS.
I. AM. NOT. A. LESBIAN.
In the last classes before the exams, none of my friends would even talk to me.

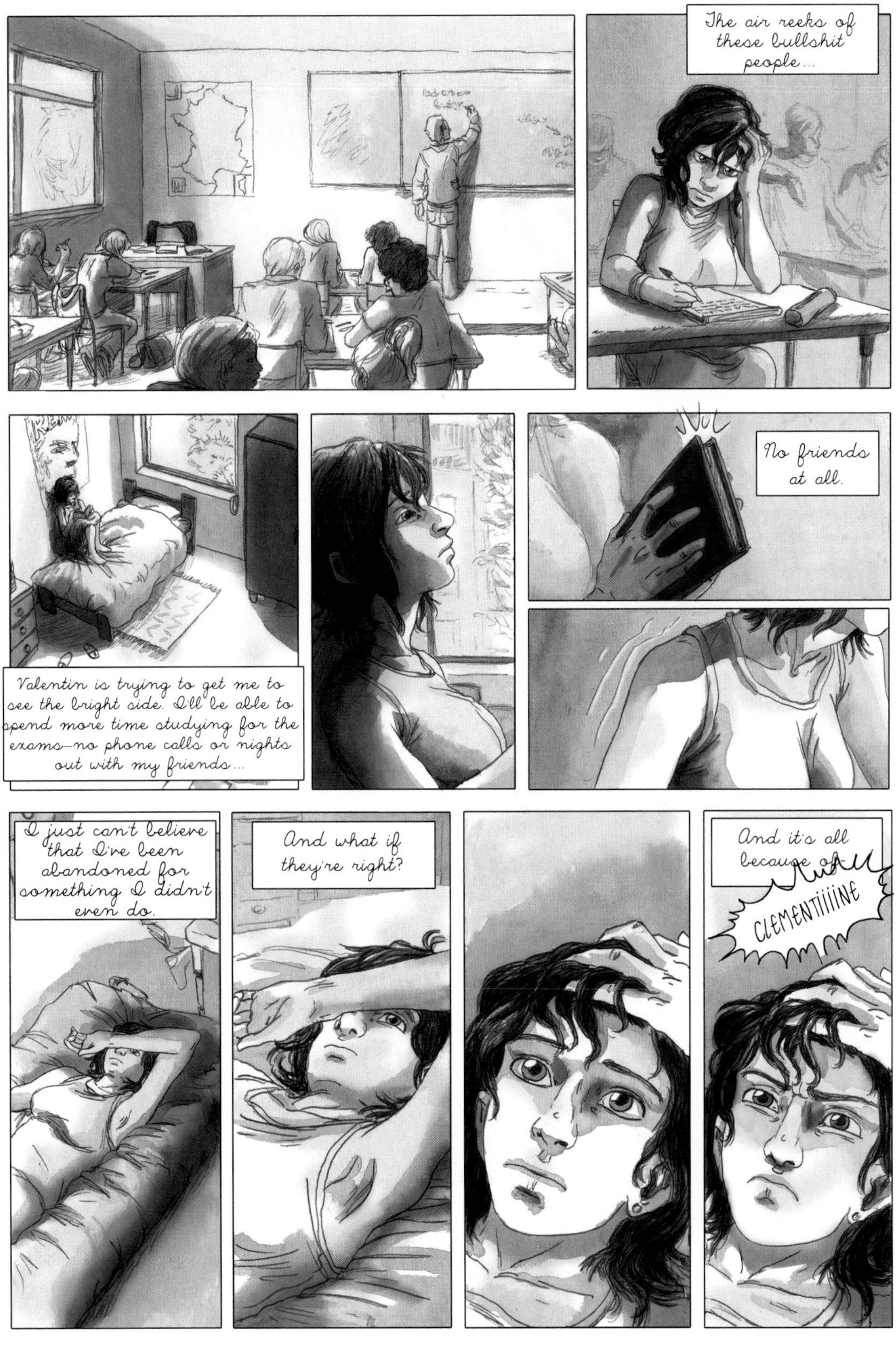
The air reeks of these bullshit people...
Valentin is trying to get me to see the bright side. I'll be able to spend more time studying for the exams—no phone calls or nights out with my friends...
No friends at all.
I just can't believe that I've been abandoned for something I didn't even do.
And what if they're right?
And it's all because of
CLEMENTIIIINE

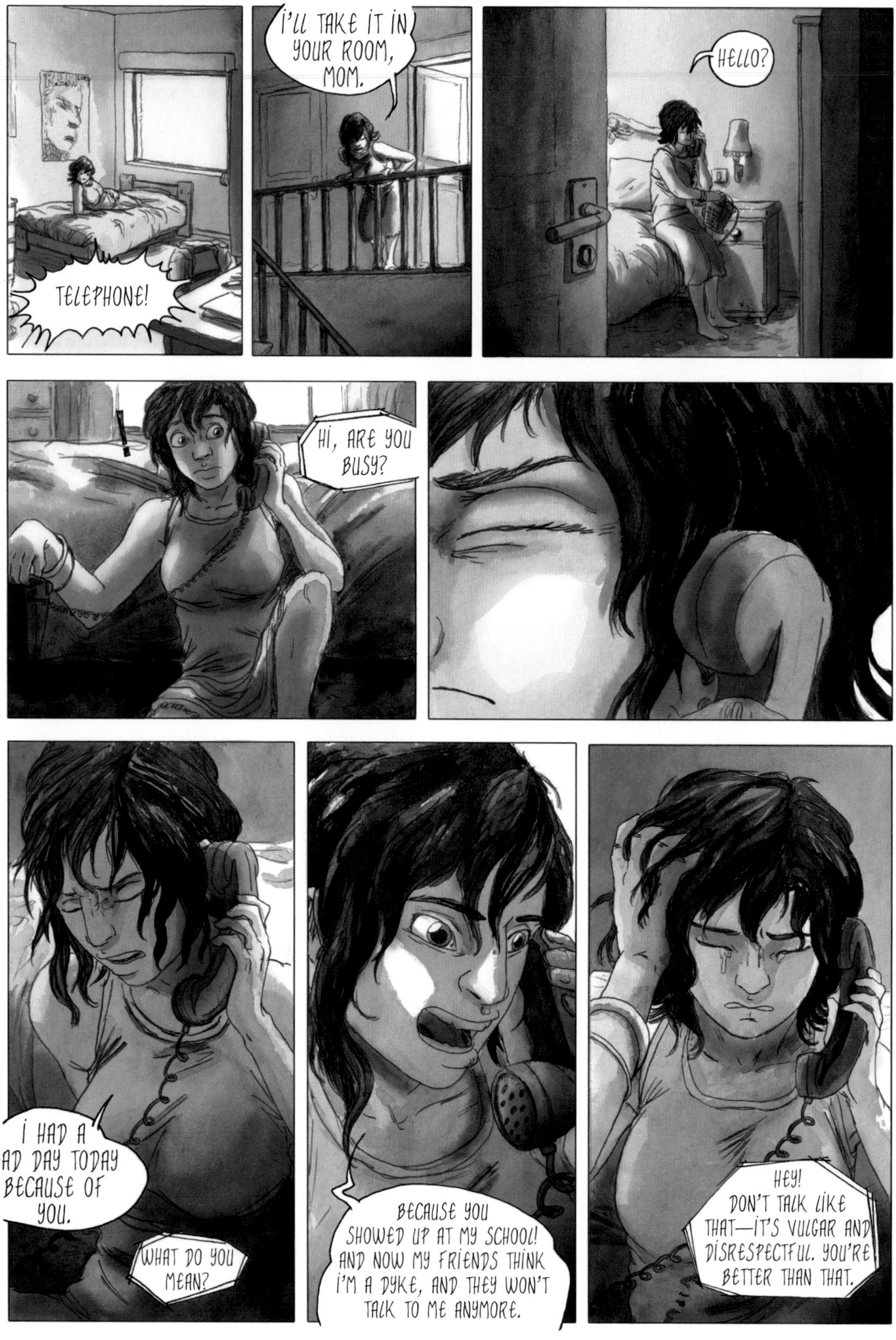
TELEPHONE!
I'LL TAKE IT IN YOUR ROOM, MOM.
HELLO?
HI, ARE YOU BUSY?
I HAD A BAD DAY TODAY BECAUSE OF YOU.
WHAT DO YOU MEAN?
BECAUSE YOU SHOWED UP AT MY SCHOOL! AND NOW MY FRIENDS THINK I'M A DYKE, AND THEY WON'T TALK TO ME ANYMORE.
HEY! DON'T TALK LIKE THAT—IT'S VULGAR AND DISRESPECTFUL. YOU'RE BETTER THAN THAT.

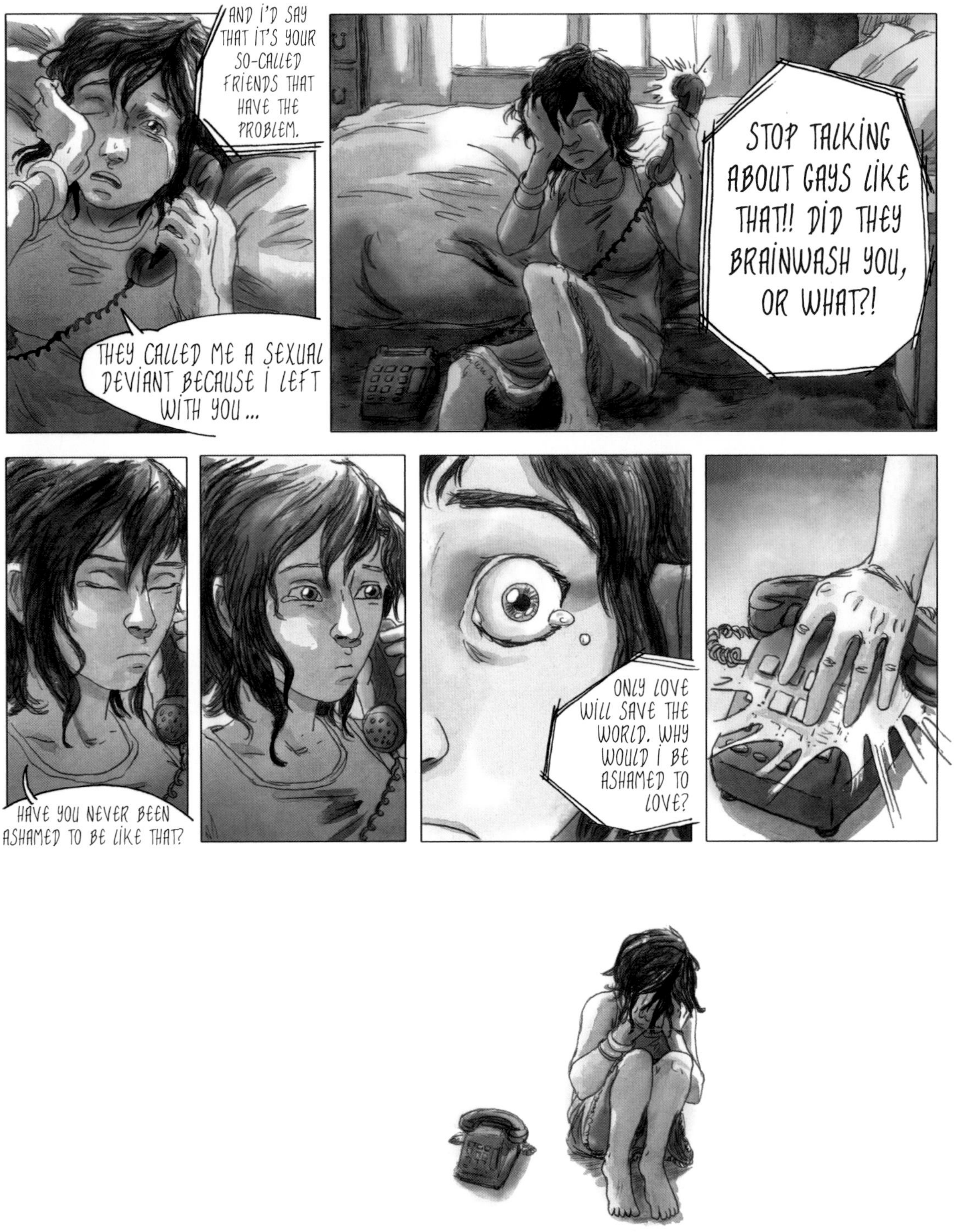
AND I'D SAY THAT IT'S YOUR SO-CALLED FRIENDS THAT HAVE THE PROBLEM.
THEY CALLED ME A SEXUAL DEVIANT BECAUSE I LEFT WITH YOU...
STOP TALKING ABOUT GAYS LIKE THAT!! DID THEY BRAINWASH YOU, OR WHAT?!
HAVE YOU NEVER BEEN ASHAMED TO BE LIKE THAT?
ONLY LOVE WILL SAVE THE WORLD. WHY WOULD I BE ASHAMED TO LOVE?

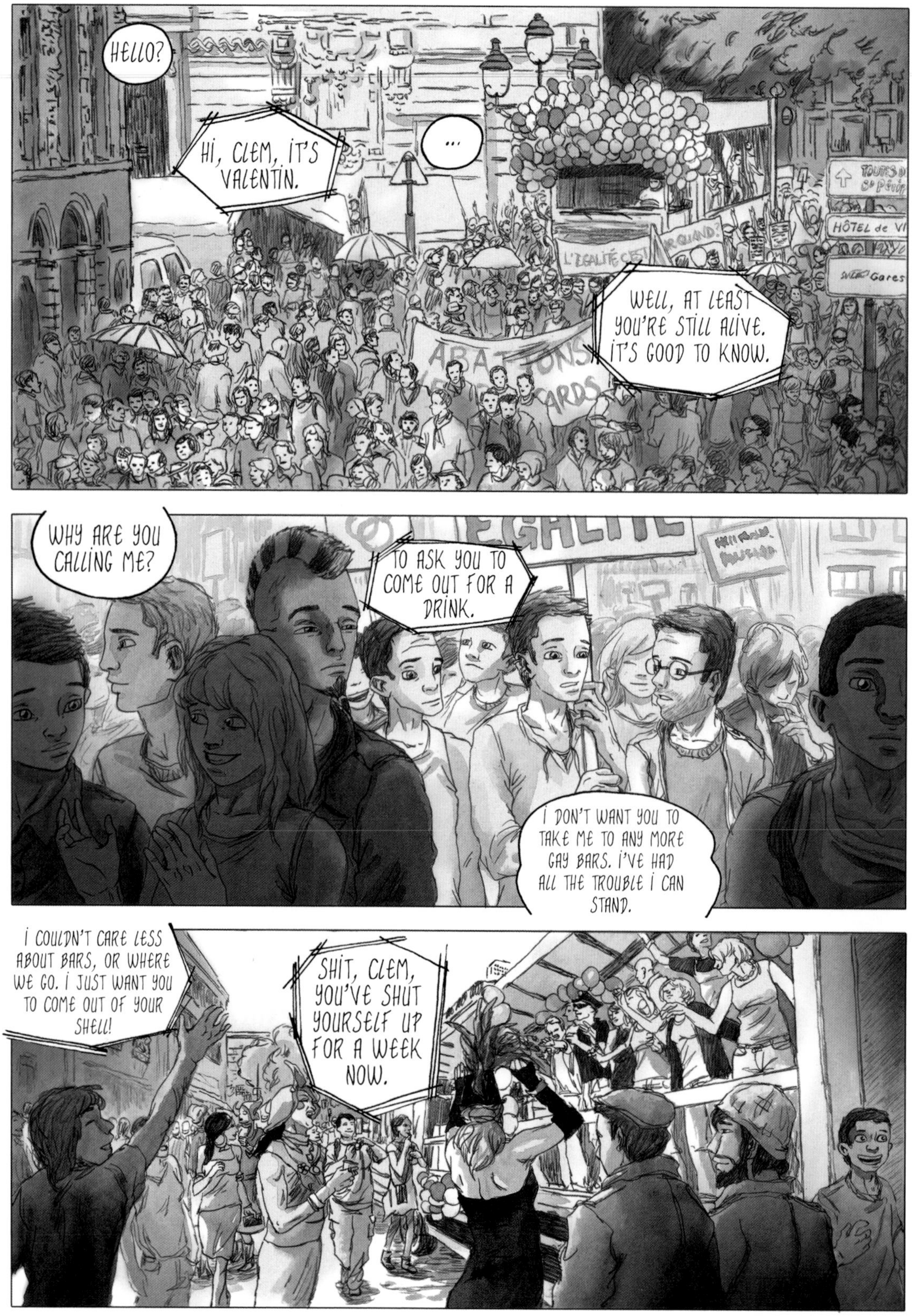
HELLO?
HI, CLEM, IT'S VALENTIN.
...
WELL, AT LEAST YOU'RE STILL ALIVE. IT'S GOOD TO KNOW.
WHY ARE YOU CALLING ME?
TO ASK YOU TO COME OUT FOR A DRINK.
I DON'T WANT YOU TO TAKE ME TO ANY MORE GAY BARS. I'VE HAD ALL THE TROUBLE I CAN STAND.
I COULDN'T CARE LESS ABOUT BARS, OR WHERE WE GO. I JUST WANT YOU TO COME OUT OF YOUR SHELL!
SHIT, CLEM, YOU'VE SHUT YOURSELF UP FOR A WEEK NOW.

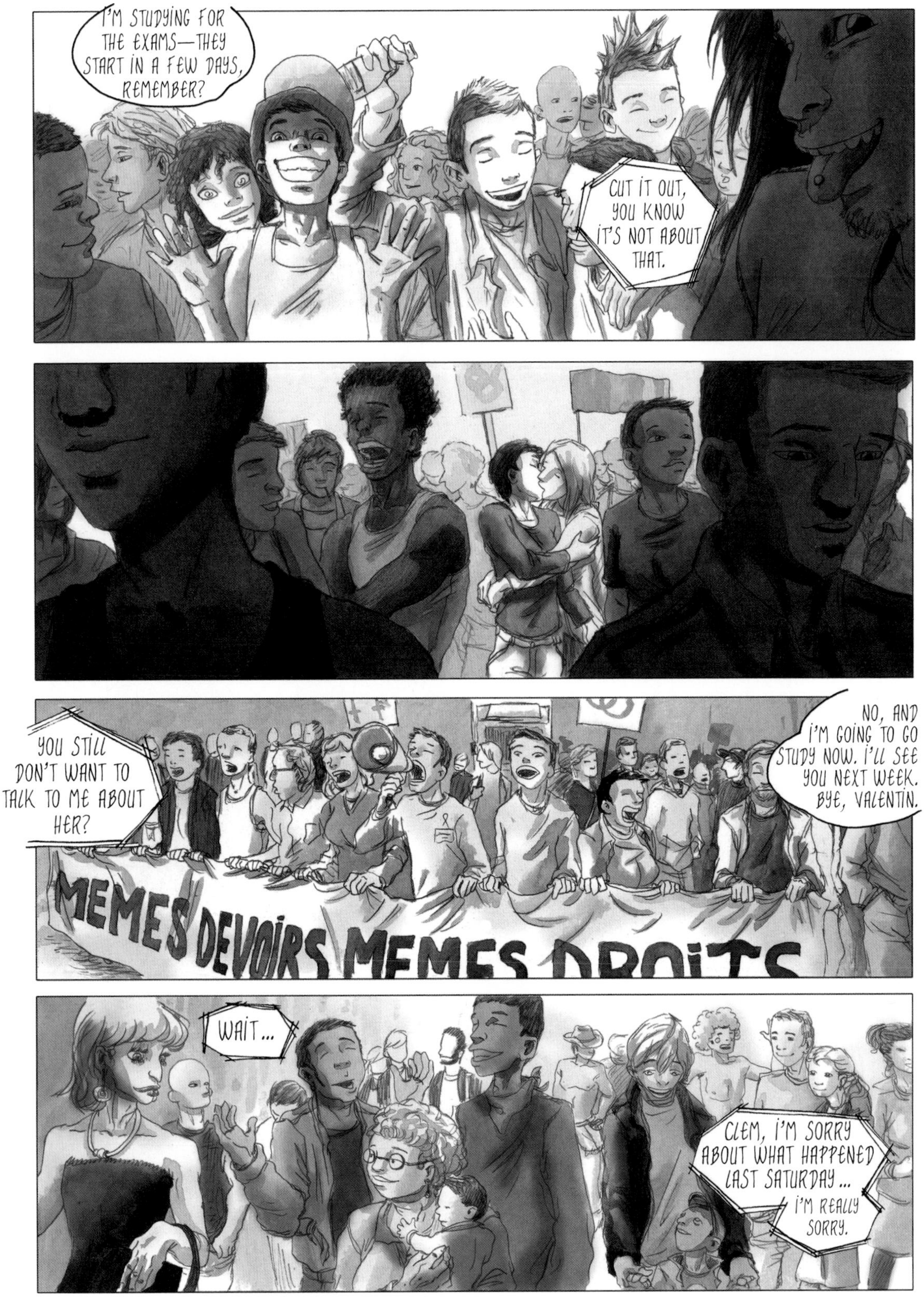
I'M STUDYING FOR THE EXAMS—THEY START IN A FEW DAYS, REMEMBER?
CUT IT OUT, YOU KNOW IT'S NOT ABOUT THAT.
YOU STILL DON'T WANT TO TALK TO ME ABOUT HER?
NO, AND I'M GOING TO GO STUDY NOW. I'LL SEE YOU NEXT WEEK. BYE, VALENTIN.
MEMES DEVOIRS MEMES DROITS
WAIT...
CLEM, I'M SORRY ABOUT WHAT HAPPENED LAST SATURDAY...
I'M REALLY SORRY.

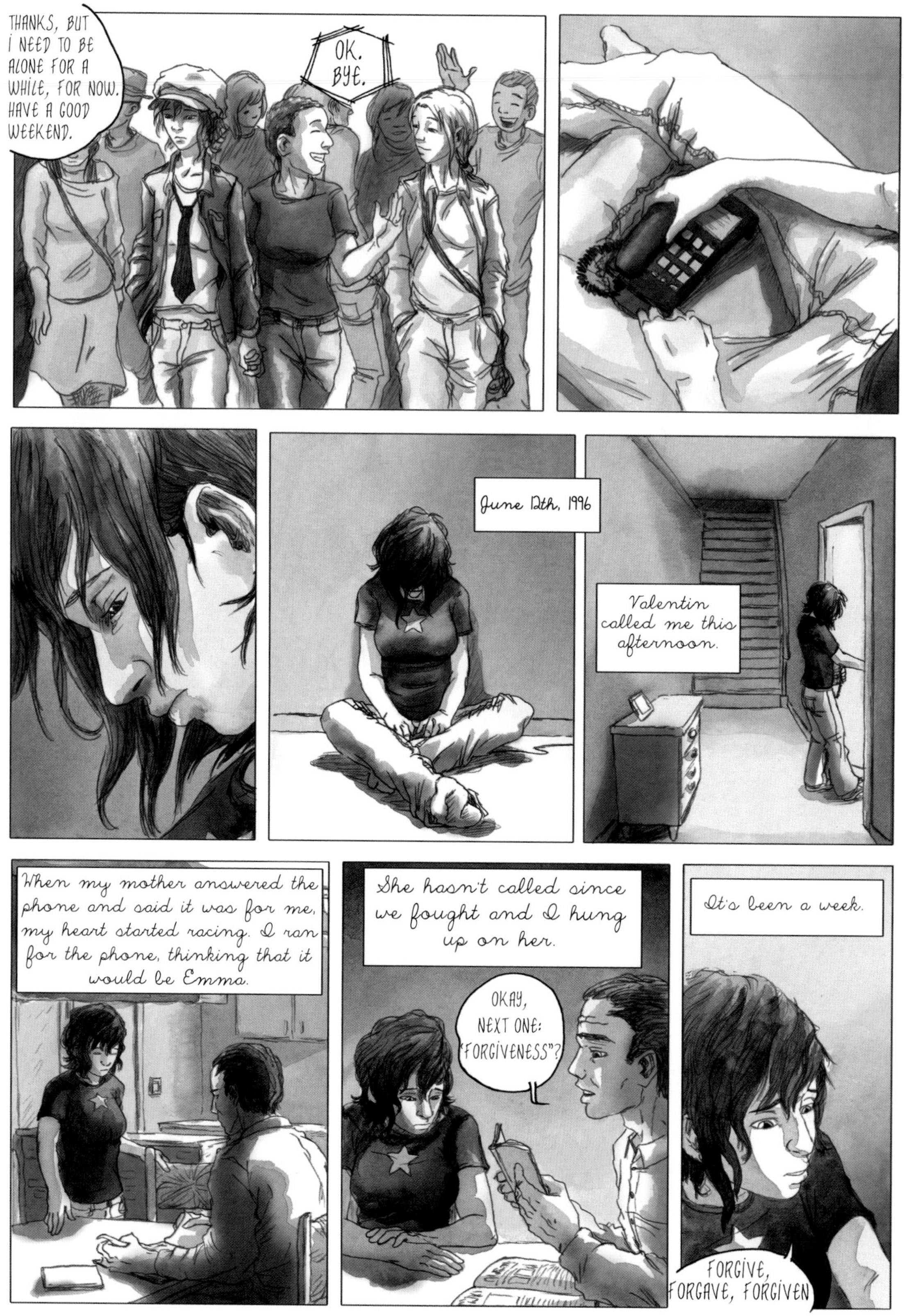
THANKS, BUT I NEED TO BE ALONE FOR A WHILE, FOR NOW. HAVE A GOOD WEEKEND.
OK. BYE.
June 12th, 1996
Valentin called me this afternoon.
When my mother answered the phone and said it was for me, my heart started racing. I ran for the phone, thinking that it would be Emma.
She hasn't called since we fought and I hung up on her.
OKAY, NEXT ONE: "FORGIVENESS"?
It's been a week.
FORGIVE, FORGAVE, FORGIVEN

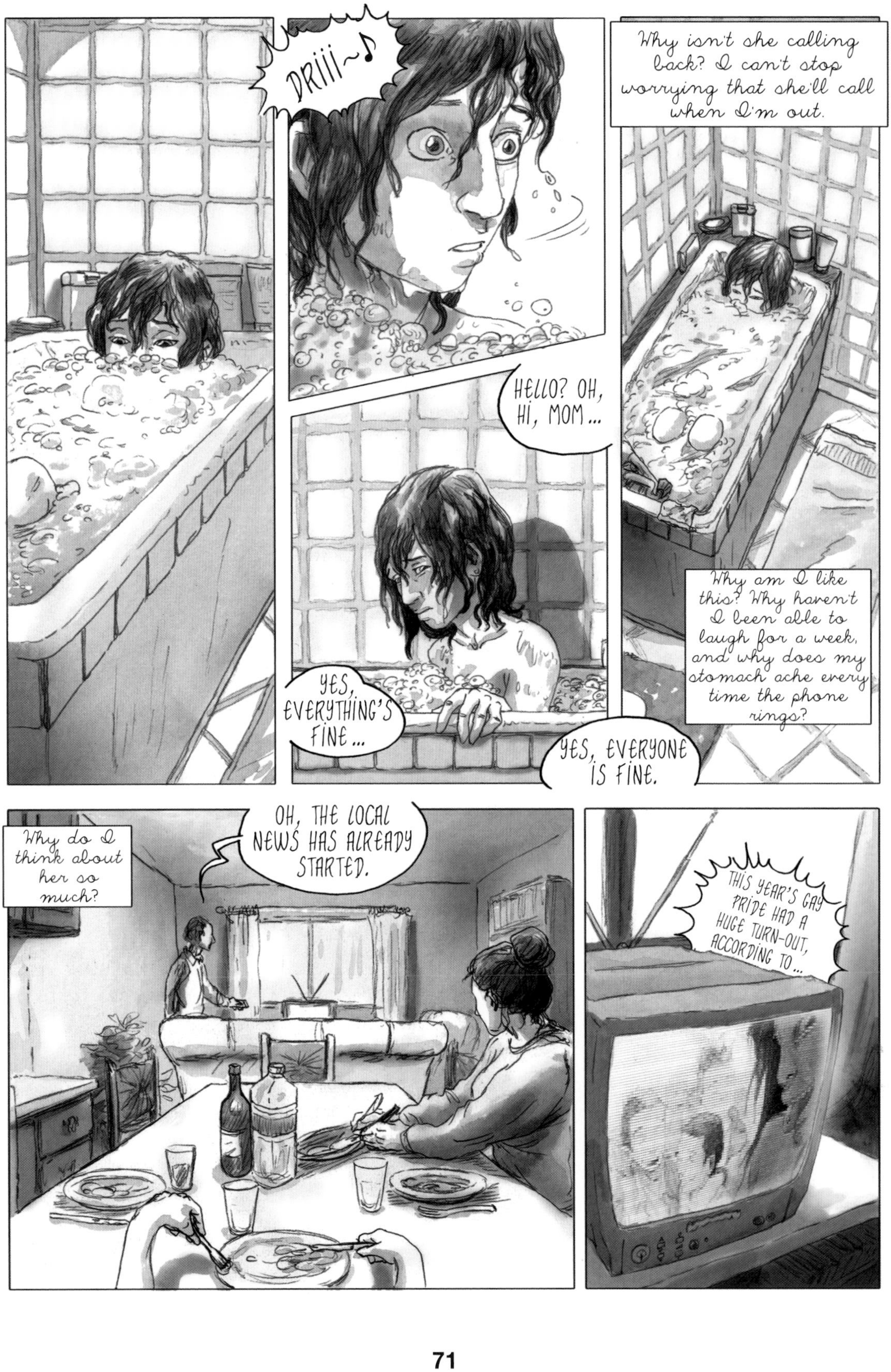
DRIIII~♪
Why isn't she calling back? I can't stop worrying that she'll call when I'm out.
HELLO? OH, HI, MOM...
YES, EVERYTHING'S FINE...
YES, EVERYONE IS FINE.
Why am I like this? Why haven't I been able to laugh for a week, and why does my stomach ache every time the phone rings?
Why do I think about her so much?
OH, THE LOCAL NEWS HAS ALREADY STARTED.
THIS YEAR'S GAY PRIDE HAD A HUGE TURN-OUT, ACCORDING TO...

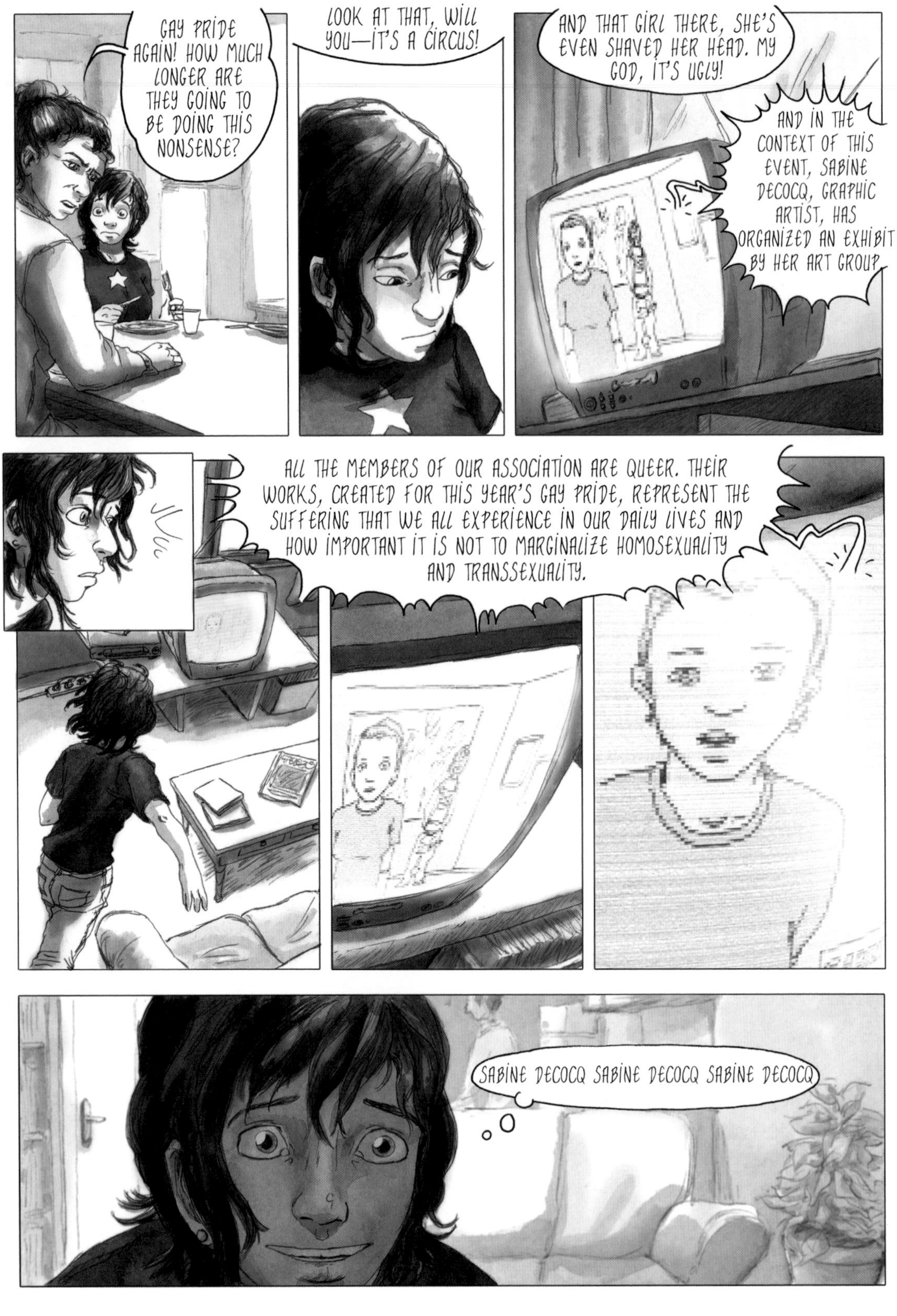
GAY PRIDE AGAIN! HOW MUCH LONGER ARE THEY GOING TO BE DOING THIS NONSENSE?
LOOK AT THAT, WILL YOU—IT'S A CIRCUS!
AND THAT GIRL THERE, SHE'S EVEN SHAVED HER HEAD. MY GOD, IT'S UGLY!
AND IN THE CONTEXT OF THIS EVENT, SABINE DECOCQ, GRAPHIC ARTIST, HAS ORGANIZED AN EXHIBIT BY HER ART GROUP.
ALL THE MEMBERS OF OUR ASSOCIATION ARE QUEER. THEIR WORKS, CREATED FOR THIS YEAR'S GAY PRIDE, REPRESENT THE SUFFERING THAT WE ALL EXPERIENCE IN OUR DAILY LIVES AND HOW IMPORTANT IT IS NOT TO MARGINALIZE HOMOSEXUALITY AND TRANSSEXUALITY.
SABINE DECOCQ SABINE DECOCQ SABINE DECOCQ

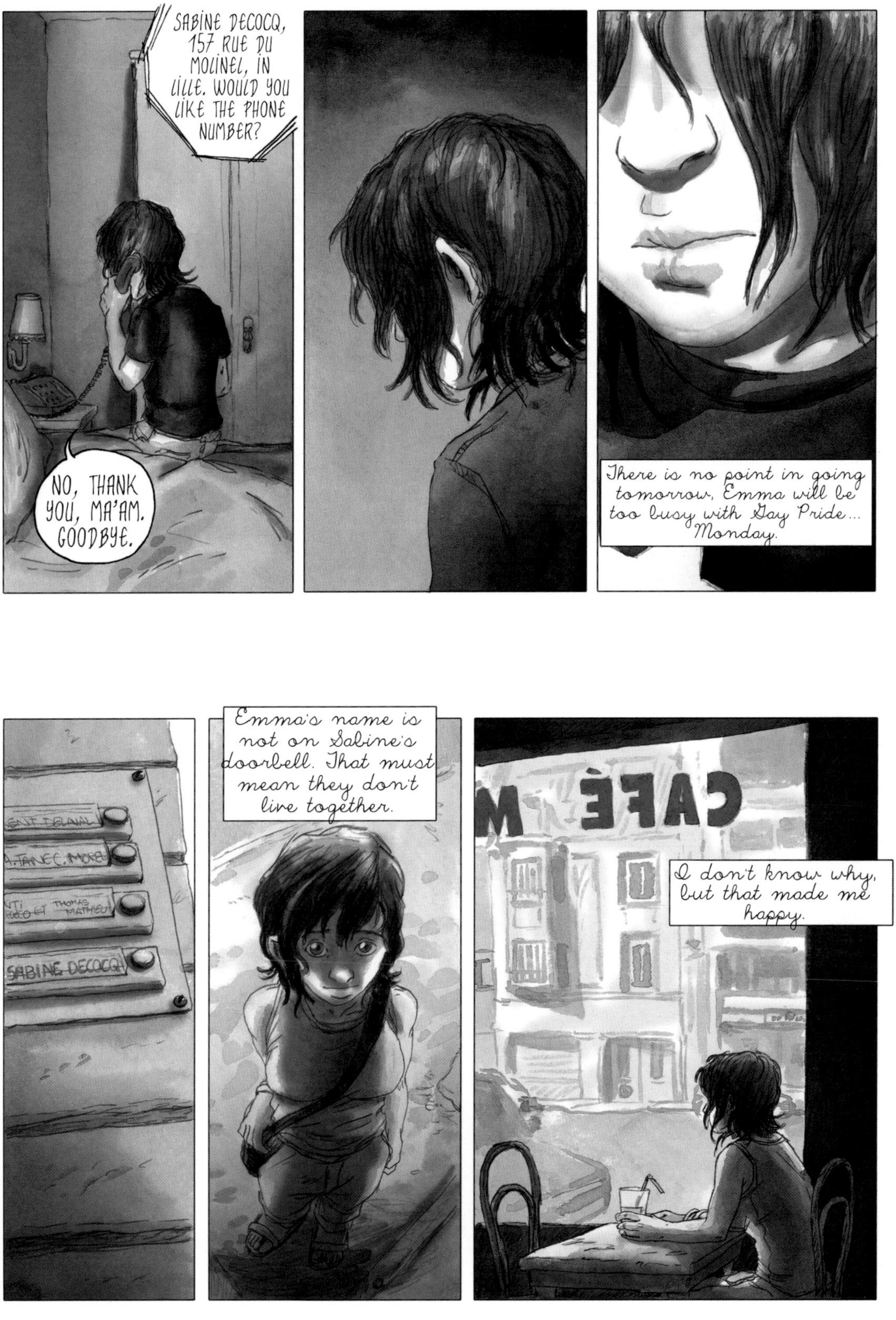
SABINE DECOCQ, 157 RUE DU MOLINEL, IN LILLE. WOULD YOU LIKE THE PHONE NUMBER?
NO, THANK YOU, MA'AM. GOODBYE.
There is no point in going tomorrow, Emma will be too busy with Gay Pride... Monday.
SABINE DECOCQ
Emma's name is not on Sabine's doorbell. That must mean they don't live together.
I don't know why, but that made me happy.

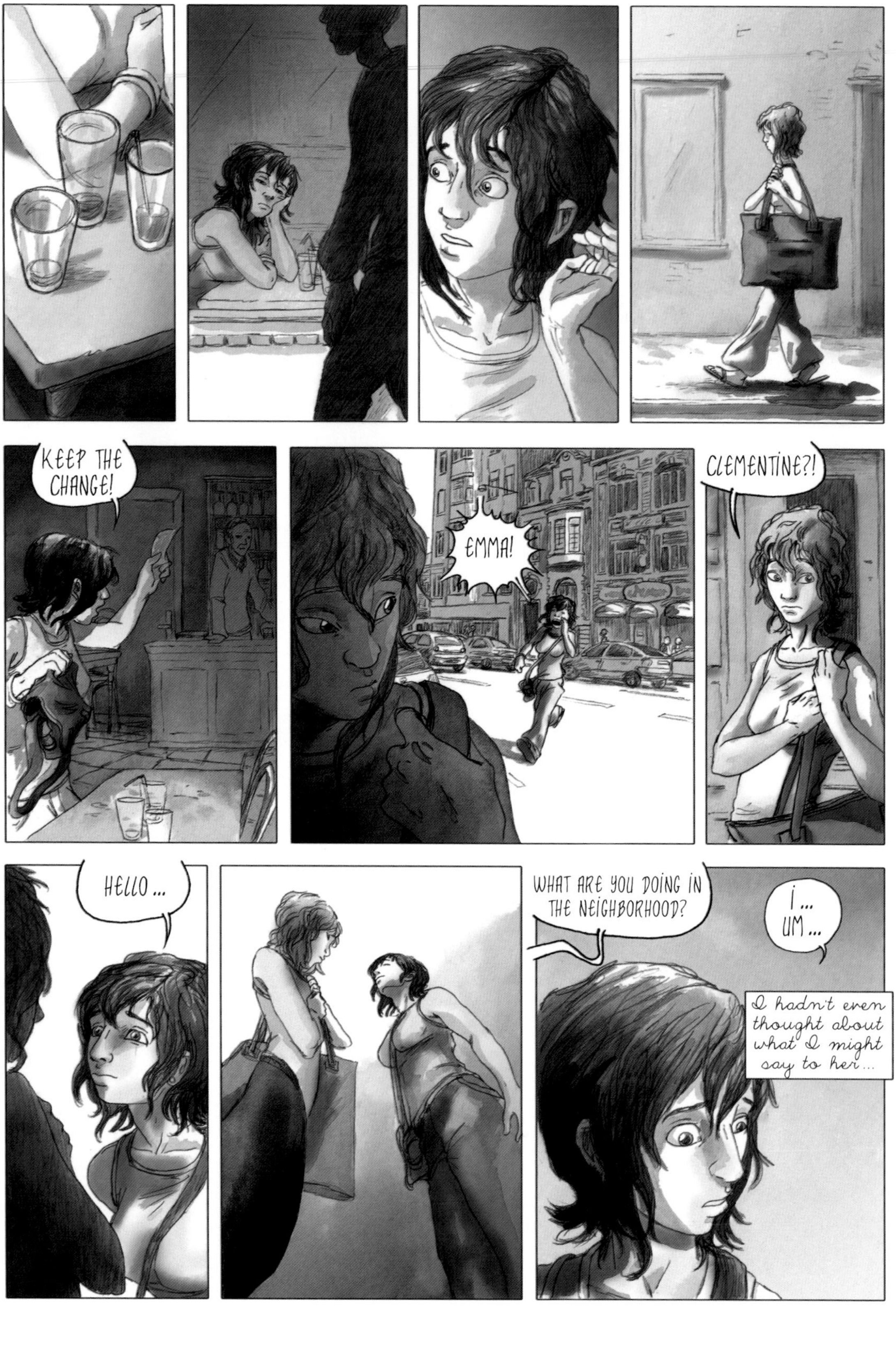
KEEP THE CHANGE!
EMMA!
CLEMENTINE?!
HELLO...
WHAT ARE YOU DOING IN THE NEIGHBORHOOD?
I... UM...
I hadn't even thought about what I might say to her...

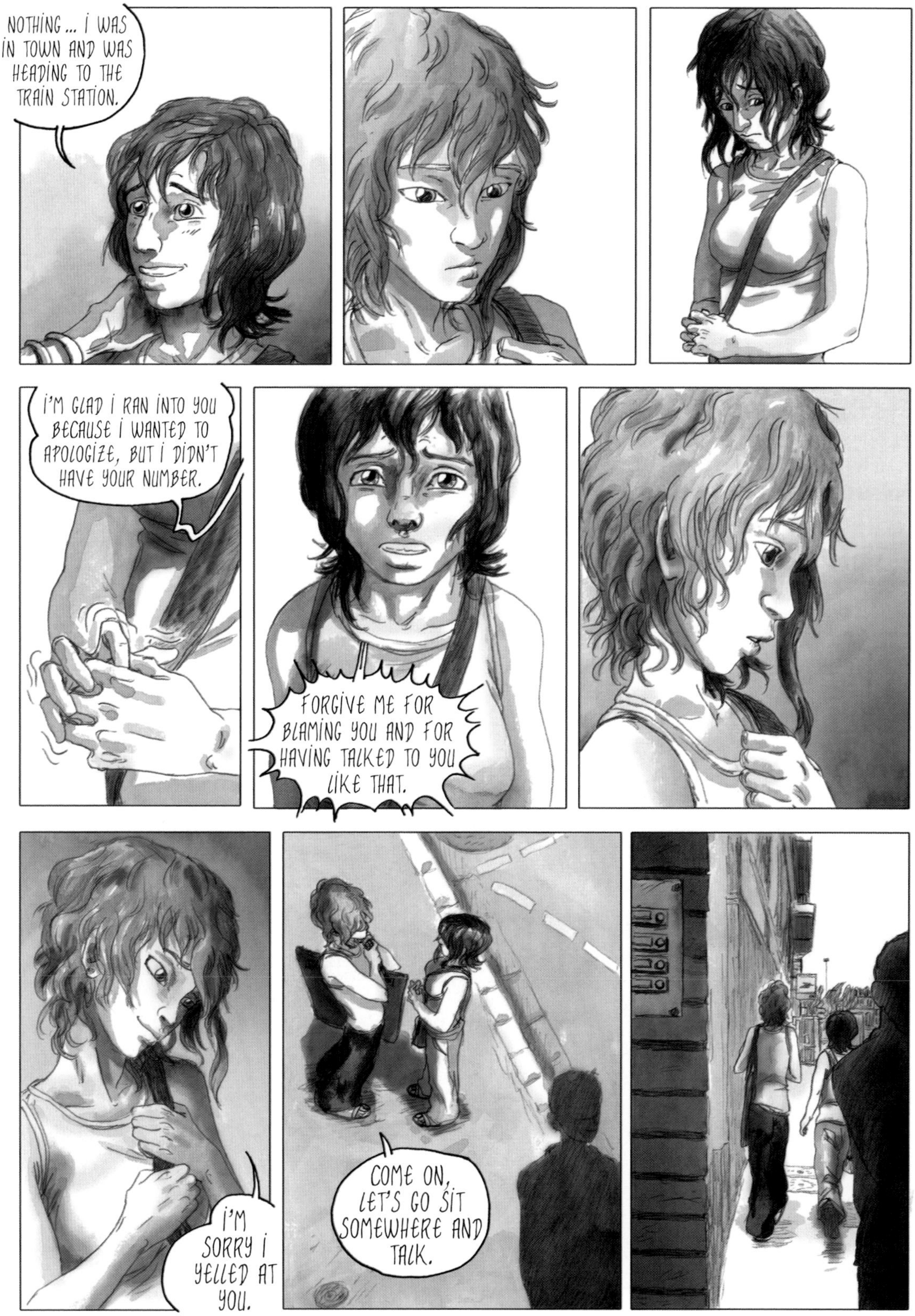
NOTHING... I WAS IN TOWN AND WAS HEADING TO THE TRAIN STATION.
I'M GLAD I RAN INTO YOU BECAUSE I WANTED TO APOLOGIZE, BUT I DIDN'T HAVE YOUR NUMBER.
FORGIVE ME FOR BLAMING YOU AND FOR HAVING TALKED TO YOU LIKE THAT.
I'M SORRY I YELLED AT YOU.
COME ON, LET'S GO SIT SOMEWHERE AND TALK.

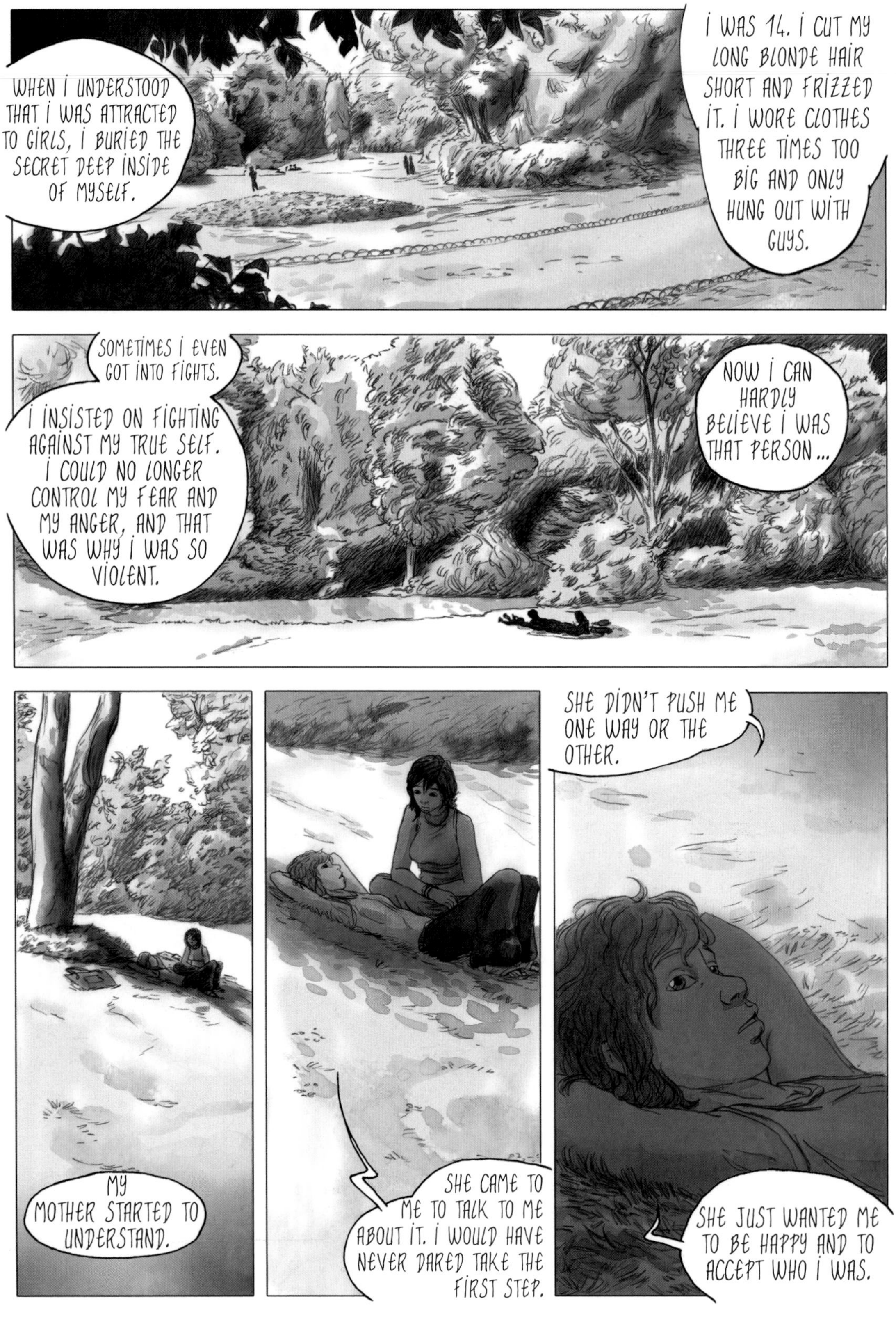
WHEN I UNDERSTOOD THAT I WAS ATTRACTED TO GIRLS, I BURIED THE SECRET DEEP INSIDE OF MYSELF.
I WAS 14. I CUT MY LONG BLONDE HAIR SHORT AND FRIZZED IT. I WORE CLOTHES THREE TIMES TOO BIG AND ONLY HUNG OUT WITH GUYS.
SOMETIMES I EVEN GOT INTO FIGHTS.
I INSISTED ON FIGHTING AGAINST MY TRUE SELF. I COULD NO LONGER CONTROL MY FEAR AND MY ANGER, AND THAT WAS WHY I WAS SO VIOLENT.
NOW I CAN HARDLY BELIEVE I WAS THAT PERSON...
MY MOTHER STARTED TO UNDERSTAND.
SHE CAME TO ME TO TALK TO ME ABOUT IT. I WOULD HAVE NEVER DARED TAKE THE FIRST STEP.
SHE DIDN'T PUSH ME ONE WAY OR THE OTHER.
SHE JUST WANTED ME TO BE HAPPY AND TO ACCEPT WHO I WAS.

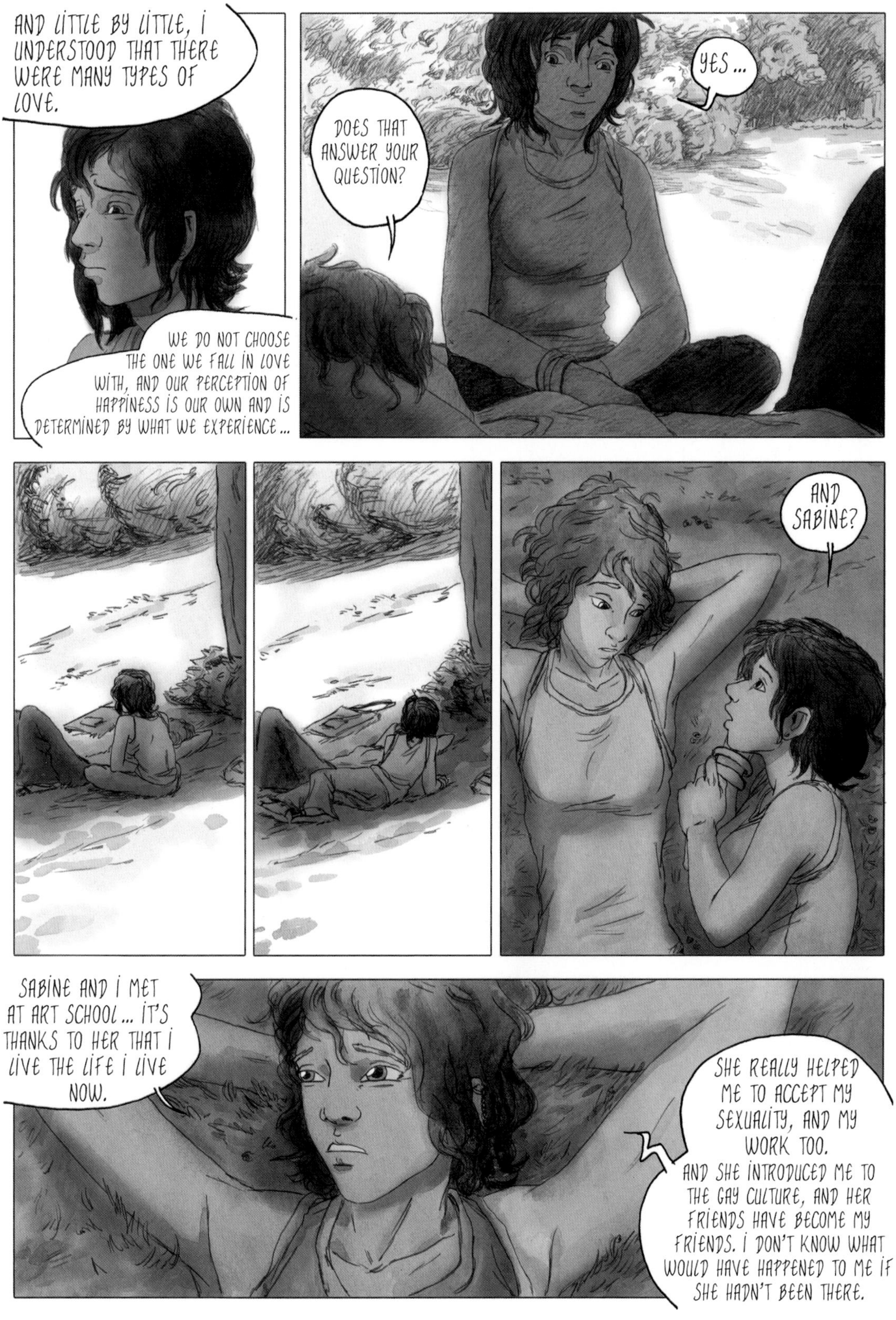
AND LITTLE BY LITTLE, I UNDERSTOOD THAT THERE WERE MANY TYPES OF LOVE.
WE DO NOT CHOOSE THE ONE WE FALL IN LOVE WITH, AND OUR PERCEPTION OF HAPPINESS IS OUR OWN AND IS DETERMINED BY WHAT WE EXPERIENCE...
DOES THAT ANSWER YOUR QUESTION?
YES...
AND SABINE?
SABINE AND I MET AT ART SCHOOL... IT'S THANKS TO HER THAT I LIVE THE LIFE I LIVE NOW.
SHE REALLY HELPED ME TO ACCEPT MY SEXUALITY, AND MY WORK TOO.
AND SHE INTRODUCED ME TO THE GAY CULTURE, AND HER FRIENDS HAVE BECOME MY FRIENDS. I DON'T KNOW WHAT WOULD HAVE HAPPENED TO ME IF SHE HADN'T BEEN THERE.

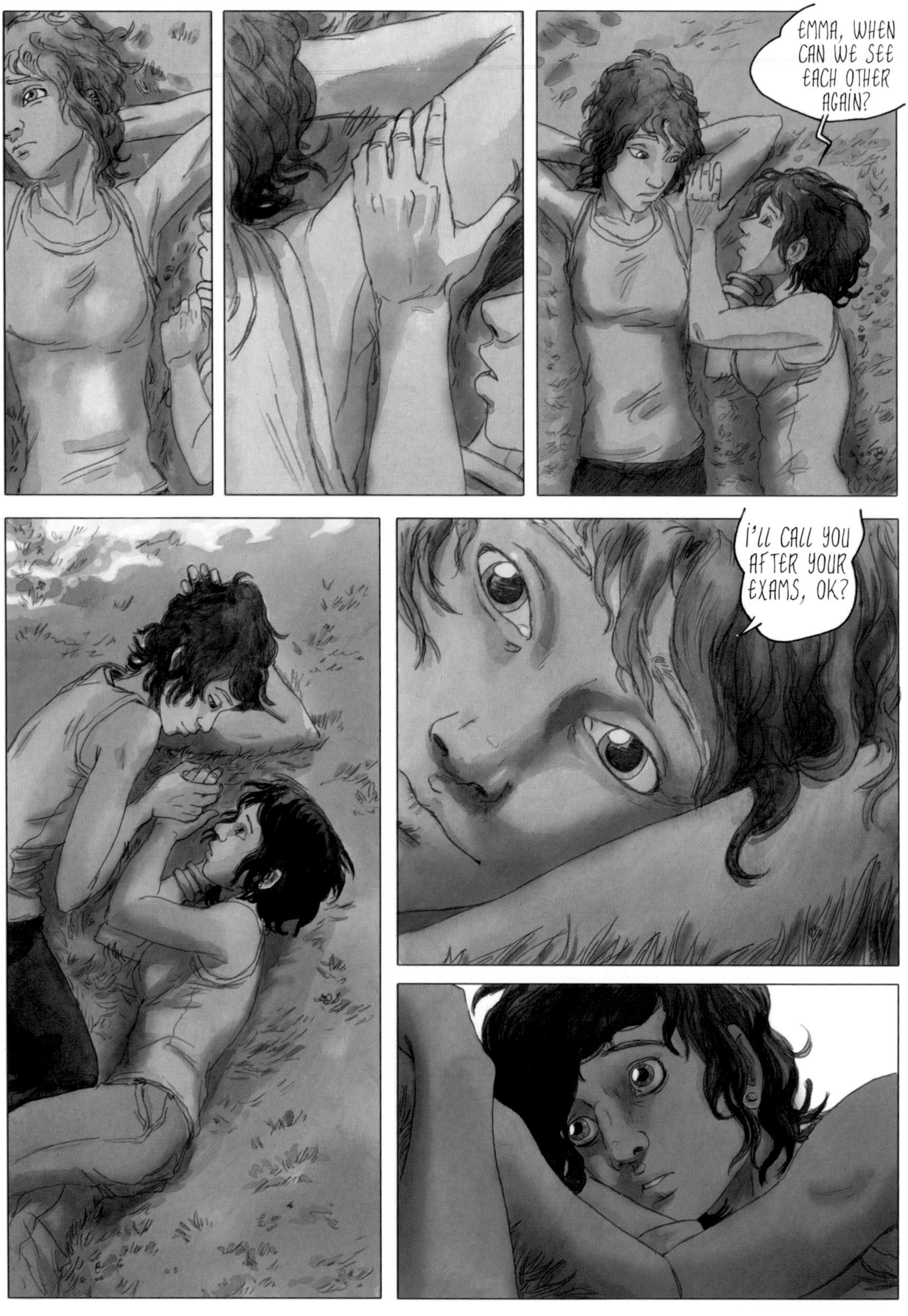
EMMA, WHEN CAN WE SEE EACH OTHER AGAIN?
I'LL CALL YOU AFTER YOUR EXAMS, OK?

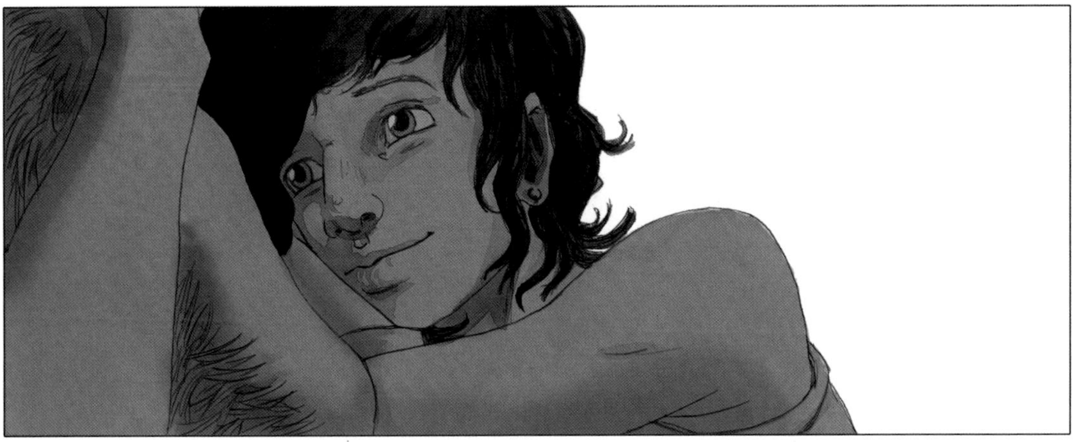

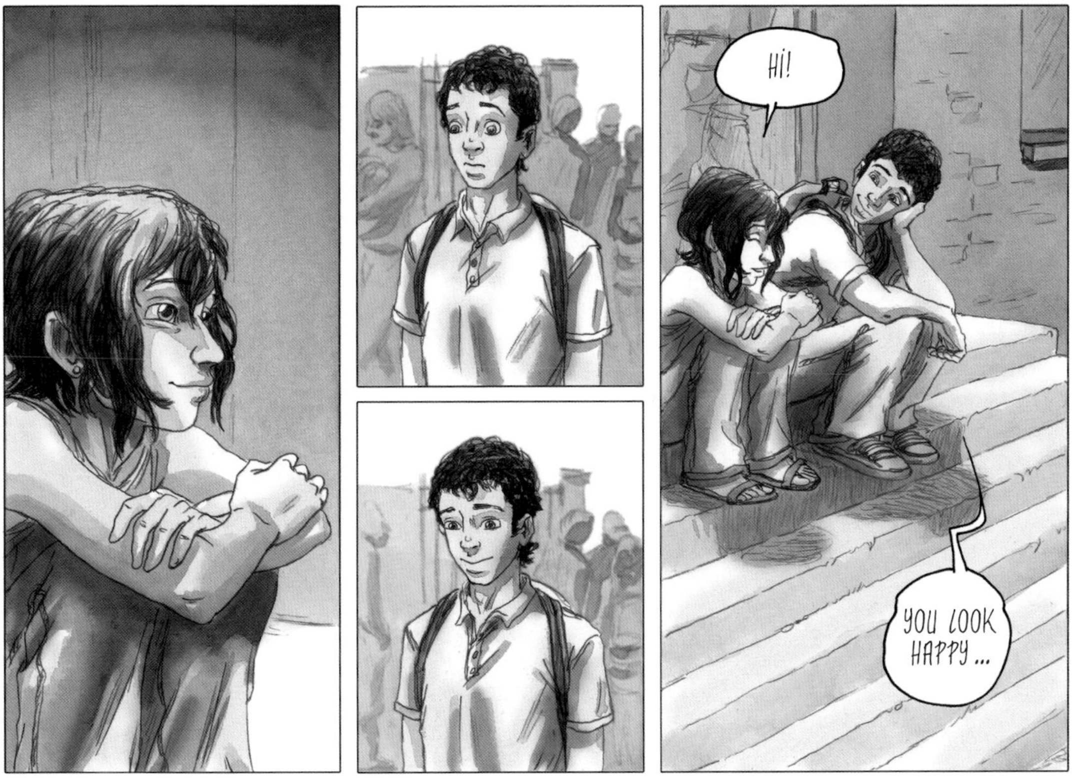
HI!
YOU LOOK HAPPY...

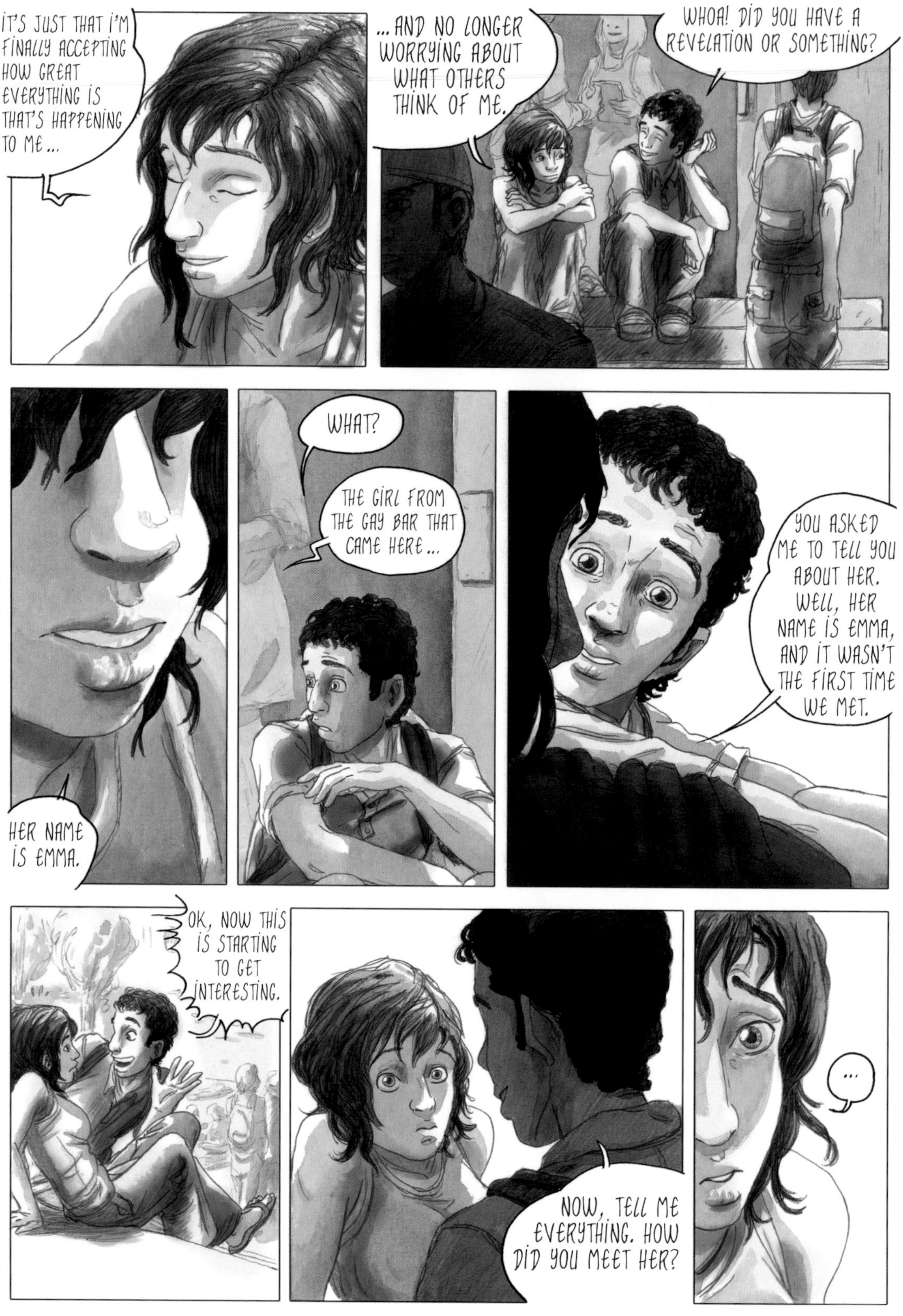
IT'S JUST THAT I'M FINALLY ACCEPTING HOW GREAT EVERYTHING IS THAT'S HAPPENING TO ME...
...AND NO LONGER WORRYING ABOUT WHAT OTHERS THINK OF ME.
WHOA! DID YOU HAVE A REVELATION OR SOMETHING?
HER NAME IS EMMA.
WHAT?
THE GIRL FROM THE GAY BAR THAT CAME HERE...
YOU ASKED ME TO TELL YOU ABOUT HER. WELL, HER NAME IS EMMA, AND IT WASN'T THE FIRST TIME WE MET.
OK, NOW THIS IS STARTING TO GET INTERESTING.
NOW, TELL ME EVERYTHING. HOW DID YOU MEET HER?
...

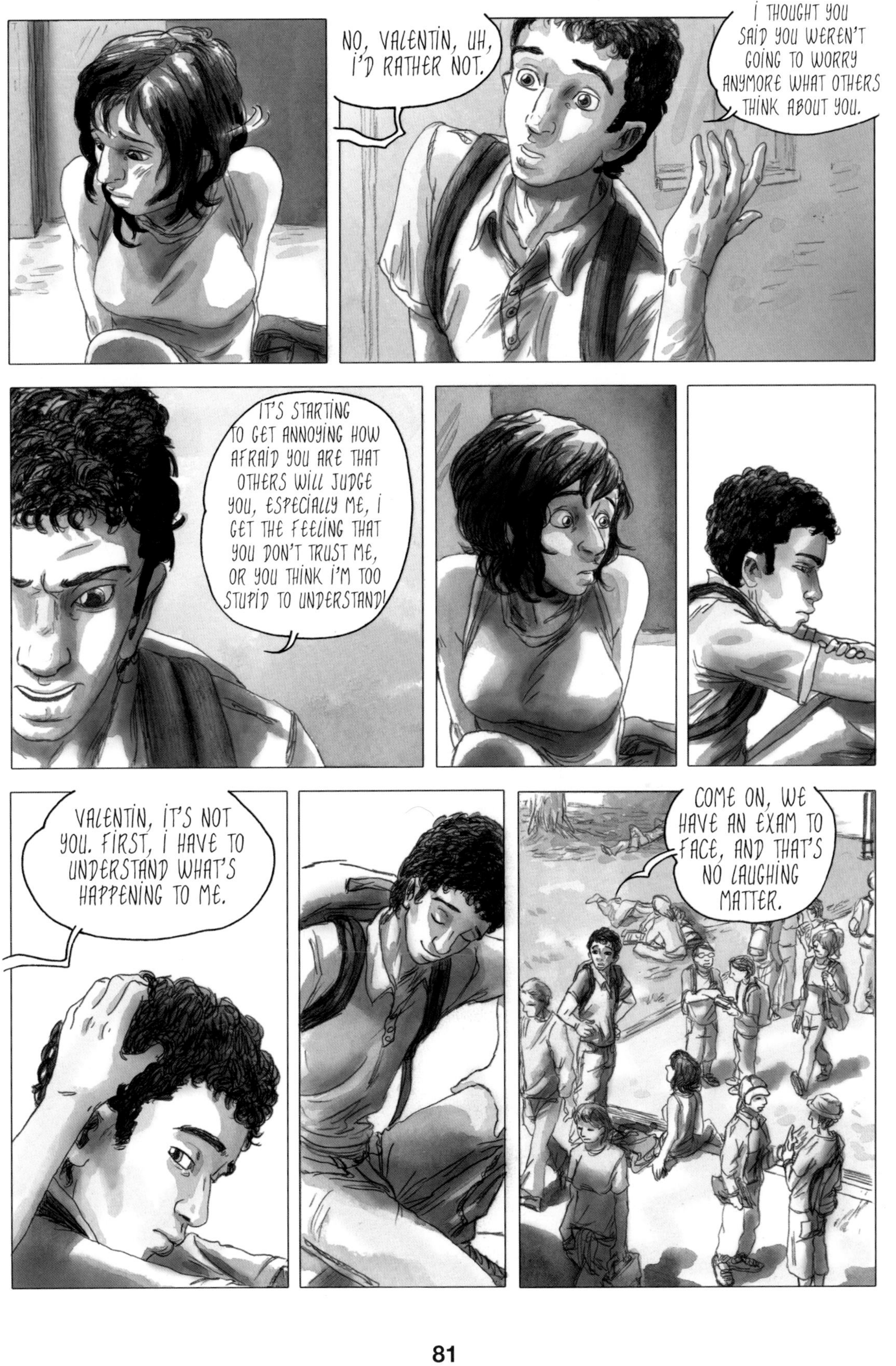
NO, VALENTIN, UH, I'D RATHER NOT.
I THOUGHT YOU SAID YOU WEREN'T GOING TO WORRY ANYMORE WHAT OTHERS THINK ABOUT YOU.
IT'S STARTING TO GET ANNOYING HOW AFRAID YOU ARE THAT OTHERS WILL JUDGE YOU, ESPECIALLY ME, I GET THE FEELING THAT YOU DON'T TRUST ME, OR YOU THINK I'M TOO STUPID TO UNDERSTAND!
VALENTIN, IT'S NOT YOU. FIRST, I HAVE TO UNDERSTAND WHAT'S HAPPENING TO ME.
COME ON, WE HAVE AN EXAM TO FACE, AND THAT'S NO LAUGHING MATTER.

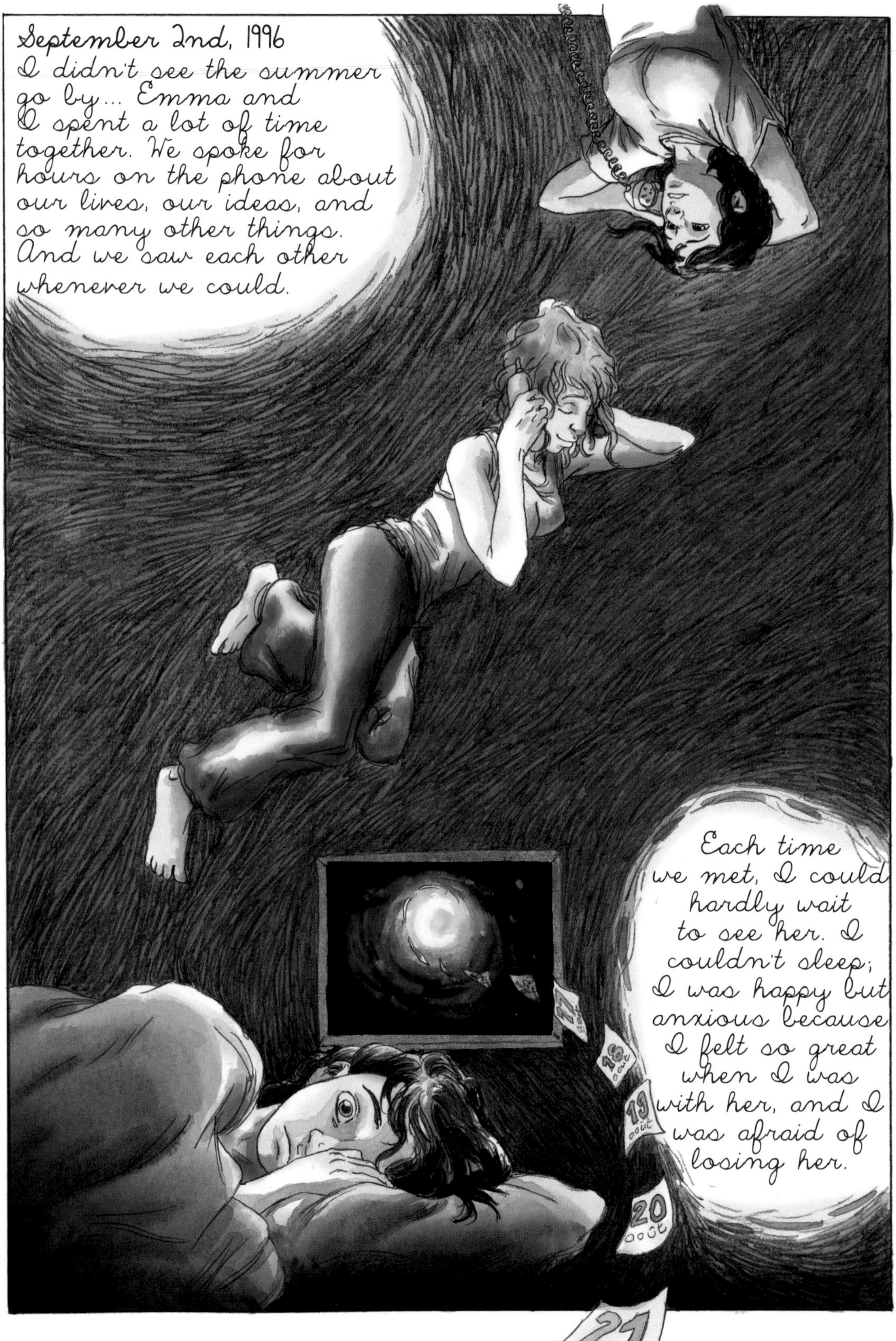
September 2nd, 1996
I didn't see the summer go by... Emma and I spent a lot of time together. We spoke for hours on the phone about our lives, our ideas, and so many other things. And we saw each other whenever we could.
Each time we met, I could hardly wait to see her. I couldn't sleep; I was happy but anxious because I felt so great when I was with her, and I was afraid of losing her.

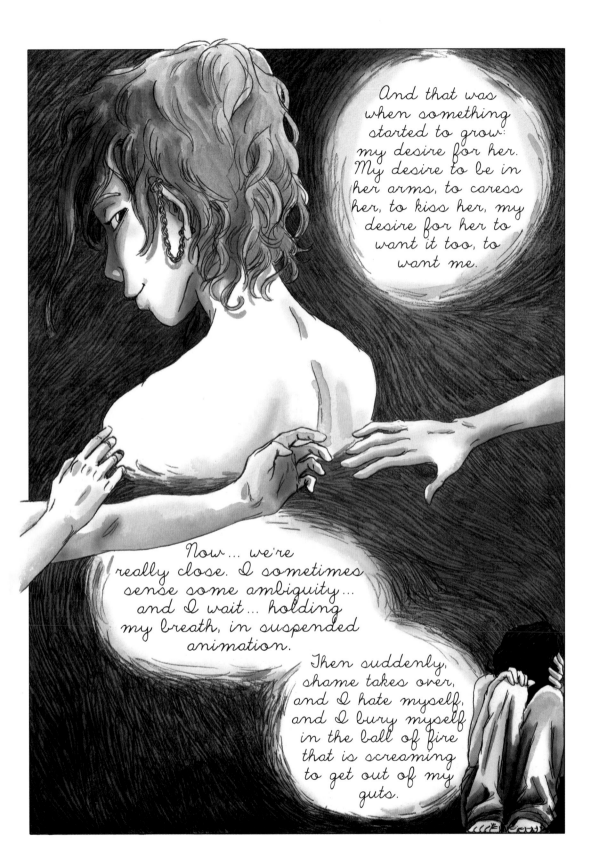

And that was when something started to grow: my desire for her. My desire to be in her arms, to caress her, to kiss her, my desire for her to want it too, to want me.

Now... we're really close. I sometimes sense some ambiguity... and I wait... holding my breath, in suspended animation.

Then suddenly, shame takes over, and I hate myself, and I bury myself in the ball of fire that is screaming to get out of my guts.

83

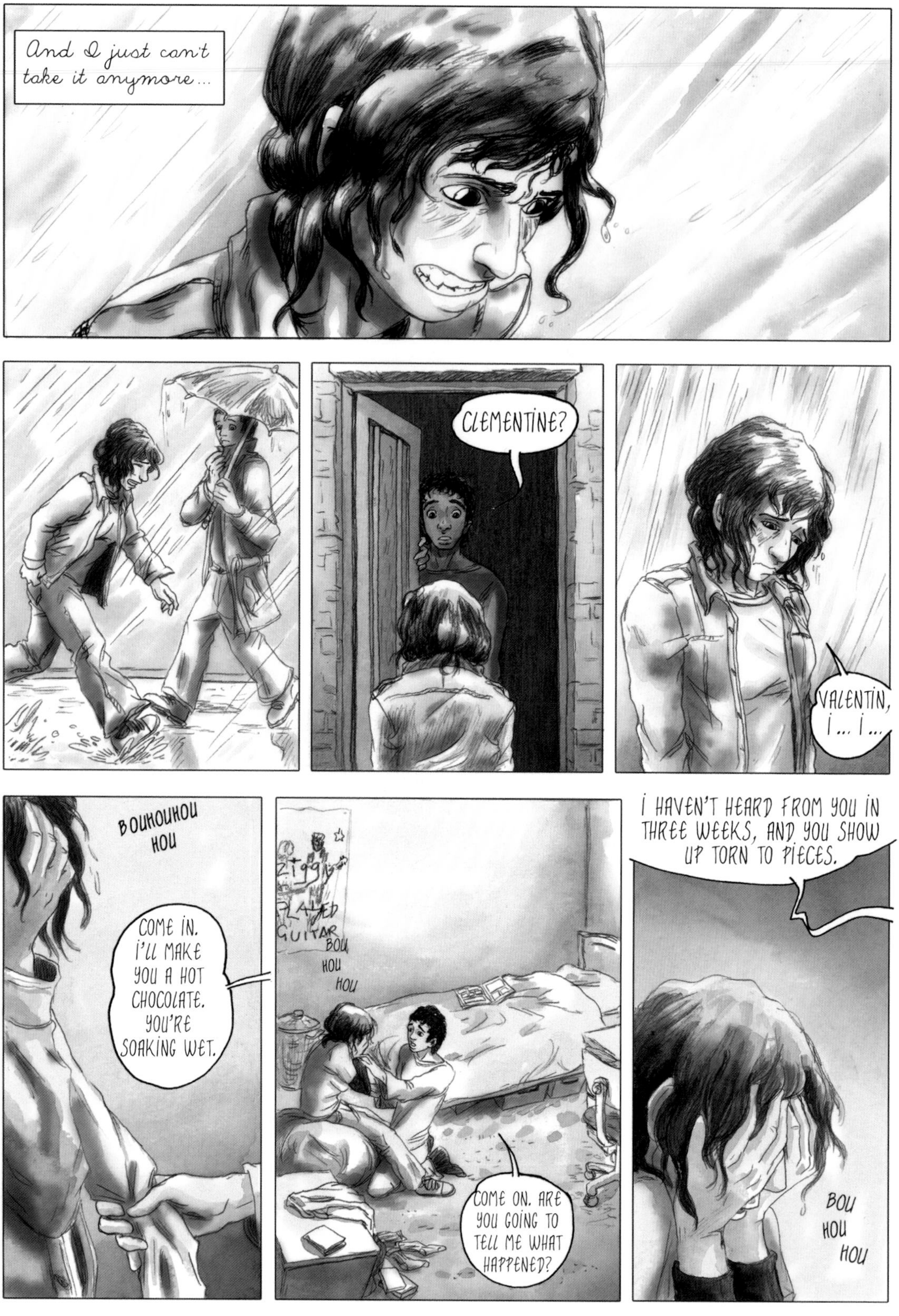
And I just can't take it anymore...
CLEMENTINE?
VALENTIN, I... I...
BOUHOUHOU HOU
COME IN. I'LL MAKE YOU A HOT CHOCOLATE. YOU'RE SOAKING WET.
BOU HOU HOU
COME ON. ARE YOU GOING TO TELL ME WHAT HAPPENED?
I HAVEN'T HEARD FROM YOU IN THREE WEEKS, AND YOU SHOW UP TORN TO PIECES.
BOU HOU HOU

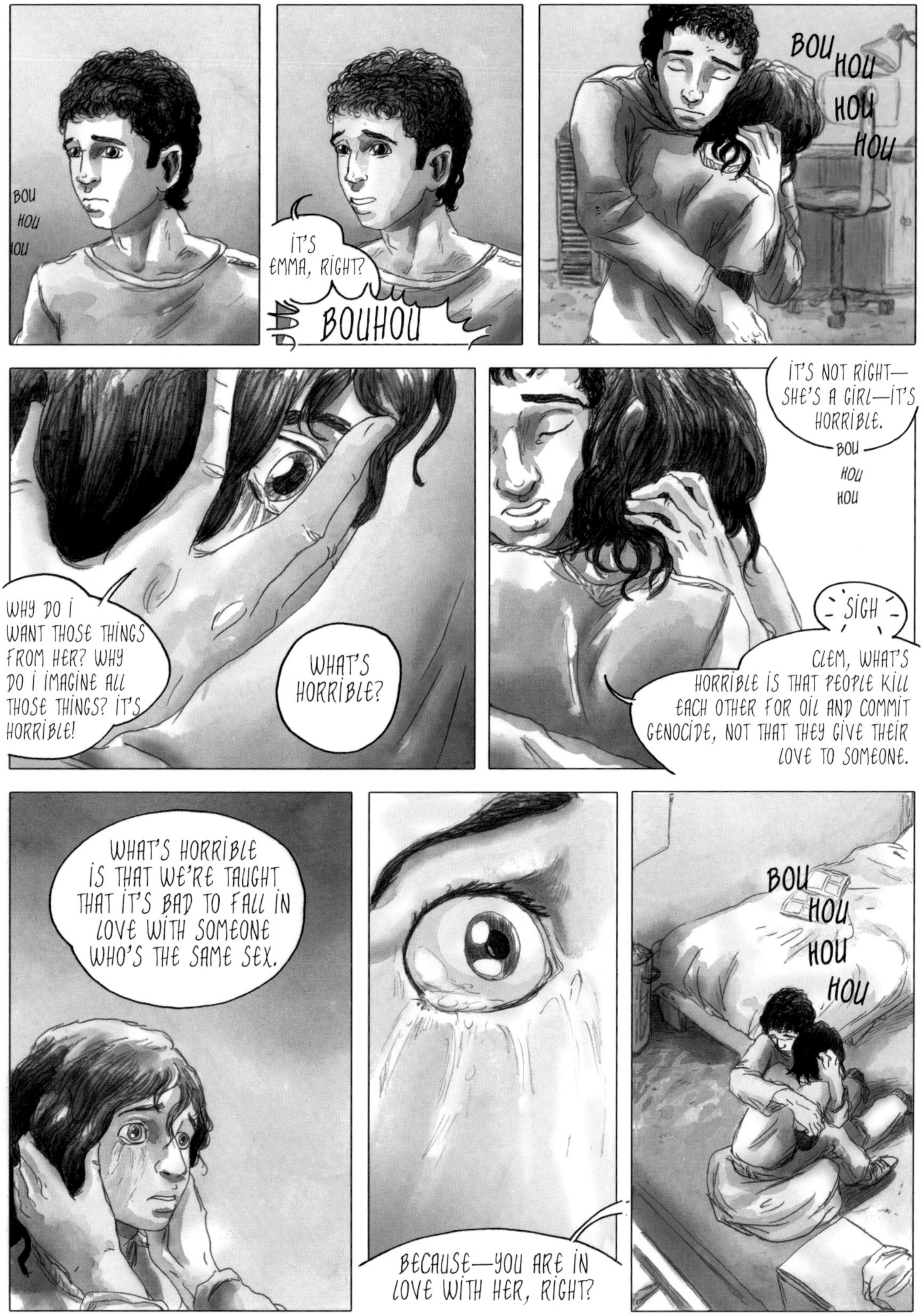
BOU
HOU
HOU
IT'S EMMA, RIGHT?
BOUHOU
BOU HOU HOU HOU
WHY DO I WANT THOSE THINGS FROM HER? WHY DO I IMAGINE ALL THOSE THINGS? IT'S HORRIBLE!
WHAT'S HORRIBLE?
IT'S NOT RIGHT—SHE'S A GIRL—IT'S HORRIBLE.
BOU
HOU
HOU
SIGH
CLEM, WHAT'S HORRIBLE IS THAT PEOPLE KILL EACH OTHER FOR OIL AND COMMIT GENOCIDE, NOT THAT THEY GIVE THEIR LOVE TO SOMEONE.
WHAT'S HORRIBLE IS THAT WE'RE TAUGHT THAT IT'S BAD TO FALL IN LOVE WITH SOMEONE WHO'S THE SAME SEX.
BECAUSE—YOU ARE IN LOVE WITH HER, RIGHT?
BOU HOU HOU HOU

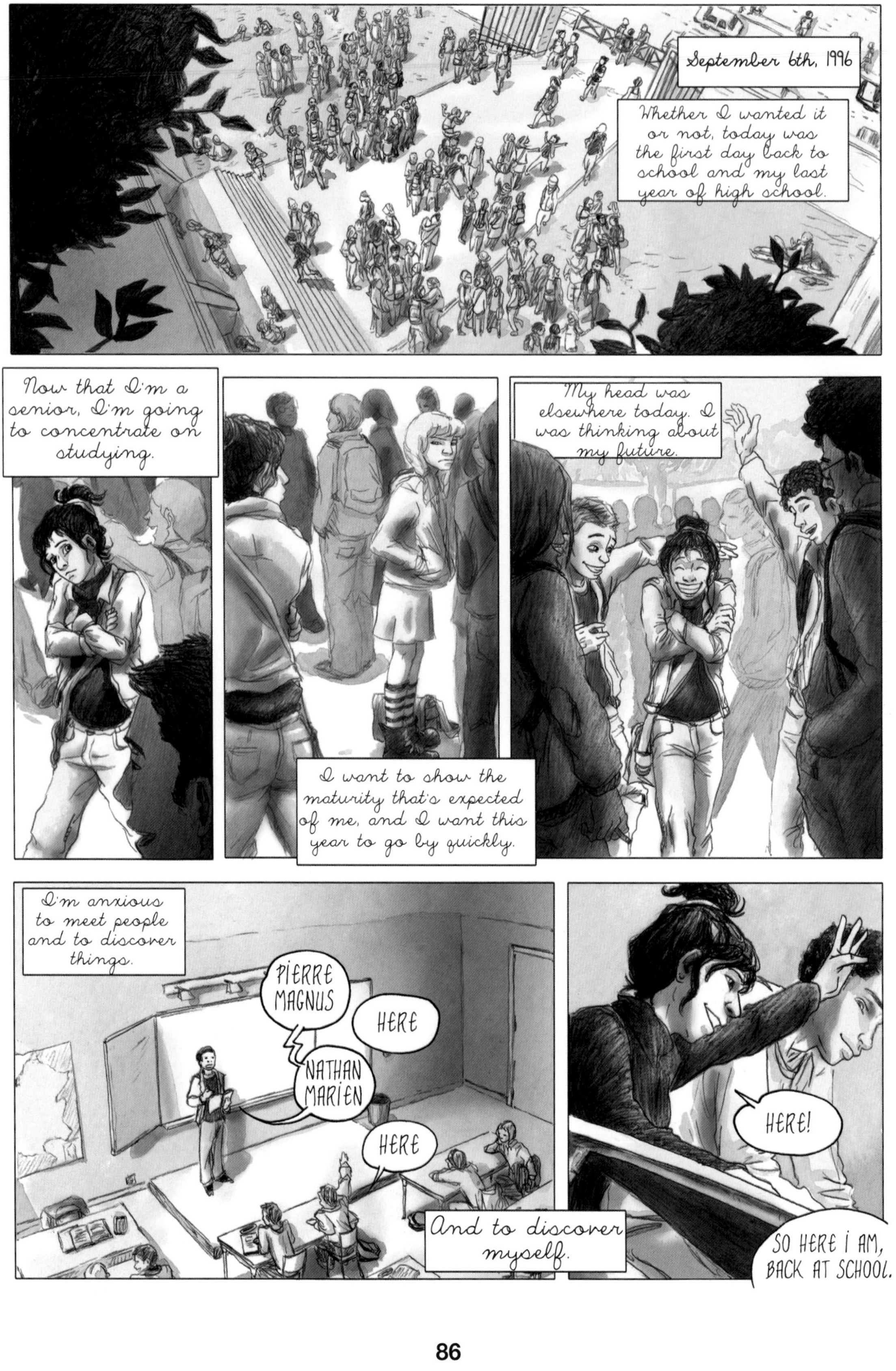
September 6th, 1996
Whether I wanted it or not, today was the first day back to school and my last year of high school.
Now that I'm a senior, I'm going to concentrate on studying.
I want to show the maturity that's expected of me, and I want this year to go by quickly.
My head was elsewhere today. I was thinking about my future.
I'm anxious to meet people and to discover things.
PIERRE MAGNUS
HERE
NATHAN MARIEN
HERE
And to discover myself.
HERE!
SO HERE I AM, BACK AT SCHOOL.

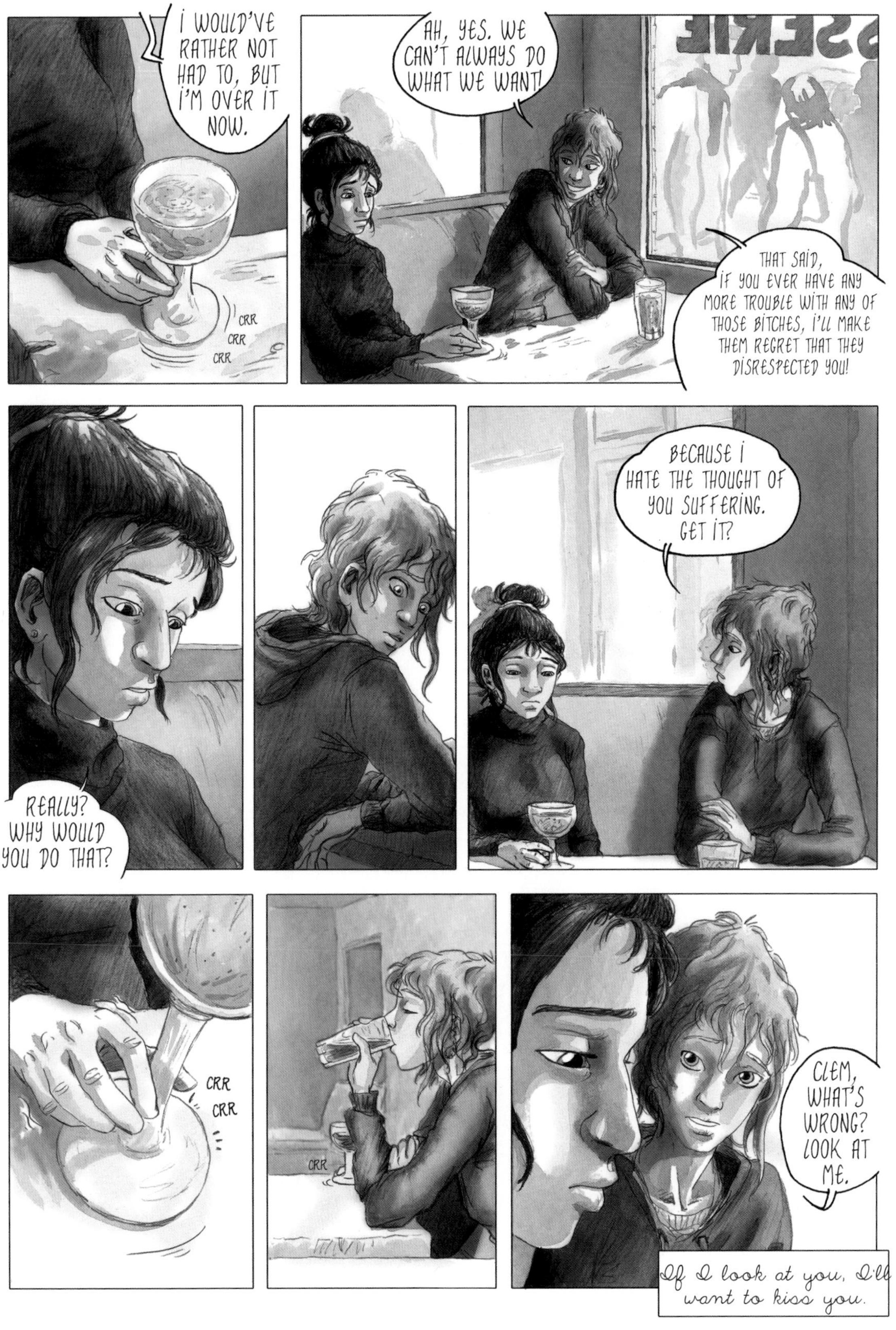
I WOULD'VE RATHER NOT HAD TO, BUT I'M OVER IT NOW.
CRR
CRR
CRR
AH, YES. WE CAN'T ALWAYS DO WHAT WE WANT!
THAT SAID, IF YOU EVER HAVE ANY MORE TROUBLE WITH ANY OF THOSE BITCHES, I'LL MAKE THEM REGRET THAT THEY DISRESPECTED YOU!
REALLY? WHY WOULD YOU DO THAT?
BECAUSE I HATE THE THOUGHT OF YOU SUFFERING. GET IT?
CRR
CRR
CRR
CLEM, WHAT'S WRONG? LOOK AT ME.
If I look at you, I'll want to kiss you.

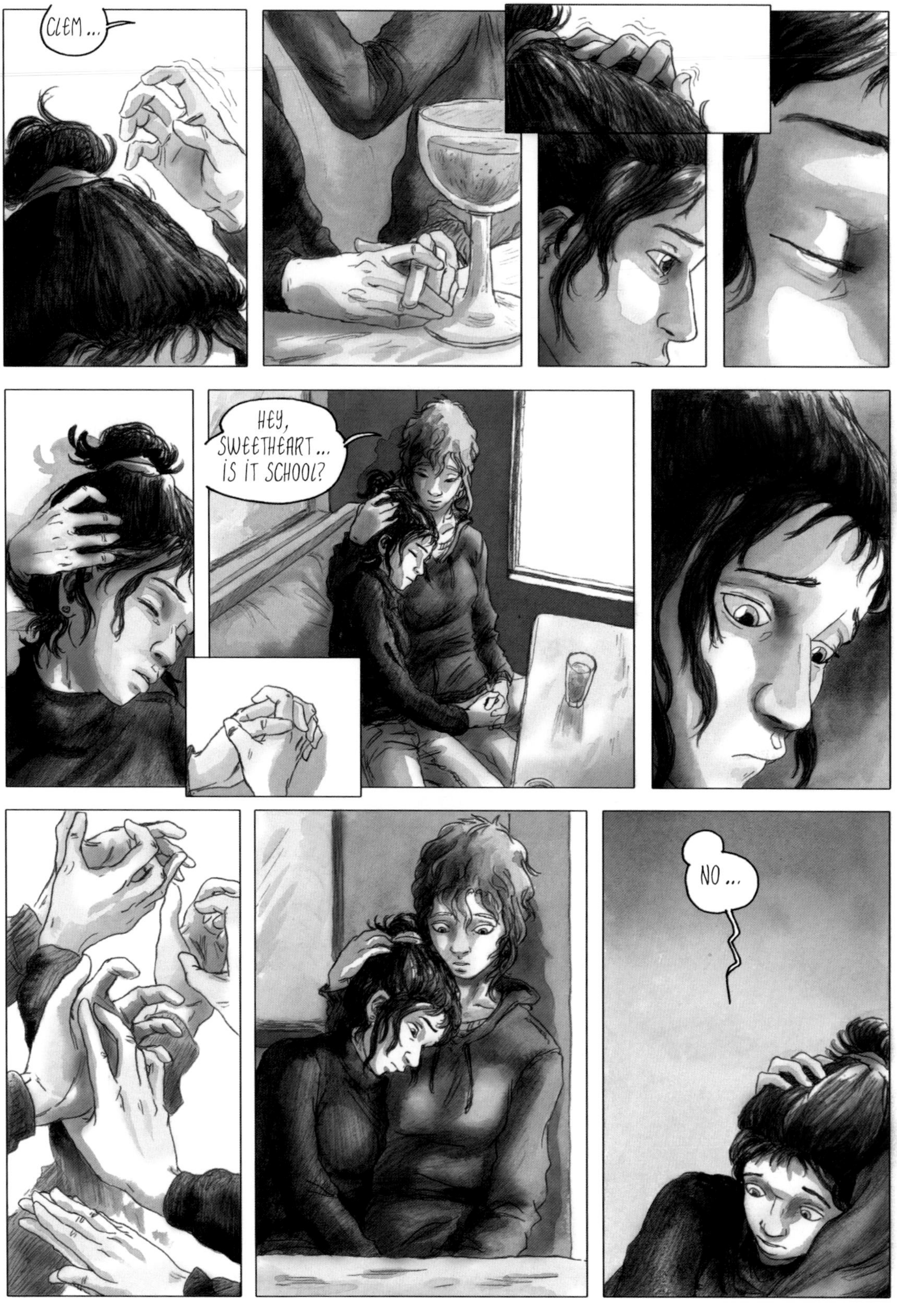
CLEM...
HEY, SWEETHEART... IS IT SCHOOL?
NO...

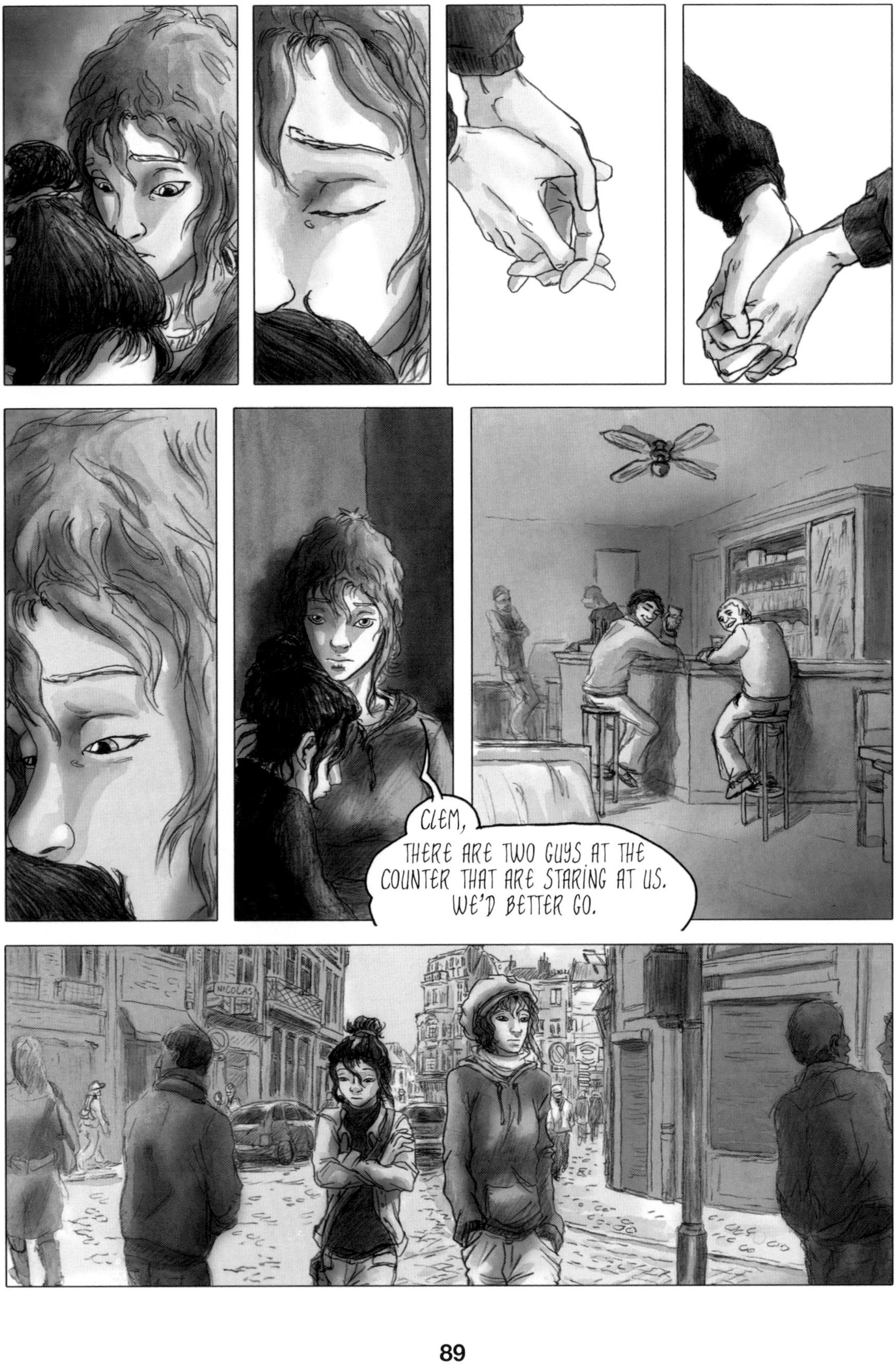
CLEM,
THERE ARE TWO GUYS AT THE COUNTER THAT ARE STARING AT US. WE'D BETTER GO.
NICOLAS

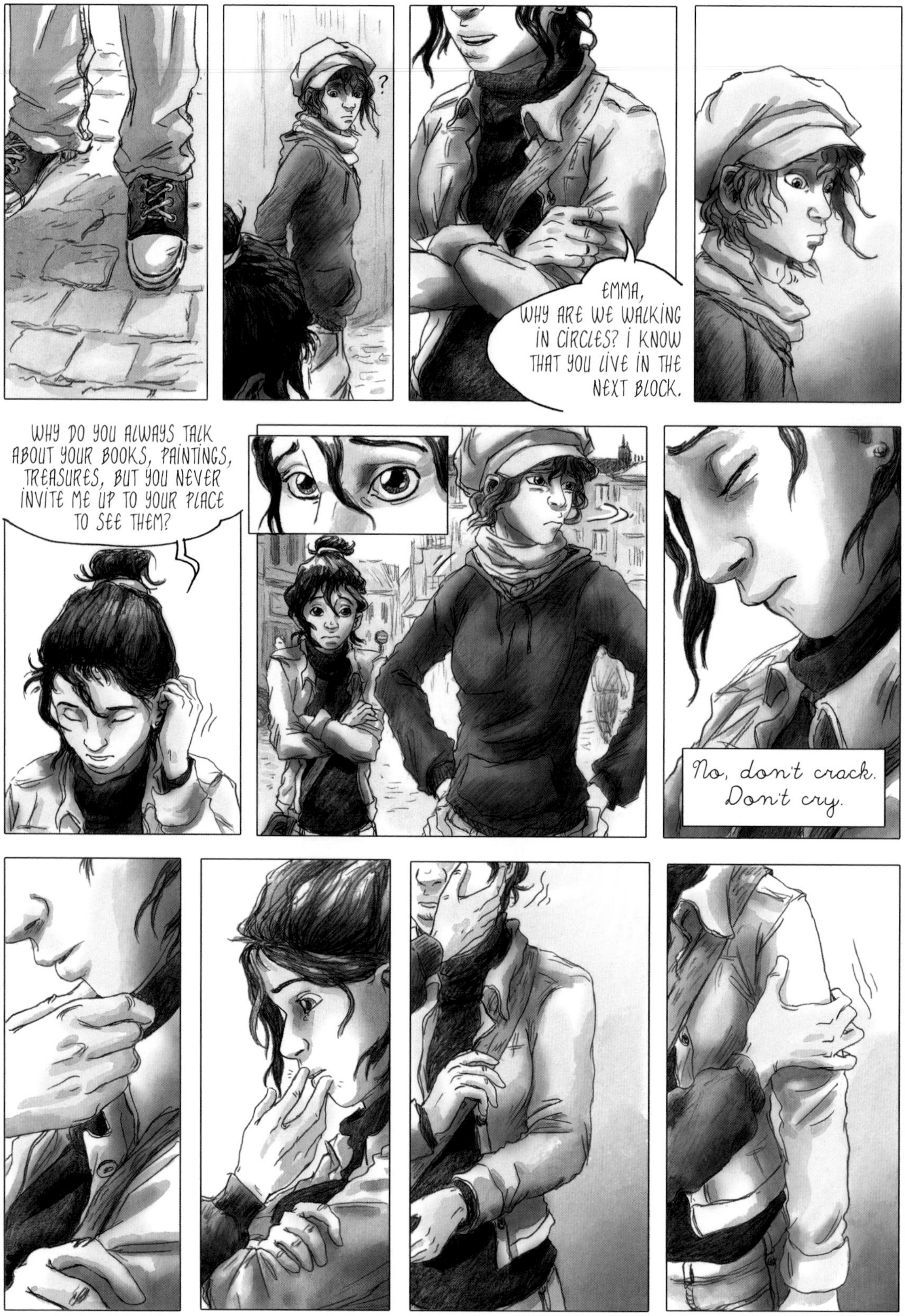
?
EMMA, WHY ARE WE WALKING IN CIRCLES? I KNOW THAT YOU LIVE IN THE NEXT BLOCK.
WHY DO YOU ALWAYS TALK ABOUT YOUR BOOKS, PAINTINGS, TREASURES, BUT YOU NEVER INVITE ME UP TO YOUR PLACE TO SEE THEM?
No, don't crack. Don't cry.

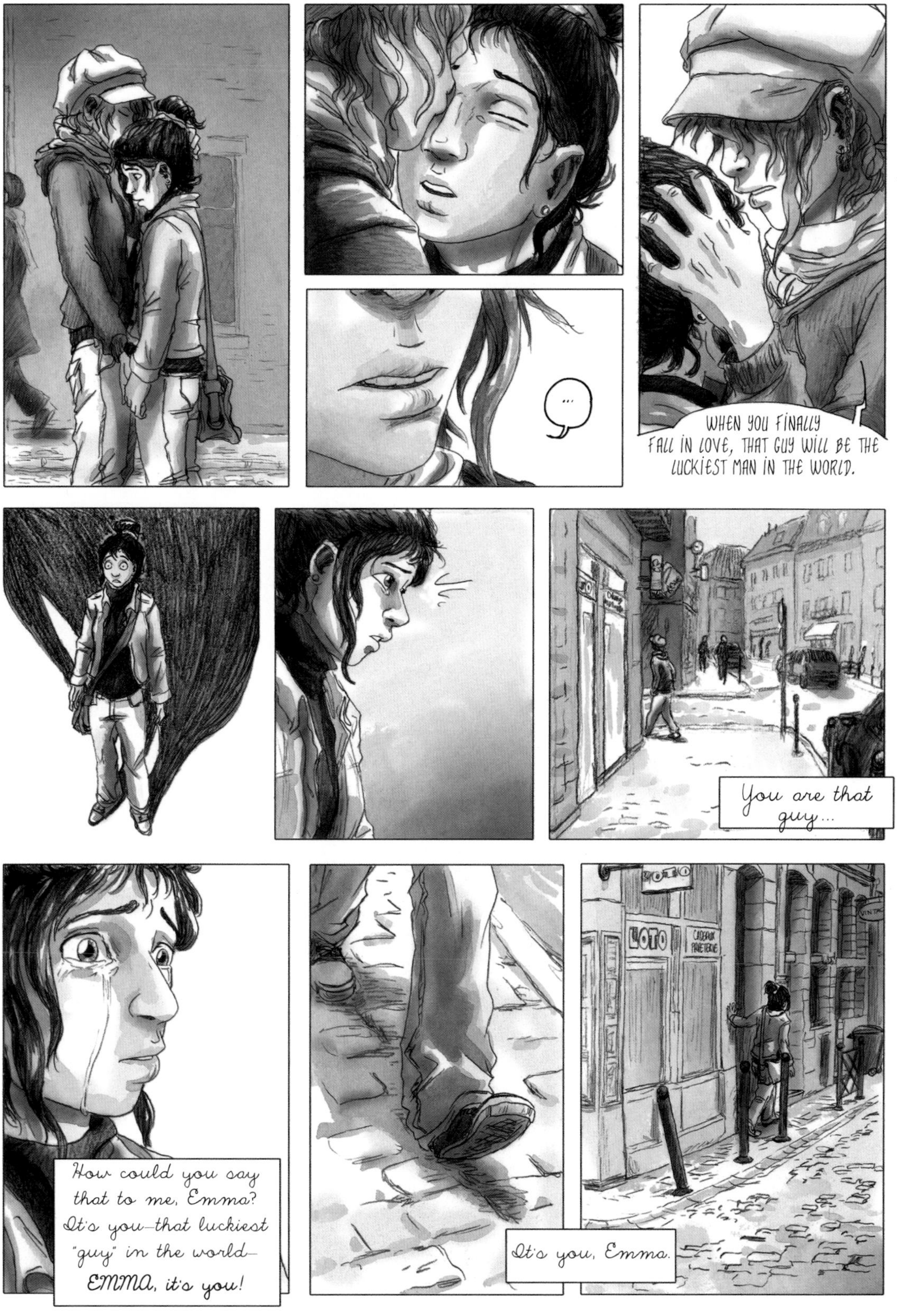
...
WHEN YOU FINALLY FALL IN LOVE, THAT GUY WILL BE THE LUCKIEST MAN IN THE WORLD.
You are that guy...
How could you say that to me, Emma? It's you—that luckiest "guy" in the world— EMMA, it's you!
It's you, Emma.
LOTO
CADEAUX PAPETERIE

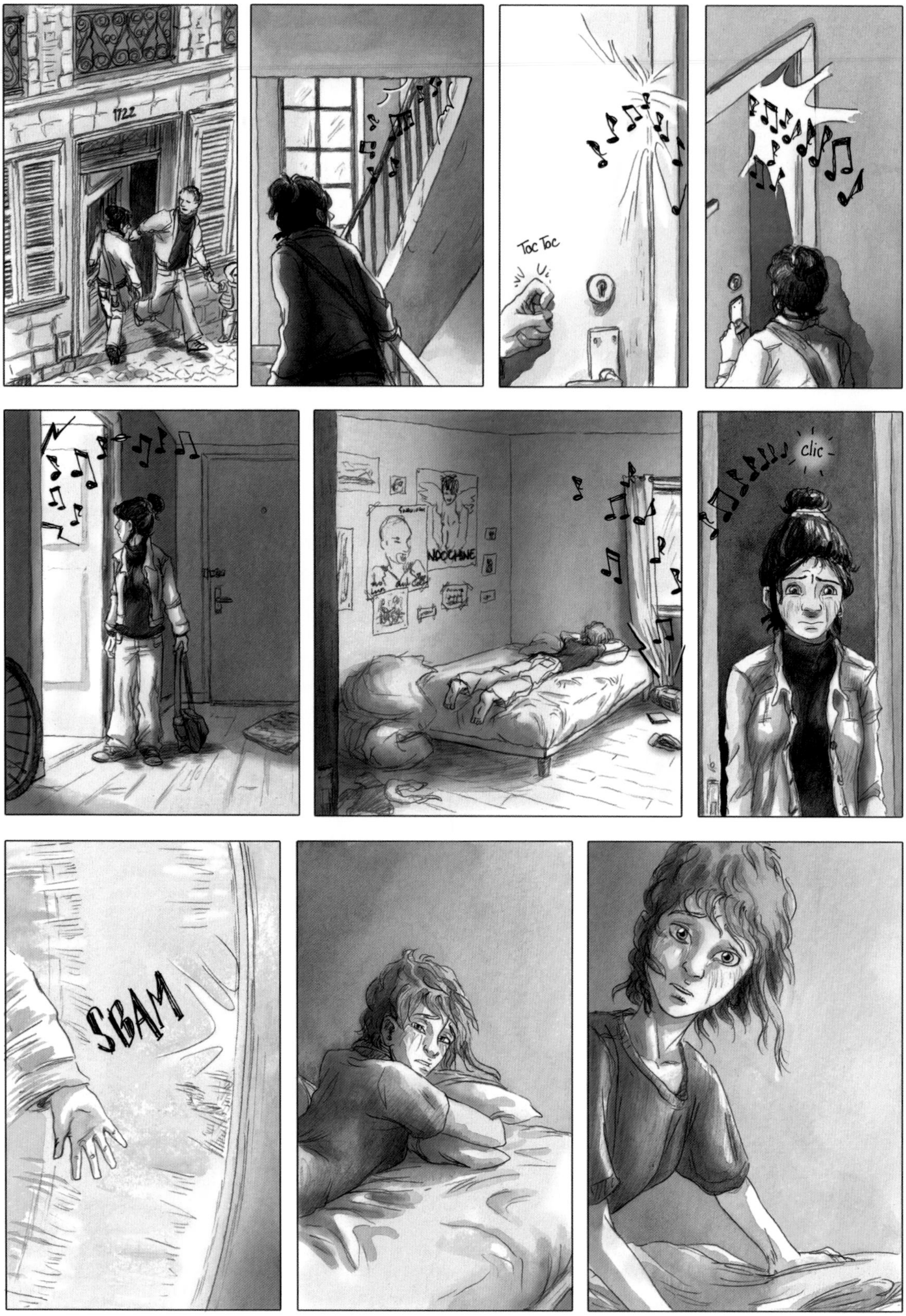
1722
Toc Toc
INDOCHINE
clic
SBAM

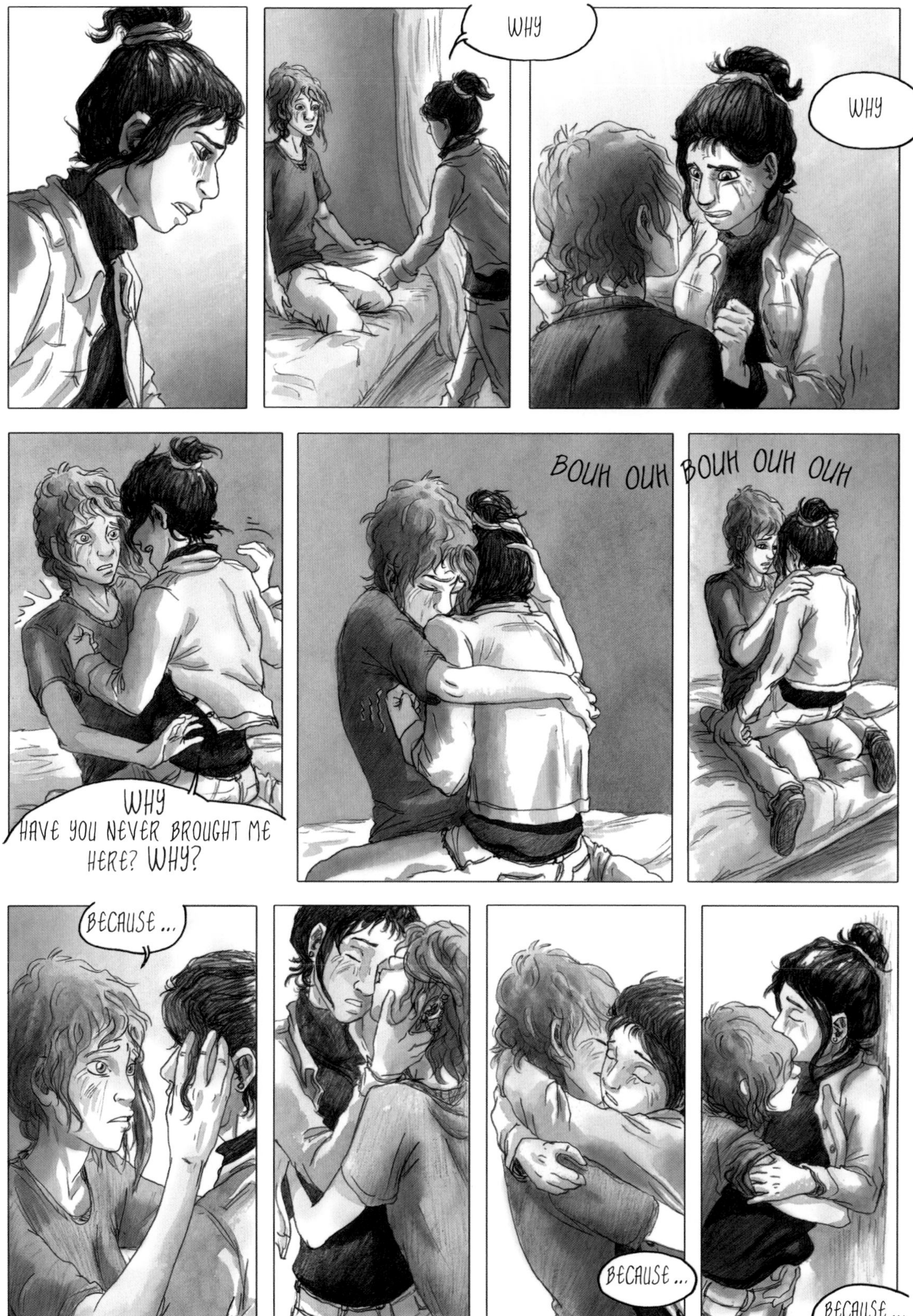

WHY
WHY
BOUH OUH BOUH OUH OUH
WHY HAVE YOU NEVER BROUGHT ME HERE? WHY?
BECAUSE ...
BECAUSE ...
BECAUSE ...

BECAUSE I COULDN'T HAVE CONTROLLED MY DESIRE TO MAKE LOVE TO YOU.

My stomach, my heart, my throat—my whole body was screaming.

You, you, you There is only you

I love you

I love you, I love you, I love you

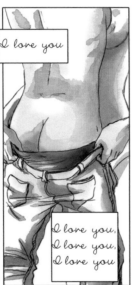

My God, her sex, her sex, naked against mine.

I'm going to go crazy. I don't want to live unless I can be with her

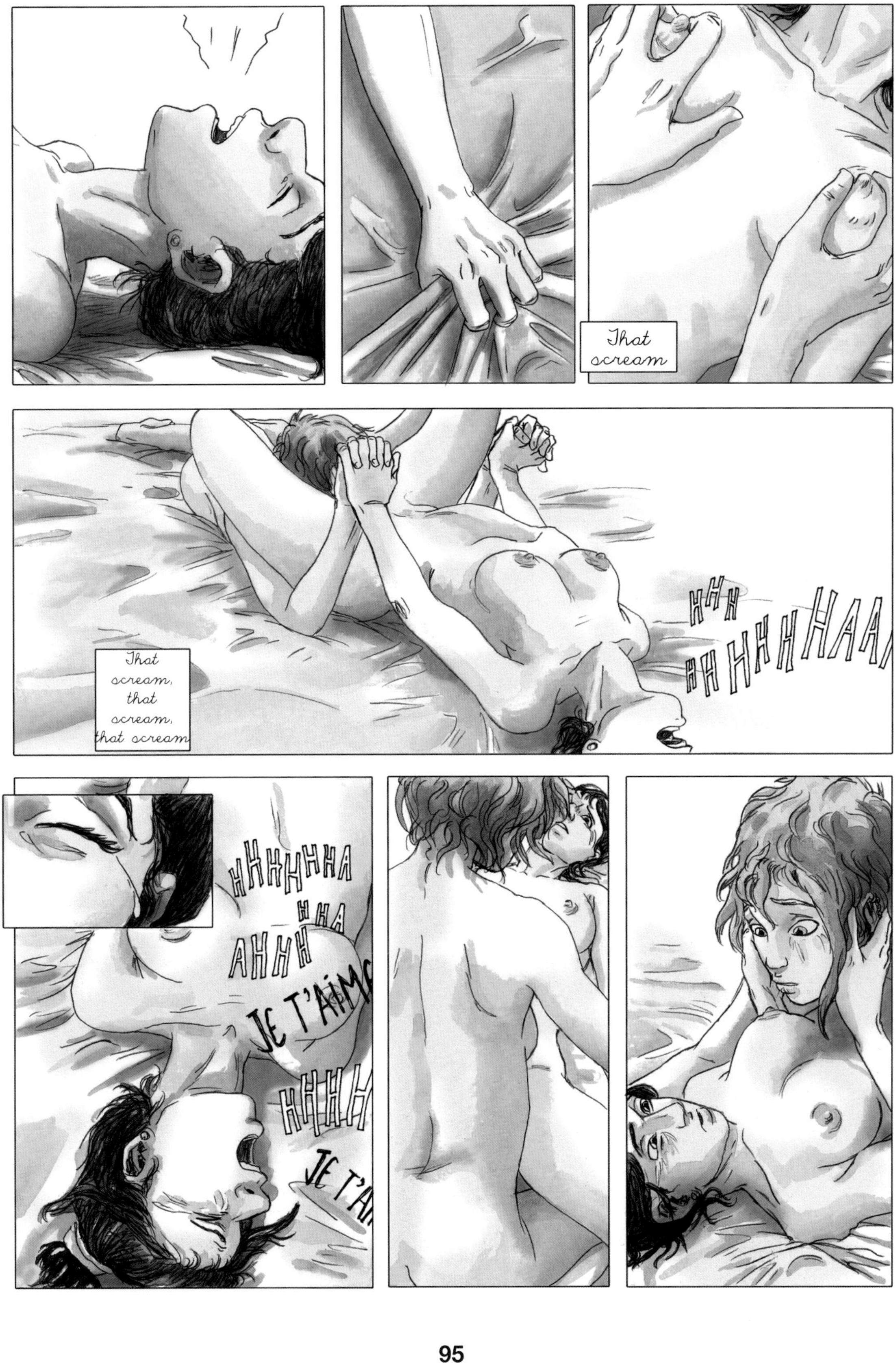
That scream
That scream, that scream, that scream
HHH
HHHHHHHHAA
HHHHHHA
HHA
AHHH
JE T'AIM
HHHH
JE T'A

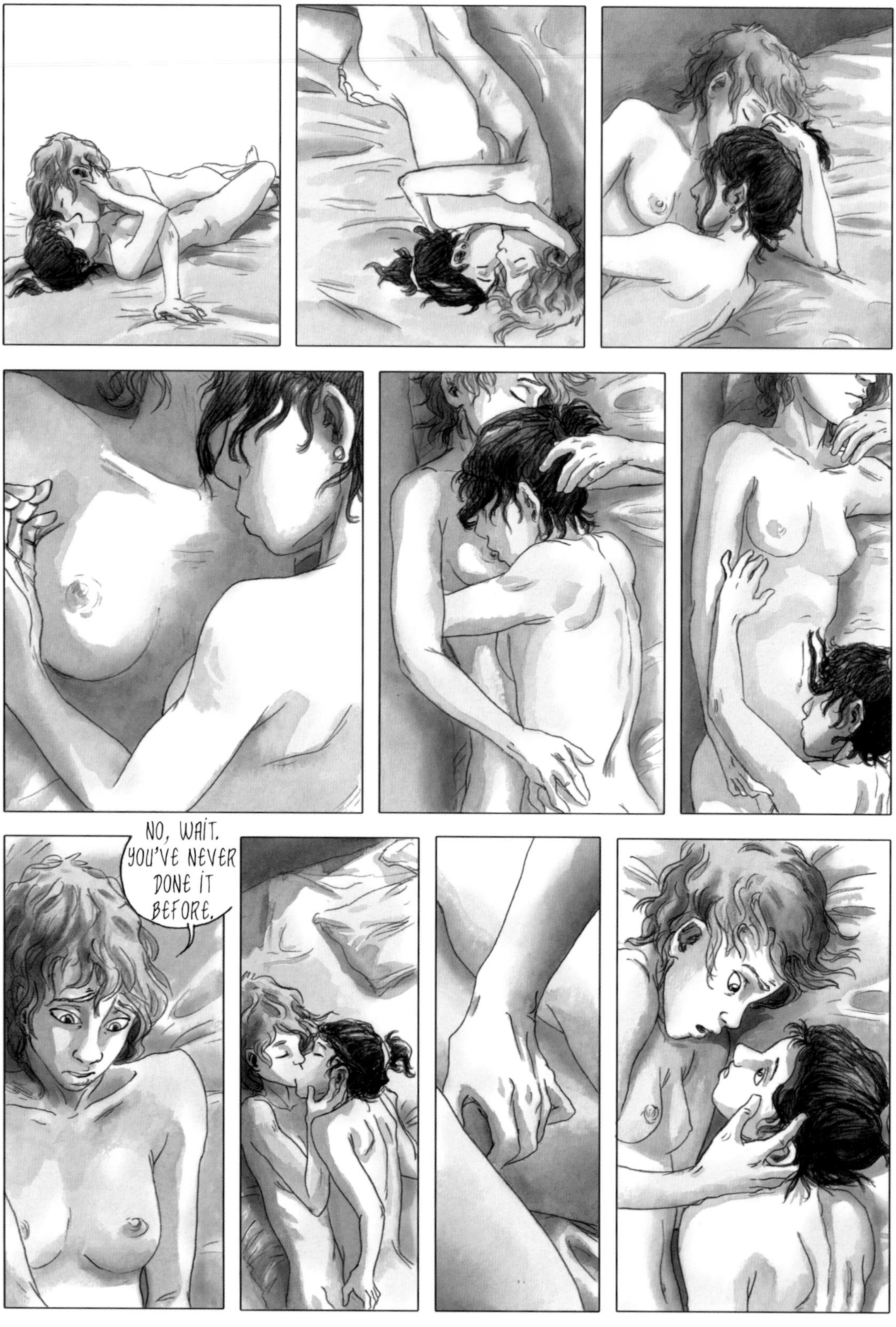
NO, WAIT. YOU'VE NEVER DONE IT BEFORE.

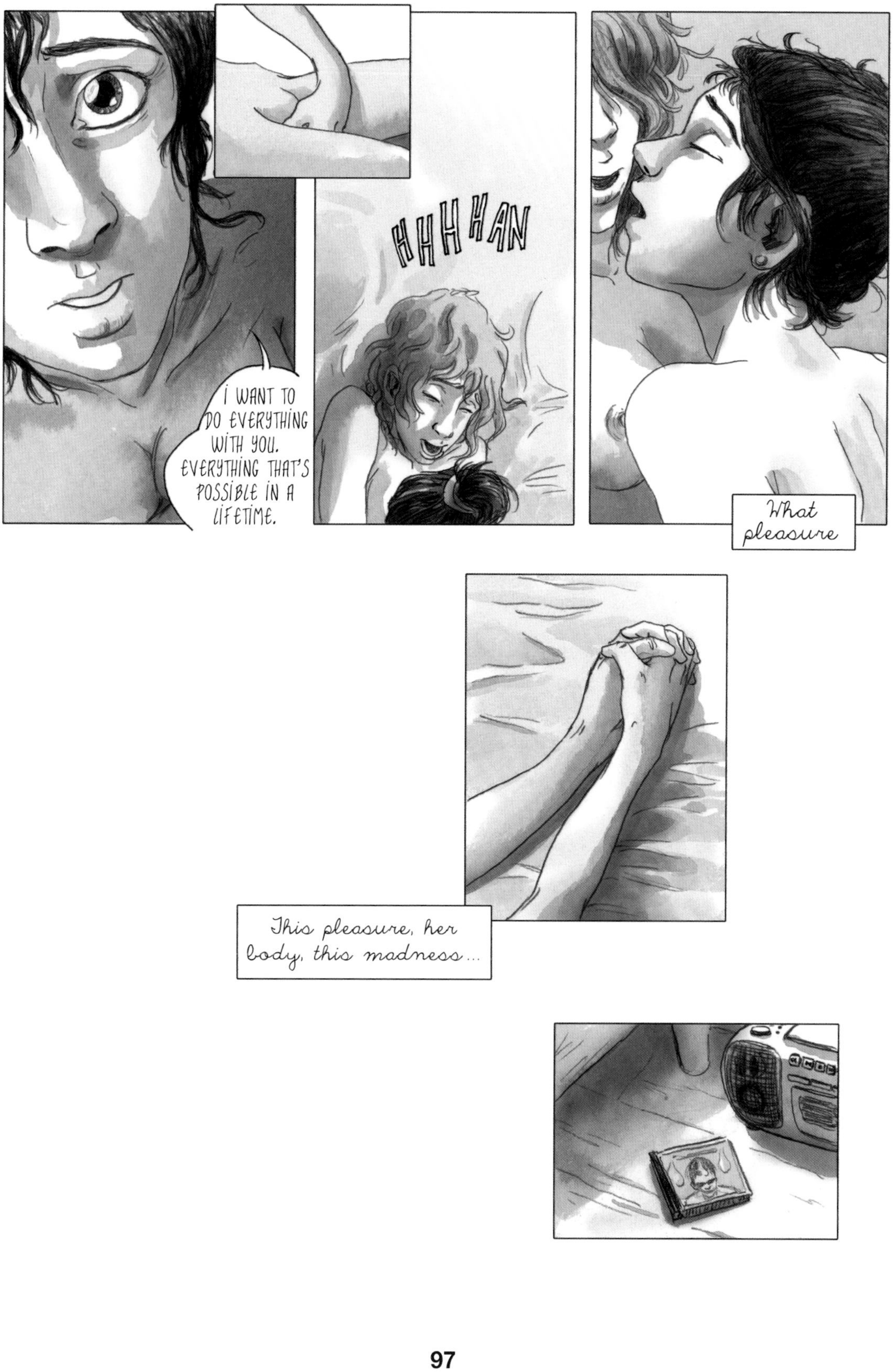
I WANT TO DO EVERYTHING WITH YOU. EVERYTHING THAT'S POSSIBLE IN A LIFETIME.
HHHHAN
What pleasure
This pleasure, her body, this madness...

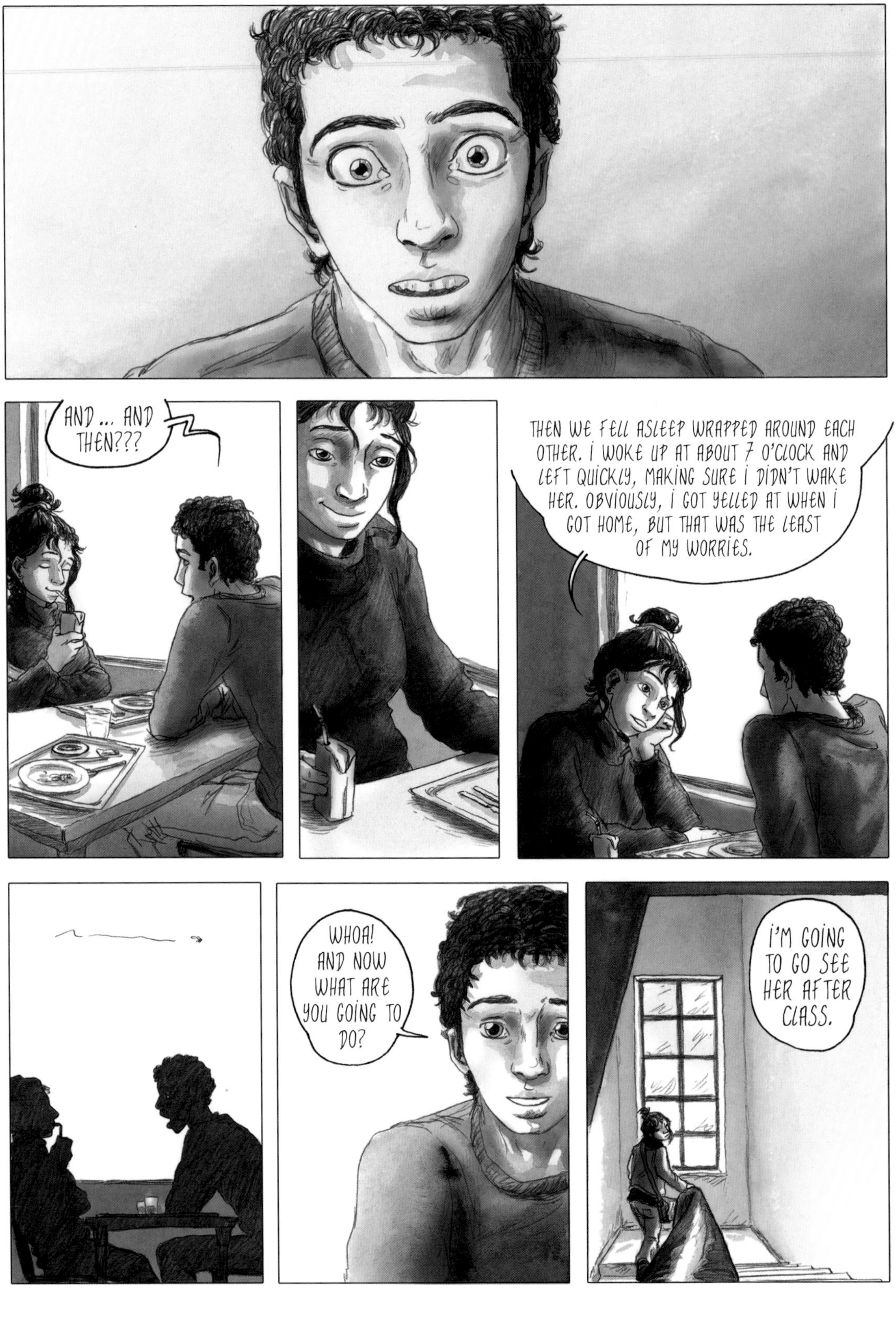
AND ... AND THEN???
THEN WE FELL ASLEEP WRAPPED AROUND EACH OTHER. I WOKE UP AT ABOUT 7 O'CLOCK AND LEFT QUICKLY, MAKING SURE I DIDN'T WAKE HER. OBVIOUSLY, I GOT YELLED AT WHEN I GOT HOME, BUT THAT WAS THE LEAST OF MY WORRIES.
WHOA! AND NOW WHAT ARE YOU GOING TO DO?
I'M GOING TO GO SEE HER AFTER CLASS.

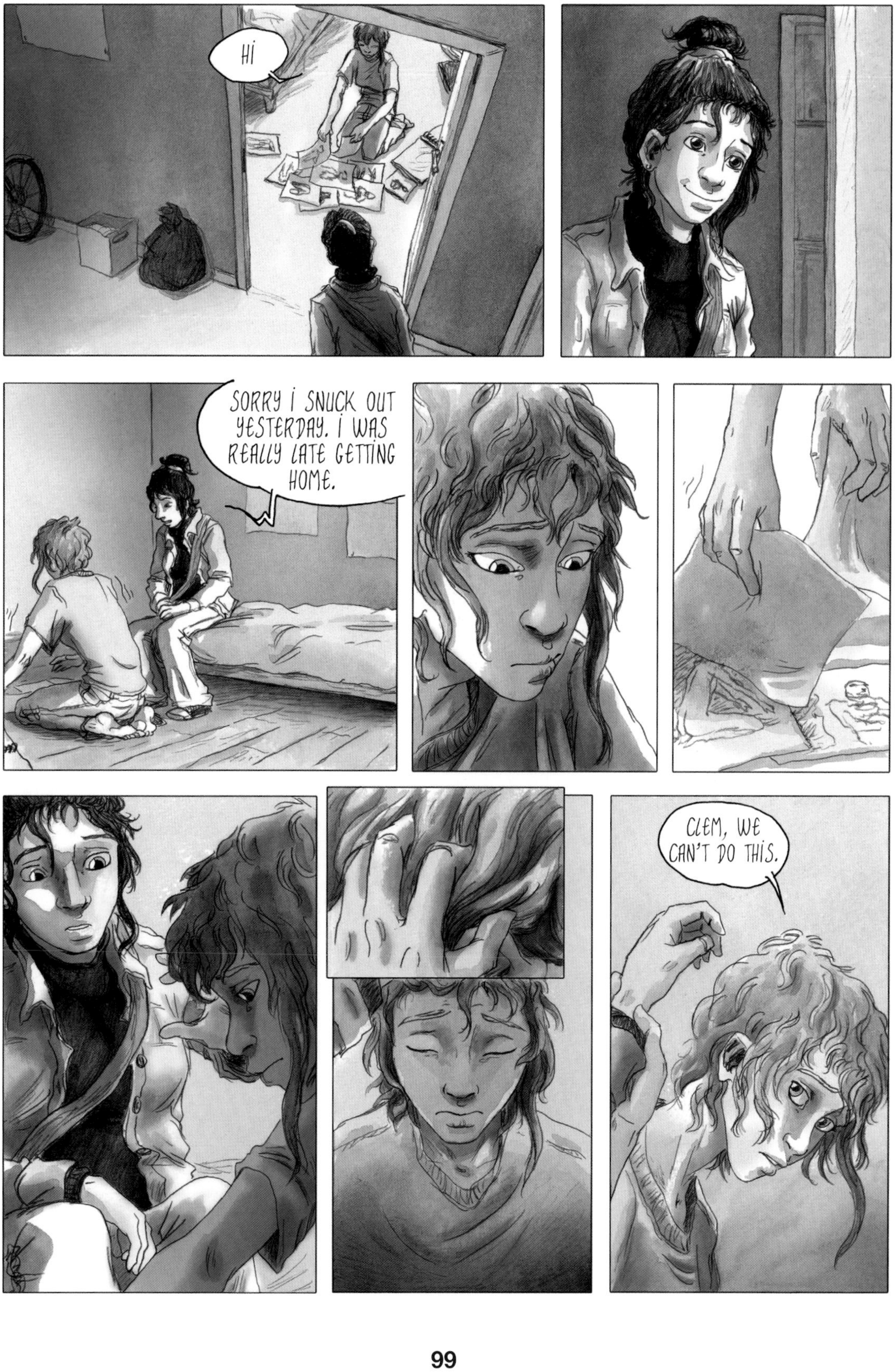
Hi
SORRY I SNUCK OUT YESTERDAY. I WAS REALLY LATE GETTING HOME.
CLEM, WE CAN'T DO THIS.

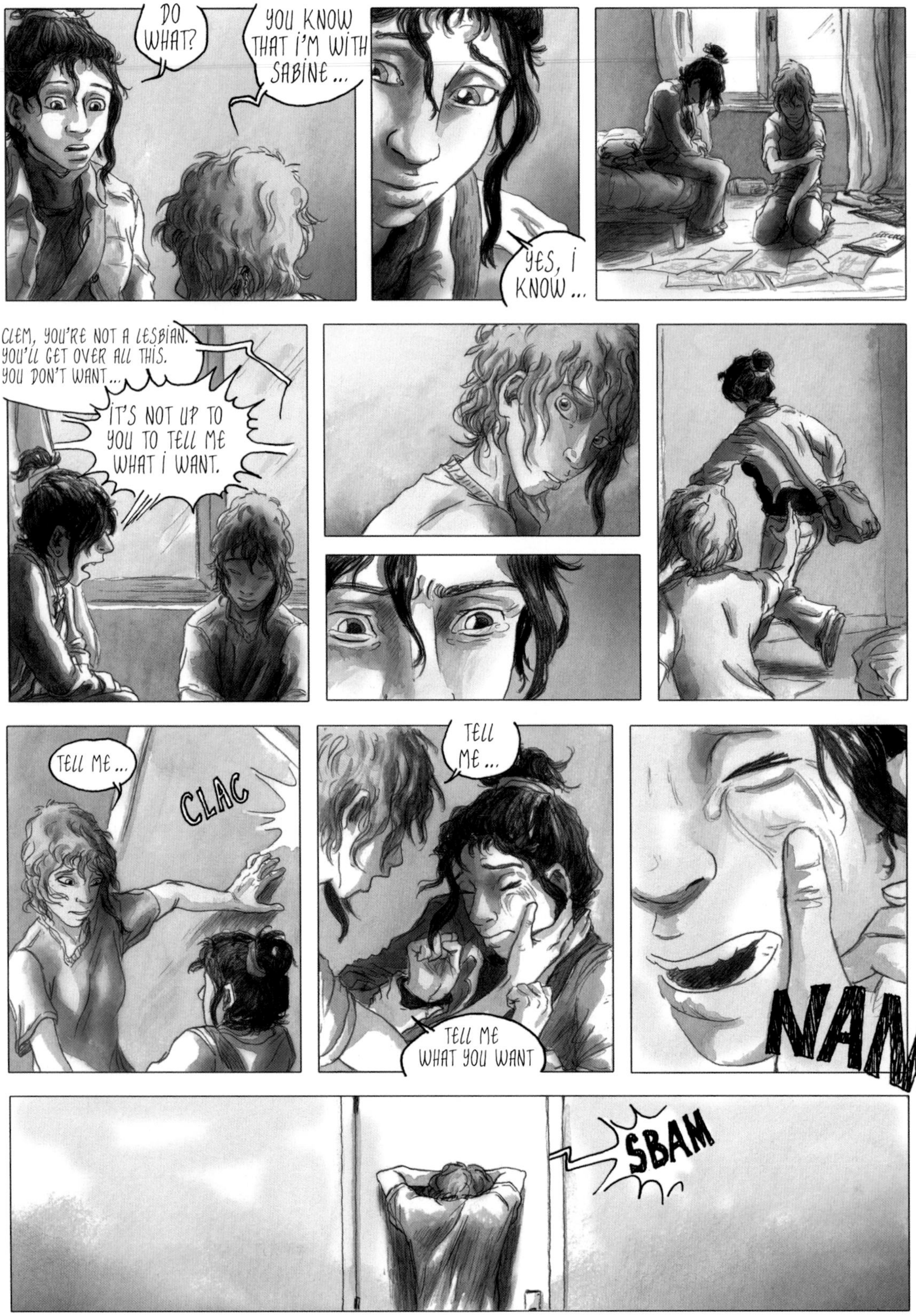
DO WHAT?
YOU KNOW THAT I'M WITH SABINE...
YES, I KNOW...
CLEM, YOU'RE NOT A LESBIAN. YOU'LL GET OVER ALL THIS. YOU DON'T WANT...
IT'S NOT UP TO YOU TO TELL ME WHAT I WANT.
TELL ME...
CLAC
TELL ME...
TELL ME WHAT YOU WANT
NAN
SBAM

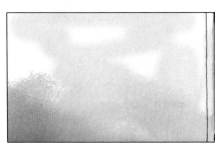

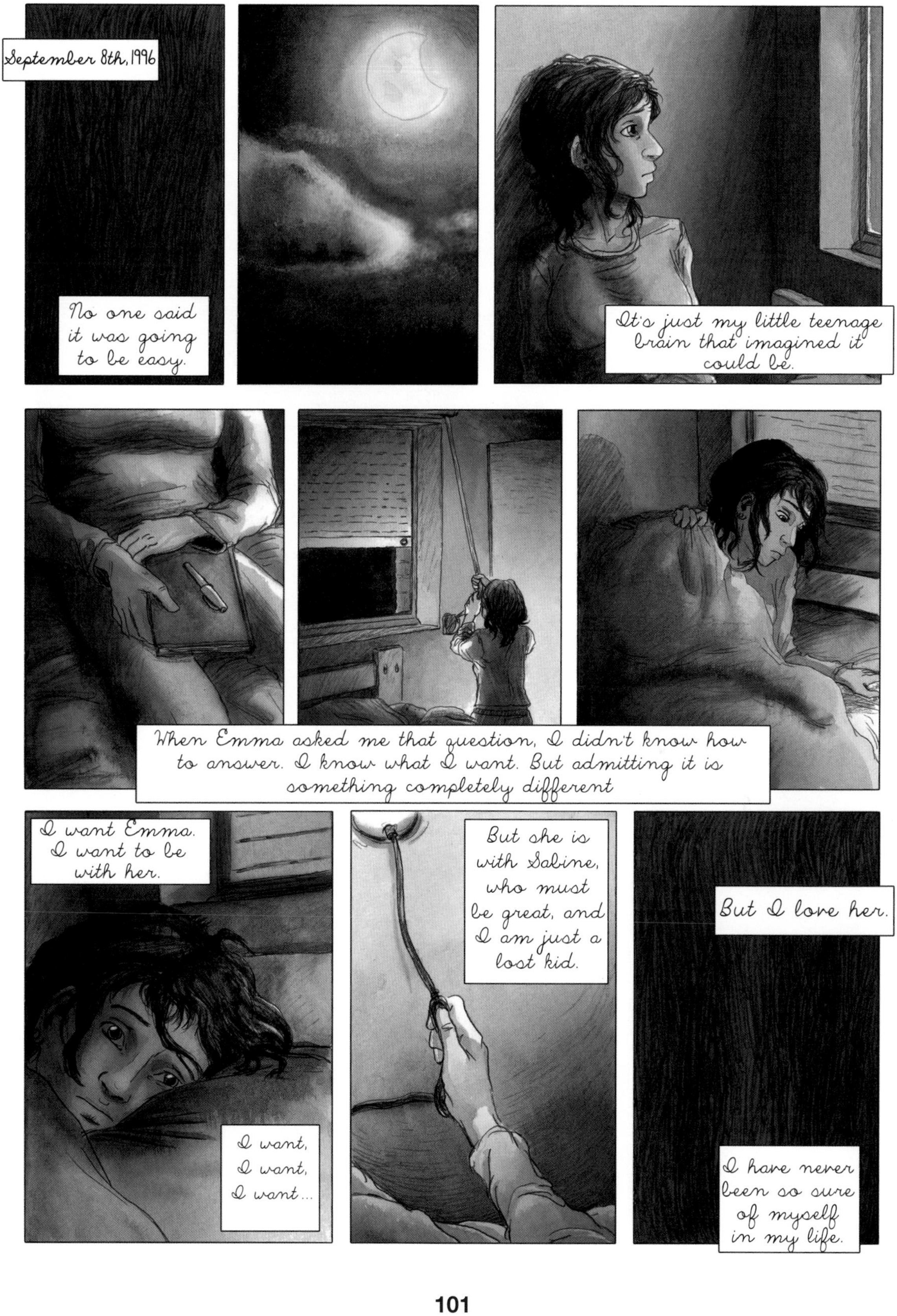
September 8th, 1996
No one said it was going to be easy.
It's just my little teenage brain that imagined it could be.
When Emma asked me that question, I didn't know how to answer. I know what I want. But admitting it is something completely different
I want Emma. I want to be with her.
I want, I want, I want...
But she is with Sabine, who must be great, and I am just a lost kid.
But I love her.
I have never been so sure of myself in my life.

October 12th, 1996
I turned 17 today.

Valentin organized a surprise party for me with my parents' help.

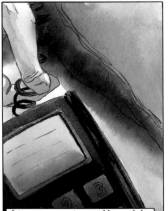

Friends from school and family came.

And then...
Emma called.

We hadn't been in touch since the scene at her place. She called to wish me happy birthday.

We weren't really able to talk... I couldn't get myself to relax, and she couldn't either. She wanted to know if we could meet.

The truth is, I wanted to avoid her, but I couldn't think of a reason not to meet.

So I said yes, and the day after tomorrow I'm going to eat at her place. She insisted on cooking me dinner in honor of my birthday.

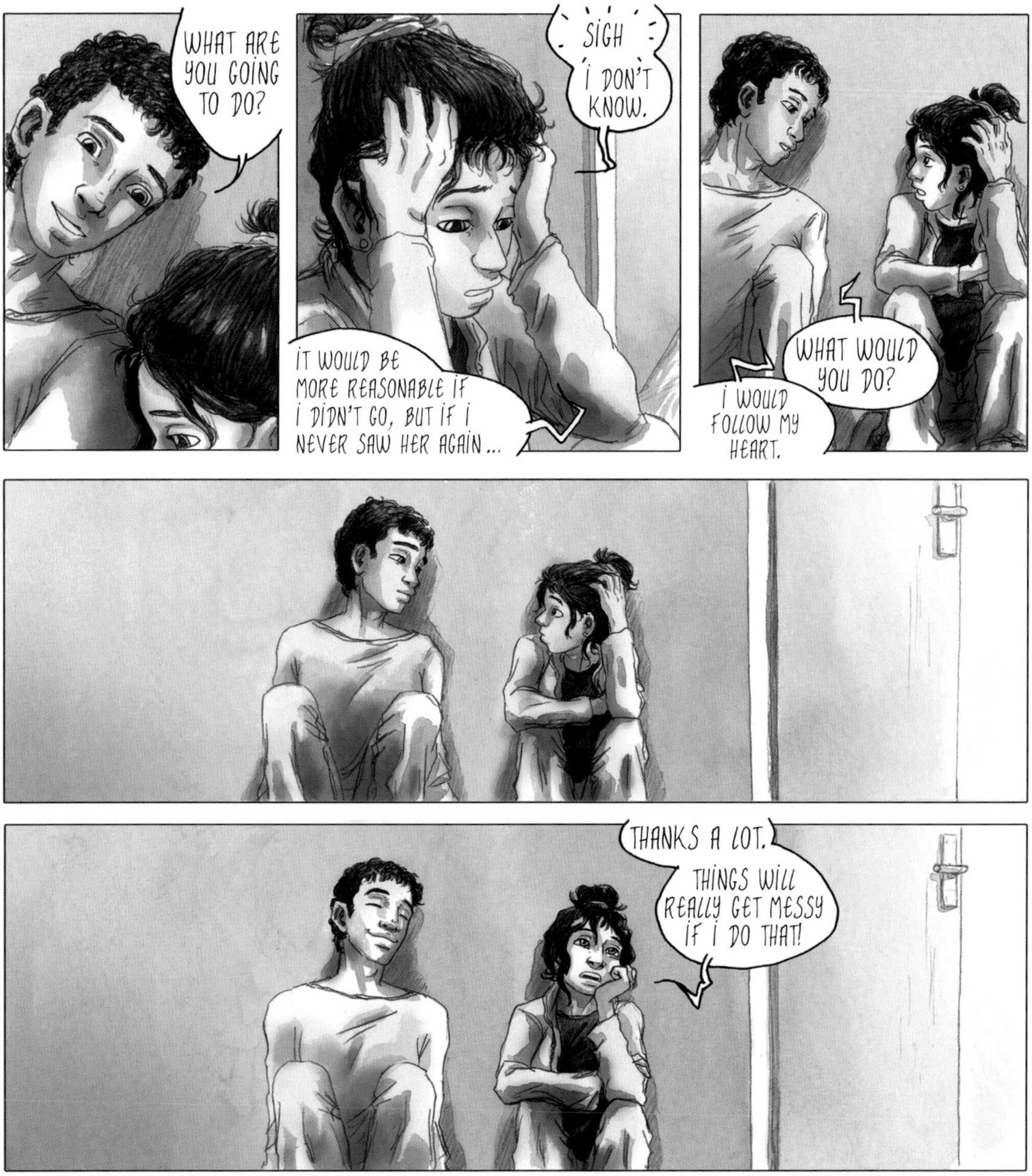
WHAT ARE YOU GOING TO DO?
SIGH
I DON'T KNOW.
IT WOULD BE MORE REASONABLE IF I DIDN'T GO, BUT IF I NEVER SAW HER AGAIN...
WHAT WOULD YOU DO?
I WOULD FOLLOW MY HEART.
THANKS A LOT.
THINGS WILL REALLY GET MESSY IF I DO THAT!

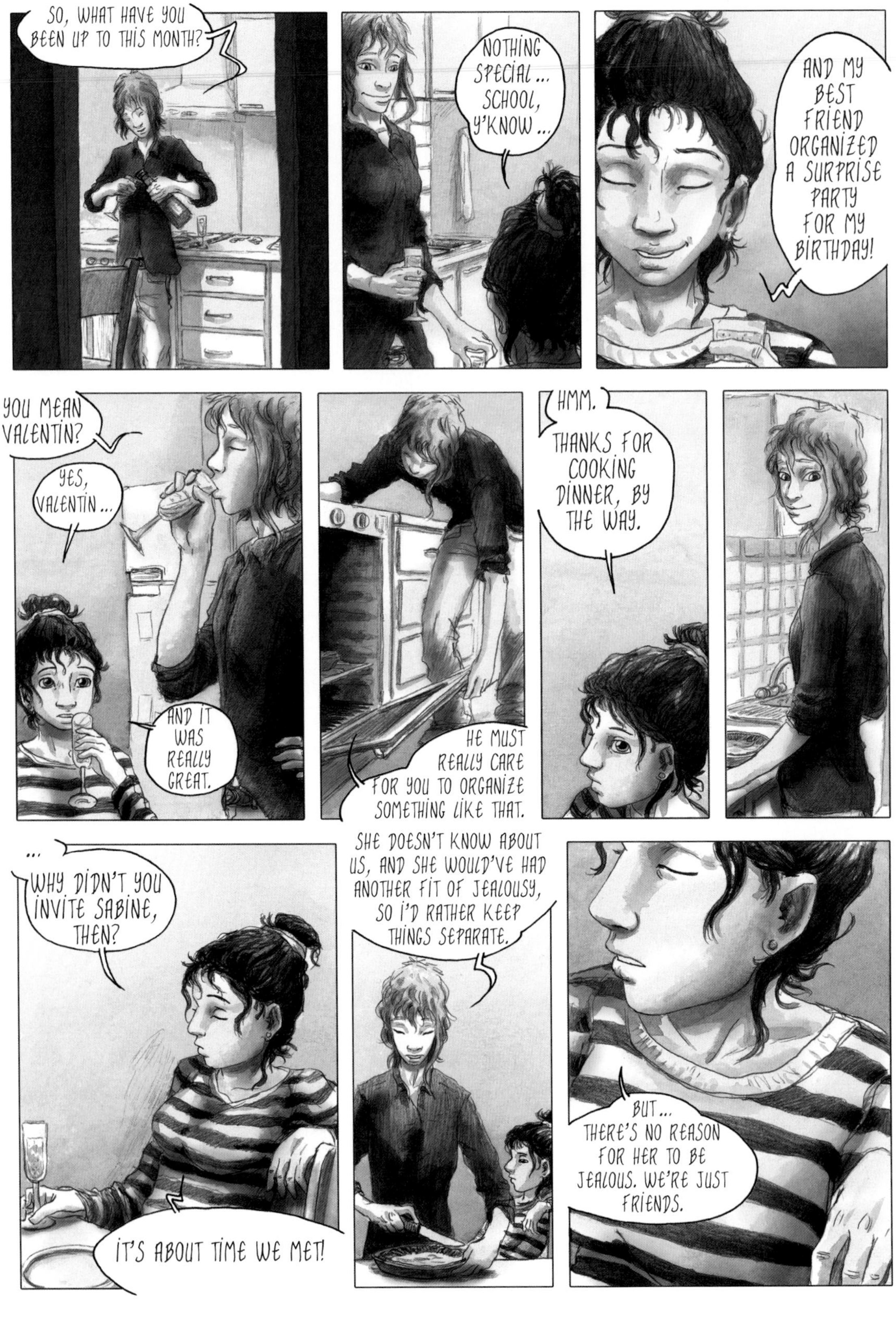
SO, WHAT HAVE YOU BEEN UP TO THIS MONTH?
NOTHING SPECIAL... SCHOOL, Y'KNOW...
AND MY BEST FRIEND ORGANIZED A SURPRISE PARTY FOR MY BIRTHDAY!
YOU MEAN VALENTIN?
YES, VALENTIN...
AND IT WAS REALLY GREAT.
HE MUST REALLY CARE FOR YOU TO ORGANIZE SOMETHING LIKE THAT.
HMM.
THANKS FOR COOKING DINNER, BY THE WAY.
...
WHY DIDN'T YOU INVITE SABINE, THEN?
IT'S ABOUT TIME WE MET!
SHE DOESN'T KNOW ABOUT US, AND SHE WOULD'VE HAD ANOTHER FIT OF JEALOUSY, SO I'D RATHER KEEP THINGS SEPARATE.
BUT... THERE'S NO REASON FOR HER TO BE JEALOUS. WE'RE JUST FRIENDS.

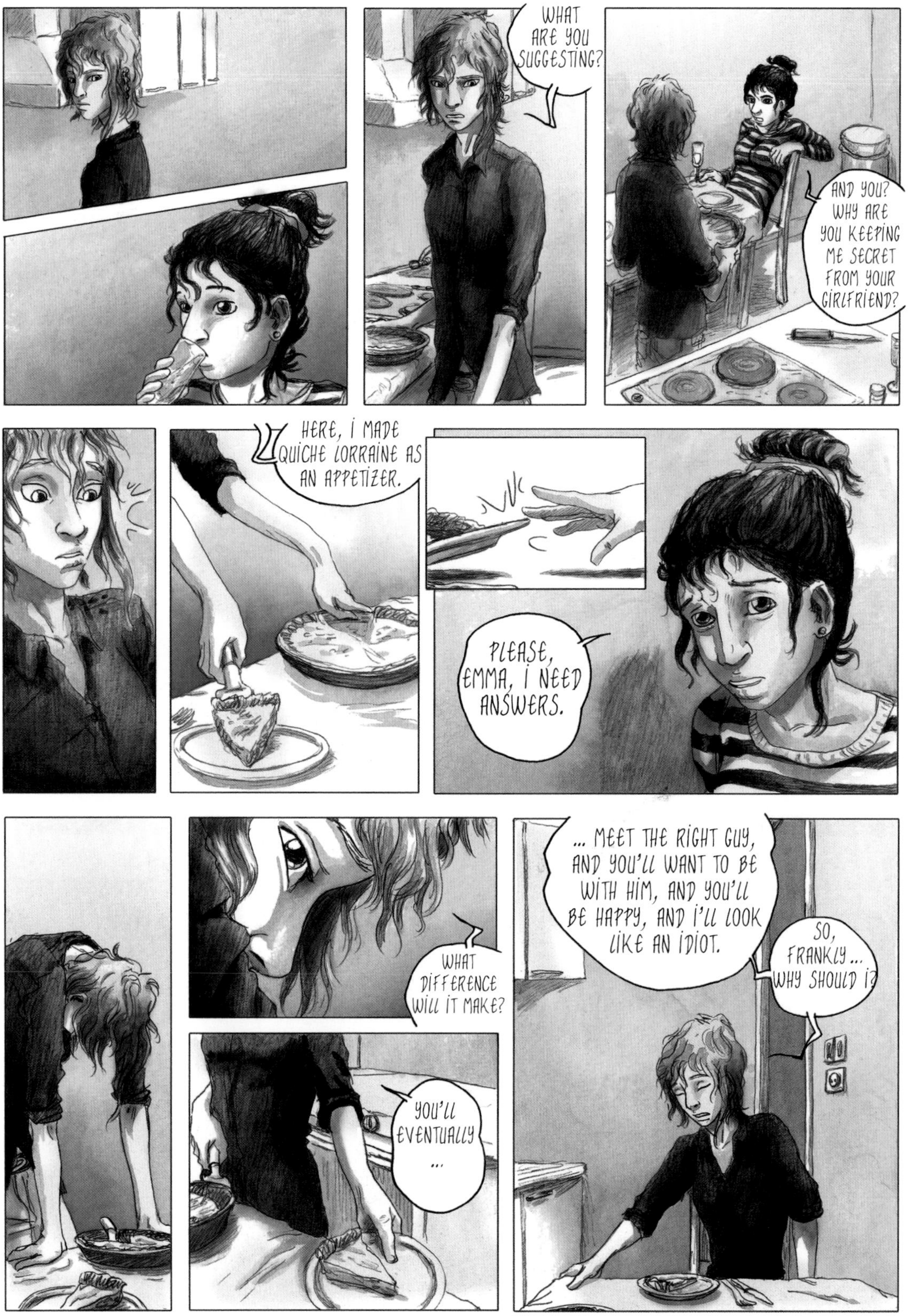
WHAT ARE YOU SUGGESTING?
AND YOU? WHY ARE YOU KEEPING ME SECRET FROM YOUR GIRLFRIEND?
HERE, I MADE QUICHE LORRAINE AS AN APPETIZER.
PLEASE, EMMA, I NEED ANSWERS.
WHAT DIFFERENCE WILL IT MAKE?
YOU'LL EVENTUALLY ...
... MEET THE RIGHT GUY, AND YOU'LL WANT TO BE WITH HIM, AND YOU'LL BE HAPPY, AND I'LL LOOK LIKE AN IDIOT.
SO, FRANKLY... WHY SHOULD I?

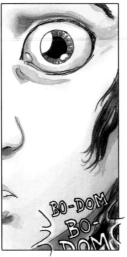

BO-DOM
BO-DOM

BUT... BUT...

SO, IT'S BECAUSE YOU'RE PROTECTING YOURSELF THAT YOU DON'T WANT TO MAKE A PLACE FOR ME IN YOUR LIFE?

i...

i...

THAT EXCUSE YOU JUST GAVE ME—I NEVER WANT TO HEAR THAT AGAIN!

NO ...
NO ... I CAN'T.

106

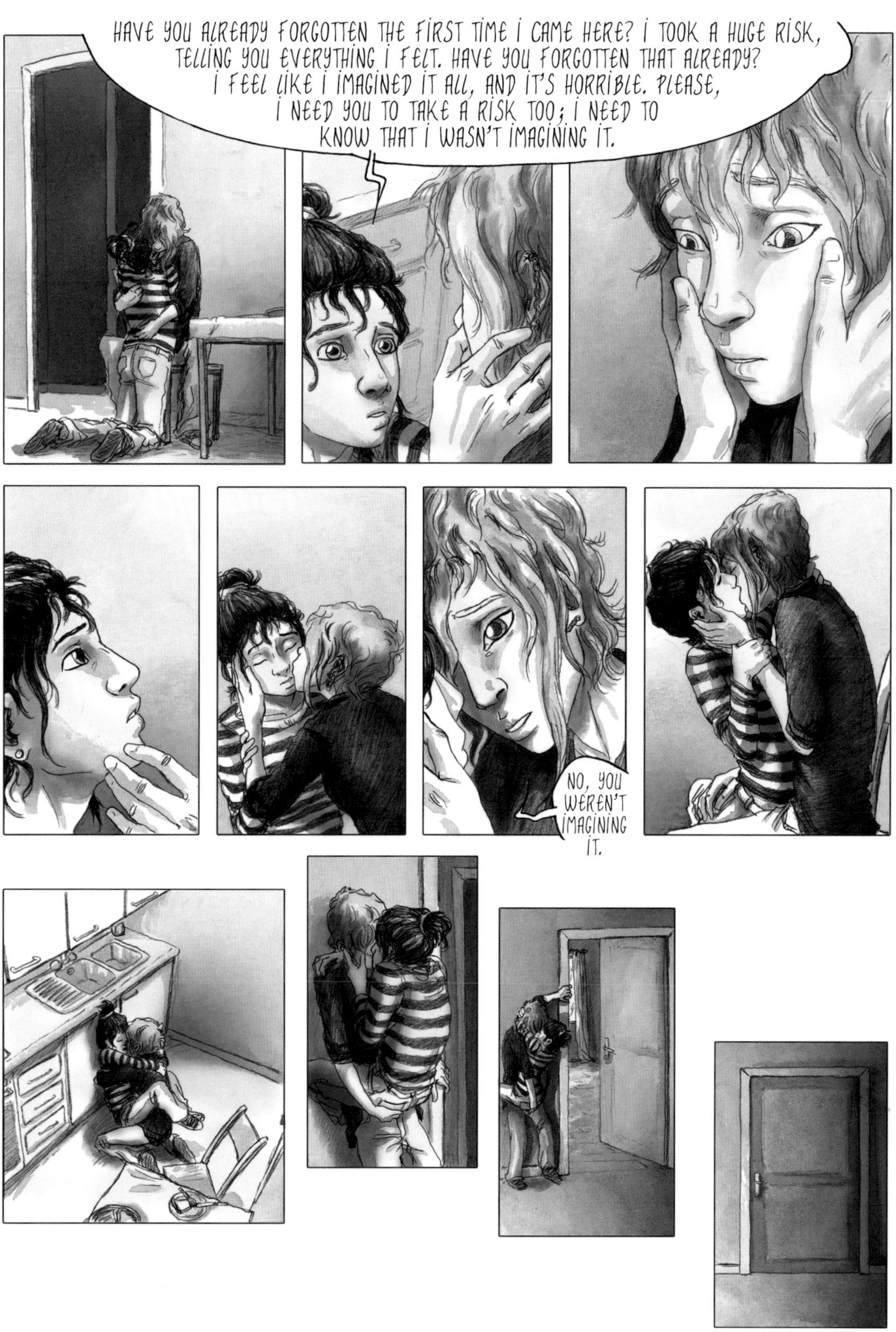
HAVE YOU ALREADY FORGOTTEN THE FIRST TIME I CAME HERE? I TOOK A HUGE RISK, TELLING YOU EVERYTHING I FELT. HAVE YOU FORGOTTEN THAT ALREADY? I FEEL LIKE I IMAGINED IT ALL, AND IT'S HORRIBLE. PLEASE, I NEED YOU TO TAKE A RISK TOO; I NEED TO KNOW THAT I WASN'T IMAGINING IT.
NO, YOU WEREN'T IMAGINING IT.

February 2nd, 1997
That's how it all started. That's how I started to have a secret life. Only Valentin knew. I made up excuses so I could spend time with Emma. "Sorry, guys, I have to go visit my grandmother, I can't go to the movies tomorrow."

Or, "Mom, I'm sleeping over at a friend's house tonight. We're going to study together."

Needless to say, I've lied a lot in the last few months.

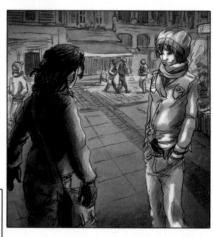

But for now I have to, because the way Laetitia humiliated me was more than I could stand.

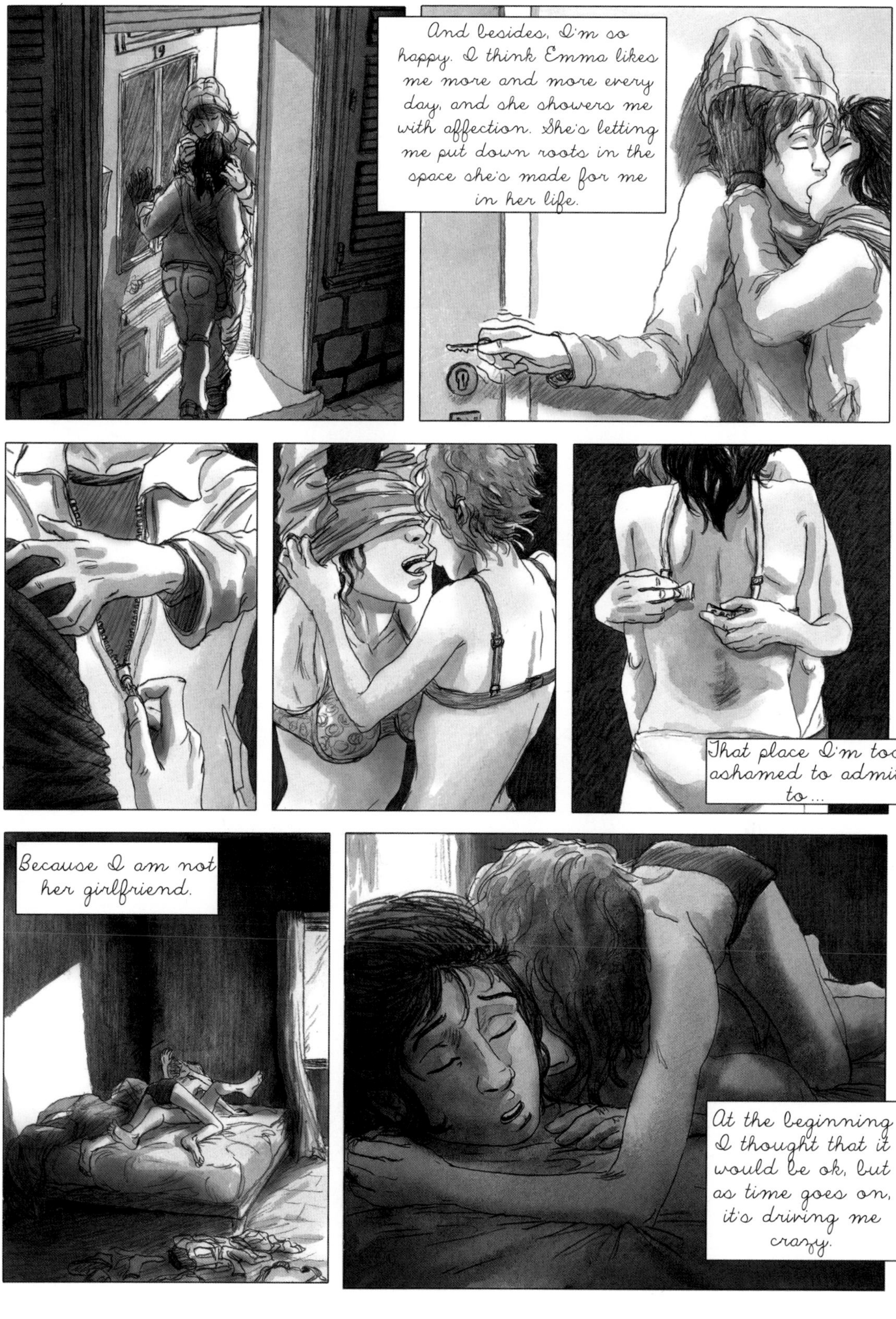
And besides, I'm so happy. I think Emma likes me more and more every day, and she showers me with affection. She's letting me put down roots in the space she's made for me in her life.
That place I'm too ashamed to admit to...
Because I am not her girlfriend.
At the beginning I thought that it would be ok, but as time goes on, it's driving me crazy.

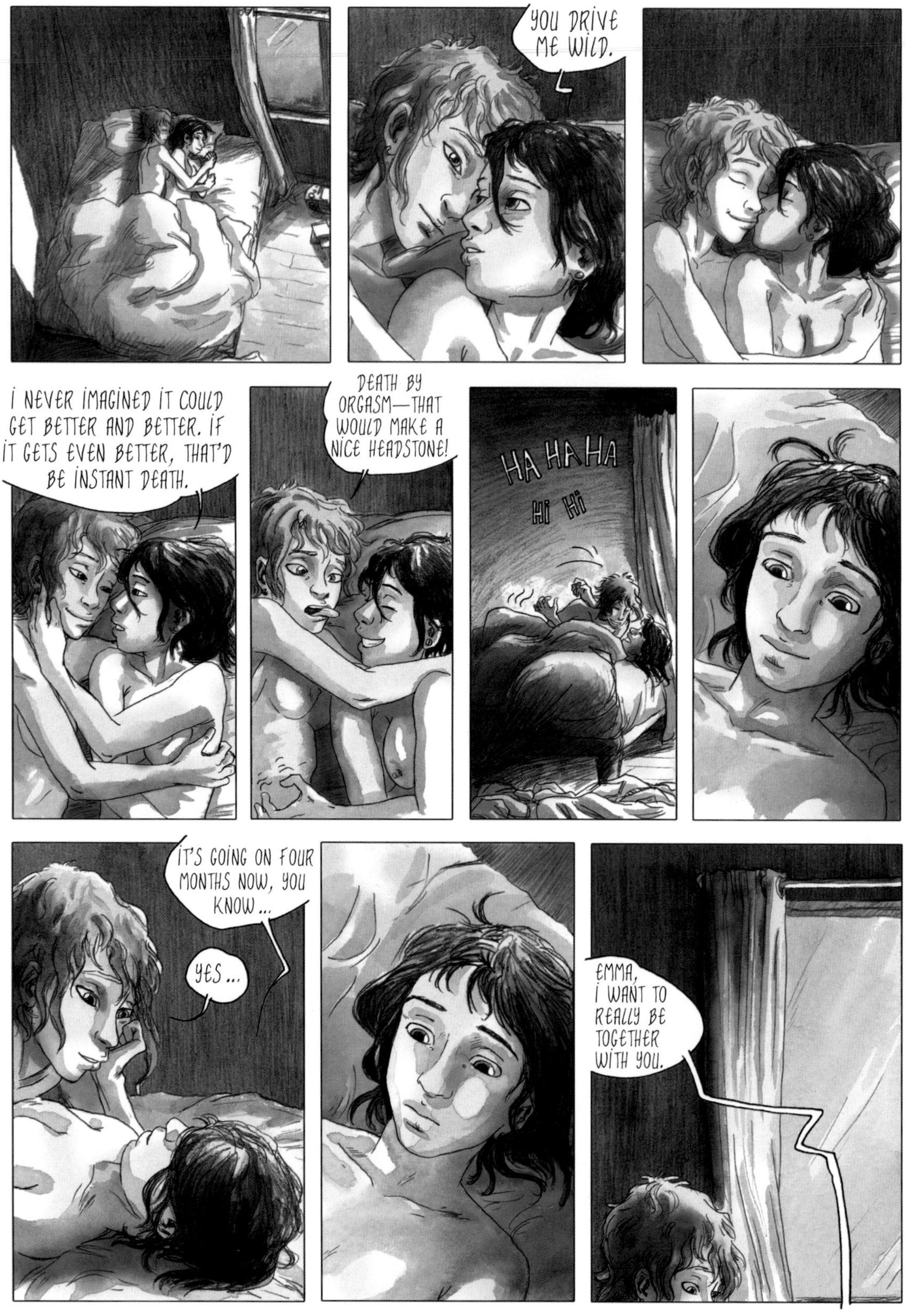
YOU DRIVE ME WILD.
I NEVER IMAGINED IT COULD GET BETTER AND BETTER. IF IT GETS EVEN BETTER, THAT'D BE INSTANT DEATH.
DEATH BY ORGASM—THAT WOULD MAKE A NICE HEADSTONE!
HA HA HA
Hi Hi
IT'S GOING ON FOUR MONTHS NOW, YOU KNOW...
YES...
EMMA, I WANT TO REALLY BE TOGETHER WITH YOU.

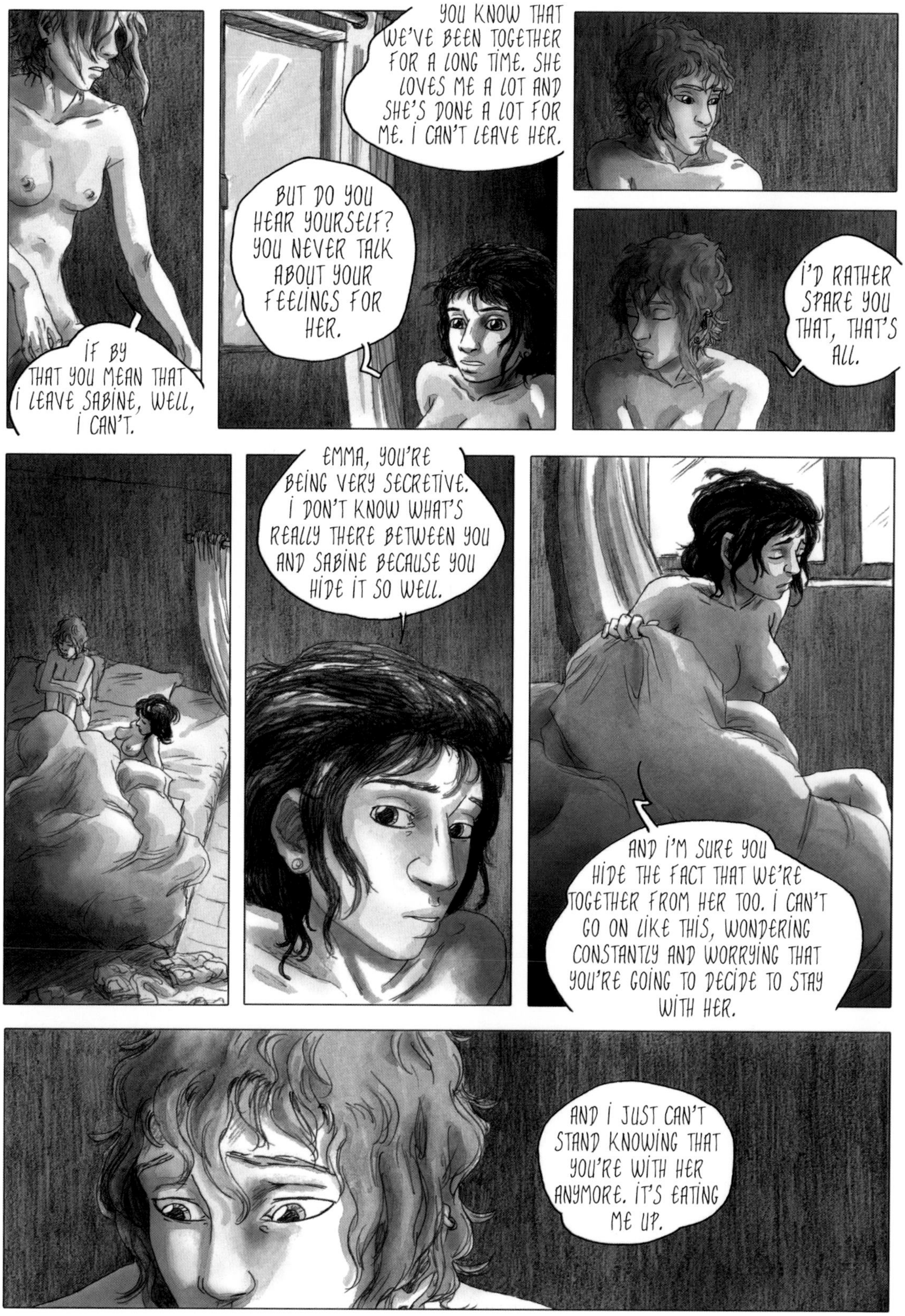
IF BY THAT YOU MEAN THAT I LEAVE SABINE, WELL, I CAN'T.
YOU KNOW THAT WE'VE BEEN TOGETHER FOR A LONG TIME. SHE LOVES ME A LOT AND SHE'S DONE A LOT FOR ME. I CAN'T LEAVE HER.
BUT DO YOU HEAR YOURSELF? YOU NEVER TALK ABOUT YOUR FEELINGS FOR HER.
I'D RATHER SPARE YOU THAT, THAT'S ALL.
EMMA, YOU'RE BEING VERY SECRETIVE. I DON'T KNOW WHAT'S REALLY THERE BETWEEN YOU AND SABINE BECAUSE YOU HIDE IT SO WELL.
AND I'M SURE YOU HIDE THE FACT THAT WE'RE TOGETHER FROM HER TOO. I CAN'T GO ON LIKE THIS, WONDERING CONSTANTLY AND WORRYING THAT YOU'RE GOING TO DECIDE TO STAY WITH HER.
AND I JUST CAN'T STAND KNOWING THAT YOU'RE WITH HER ANYMORE. IT'S EATING ME UP.

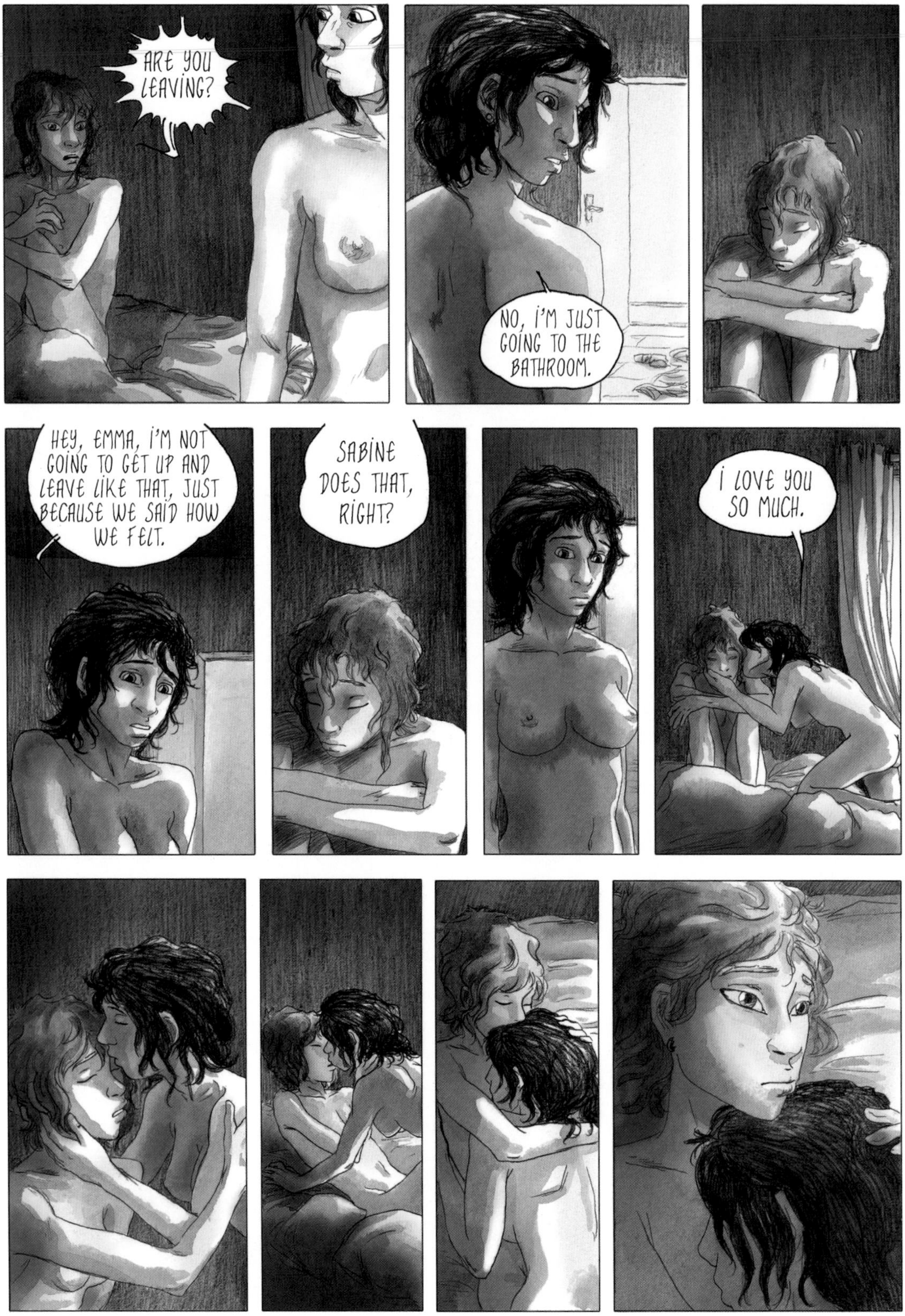
ARE YOU LEAVING?
NO, I'M JUST GOING TO THE BATHROOM.
HEY, EMMA, I'M NOT GOING TO GET UP AND LEAVE LIKE THAT, JUST BECAUSE WE SAID HOW WE FELT.
SABINE DOES THAT, RIGHT?
I LOVE YOU SO MUCH.

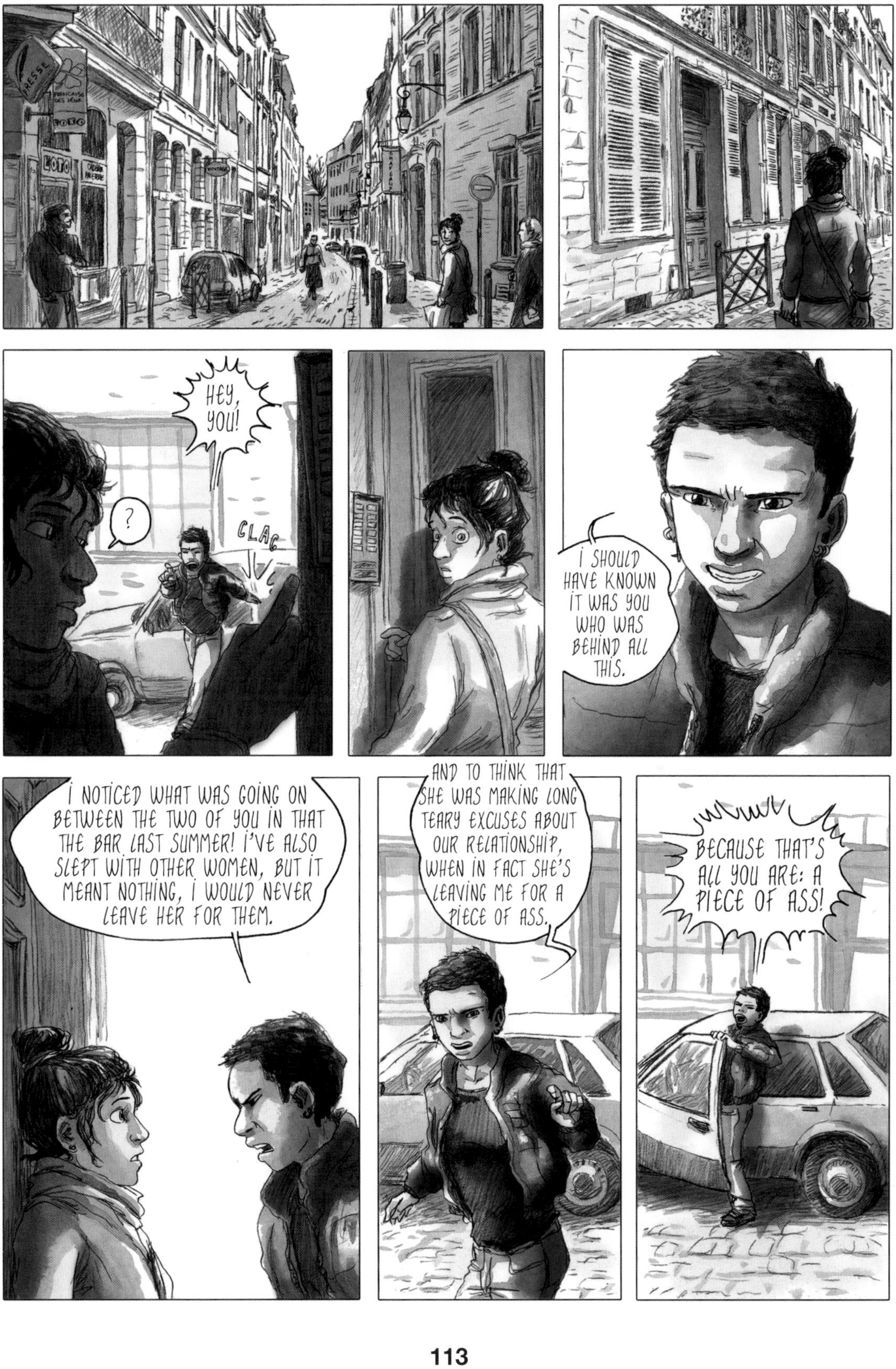
HEY, YOU!
?
CLAG
I SHOULD HAVE KNOWN IT WAS YOU WHO WAS BEHIND ALL THIS.
I NOTICED WHAT WAS GOING ON BETWEEN THE TWO OF YOU IN THAT THE BAR LAST SUMMER! I'VE ALSO SLEPT WITH OTHER WOMEN, BUT IT MEANT NOTHING, I WOULD NEVER LEAVE HER FOR THEM.
AND TO THINK THAT SHE WAS MAKING LONG TEARY EXCUSES ABOUT OUR RELATIONSHIP, WHEN IN FACT SHE'S LEAVING ME FOR A PIECE OF ASS.
BECAUSE THAT'S ALL YOU ARE: A PIECE OF ASS!

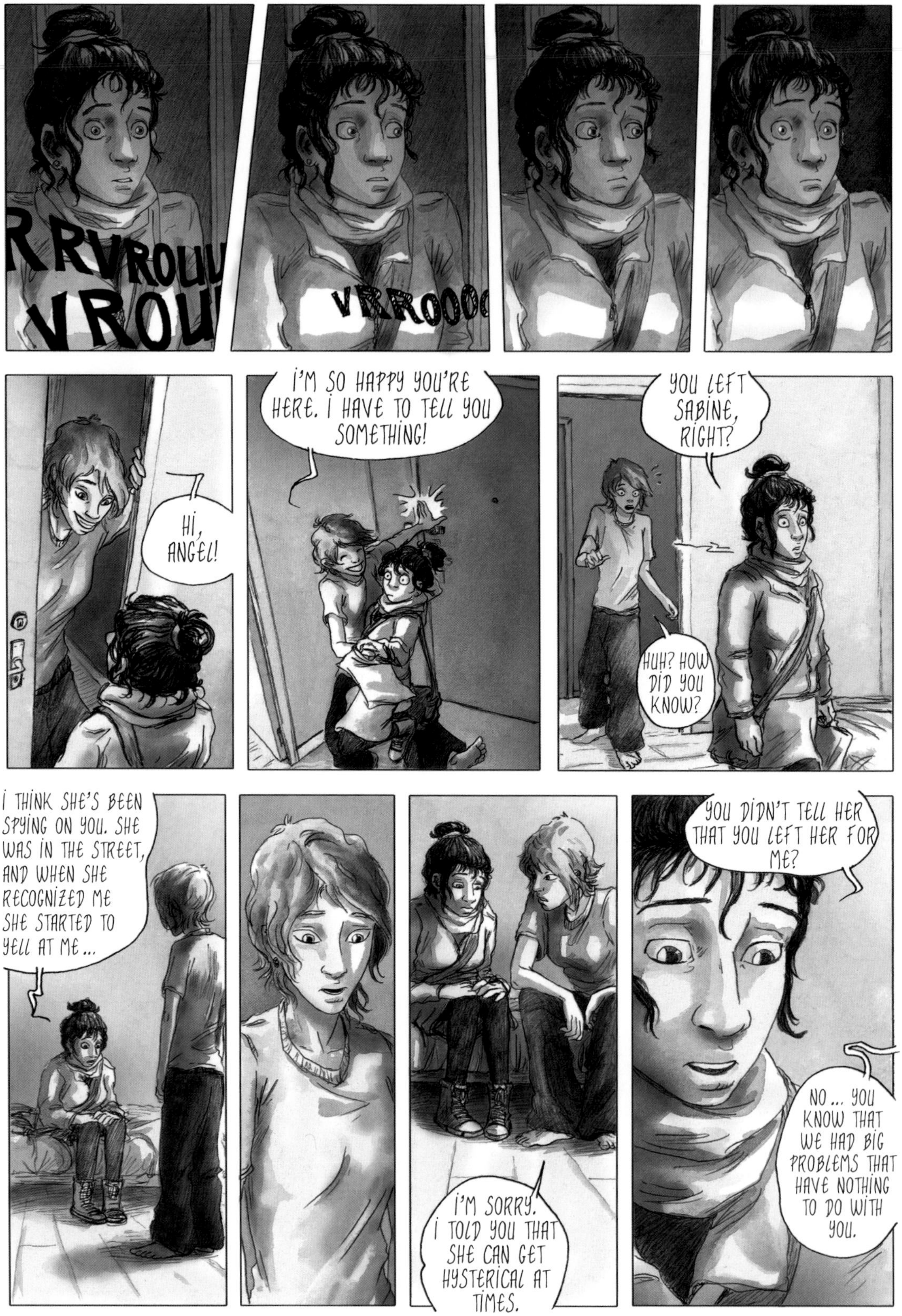
RRVROUU
VROU
VRROOOO
HI, ANGEL!
I'M SO HAPPY YOU'RE HERE. I HAVE TO TELL YOU SOMETHING!
YOU LEFT SABINE, RIGHT?
HUH? HOW DID YOU KNOW?
I THINK SHE'S BEEN SPYING ON YOU. SHE WAS IN THE STREET, AND WHEN SHE RECOGNIZED ME SHE STARTED TO YELL AT ME...
I'M SORRY. I TOLD YOU THAT SHE CAN GET HYSTERICAL AT TIMES.
YOU DIDN'T TELL HER THAT YOU LEFT HER FOR ME?
NO... YOU KNOW THAT WE HAD BIG PROBLEMS THAT HAVE NOTHING TO DO WITH YOU.

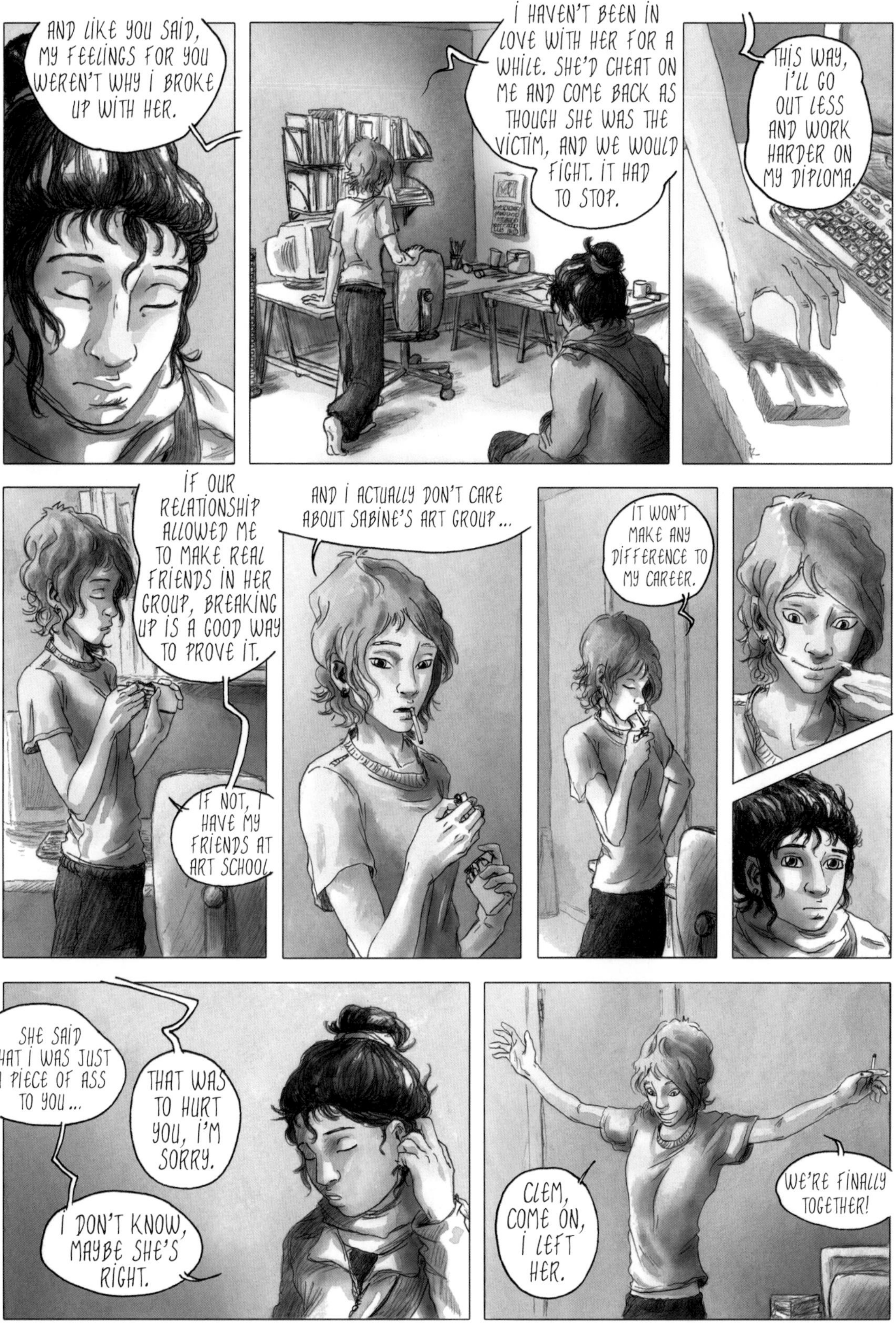
AND LIKE YOU SAID, MY FEELINGS FOR YOU WEREN'T WHY I BROKE UP WITH HER.
I HAVEN'T BEEN IN LOVE WITH HER FOR A WHILE. SHE'D CHEAT ON ME AND COME BACK AS THOUGH SHE WAS THE VICTIM, AND WE WOULD FIGHT. IT HAD TO STOP.
THIS WAY, I'LL GO OUT LESS AND WORK HARDER ON MY DIPLOMA.
IF OUR RELATIONSHIP ALLOWED ME TO MAKE REAL FRIENDS IN HER GROUP, BREAKING UP IS A GOOD WAY TO PROVE IT.
IF NOT, I HAVE MY FRIENDS AT ART SCHOOL
AND I ACTUALLY DON'T CARE ABOUT SABINE'S ART GROUP...
IT WON'T MAKE ANY DIFFERENCE TO MY CAREER.
SHE SAID THAT I WAS JUST A PIECE OF ASS TO YOU...
THAT WAS TO HURT YOU, I'M SORRY.
I DON'T KNOW, MAYBE SHE'S RIGHT.
CLEM, COME ON, I LEFT HER.
WE'RE FINALLY TOGETHER!

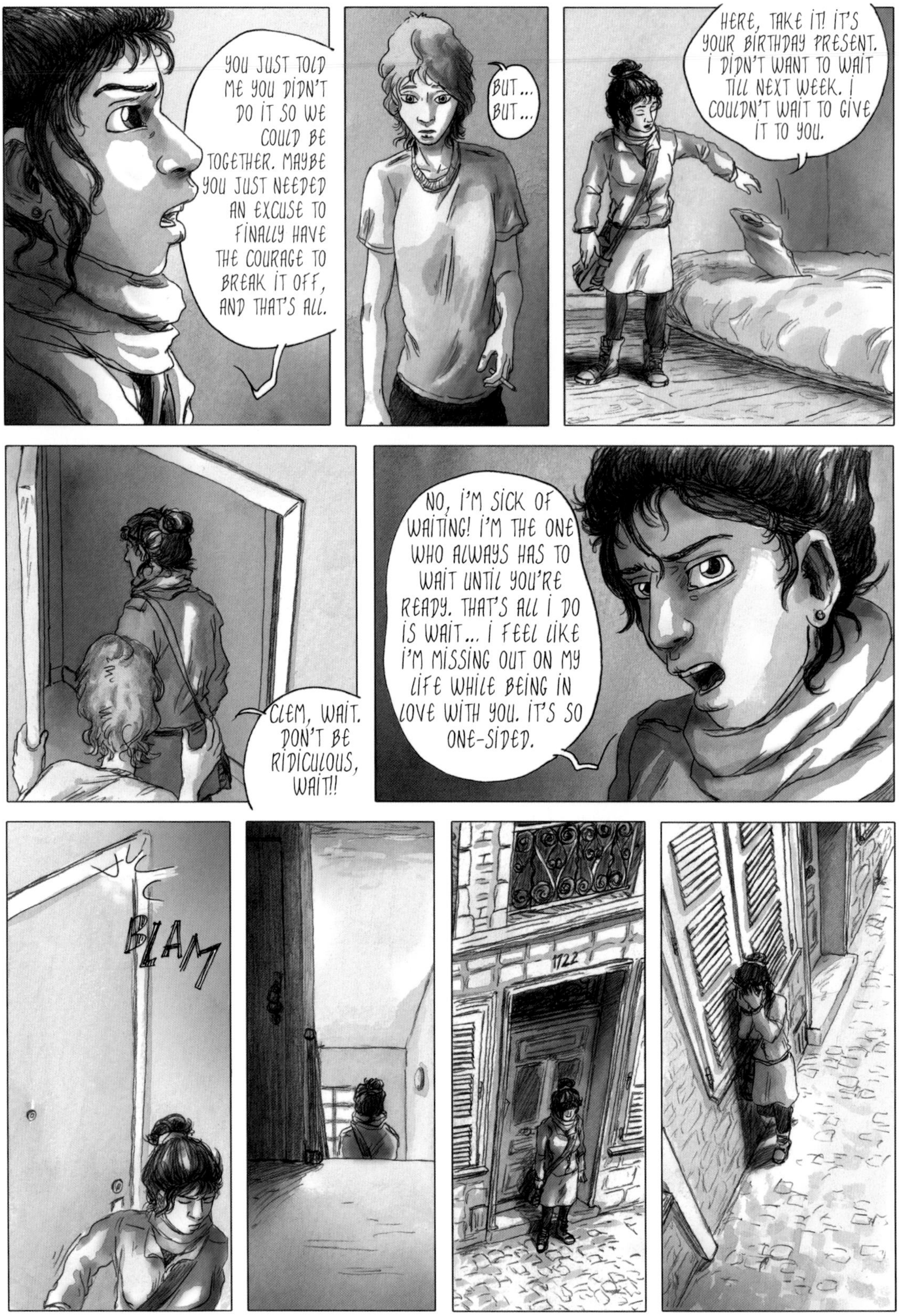
YOU JUST TOLD ME YOU DIDN'T DO IT SO WE COULD BE TOGETHER. MAYBE YOU JUST NEEDED AN EXCUSE TO FINALLY HAVE THE COURAGE TO BREAK IT OFF, AND THAT'S ALL.
BUT... BUT...
HERE, TAKE IT! IT'S YOUR BIRTHDAY PRESENT. I DIDN'T WANT TO WAIT TILL NEXT WEEK. I COULDN'T WAIT TO GIVE IT TO YOU.
CLEM, WAIT. DON'T BE RIDICULOUS, WAIT!!
NO, I'M SICK OF WAITING! I'M THE ONE WHO ALWAYS HAS TO WAIT UNTIL YOU'RE READY. THAT'S ALL I DO IS WAIT... I FEEL LIKE I'M MISSING OUT ON MY LIFE WHILE BEING IN LOVE WITH YOU. IT'S SO ONE-SIDED.
BLAM
1722

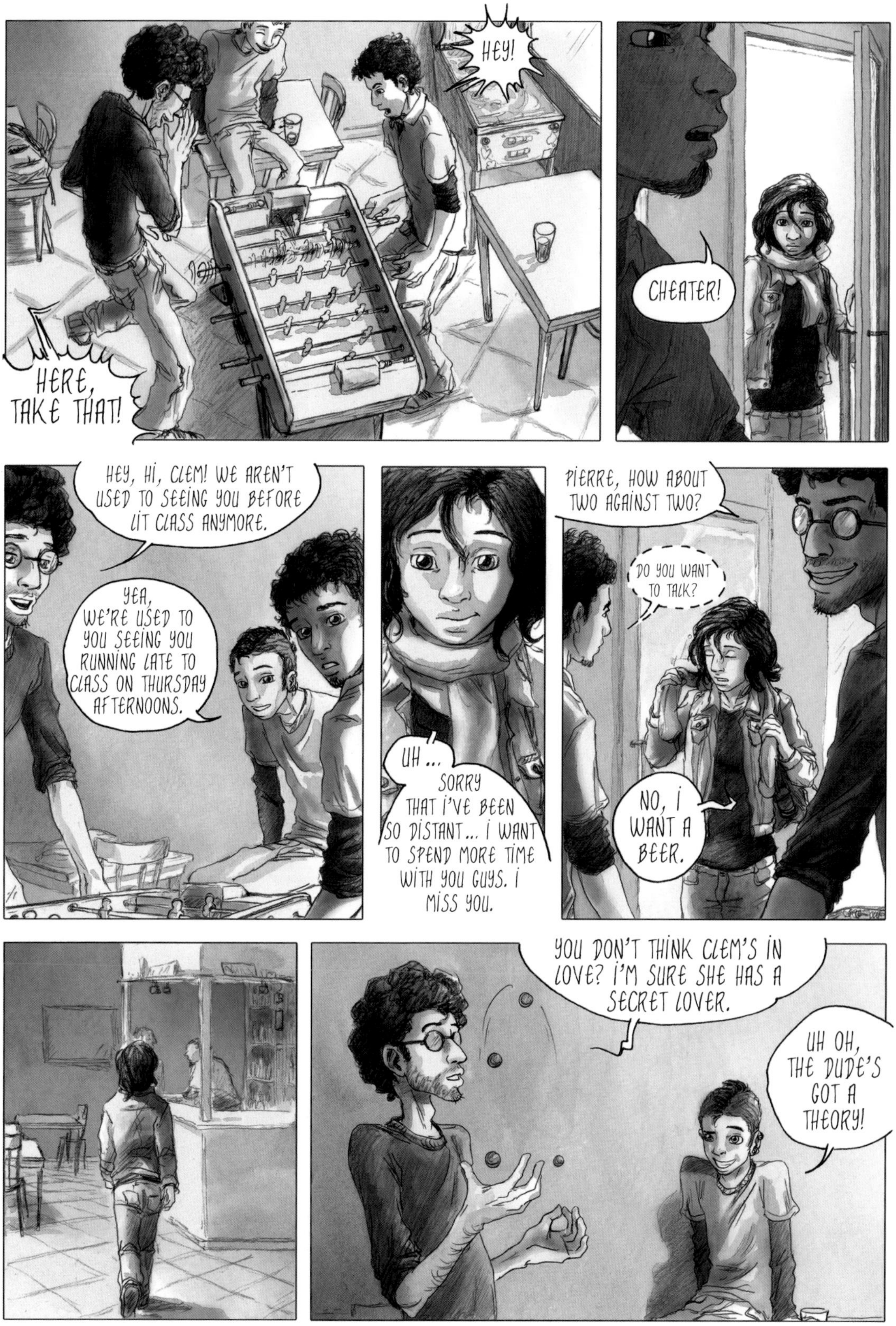
HEY!
HERE, TAKE THAT!
CHEATER!
HEY, HI, CLEM! WE AREN'T USED TO SEEING YOU BEFORE LIT CLASS ANYMORE.
YEA, WE'RE USED TO YOU SEEING YOU RUNNING LATE TO CLASS ON THURSDAY AFTERNOONS.
UH ...
SORRY THAT I'VE BEEN SO DISTANT... I WANT TO SPEND MORE TIME WITH YOU GUYS. I MISS YOU.
PIERRE, HOW ABOUT TWO AGAINST TWO?
DO YOU WANT TO TALK?
NO, I WANT A BEER.
YOU DON'T THINK CLEM'S IN LOVE? I'M SURE SHE HAS A SECRET LOVER.
UH OH, THE DUDE'S GOT A THEORY!

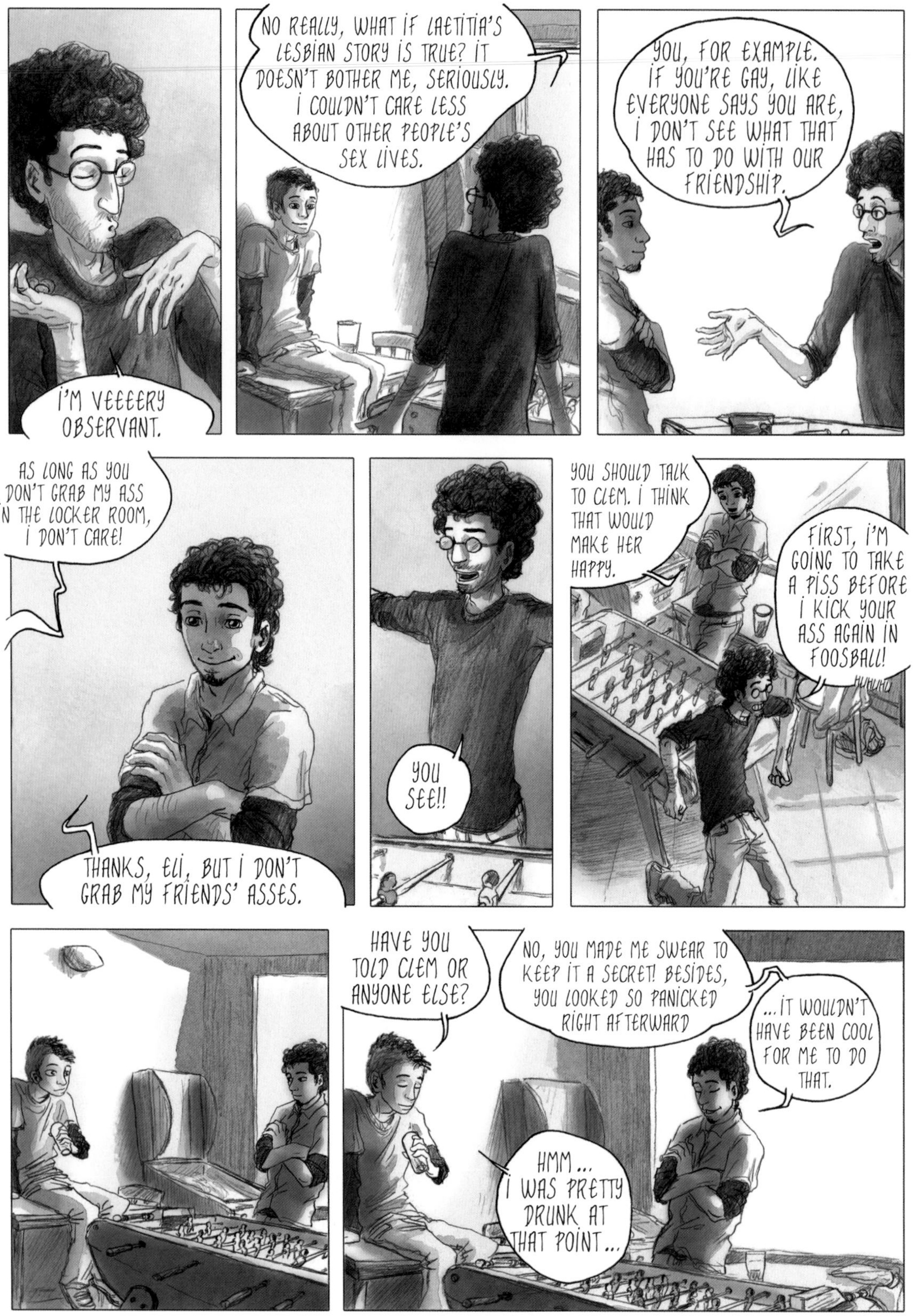
I'M VEEEERY OBSERVANT.
NO REALLY, WHAT IF LAETITIA'S LESBIAN STORY IS TRUE? IT DOESN'T BOTHER ME, SERIOUSLY. I COULDN'T CARE LESS ABOUT OTHER PEOPLE'S SEX LIVES.
YOU, FOR EXAMPLE. IF YOU'RE GAY, LIKE EVERYONE SAYS YOU ARE, I DON'T SEE WHAT THAT HAS TO DO WITH OUR FRIENDSHIP.
AS LONG AS YOU DON'T GRAB MY ASS IN THE LOCKER ROOM, I DON'T CARE!
THANKS, ELI, BUT I DON'T GRAB MY FRIENDS' ASSES.
YOU SEE!!
YOU SHOULD TALK TO CLEM. I THINK THAT WOULD MAKE HER HAPPY.
FIRST, I'M GOING TO TAKE A PISS BEFORE I KICK YOUR ASS AGAIN IN FOOSBALL!
HAVE YOU TOLD CLEM OR ANYONE ELSE?
NO, YOU MADE ME SWEAR TO KEEP IT A SECRET! BESIDES, YOU LOOKED SO PANICKED RIGHT AFTERWARD
...IT WOULDN'T HAVE BEEN COOL FOR ME TO DO THAT.
HMM... I WAS PRETTY DRUNK AT THAT POINT...

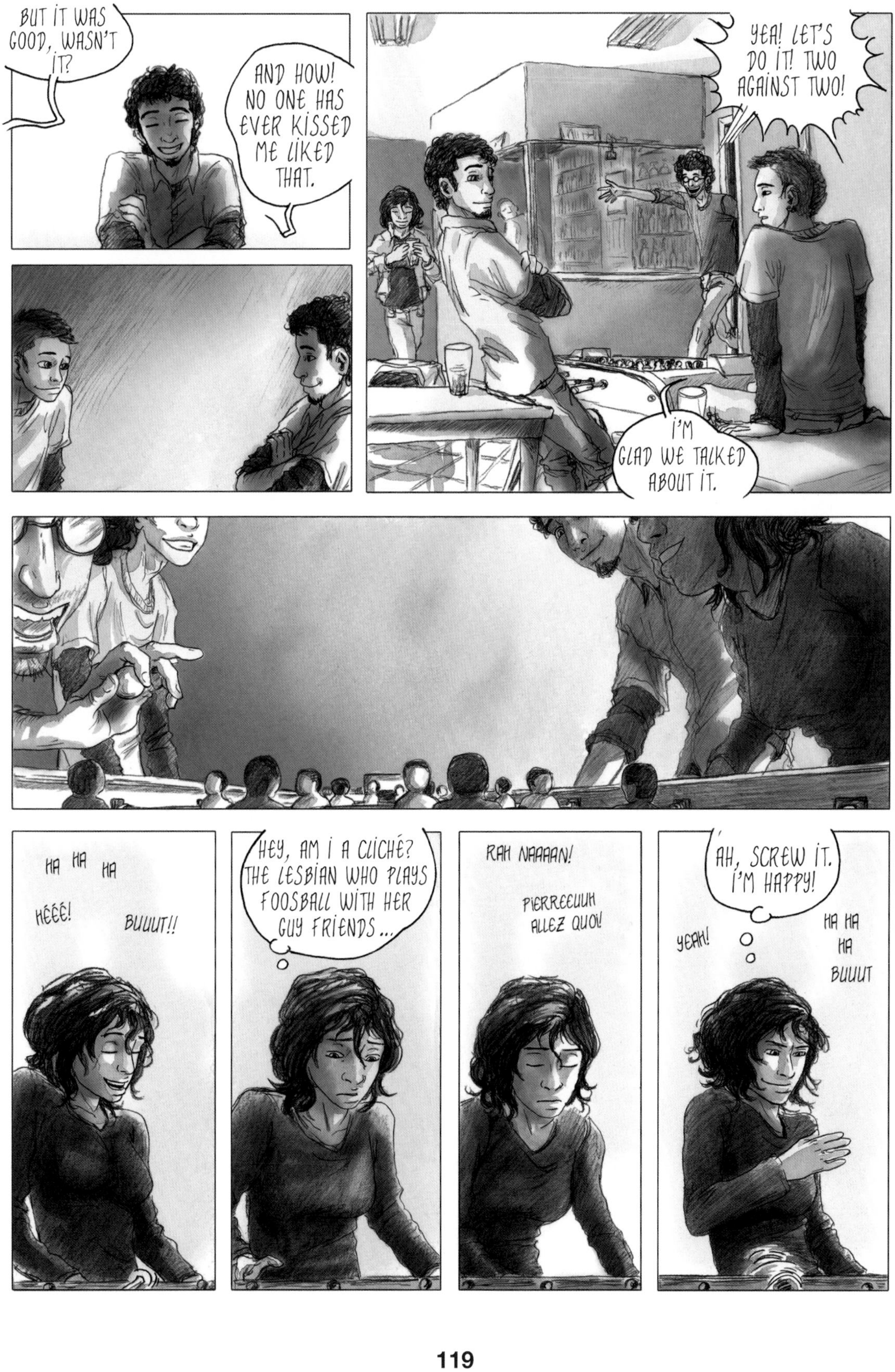
BUT IT WAS GOOD, WASN'T IT?
AND HOW! NO ONE HAS EVER KISSED ME LIKED THAT.
YEA! LET'S DO IT! TWO AGAINST TWO!
I'M GLAD WE TALKED ABOUT IT.
HA HA HA
HÉÉÉ!
BUUUT!!
HEY, AM I A CLICHÉ? THE LESBIAN WHO PLAYS FOOSBALL WITH HER GUY FRIENDS...
RAH NAAAAAN!
PIERREEUUH ALLEZ QUOI!
AH, SCREW IT. I'M HAPPY!
YEAH!
HA HA HA
BUUUT

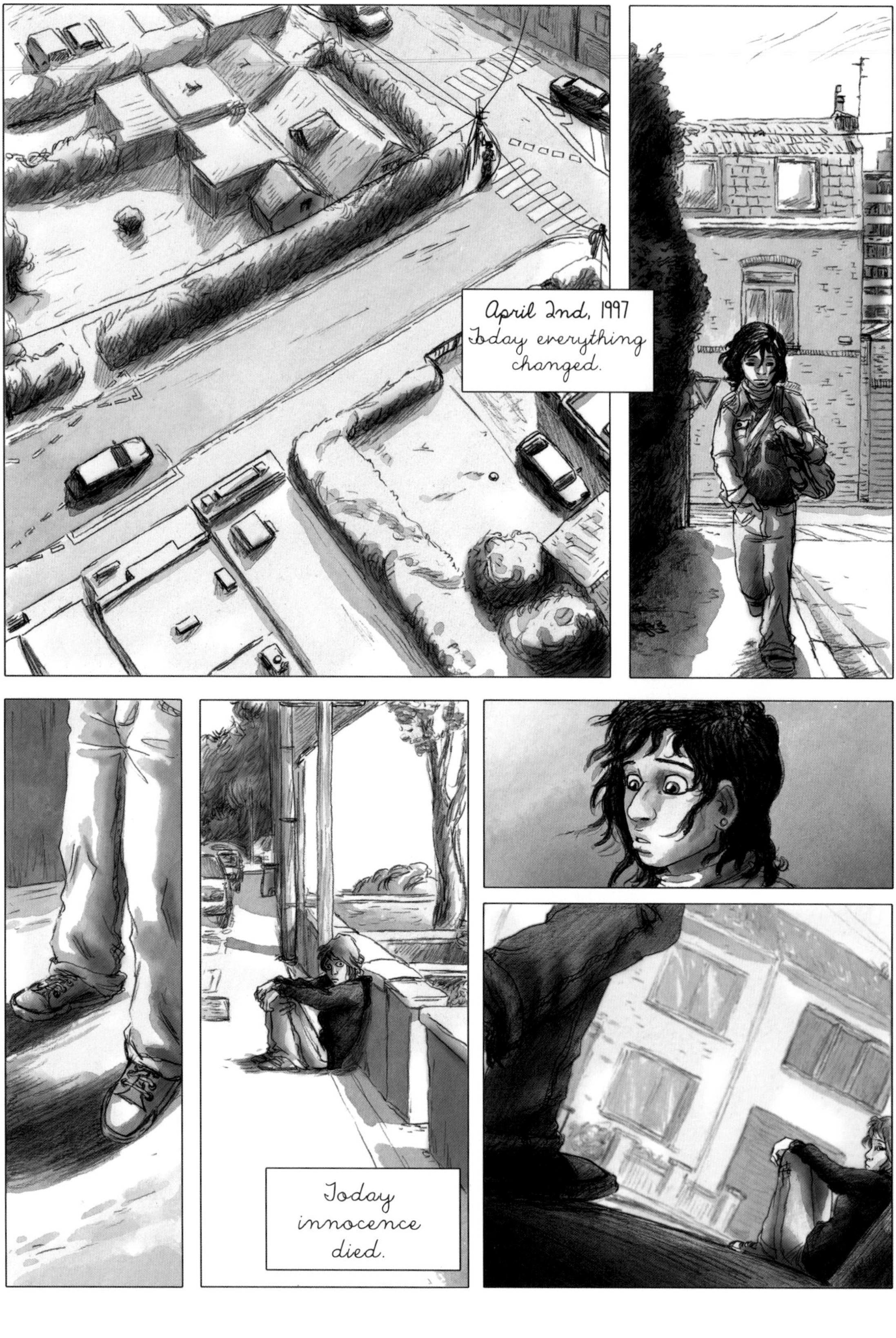
April 2nd, 1997
Today everything changed.
Today innocence died.

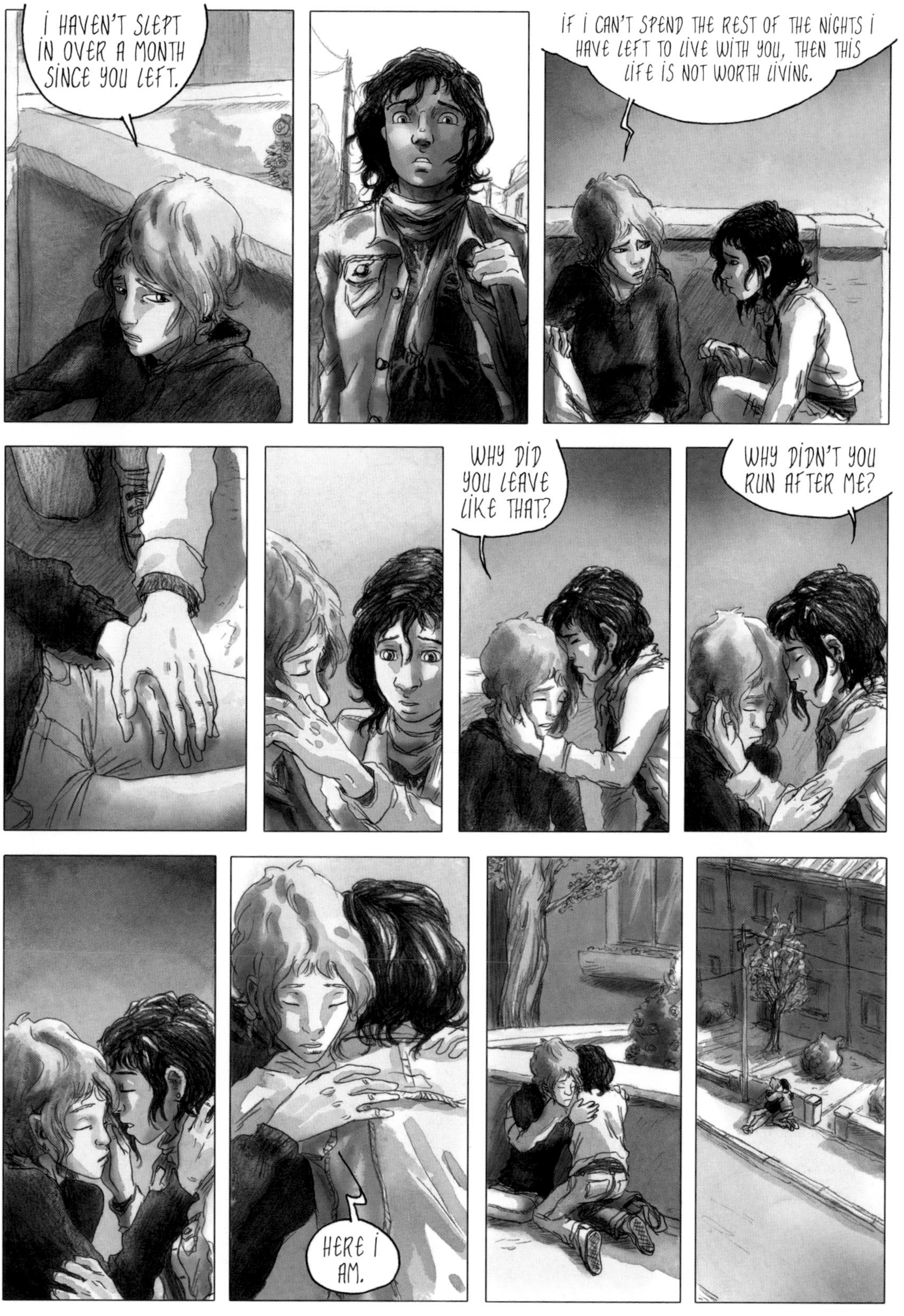
I HAVEN'T SLEPT IN OVER A MONTH SINCE YOU LEFT.
IF I CAN'T SPEND THE REST OF THE NIGHTS I HAVE LEFT TO LIVE WITH YOU, THEN THIS LIFE IS NOT WORTH LIVING.
WHY DID YOU LEAVE LIKE THAT?
WHY DIDN'T YOU RUN AFTER ME?
HERE I AM.

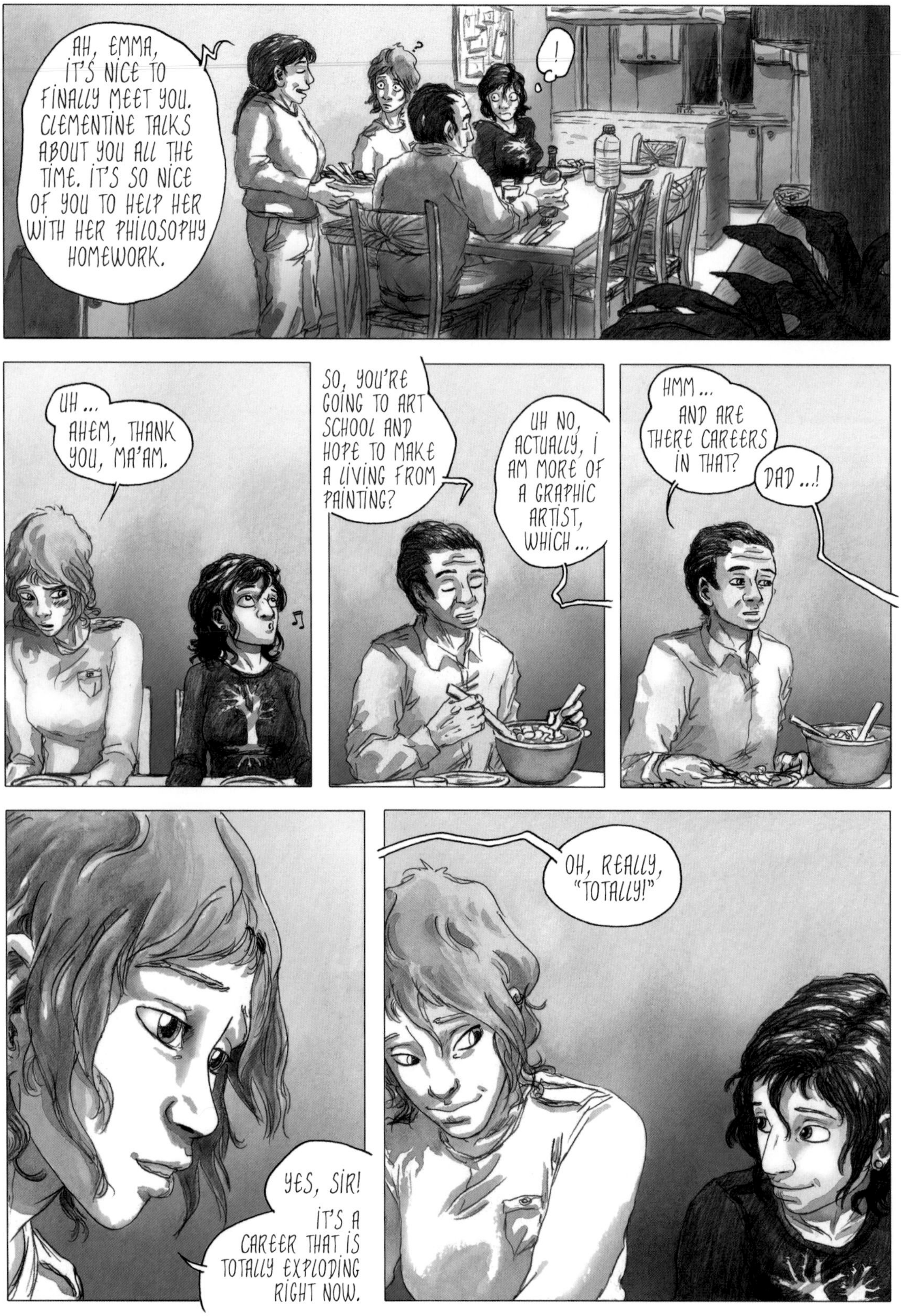
AH, EMMA, IT'S NICE TO FINALLY MEET YOU. CLEMENTINE TALKS ABOUT YOU ALL THE TIME. IT'S SO NICE OF YOU TO HELP HER WITH HER PHILOSOPHY HOMEWORK.
?
!
UH ... AHEM, THANK YOU, MA'AM.
SO, YOU'RE GOING TO ART SCHOOL AND HOPE TO MAKE A LIVING FROM PAINTING?
UH NO, ACTUALLY, I AM MORE OF A GRAPHIC ARTIST, WHICH ...
HMM ... AND ARE THERE CAREERS IN THAT?
DAD ...!
YES, SIR!
IT'S A CAREER THAT IS TOTALLY EXPLODING RIGHT NOW.
OH, REALLY, "TOTALLY!"

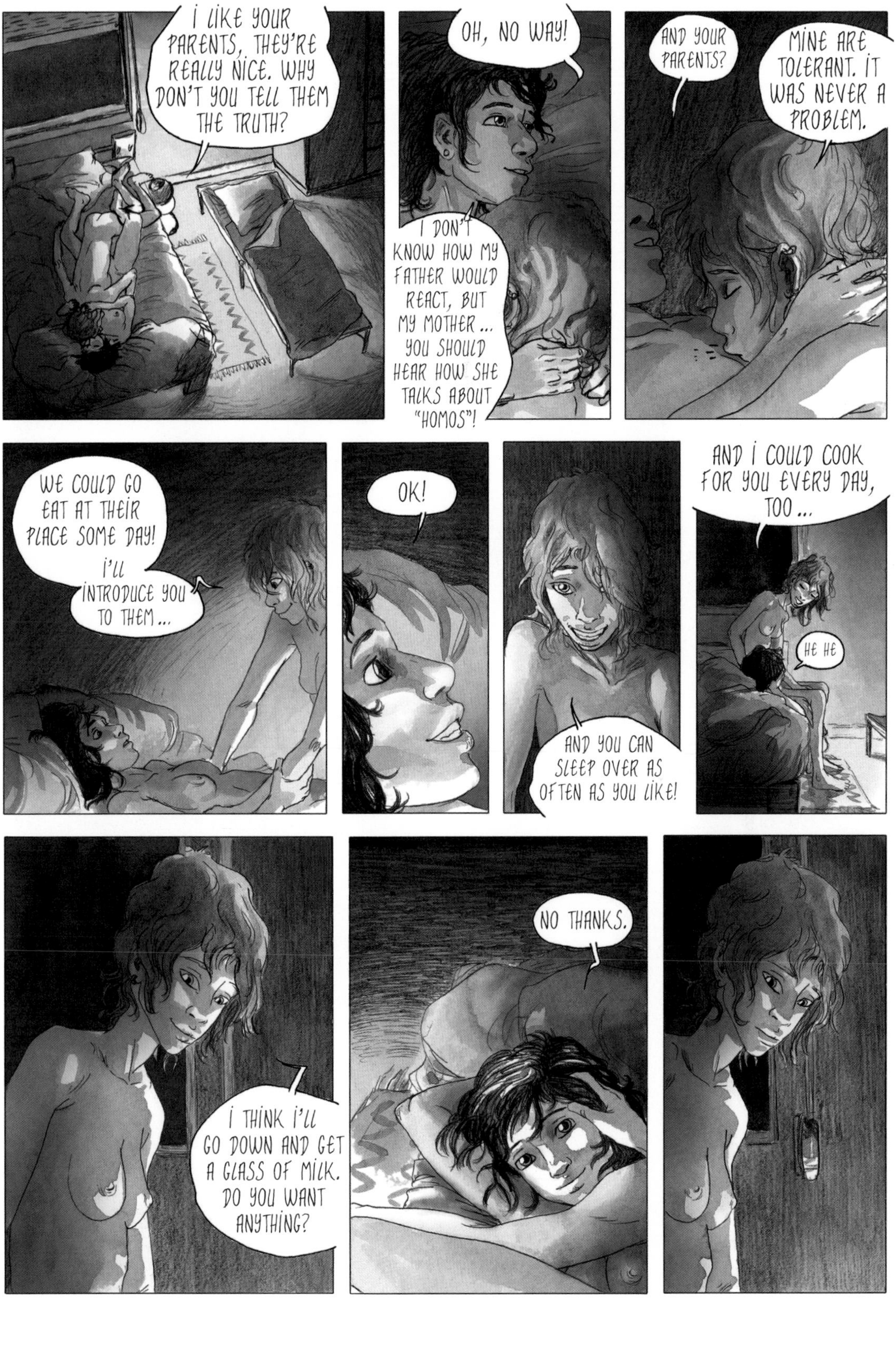
I LIKE YOUR PARENTS, THEY'RE REALLY NICE. WHY DON'T YOU TELL THEM THE TRUTH?
OH, NO WAY!
I DON'T KNOW HOW MY FATHER WOULD REACT, BUT MY MOTHER ... YOU SHOULD HEAR HOW SHE TALKS ABOUT "HOMOS"!
AND YOUR PARENTS?
MINE ARE TOLERANT. IT WAS NEVER A PROBLEM.
WE COULD GO EAT AT THEIR PLACE SOME DAY!
I'LL INTRODUCE YOU TO THEM...
OK!
AND YOU CAN SLEEP OVER AS OFTEN AS YOU LIKE!
AND I COULD COOK FOR YOU EVERY DAY, TOO ...
HE HE
I THINK I'LL GO DOWN AND GET A GLASS OF MILK. DO YOU WANT ANYTHING?
NO THANKS.

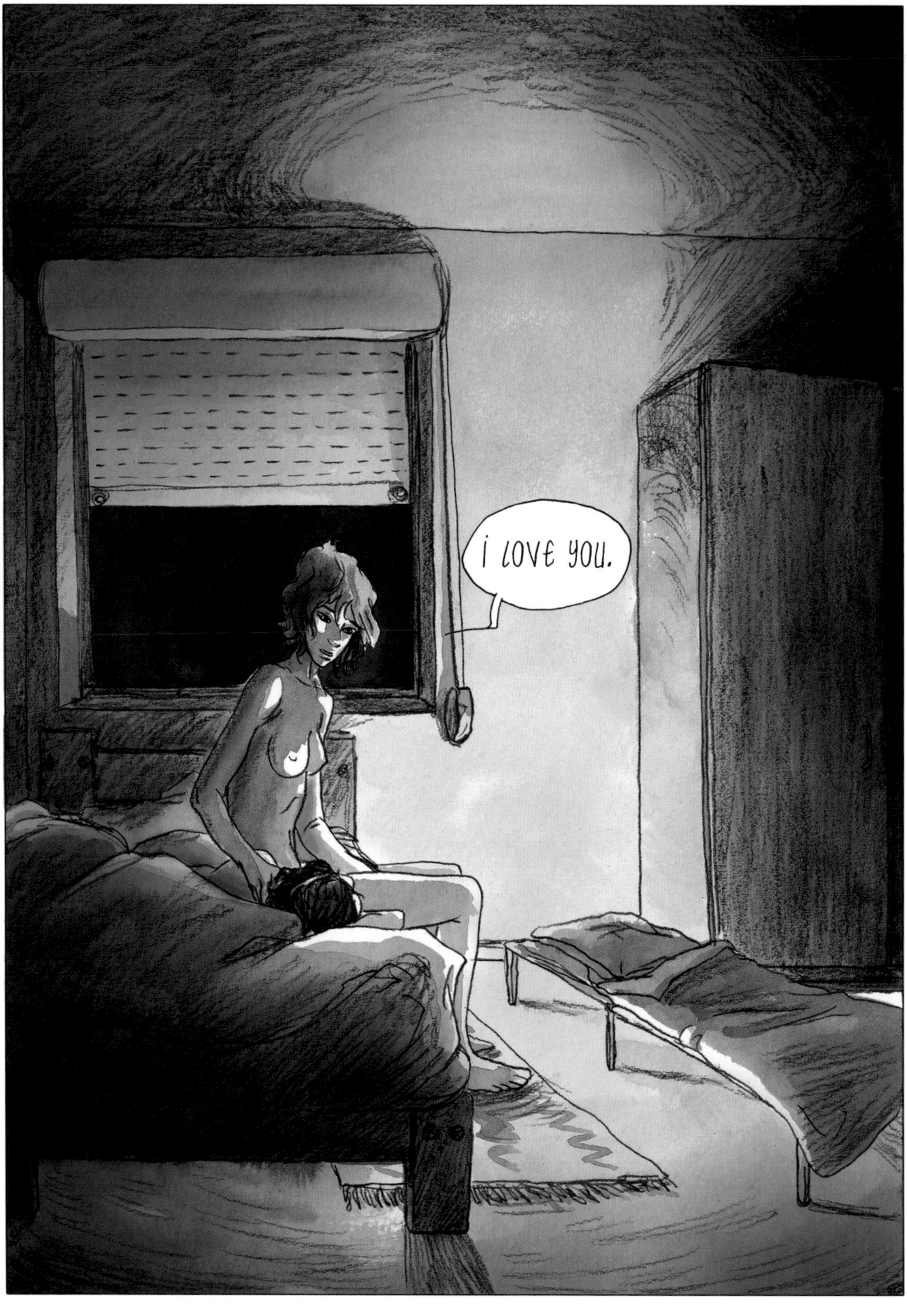
i love you.

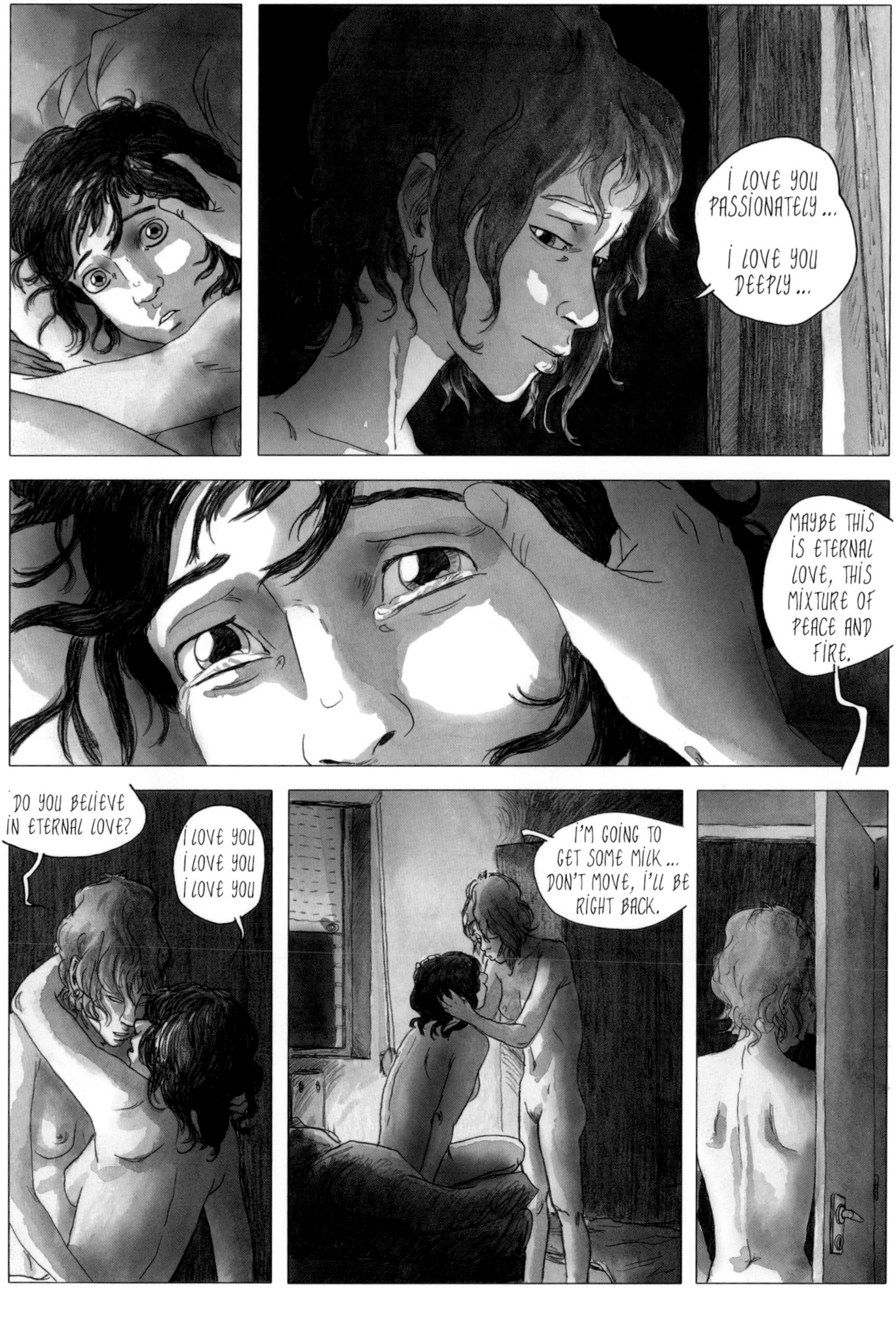
I LOVE YOU PASSIONATELY ...
I LOVE YOU DEEPLY ...
MAYBE THIS IS ETERNAL LOVE, THIS MIXTURE OF PEACE AND FIRE.
DO YOU BELIEVE IN ETERNAL LOVE?
I LOVE YOU I LOVE YOU I LOVE YOU
I'M GOING TO GET SOME MILK ... DON'T MOVE, I'LL BE RIGHT BACK.

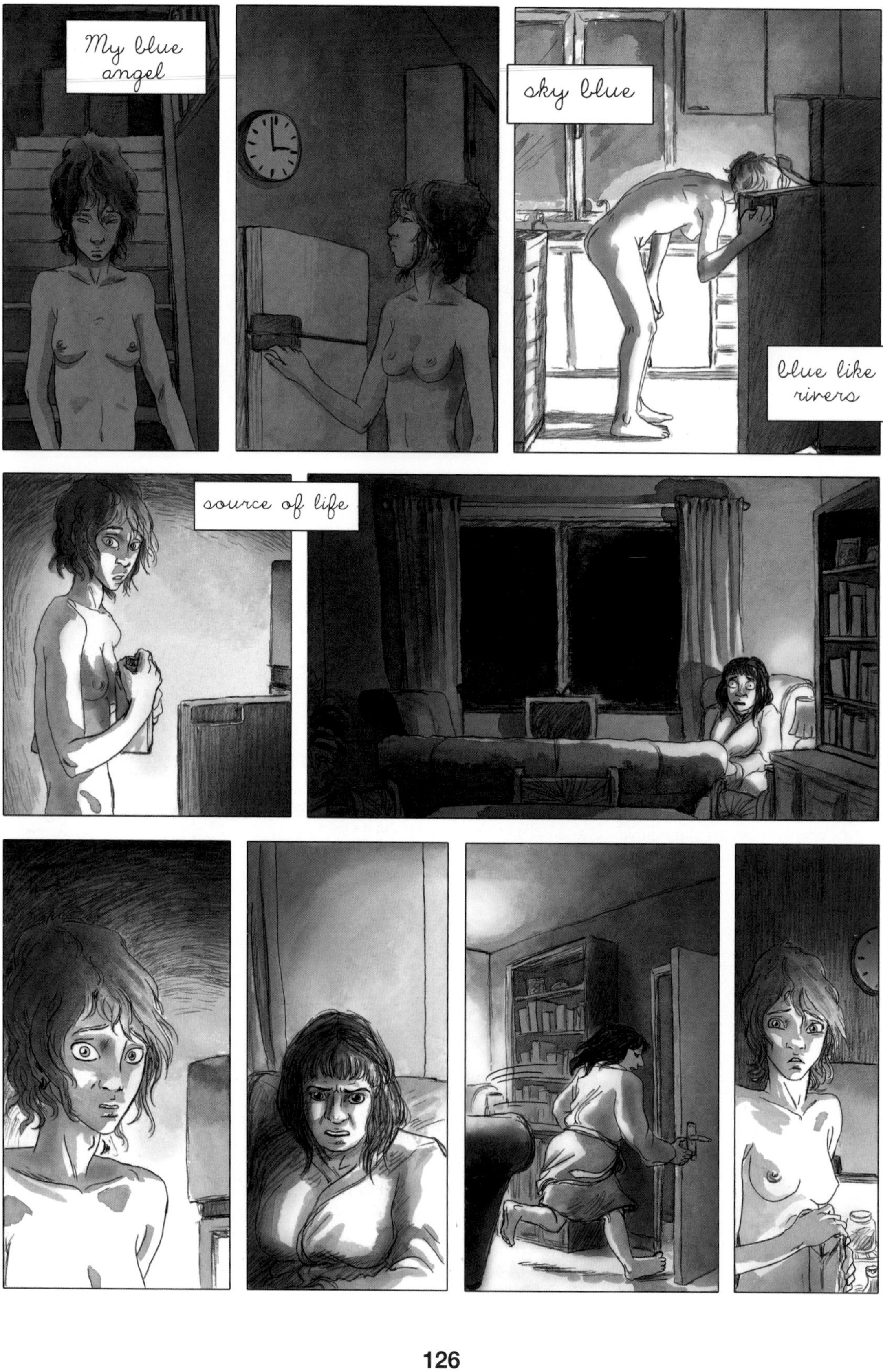
My blue angel
sky blue
blue like rivers
source of life

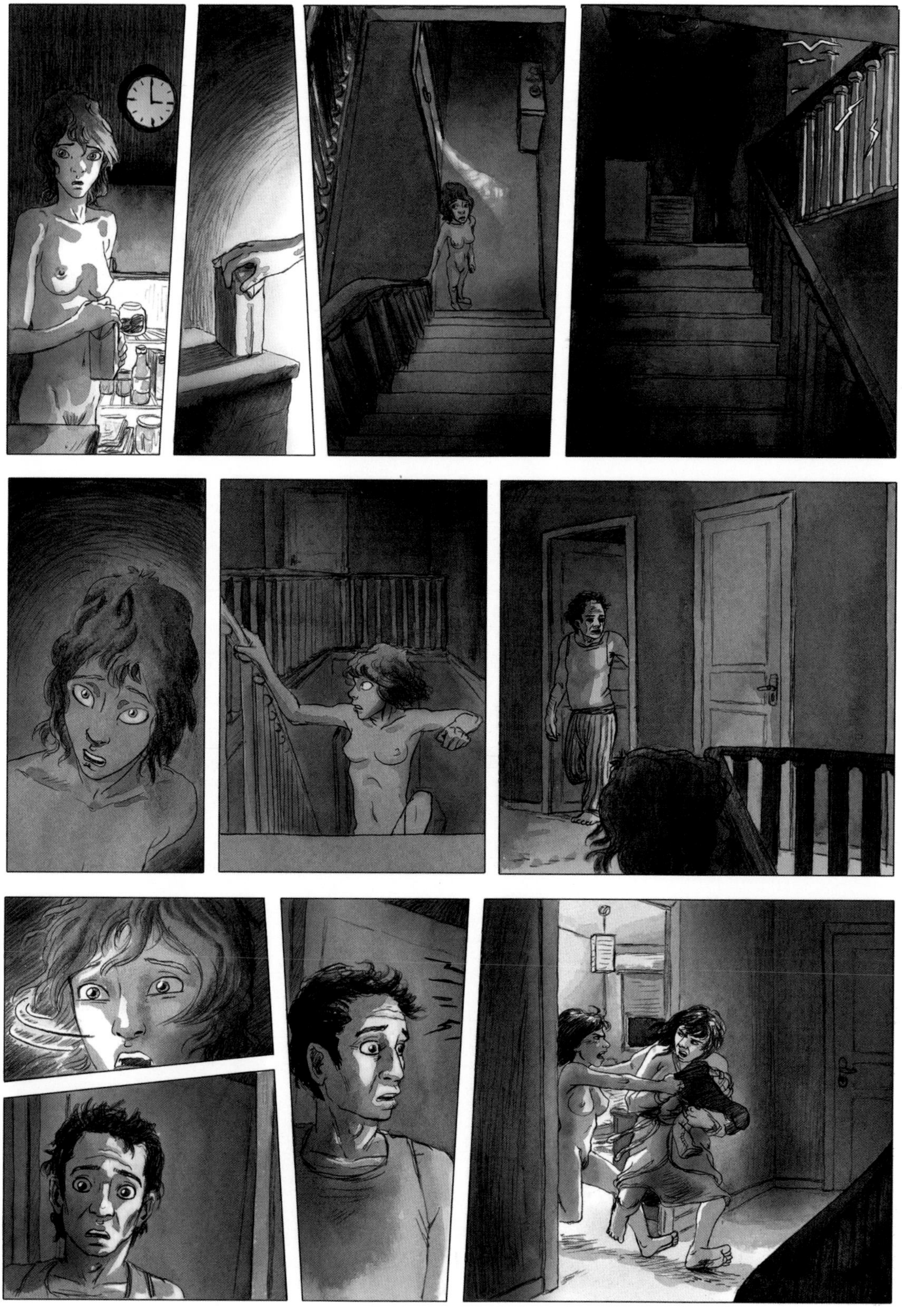

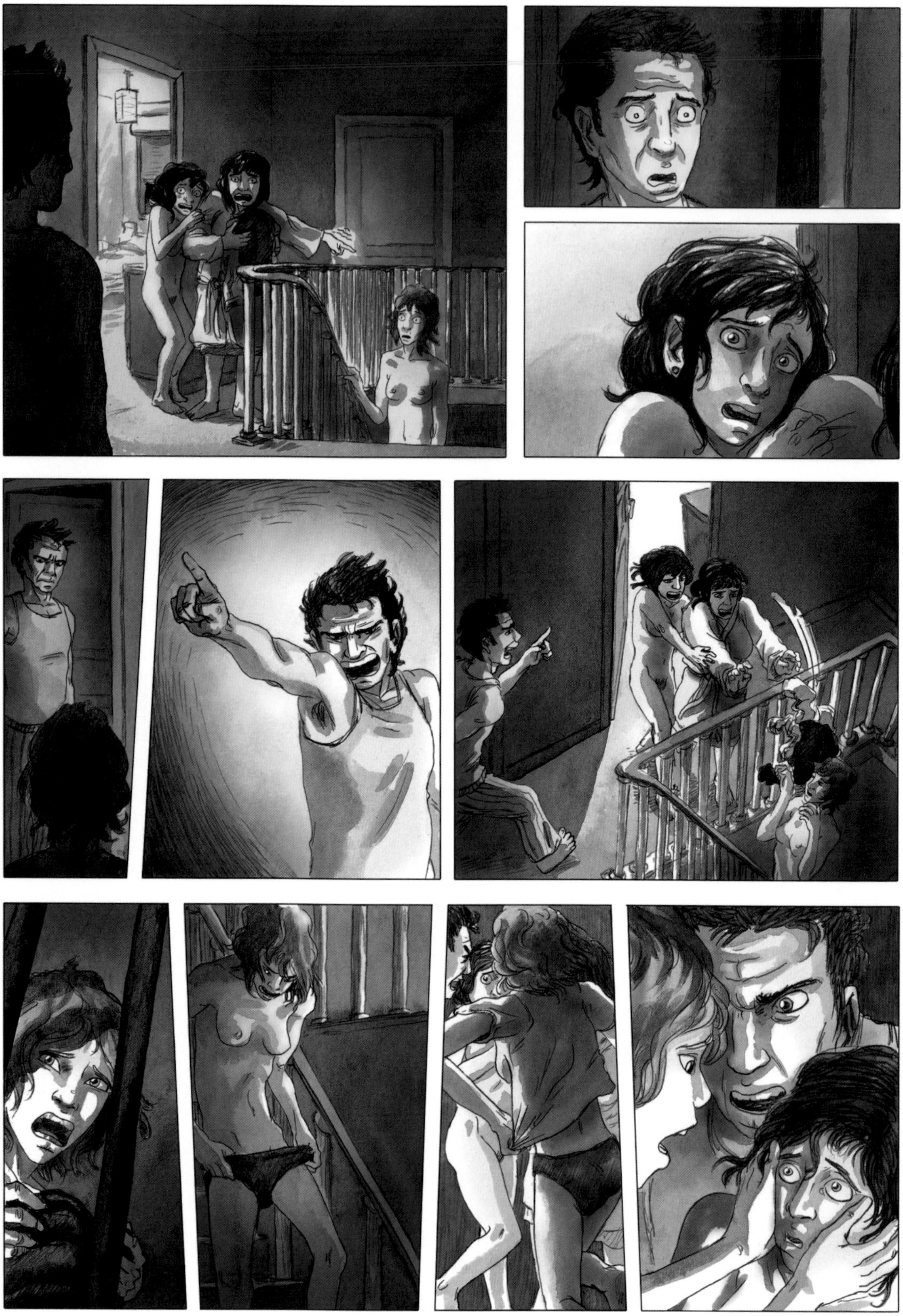

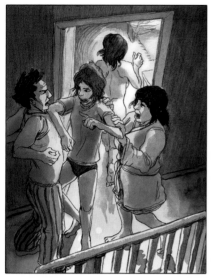

Today a crisis blew open our secrets.

mine

and my family's

And we'll never be the same.

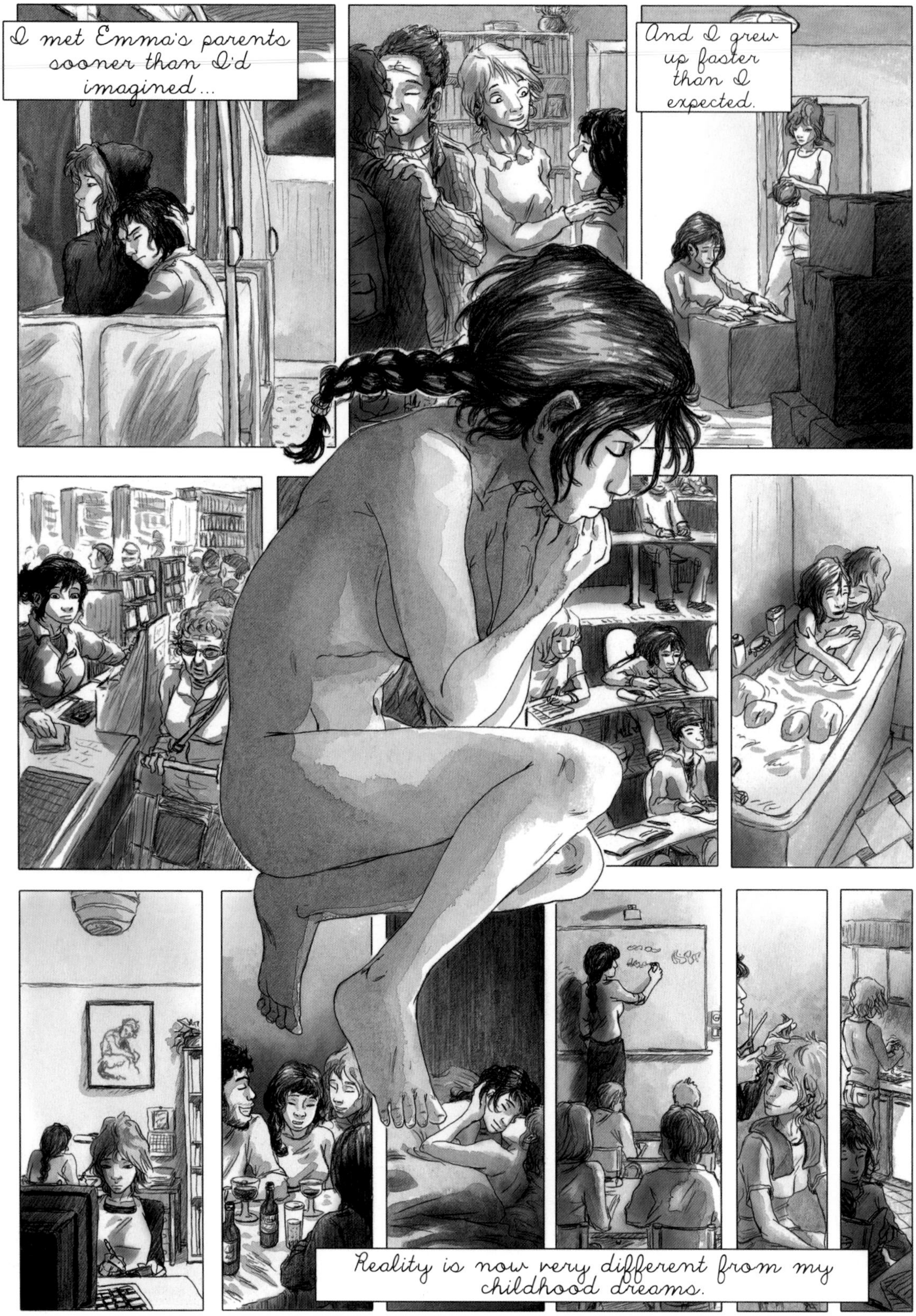
I met Emma's parents sooner than I'd imagined...
And I grew up faster than I expected.
Reality is now very different from my childhood dreams.

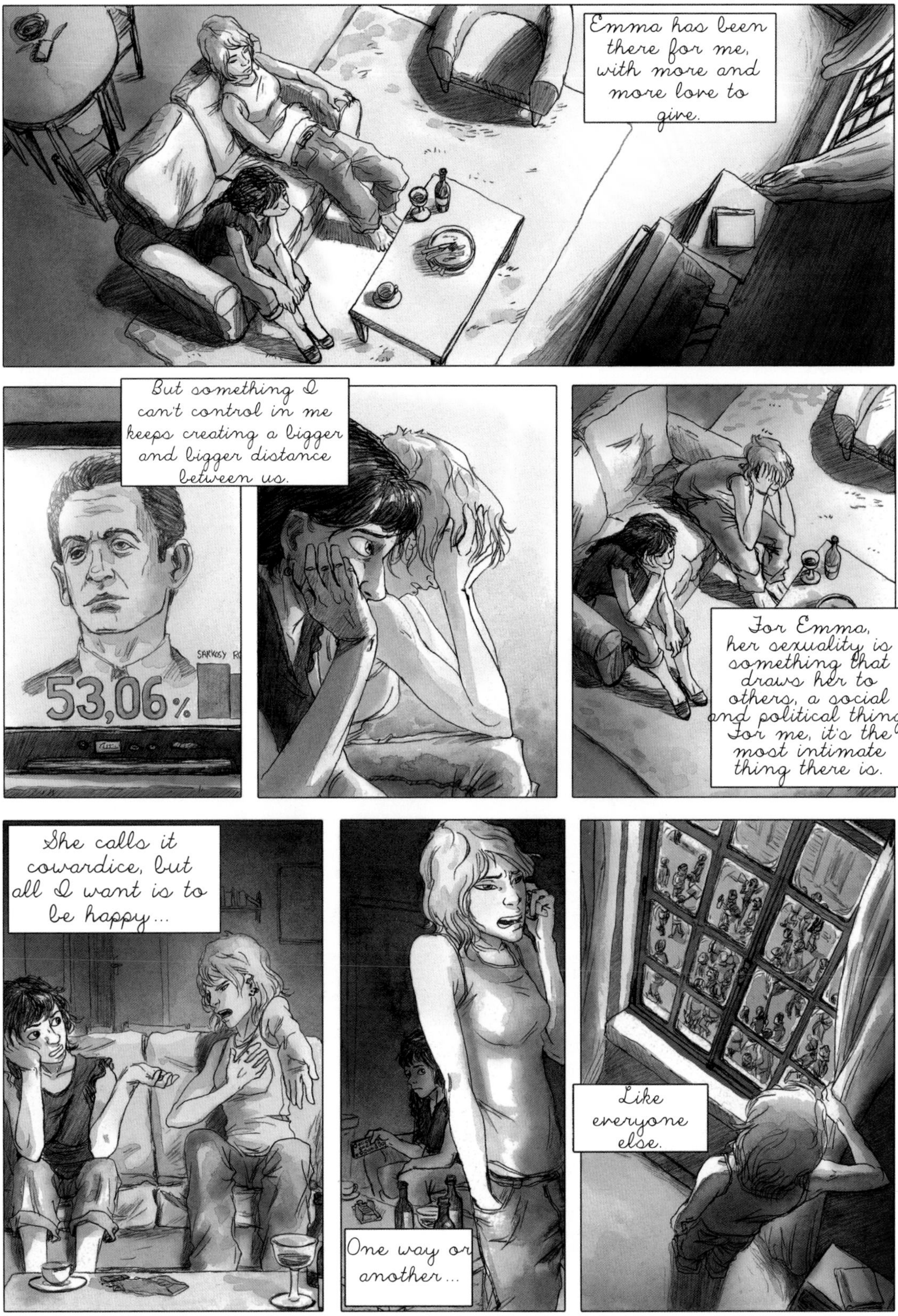
Emma has been there for me, with more and more love to give.
But something I can't control in me keeps creating a bigger and bigger distance between us.
SARKOSY
53,06%
For Emma, her sexuality is something that draws her to others, a social and political thing. For me, it's the most intimate thing there is.
She calls it cowardice, but all I want is to be happy...
One way or another...
Like everyone else.

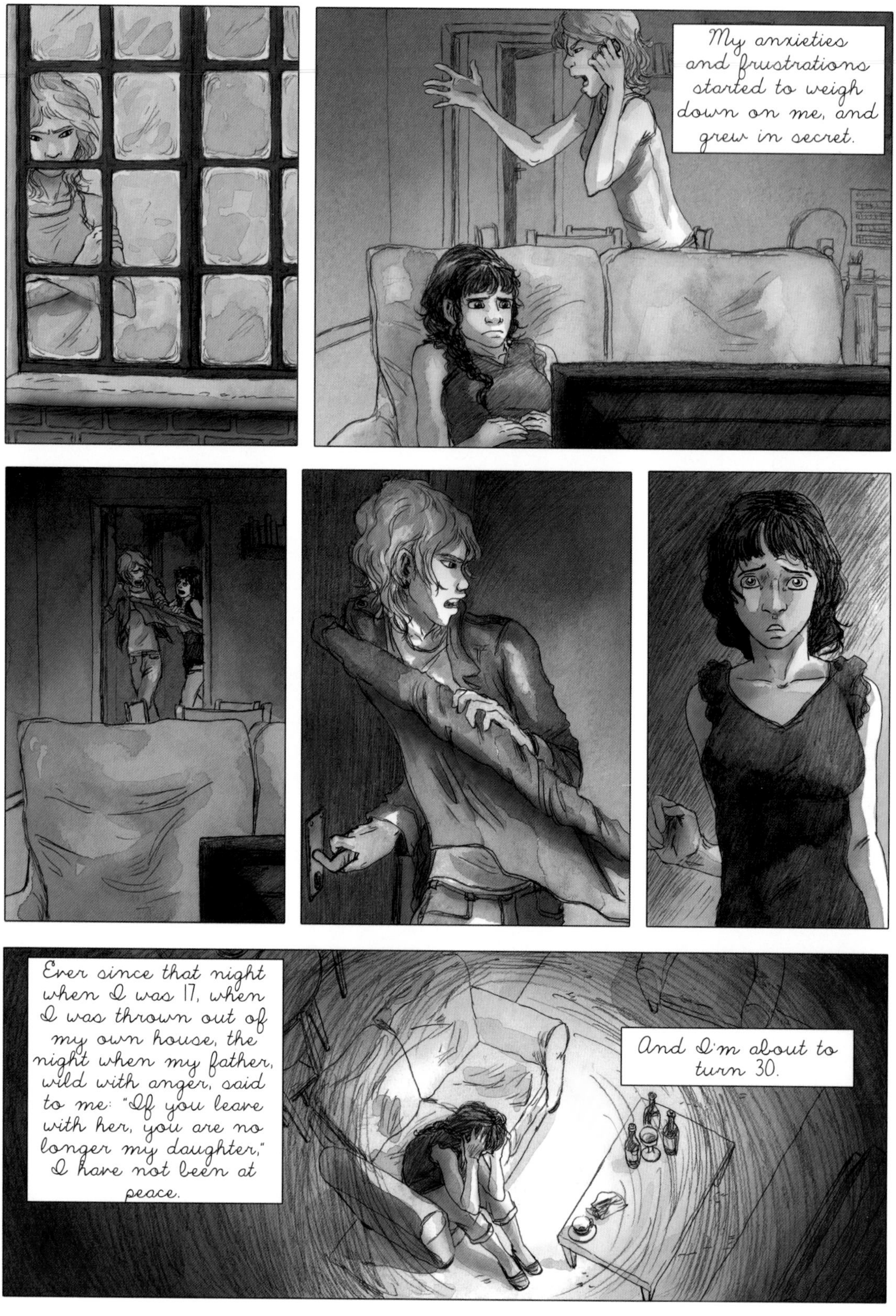
My anxieties and frustrations started to weigh down on me, and grew in secret.
Ever since that night when I was 17, when I was thrown out of my own house, the night when my father, wild with anger, said to me: "If you leave with her, you are no longer my daughter," I have not been at peace.
And I'm about to turn 30.

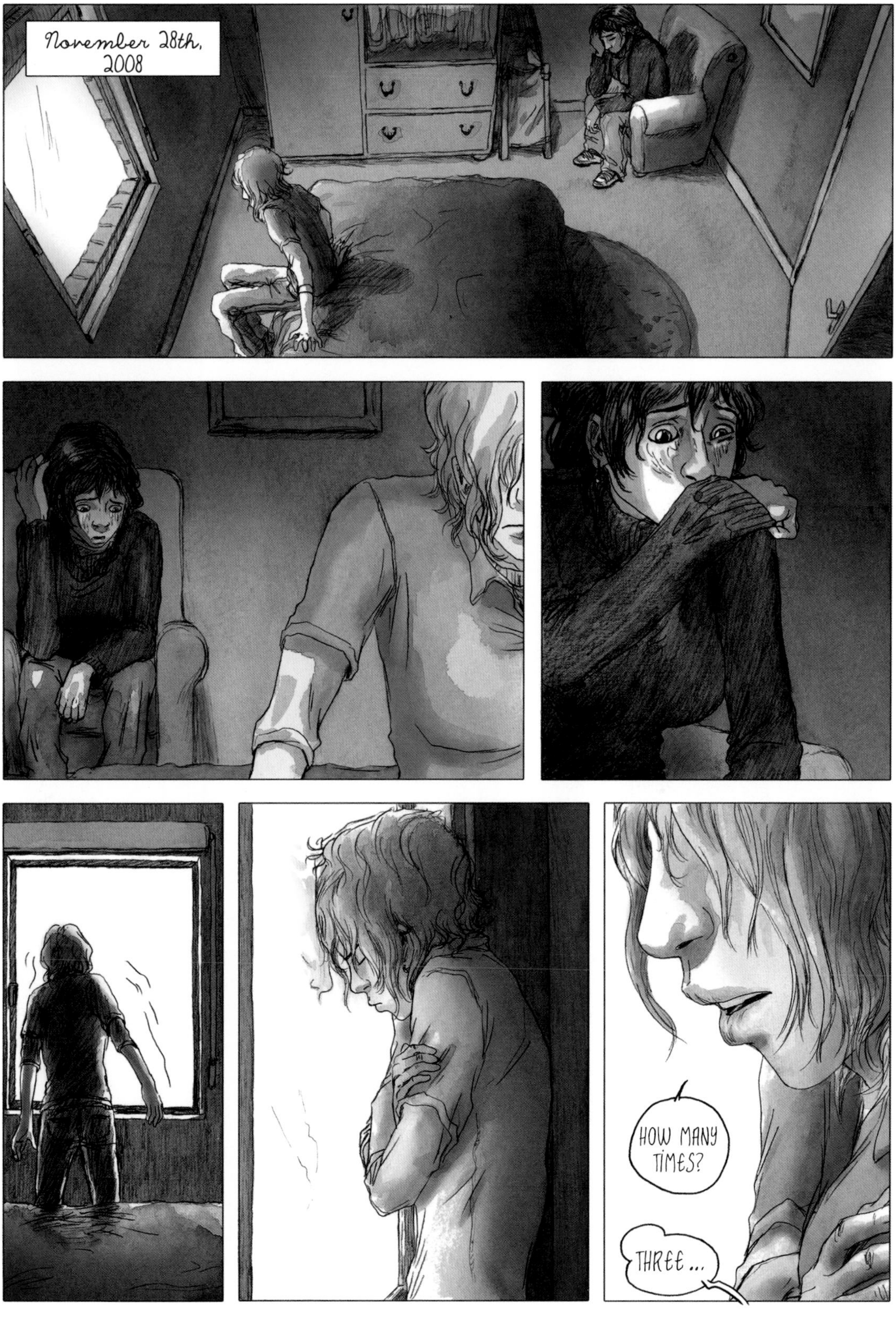
November 28th, 2008
HOW MANY TIMES?
THREE...

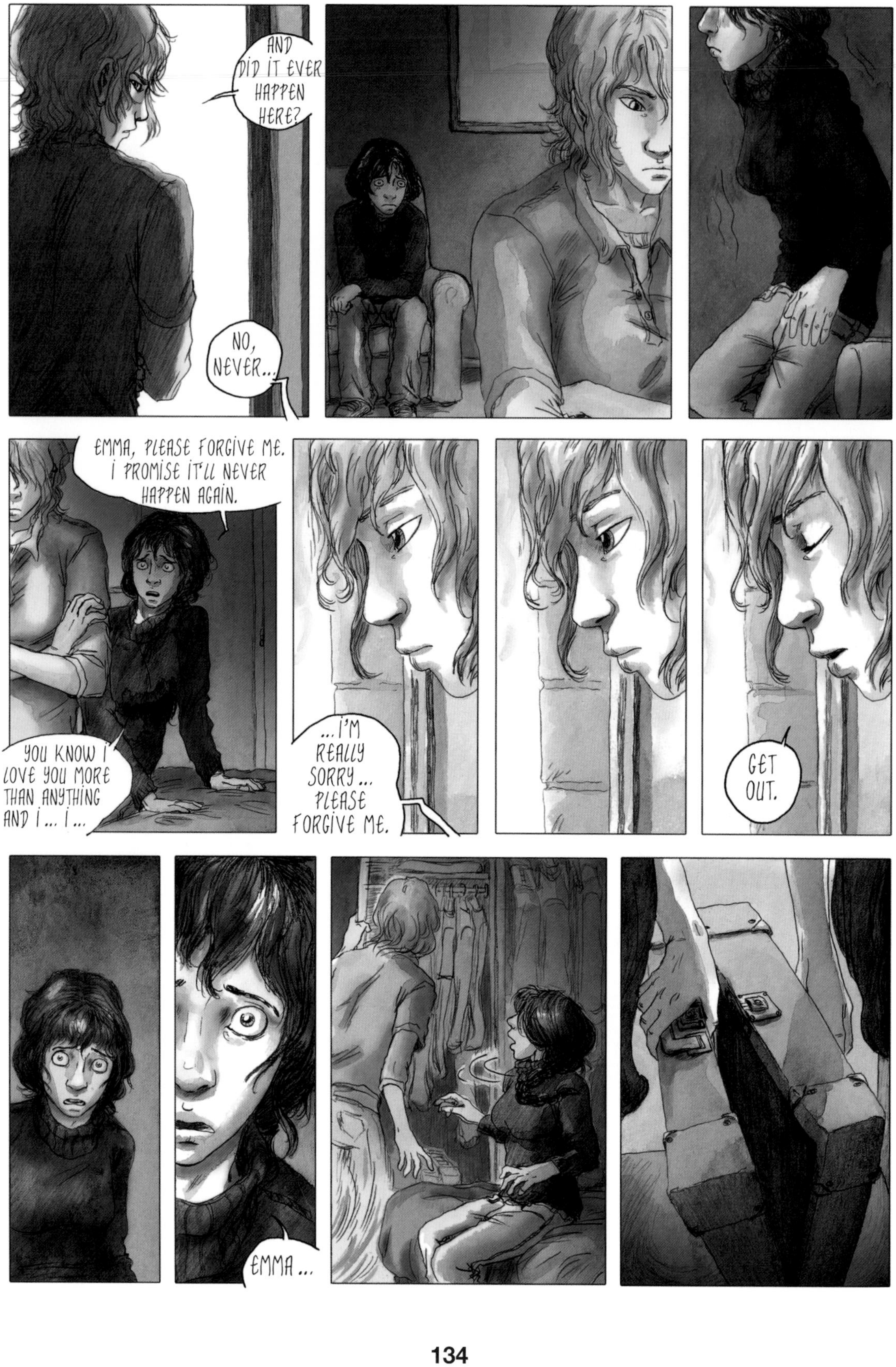
AND DID IT EVER HAPPEN HERE?
NO, NEVER...
EMMA, PLEASE FORGIVE ME. I PROMISE IT'LL NEVER HAPPEN AGAIN.
YOU KNOW I LOVE YOU MORE THAN ANYTHING AND I... I...
...I'M REALLY SORRY... PLEASE FORGIVE ME.
GET OUT.
EMMA...

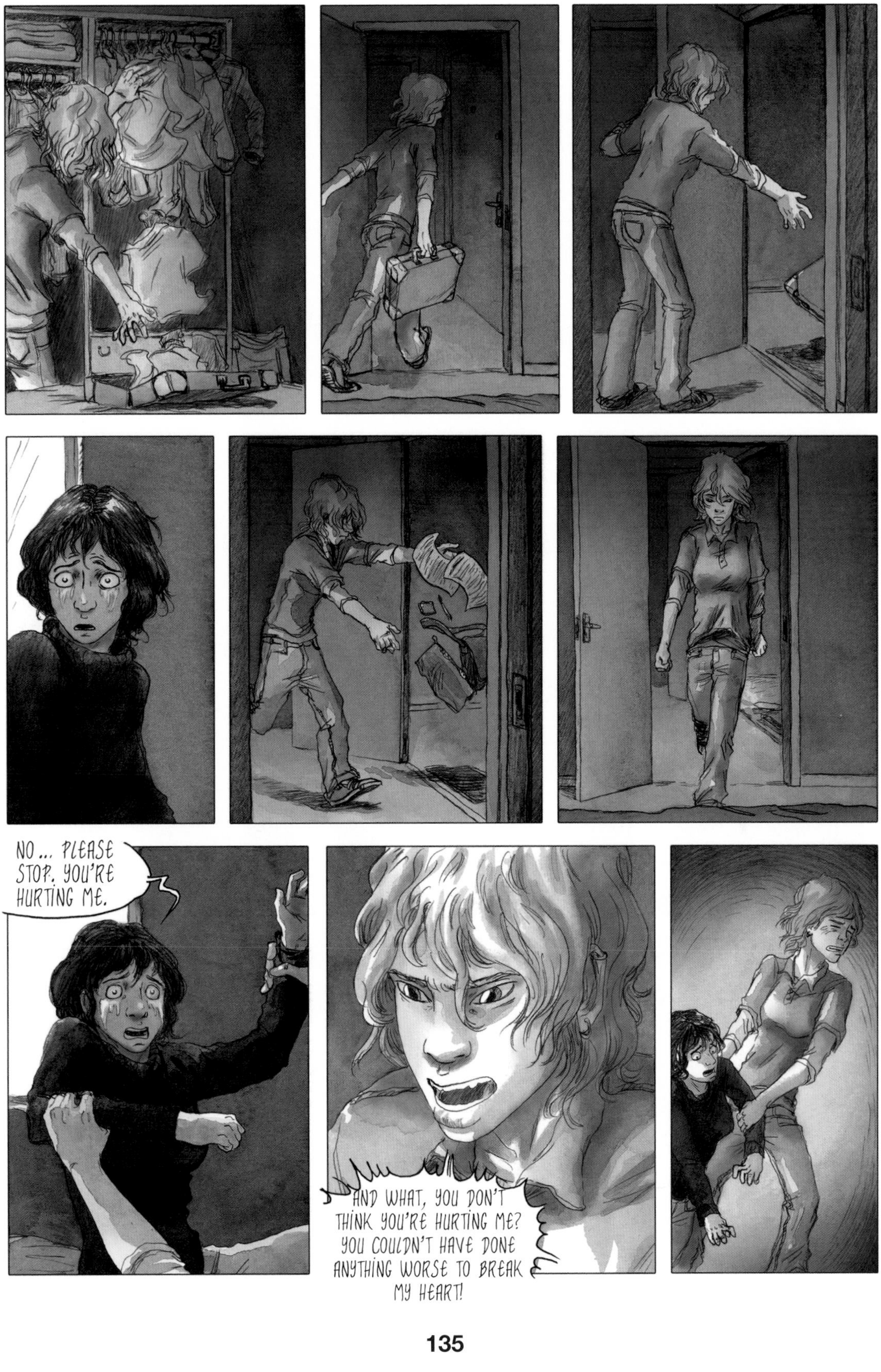
NO ... PLEASE STOP. YOU'RE HURTING ME.
AND WHAT, YOU DON'T THINK YOU'RE HURTING ME? YOU COULDN'T HAVE DONE ANYTHING WORSE TO BREAK MY HEART!

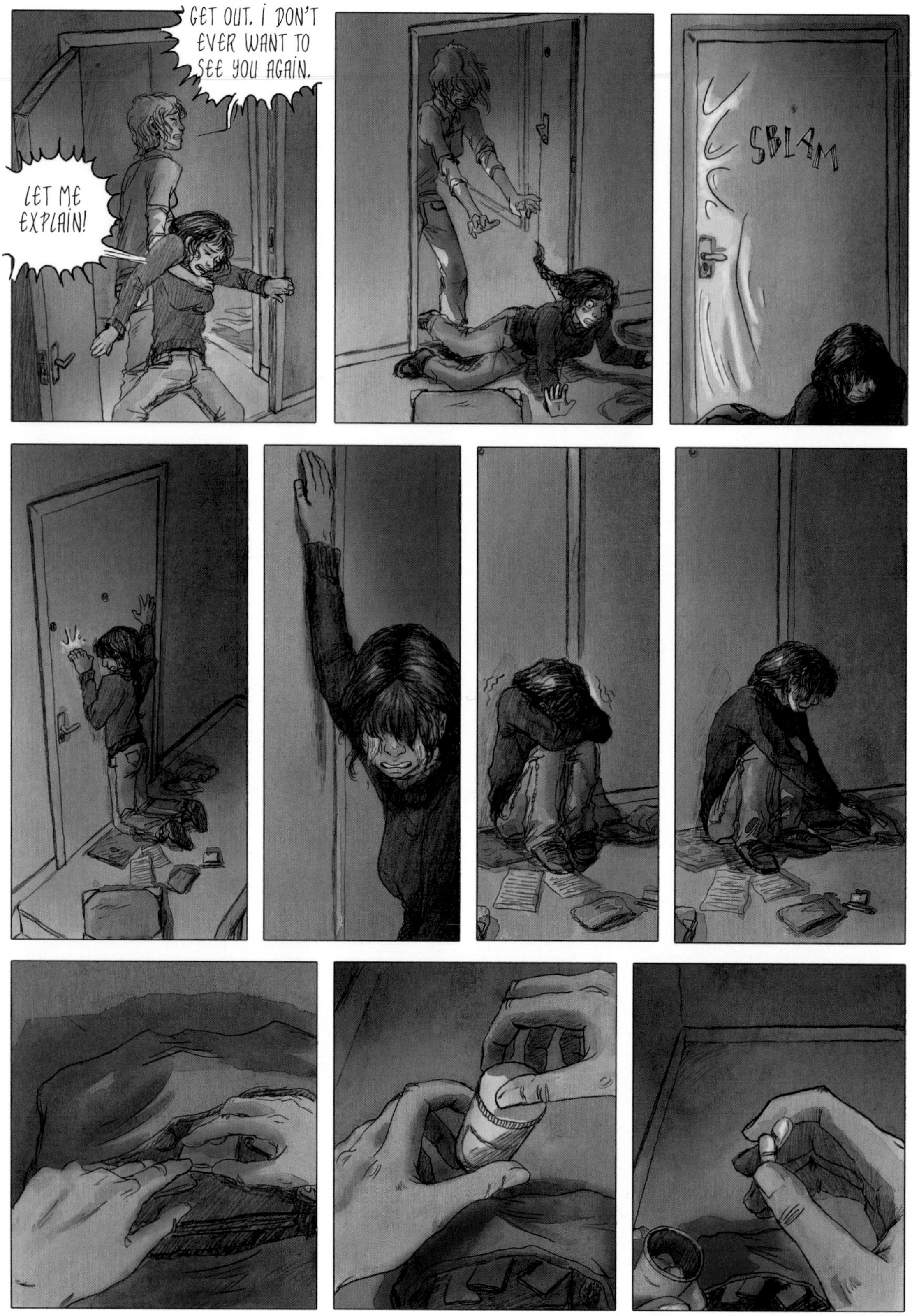
GET OUT. I DON'T EVER WANT TO SEE YOU AGAIN.
LET ME EXPLAIN!
SBLAM

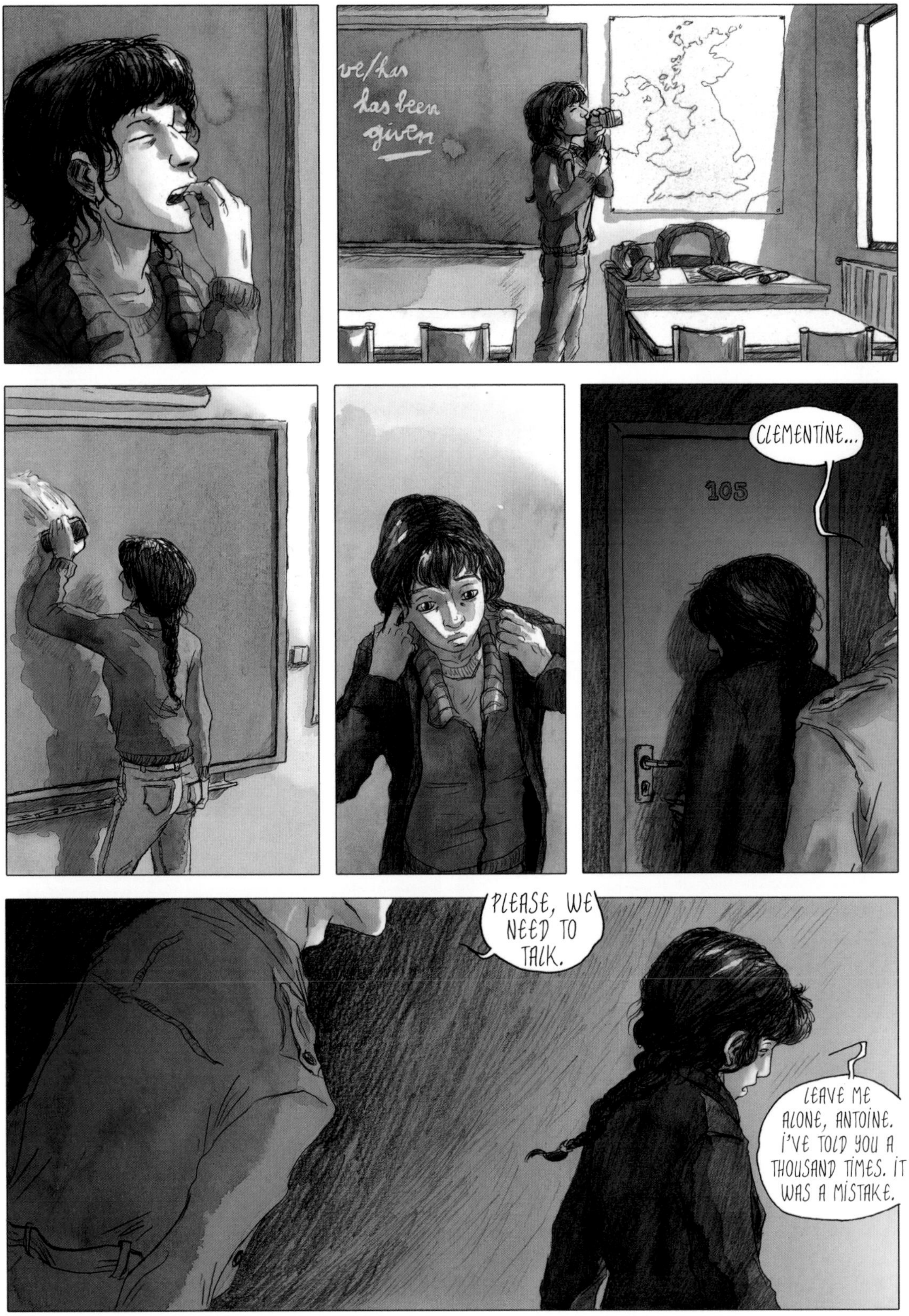
ve/has
has been
given
105
CLEMENTINE...
PLEASE, WE NEED TO TALK.
LEAVE ME ALONE, ANTOINE. I'VE TOLD YOU A THOUSAND TIMES. IT WAS A MISTAKE.

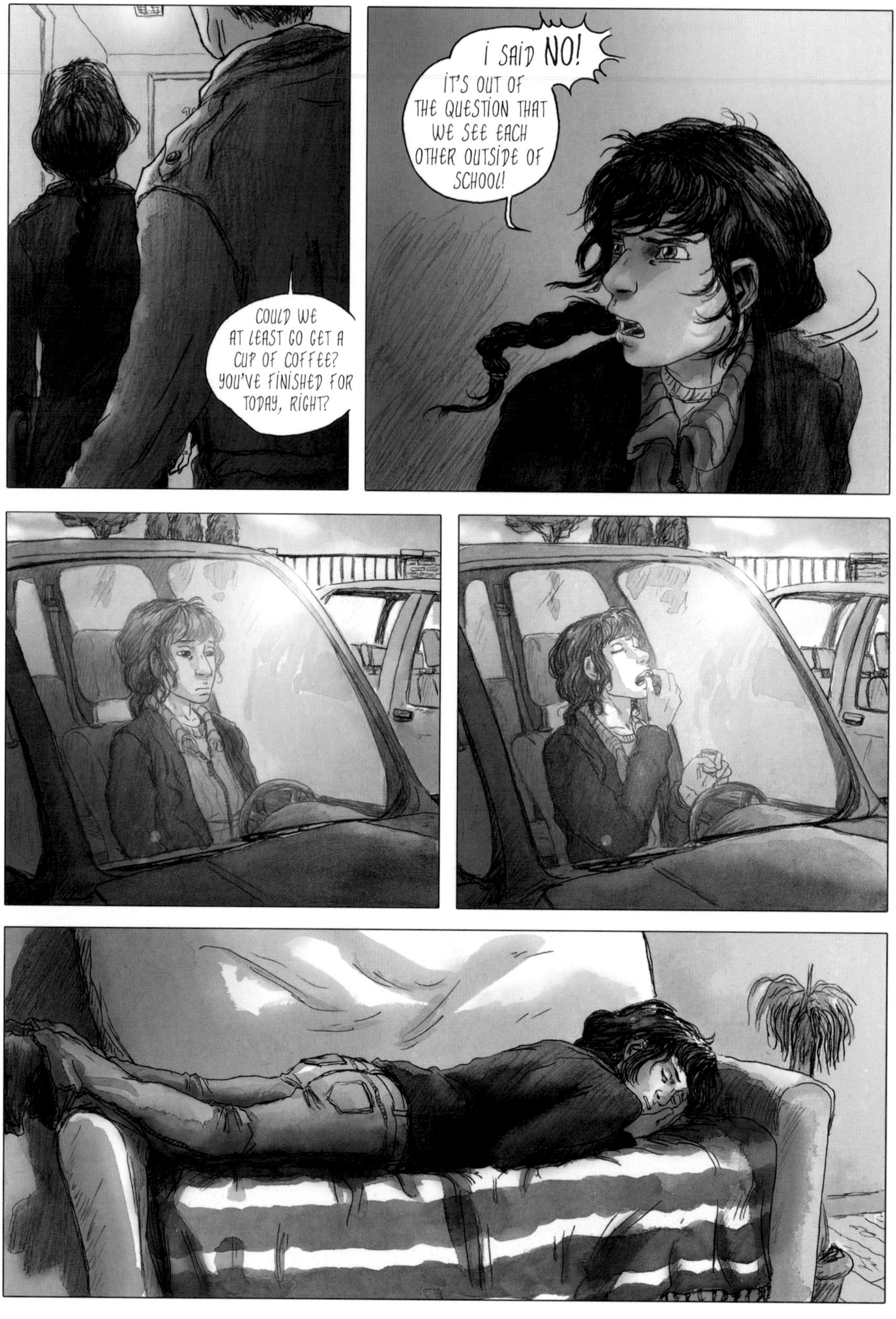
COULD WE AT LEAST GO GET A CUP OF COFFEE? YOU'VE FINISHED FOR TODAY, RIGHT?
I SAID NO!
IT'S OUT OF THE QUESTION THAT WE SEE EACH OTHER OUTSIDE OF SCHOOL!

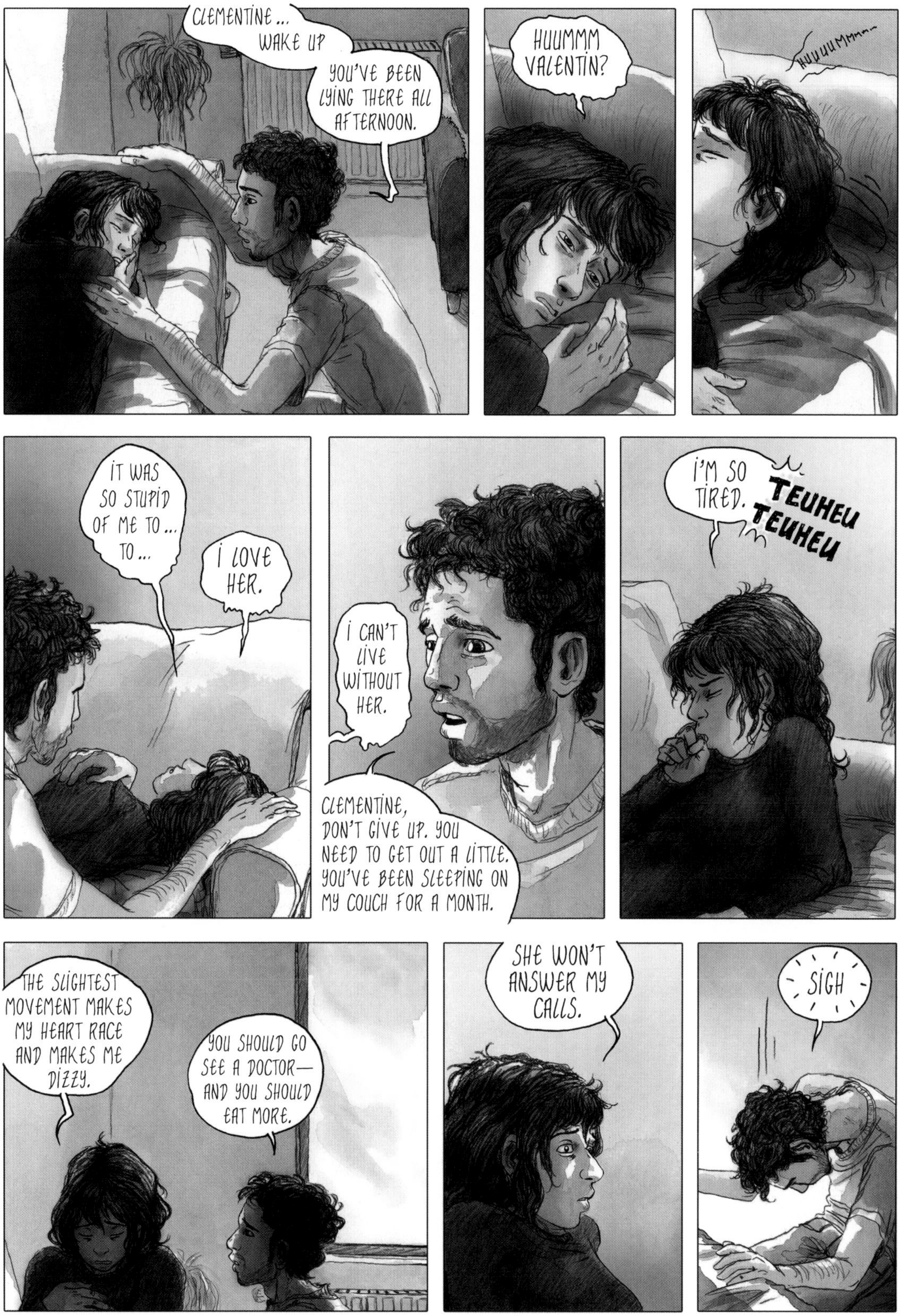

CLEMENTINE... WAKE UP
YOU'VE BEEN LYING THERE ALL AFTERNOON.
HUUMMM VALENTIN?
HUUUUMMMM
IT WAS SO STUPID OF ME TO... TO...
I LOVE HER.
I CAN'T LIVE WITHOUT HER.
CLEMENTINE, DON'T GIVE UP. YOU NEED TO GET OUT A LITTLE. YOU'VE BEEN SLEEPING ON MY COUCH FOR A MONTH.
I'M SO TIRED.
TEUHEU TEUHEU
THE SLIGHTEST MOVEMENT MAKES MY HEART RACE AND MAKES ME DIZZY.
YOU SHOULD GO SEE A DOCTOR— AND YOU SHOULD EAT MORE.
SHE WON'T ANSWER MY CALLS.
SIGH

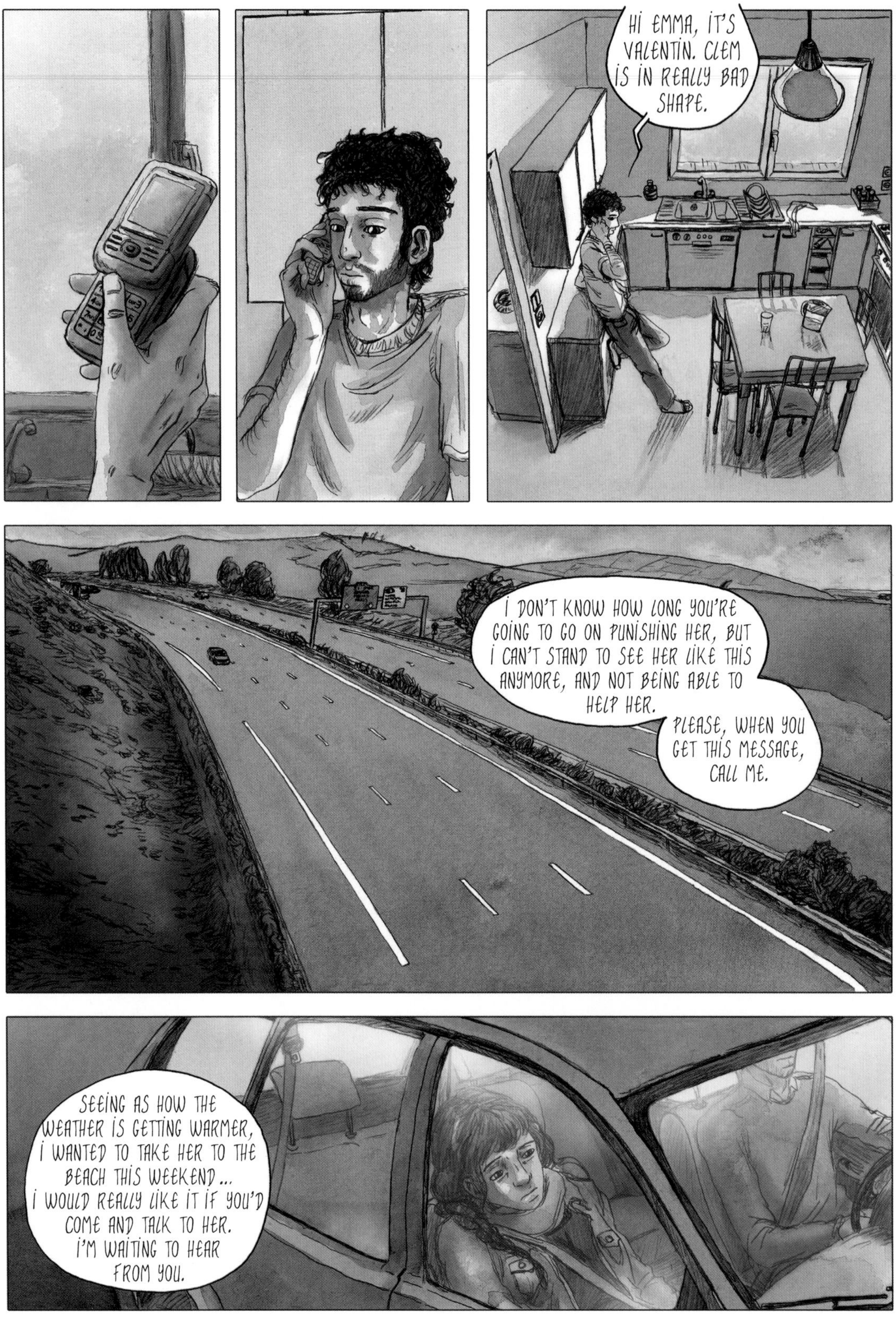
HI EMMA, IT'S VALENTIN. CLEM IS IN REALLY BAD SHAPE.
I DON'T KNOW HOW LONG YOU'RE GOING TO GO ON PUNISHING HER, BUT I CAN'T STAND TO SEE HER LIKE THIS ANYMORE, AND NOT BEING ABLE TO HELP HER.
PLEASE, WHEN YOU GET THIS MESSAGE, CALL ME.
SEEING AS HOW THE WEATHER IS GETTING WARMER, I WANTED TO TAKE HER TO THE BEACH THIS WEEKEND... I WOULD REALLY LIKE IT IF YOU'D COME AND TALK TO HER. I'M WAITING TO HEAR FROM YOU.

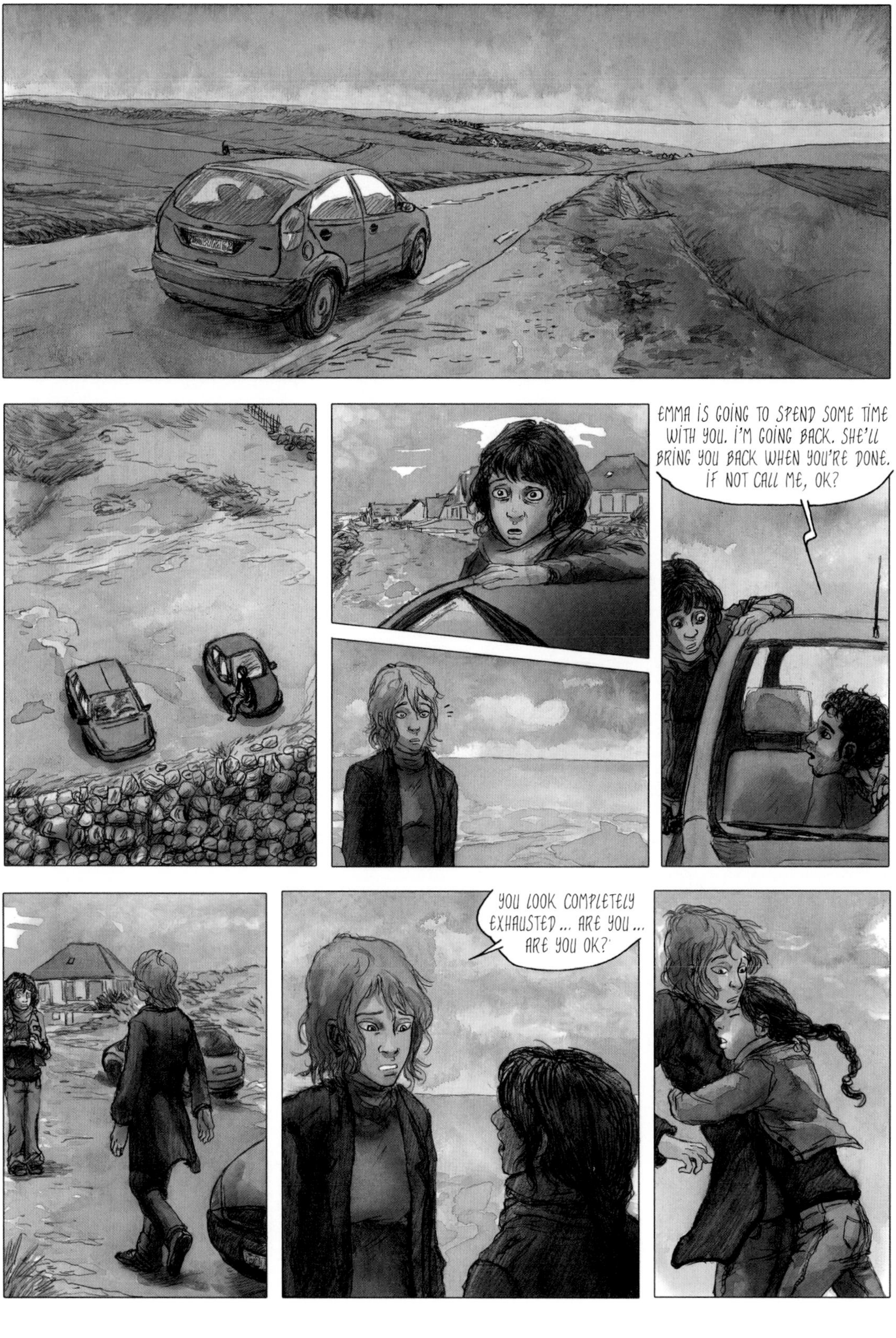
EMMA IS GOING TO SPEND SOME TIME WITH YOU. I'M GOING BACK. SHE'LL BRING YOU BACK WHEN YOU'RE DONE. IF NOT CALL ME, OK?
YOU LOOK COMPLETELY EXHAUSTED ... ARE YOU ... ARE YOU OK?

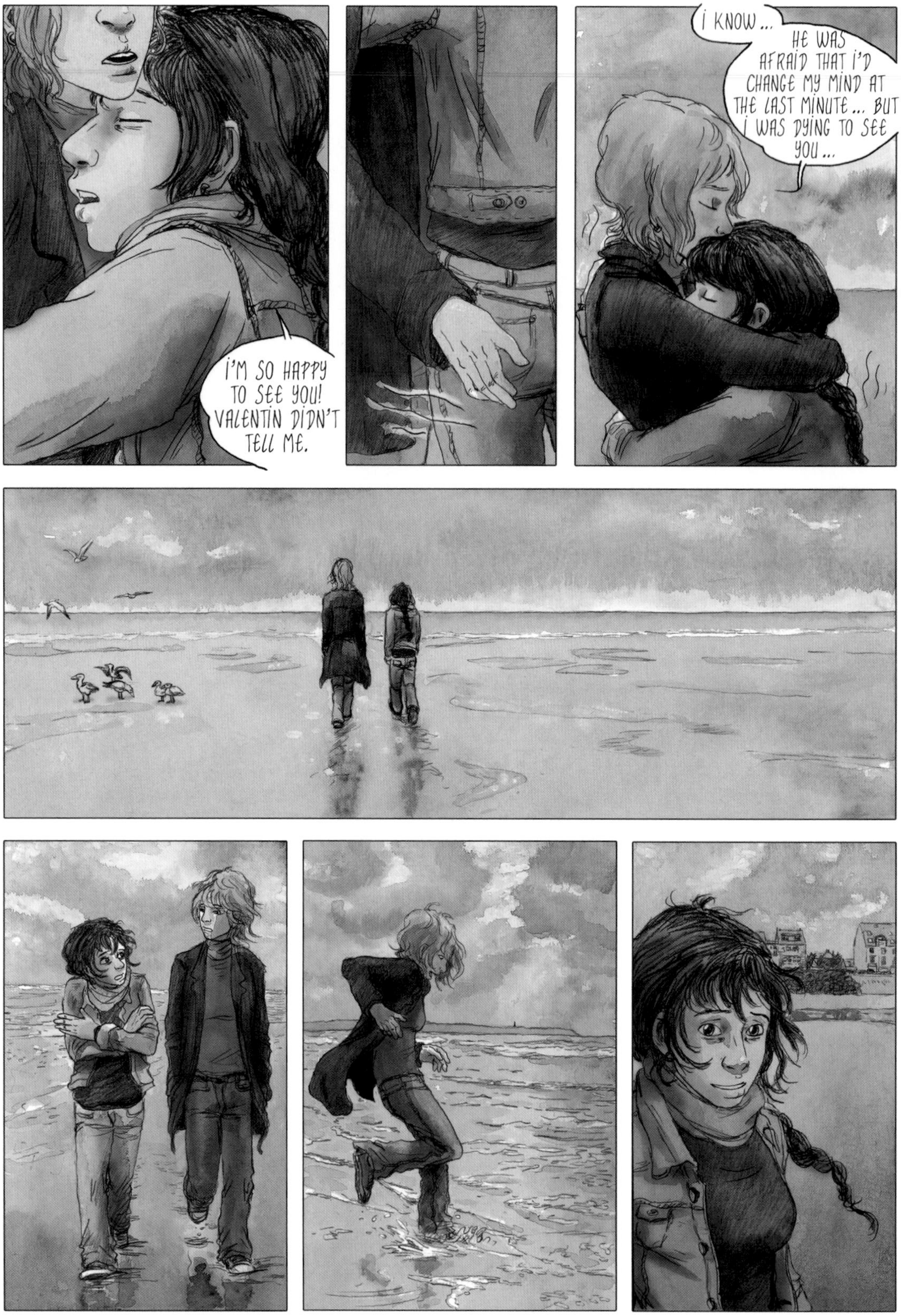
I'M SO HAPPY TO SEE YOU! VALENTIN DIDN'T TELL ME.
I KNOW...
HE WAS AFRAID THAT I'D CHANGE MY MIND AT THE LAST MINUTE... BUT I WAS DYING TO SEE YOU...

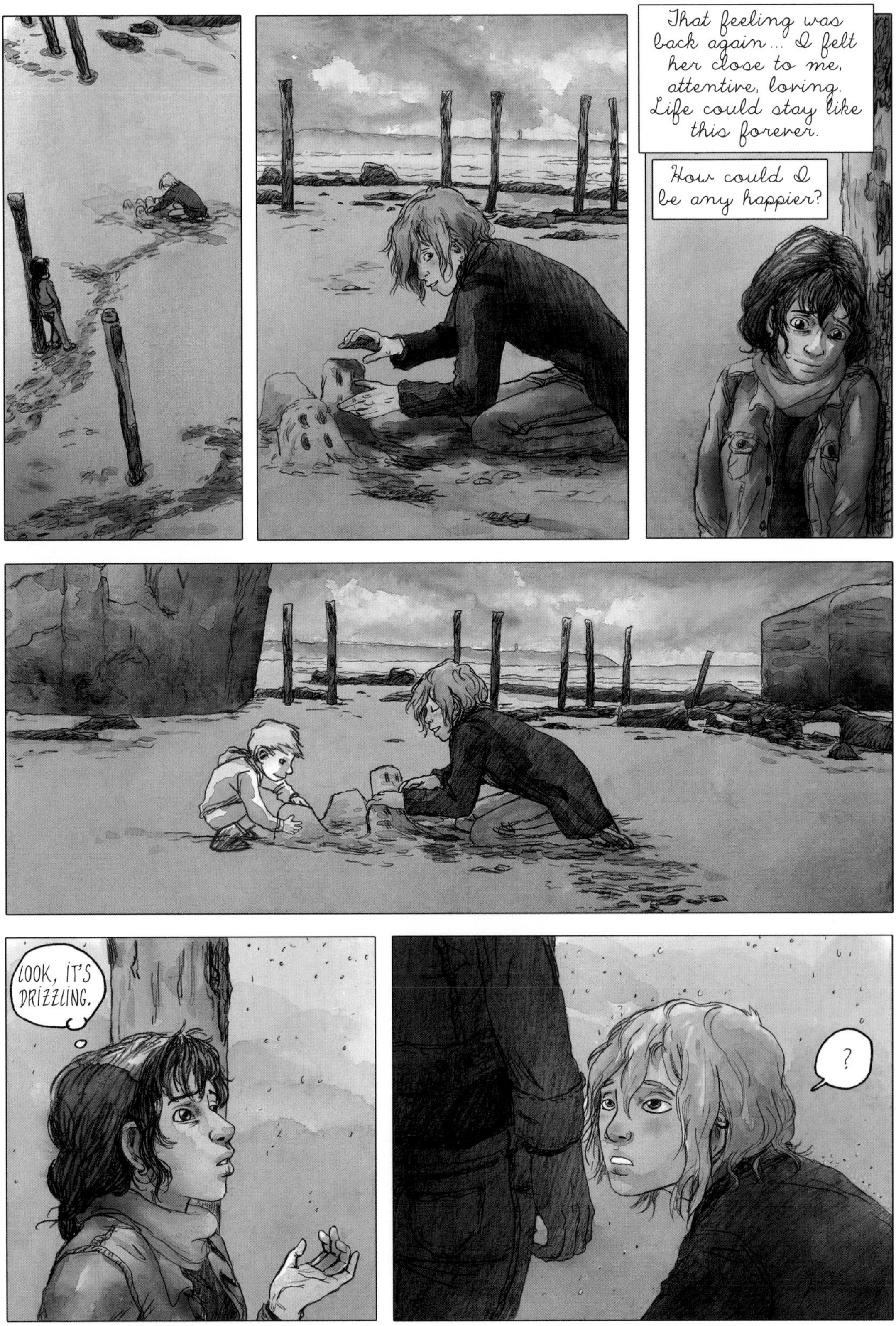
That feeling was back again... I felt her close to me, attentive, loving. Life could stay like this forever.
How could I be any happier?
LOOK, IT'S DRIZZLING.
?

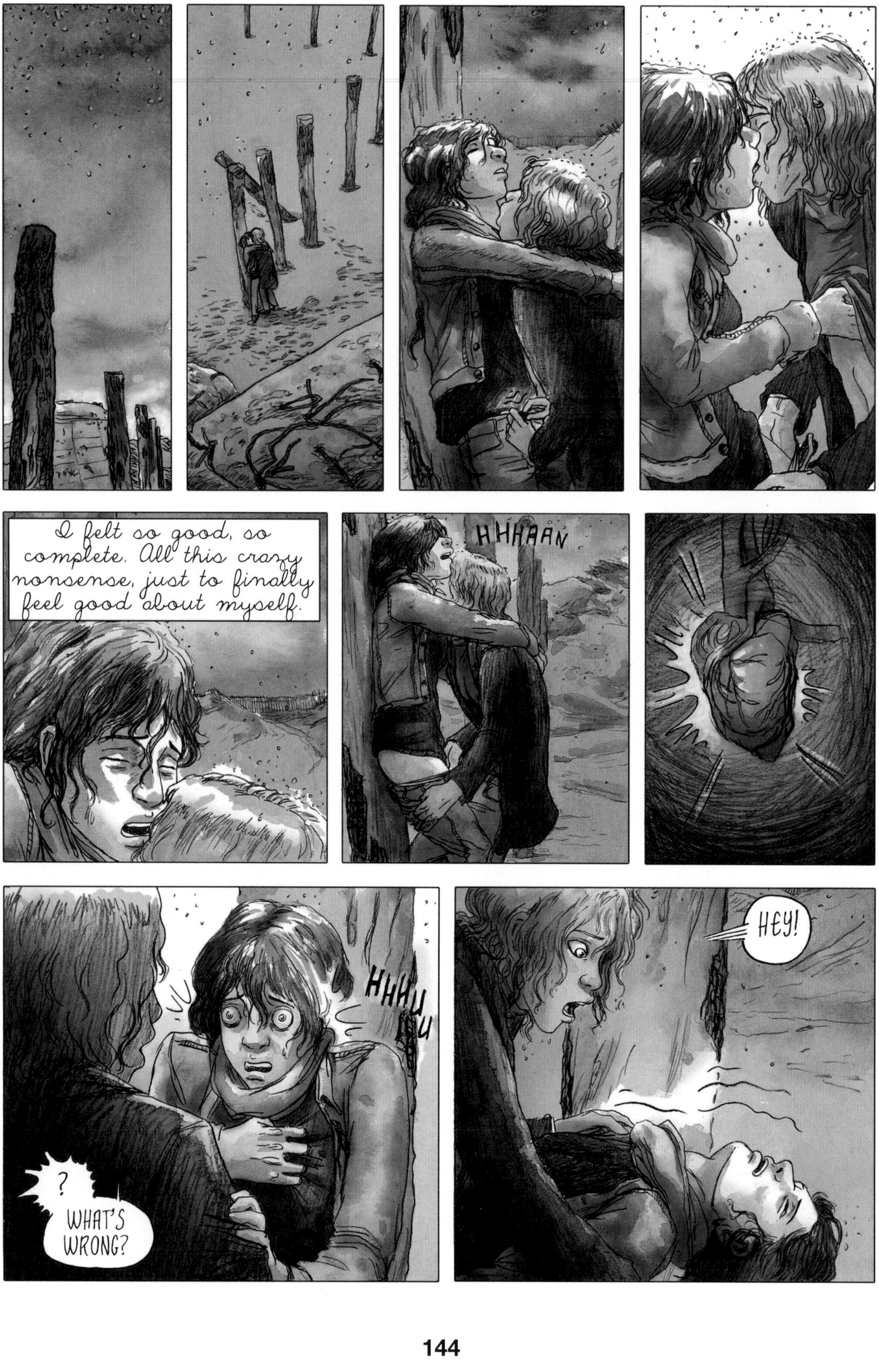
I felt so good, so complete. All this crazy nonsense, just to finally feel good about myself.
HHHAAN
HHHUU
?
WHAT'S WRONG?
HEY!

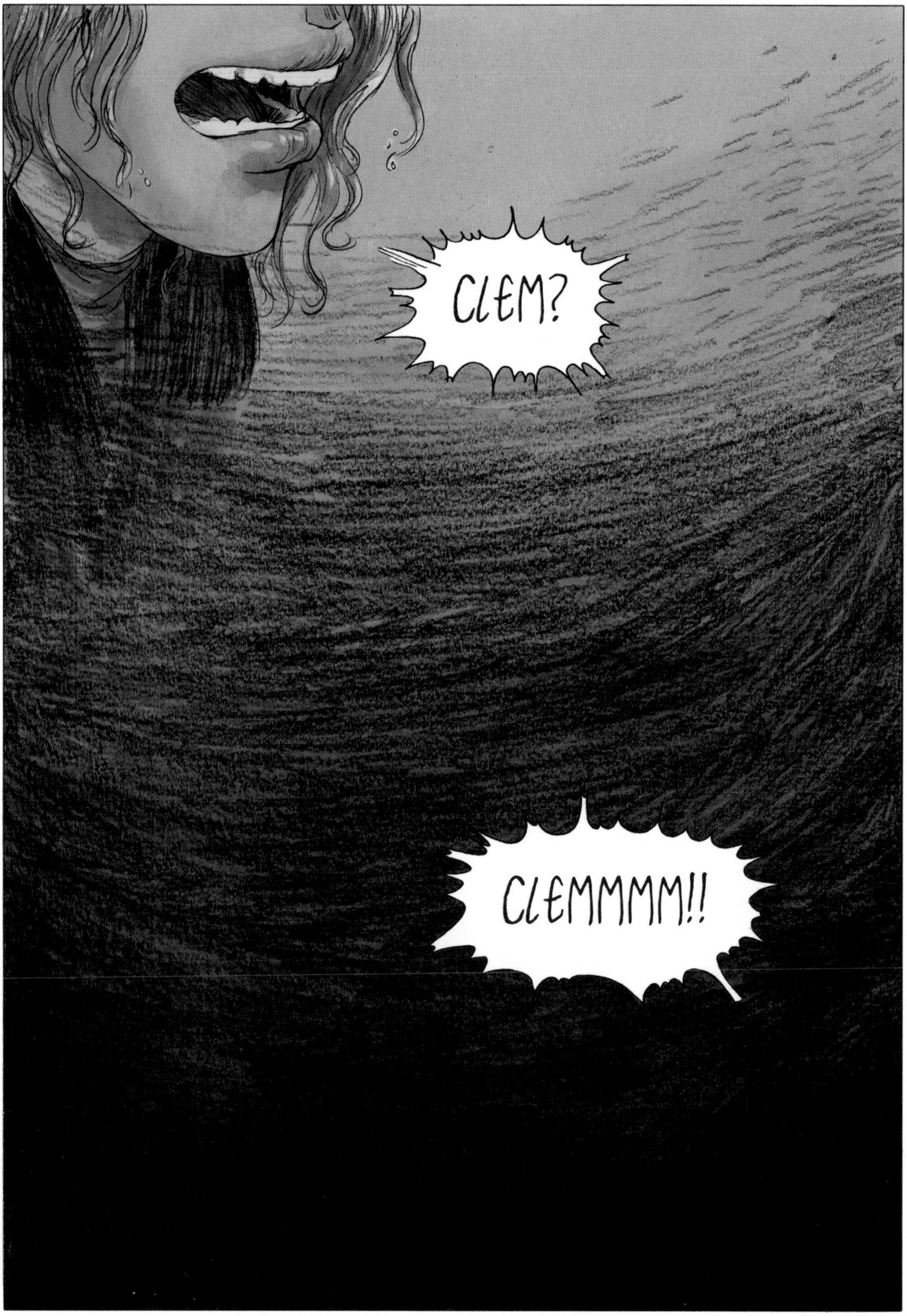
CLEM?
CLEMMMM!!

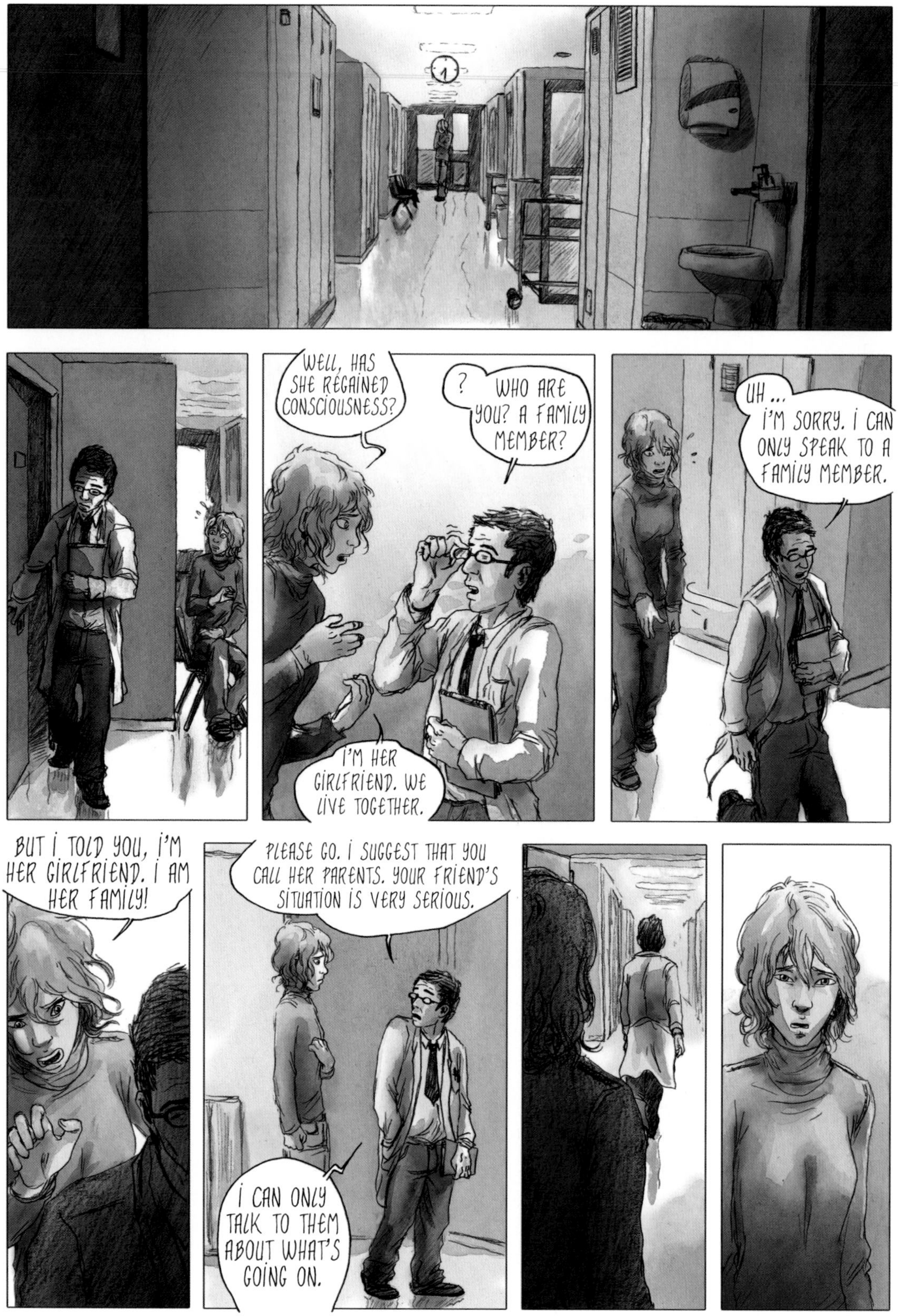
WELL, HAS SHE REGAINED CONSCIOUSNESS?
?
WHO ARE YOU? A FAMILY MEMBER?
I'M HER GIRLFRIEND. WE LIVE TOGETHER.
UH ...
I'M SORRY. I CAN ONLY SPEAK TO A FAMILY MEMBER.
BUT I TOLD YOU, I'M HER GIRLFRIEND. I AM HER FAMILY!
PLEASE GO. I SUGGEST THAT YOU CALL HER PARENTS. YOUR FRIEND'S SITUATION IS VERY SERIOUS.
I CAN ONLY TALK TO THEM ABOUT WHAT'S GOING ON.

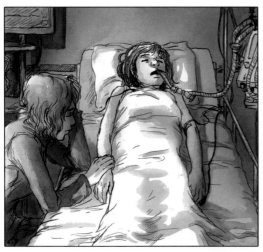

TOC
TOC

...HELLO, FABIENNE.

HELLO.

DANIEL DIDN'T COME WITH YOU?

UH... NO. HE WASN'T READY.

HELLO, DOCTOR, I'M CLEMENTINE'S MOTHER.

HELLO, MA'AM...

I'M REALLY SORRY, BUT I HAVE SOME VERY BAD NEWS.

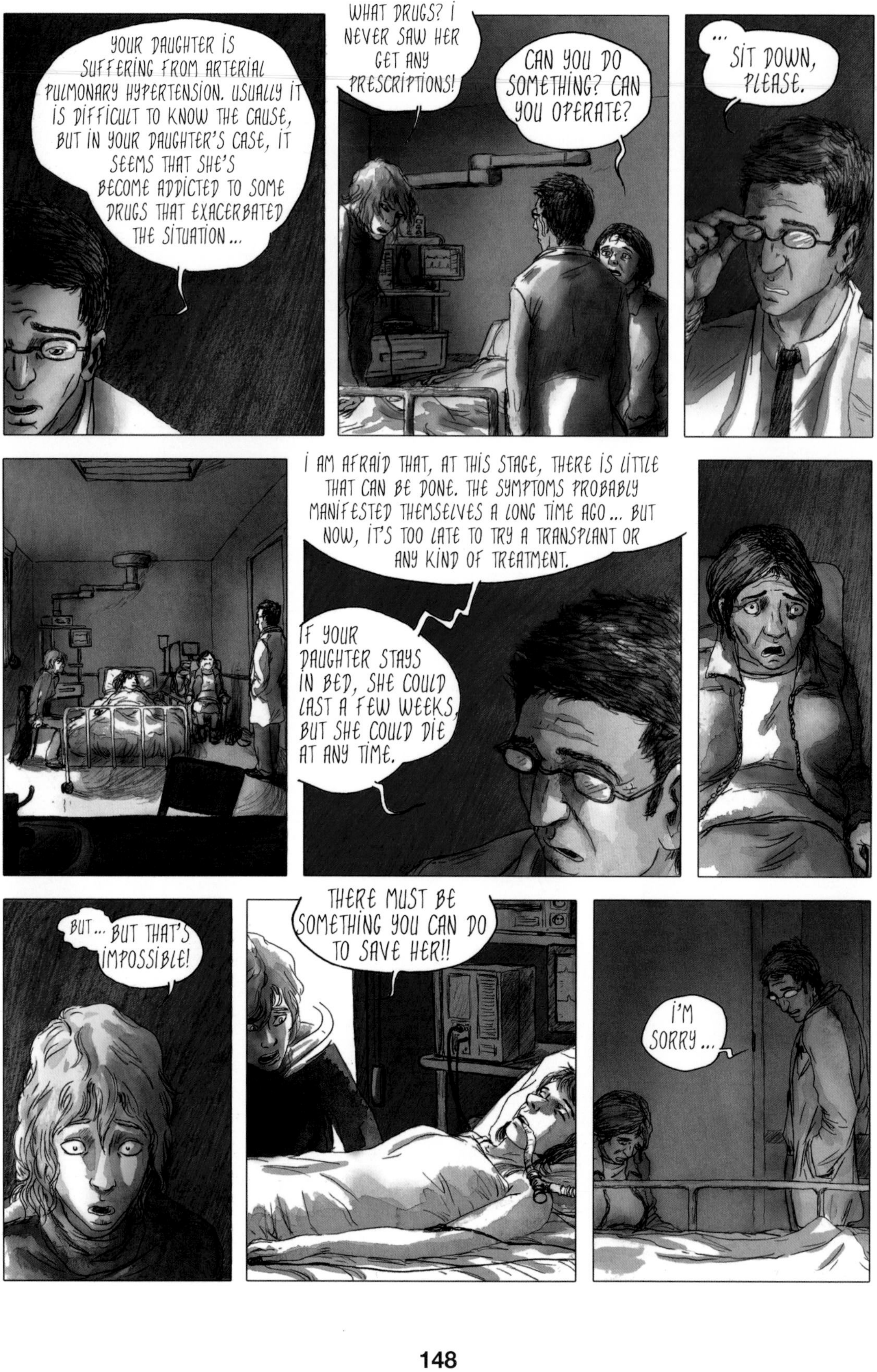
YOUR DAUGHTER IS SUFFERING FROM ARTERIAL PULMONARY HYPERTENSION. USUALLY IT IS DIFFICULT TO KNOW THE CAUSE, BUT IN YOUR DAUGHTER'S CASE, IT SEEMS THAT SHE'S BECOME ADDICTED TO SOME DRUGS THAT EXACERBATED THE SITUATION...
WHAT DRUGS? I NEVER SAW HER GET ANY PRESCRIPTIONS!
CAN YOU DO SOMETHING? CAN YOU OPERATE?
... SIT DOWN, PLEASE.
I AM AFRAID THAT, AT THIS STAGE, THERE IS LITTLE THAT CAN BE DONE. THE SYMPTOMS PROBABLY MANIFESTED THEMSELVES A LONG TIME AGO... BUT NOW, IT'S TOO LATE TO TRY A TRANSPLANT OR ANY KIND OF TREATMENT.
IF YOUR DAUGHTER STAYS IN BED, SHE COULD LAST A FEW WEEKS, BUT SHE COULD DIE AT ANY TIME.
BUT... BUT THAT'S IMPOSSIBLE!
THERE MUST BE SOMETHING YOU CAN DO TO SAVE HER!!
I'M SORRY...

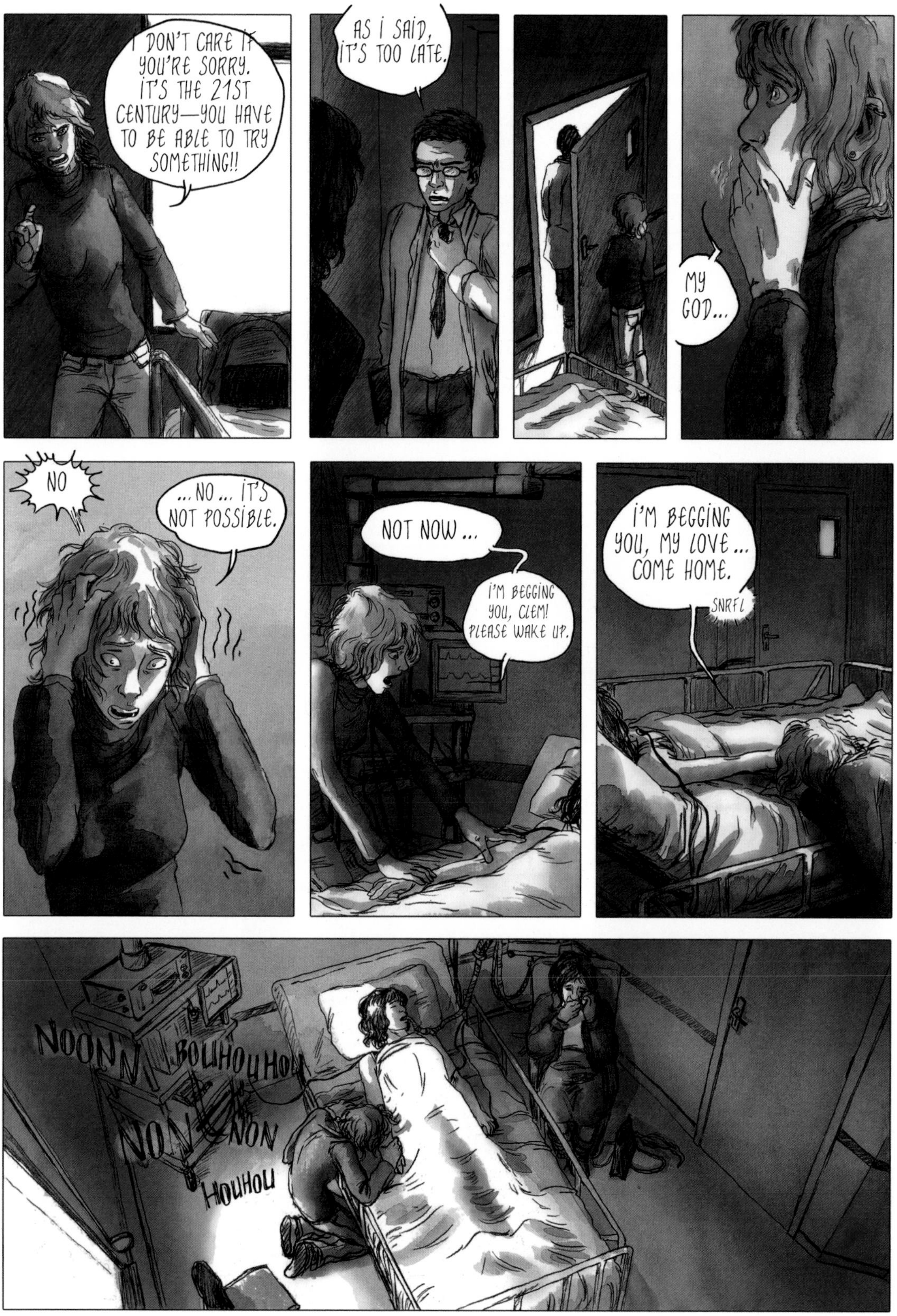
I DON'T CARE IF YOU'RE SORRY. IT'S THE 21ST CENTURY—YOU HAVE TO BE ABLE TO TRY SOMETHING!!
AS I SAID, IT'S TOO LATE.
MY GOD...
NO
...NO ... IT'S NOT POSSIBLE.
NOT NOW ...
I'M BEGGING YOU, CLEM! PLEASE WAKE UP.
I'M BEGGING YOU, MY LOVE ... COME HOME.
SNRFL
NOONN
BOUHOUHOU
NON
NON
HOUHOU

OH, YOU'RE HERE, FABIENNE ...HELLO.

HELLO, EMMA.

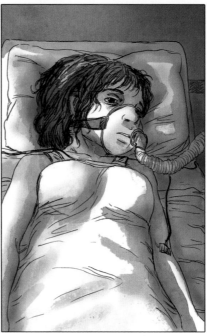

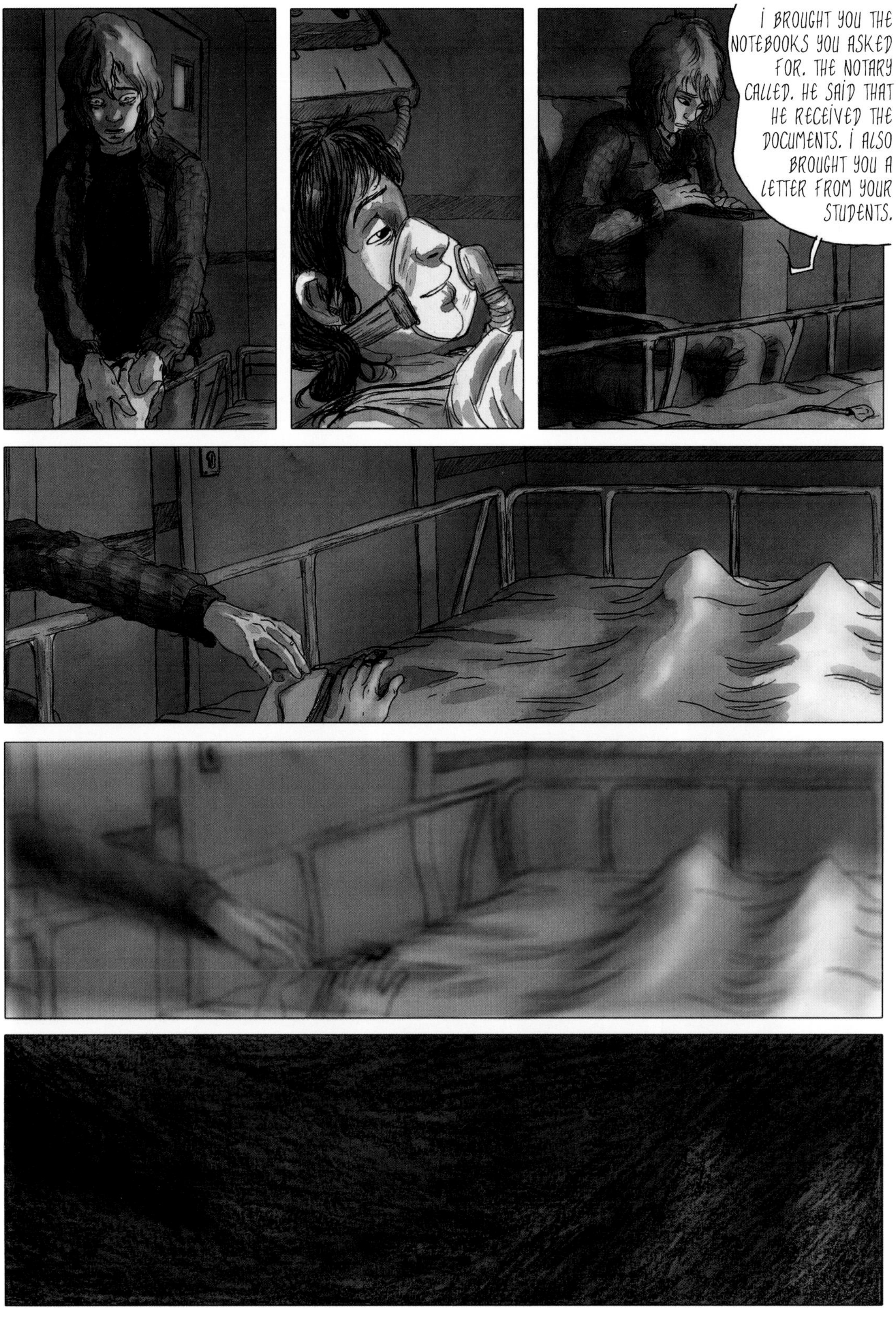
I BROUGHT YOU THE NOTEBOOKS YOU ASKED FOR. THE NOTARY CALLED. HE SAID THAT HE RECEIVED THE DOCUMENTS. I ALSO BROUGHT YOU A LETTER FROM YOUR STUDENTS.

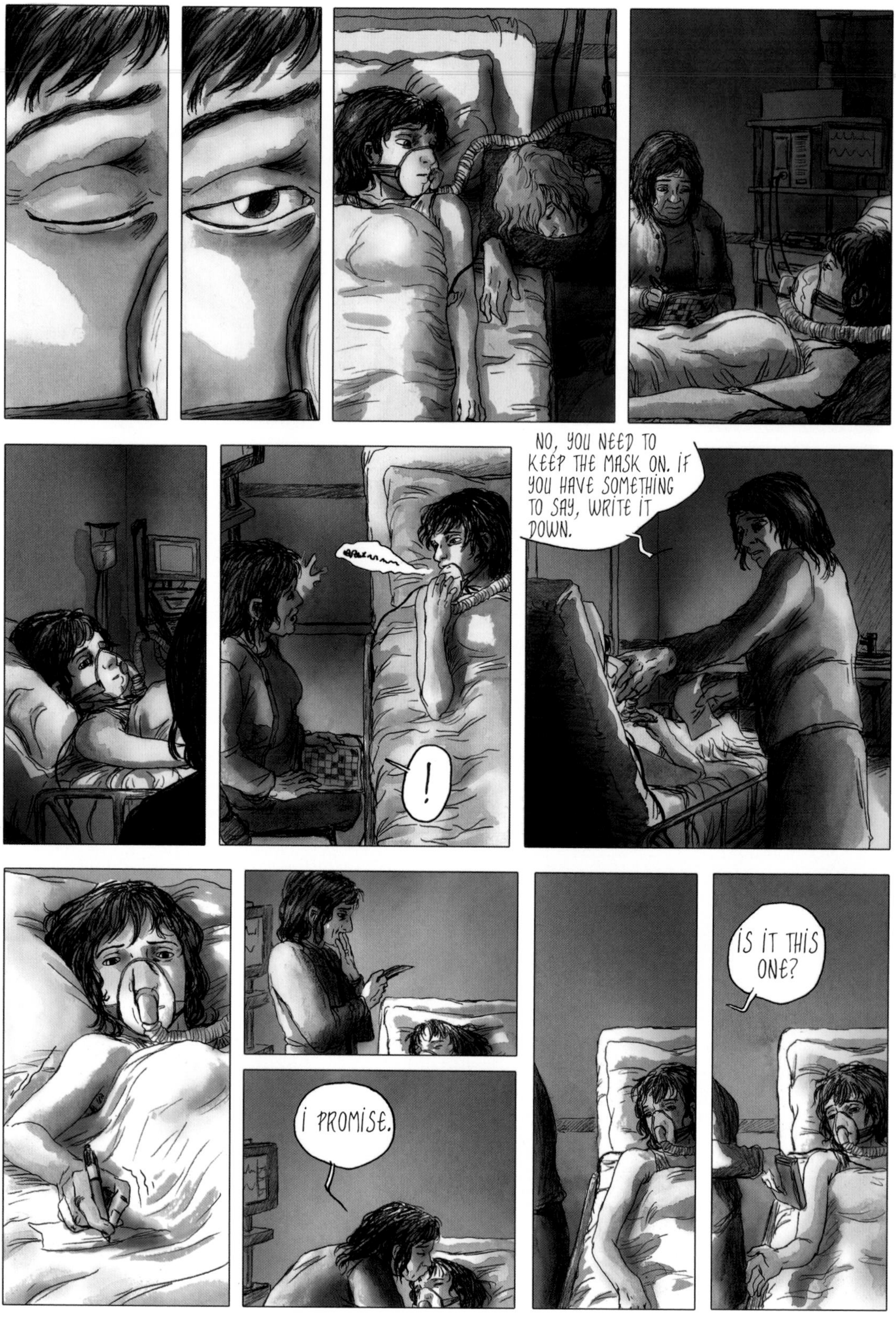
NO, YOU NEED TO KEEP THE MASK ON. IF YOU HAVE SOMETHING TO SAY, WRITE IT DOWN.
!
IS IT THIS ONE?
I PROMISE.

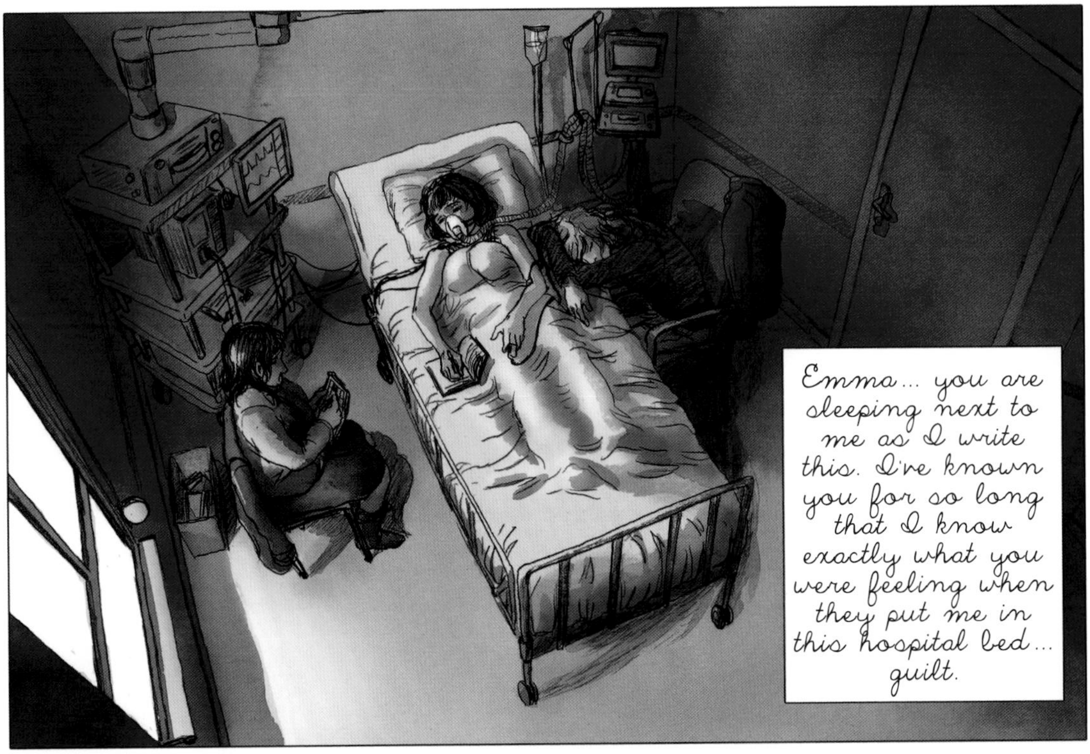
Emma... you are sleeping next to me as I write this. I've known you for so long that I know exactly what you were feeling when they put me in this hospital bed... guilt.

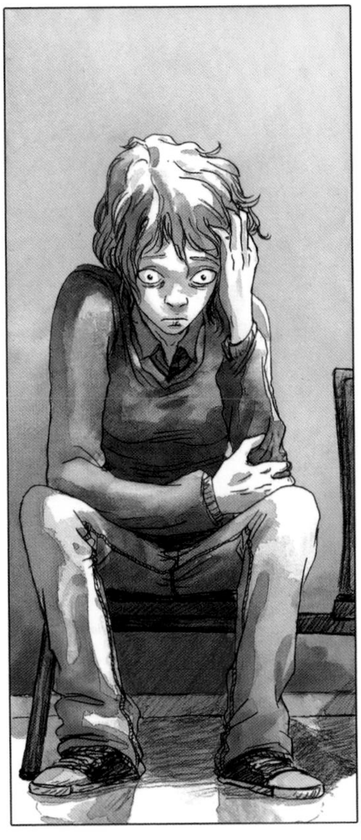

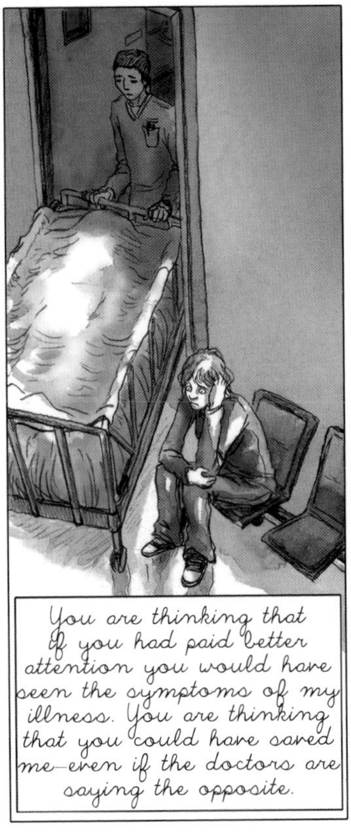
You are thinking that if you had paid better attention you would have seen the symptoms of my illness. You are thinking that you could have saved me—even if the doctors are saying the opposite.

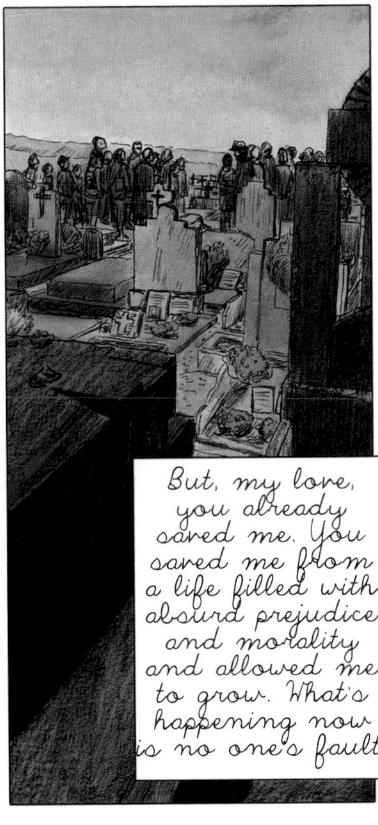
But, my love, you already saved me. You saved me from a life filled with absurd prejudice and morality and allowed me to grow. What's happening now is no one's fault.

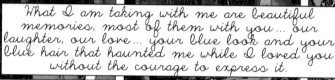

What I am taking with me are beautiful memories, most of them with you... our laughter, our love... your blue look and your blue hair that haunted me while I loved you without the courage to express it.

So, now that I am leaving, and you are staying, please live your precious life, what's left of it, to the fullest and be—as I am today, lying in this bed—without any regrets and at peace with yourself.

The life you gave me could never have been anything but happy.

154

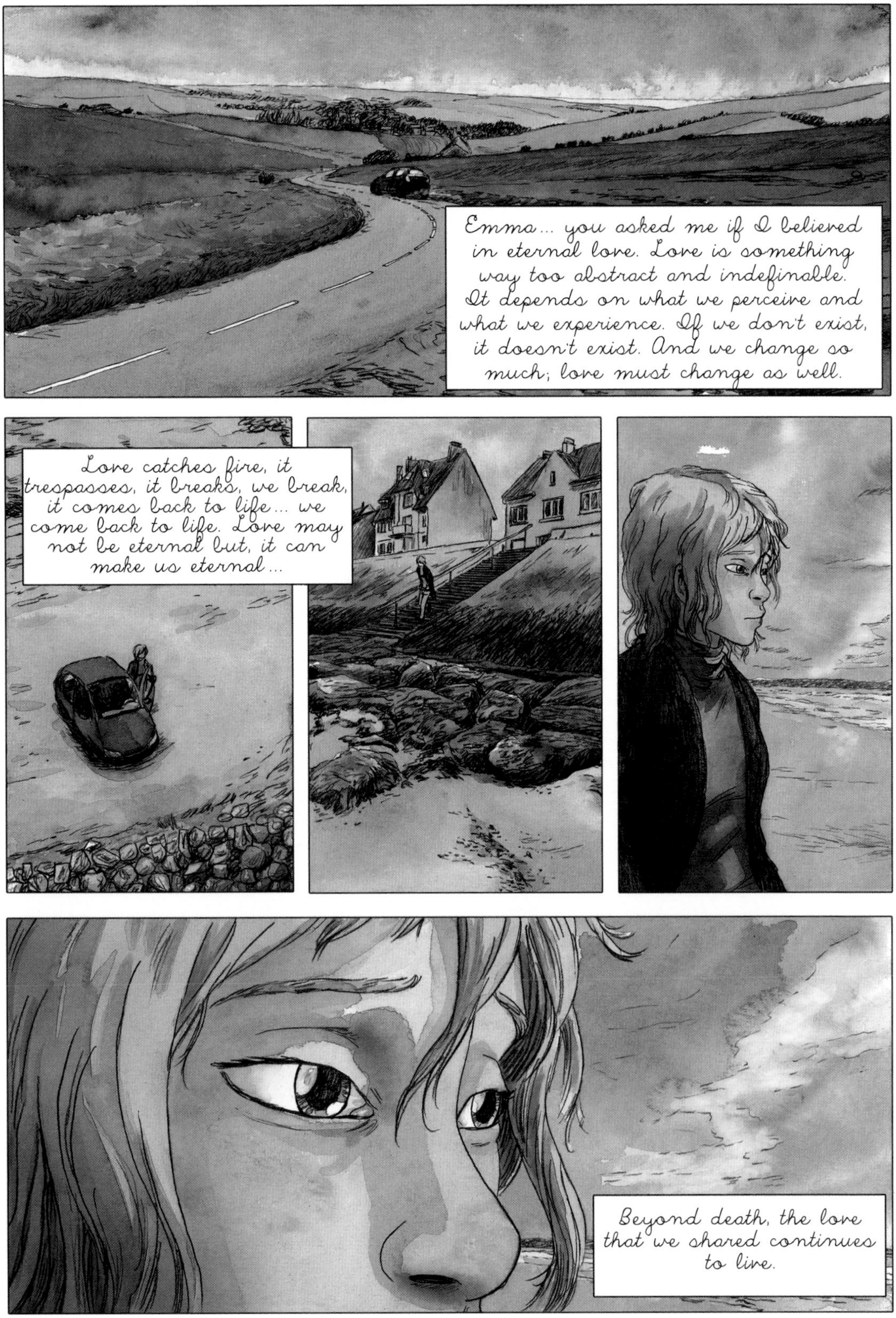
Emma... you asked me if I believed in eternal love. Love is something way too abstract and indefinable. It depends on what we perceive and what we experience. If we don't exist, it doesn't exist. And we change so much; love must change as well.
Love catches fire, it trespasses, it breaks, we break, it comes back to life... we come back to life. Love may not be eternal but, it can make us eternal...
Beyond death, the love that we shared continues to live.

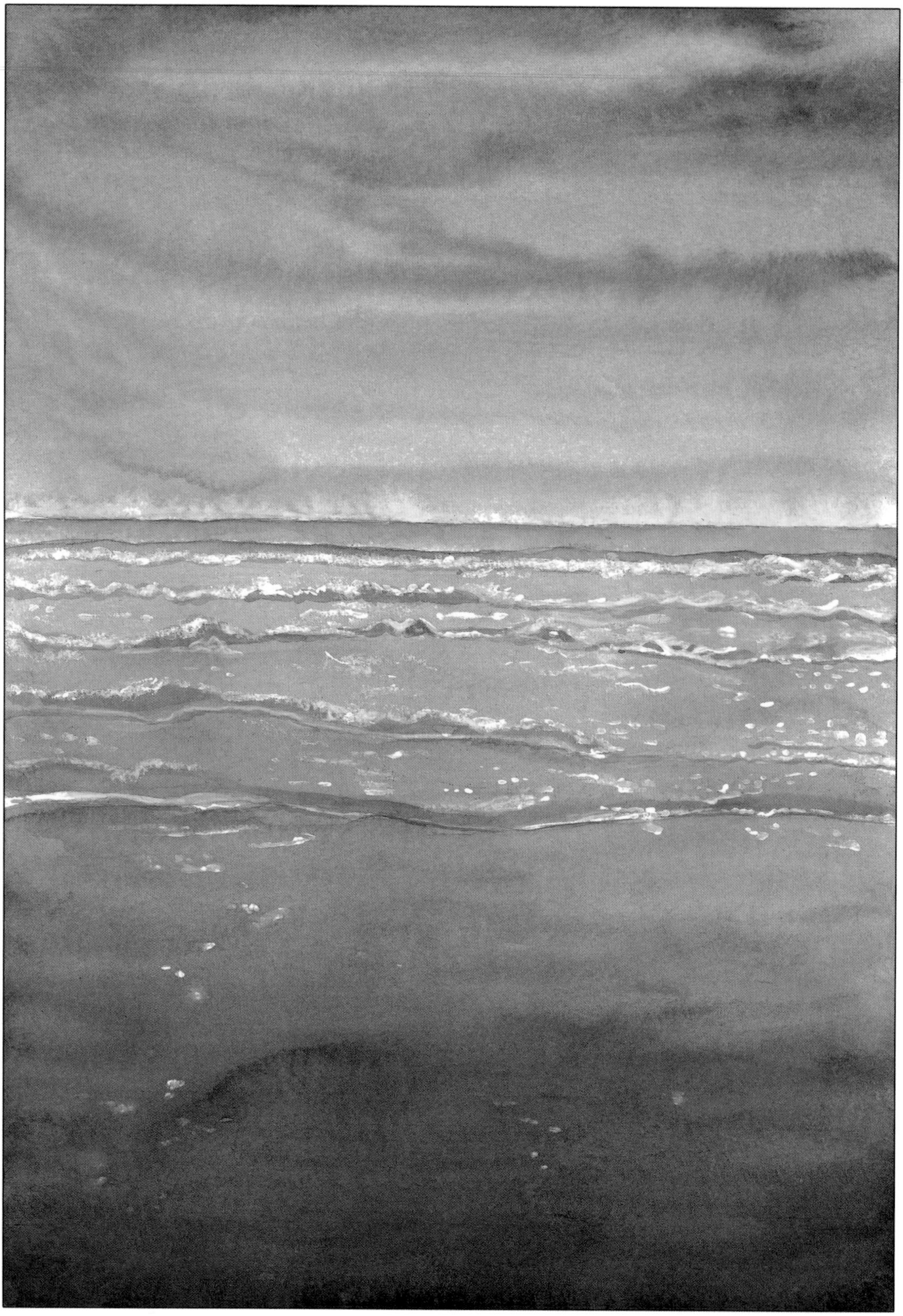

JULIE MAROH IS AN AUTHOR AND ILLUSTRATOR ORIGINALLY FROM
NORTHERN FRANCE. SHE FIRST STARTED DRAWING AT THE AGE OF
SIX, AND DREW HER FIRST COMICS AT EIGHT. SHE STUCK WITH HER
PASSION THROUGH HIGH SCHOOL, THEN STUDIED COMIC ART AT THE
INSTITUTE SAINT-LUC IN BRUSSELS AND LITHOGRAPHY AND ENGRAVING
AT THE ROYAL ACADEMY OF ARTS IN BRUSSELS, WHERE SHE STILL
LIVES. AFTER SELF-PUBLISHING THREE COMICS, IN 2010 SHE
PUBLISHED THE ORIGINAL FRENCH-LANGUAGE EDITION OF THIS BOOK,
ENTITLED *Le bleu est une couleur chaude*
(GLÉNAT), WHICH RECEIVED THE AUDIENCE AWARD AT THE 2011
ANGOULÊME INTERNATIONAL COMIC FESTIVAL. HER LATEST BOOK IN
FRENCH IS *Skandalon*, A GRAPHIC NOVEL ABOUT A ROCK 'N'
ROLL STAR, TO BE PUBLISHED IN LATE 2013.